ALL OUR
BROKEN PIECES

ALL
OUR
BROKEN
PIECES

BY L. D. CRICHTON

HYPERION

Los Angeles   New York

First Edition, May 2019
1 3 5 7 9 10 8 6 4 2
FAC-020093-19081

Printed in the United States of America

This book is set in Palatino, Arial/Monotype; Food Truck Menu/
Fontspring; Neutraface/House Industries
Designed by Torborg Davern

Library of Congress Cataloging-in-Publication Data
Names: Crichton, L. D., author.
Title: All our broken pieces / by L.D. Crichton.
Description: First edition. • Los Angeles; New York : Hyperion, 2019.
• Summary: Musically gifted seventeen-year-old Kyler and his new
neighbor Lennon, who is afflicted by OCD, discover that the strength
to survive, live, and love can be found in unexpected places.
Identifiers: LCCN 2018017987 • ISBN 9781368023962 (hardcover)
Subjects: • CYAC: Obsessive-compulsive disorder—Fiction. • Bands
(Music)—Fiction. • Dating (Social customs)—Fiction. • Family life—
Fiction. • High schools—Fiction. • Schools—Fiction.
Classification: LCC PZ7.1.C744 Al 2019 • DDC [Fic]—dc23
LC record available at https://lccn.loc.gov/2018017987

Reinforced binding

Visit www.hyperionteens.com

3361408156 0376

For all of the Auspicious Misfits.
Could be a band name. Think about it. ;)

KYLER

"LEAVE IT UP TO ME, OLD MAN, BURY ALL YOUR SINS, CLOSE
YOUR EYES AND I'LL DISGUISE THE SHAME THAT'S ON MY SKIN."
Fire to Dust, *Life-Defining Moments* EP, "Scarred"

GOALS. EVERYONE'S GOT TO HAVE them, at least that's what my dad says. For the last two years, it's been my mission—no, my *goal*—to make our front lawn resemble a football field for no other reason than to piss my father off. Don't get me wrong— guys like him don't mind having lawns that resemble football fields. Therein lies the problem. He'd *love* it. He'd *admire* it. He'd bask in its undeniable glory with unshakable pride. More than that, he'd rage. The sort of red-faced-vein-throbbing-style *pissed* because accepting the perfect lawn means I mastered something he never could. I've come close before, alternating the height of the grass in patches, but I still haven't perfected it. That *is my goal*.

Here's my theory: He likes to make me work. Thinks it'll teach me to be a real man. Maybe that's true, and hey, if the art of lawn maintenance is his vision for my future, then who am I to argue? The truth is, it isn't like that at all. He wants me to be a yuppie attorney, just like him. Guy doesn't want a kid; he wants a clone. Better luck next time, old man. I'd rather die.

I survey my work, nodding, pleased with the shifting pattern and alternating shades of light and dark green. Today is the closest I've ever come to achieving greatness. I give myself a mental high five. I should call the guys, have a good old-fashioned game of rugby in the backyard. Dad coming home to a bunch of *riffraff*, as it he calls it, might make his head explode. Not the worst idea I've ever had.

I let myself in the back door and go straight to the kitchen. The scent of garlic floats through the house, courtesy of whatever simmers on the stove, but Mom and Macy are nowhere in sight, so I ignore the growling in my stomach and grab a Coke, sliding it into the pocket of my hoodie before U-turning back outside, sidestepping the pool, and crossing my immaculate lawn until I reach the ladder to the tree house.

Yeah, a tree house. Go ahead. Laugh. Let me find the fucks I give.

Hint:

None.

That is correct. I do not give a single solitary fuck about how absurd it is. I'm seventeen. Six foot one and growing, and I still prefer to remain hidden in the trees. It's rad and if anyone knocks it, I'll knock their teeth clean out of their face, no joke.

Two wooden rungs are affixed to the tree stump near the bottom, and they're the only steps I use to enter the door. It's not a big effort for a guy my size, because during its construction, my father wanted to make sure he would fit, too, and he's not what I would call a slight man. I was six. We'd gone for a family dinner at the home of a client of my father's, who like all his A-list clients shall remain unnamed. The guy had built a tree house for his kid. A standard, run-of-the-mill kind. A few pieces of wood, a floor, and a roof.

My dad got one glimpse of it and decided that I needed one, too. But mine had to be higher, bigger, and better, so he hired contractors to build me the Taj Ma-freakin-hal of tree houses. He promised me the world that summer and I got this. My kid sister, Macy, got a motorized pink jeep. The only reason I got the better end of the deal is because Macy outgrew her SUV in a year.

Dad and I planned to spend time up here, doing all kinds of father-and-son things. He's been twice, both times before the accident.

For this reason alone, I should hate it. I should loathe the thing with the burning fire of a thousand suns, but I don't. I can't. It's my only escape. I write music up here because it reminds me of a time when life wasn't so messed up.

I pull my hoodie up and over my head, discarding it on the wooden floorboards, grateful for the relief from the oppressive heat. It's the first day of spring and sweltering already. In a week it'll be hot enough to cook eggs on the sidewalk and for me, a serial overdresser, that sucks. Cracking the can of soda, I shove my earbuds in and scroll through my playlist until I find it. Nirvana. *R.I.P., Kurt, you were a musical genius.* I lie back and stretch my legs on the small mattress tucked against the wall. A slight breeze blows in, and I watch the steel-gray curtains, sewn by my mother, catch on the wind.

I turn down the music, not because Kurt's vocals should ever be silenced, but because it seems like a nice day to catch a catnap before dinner. My eyes close, and seconds before the pull of sleep takes hold, a car with a destitute muffler rumbles not so far in the distance.

I sit up and inch closer to the small window, getting a faceful of curtain as the wind's direction shifts. A cab ambles up the drive at the house next door and parks, its muffler chugging with relief as the sputtering stops. An interesting phenomenon in a place like Bel Air. It's the kind of neighborhood infested with sports cars like mine, Range Rovers, Hummers. Status symbols on wheels. Yellow checkered taxicabs screaming for a little maintenance stick out like sore thumbs. Josh, our next-door neighbor, and proud owner of both a Corvette and Porsche's version of an SUV, steps out of the cab, reaches into his coat pocket, and whips out a pile of cash.

The driver exits the vehicle, too, and moves to the rear of the car, removing large bags of luggage and a trunk. By the looks of the trunk, they're transporting a body. I sit up straighter.

Ever see a TV show or movie and wonder how they find such good music? Well, there's a guy for that. Josh. He's a music supervisor. That's a legit job, and since we live in LA, he doesn't have to travel much, and when he does, I'm certain it's not with purple polka-dotted luggage.

The back door of the cab swings open and a female silhouette emerges. I squint and lean forward as if either of those things will give me a better view of the newcomer, but all I can make out are legs and long blond waves. She shuts the door to the cab and turns away from my line of sight.

Josh and the cabbie stand side by side, Josh holding the polka-dotted luggage pull in one hand, the body-hiding trunk sitting on the ground at their feet.

I return my attention to her. *Turn. Around. I want to see your face.*

Macy's voice pierces through my thoughts like a needle popping a balloon. "Kyler! Dinner!"

I don't respond.

"Kyler!" she shouts again. "Mom wants you to come in for supper!"

The shrill pitch of my sister hollering is surely enough to cause someone to turn to see the commotion. But no. Newcomer doesn't move.

"Ky—!"

"I'm coming. Don't get your leotard in a knot." I poke my head through the door to see Macy, standing at the bottom of the tree in her full dance gear, with one hand on her hip, the other raised high flipping me off. I descend the ladder, hesitant to leave my can of Coke and the view of the first interesting thing to happen on this street in a while. There hasn't been this much action since last year when Tim Bowman got chased around the neighborhood in his underwear after being caught making out with his brother's girlfriend.

Macy spins on her heel and stomps across the yard in front of me. I cringe as I watch her walk. She's so rigid in her posture, her skull looks like it's anchored to the sky with invisible string; her shoulders, muscled and strong, pulled back into a perfect arch. Years of conditioning from ballet, I guess, but I can't help but think my little sister needs to take a play from my book and chill out.

Mom stands at the back door, a smile plastered on her face. I wonder how much she forces that smile when she looks at me. She tilts her head and brings her fingers to brush across the left side of my cheek. She's the only person in the world permitted to do this.

"How was your day, honey?"

She holds out a wicker basket decorated with a blue ribbon on the side. A Pinterest endeavor for sure. Without hesitation, I reach into the pocket of my jeans, remove my cell phone, and drop it next to Macy's bedazzled one. No electronic devices at dinner. No exceptions. Mom instituted this rule a year ago. I'm happy to do it for her even though it means that every single night, for an hour, my family is technology free and forced to endure all the things my dad knows everything about.

When I sit at the table, Dad's drinking a glass of red wine. His beverage choice tells me one thing. He was mediating a star-studded divorce and didn't get the cheating husband whatever settlement he was after. Mom scoops a mound of seafood pasta onto his plate. Dad gives her a curt nod, the kind you'd give to the guy who bags groceries at the store.

"Thanks."

Macy is next and places a card-sized amount on her plate.

"Mae, that's two bites. Eat something. I can see your ribs."

She shakes her head and holds up a glass of water. "Tryouts

for our production of *Swan Lake* are in a few weeks. Gotta keep it trim."

"Trim is one thing. You're skeletal." She kicks my shin under the table. I take a drink of water and grin at her. "Kicking someone is much more effective when there's muscle behind it. Eat a sandwich."

She glares. "Shut up."

"That's enough," Dad says, pointing the tip of his fork at me. "If Macy needs to cut down on her intake to reach her goal, no need to chastise her for it."

I place a heaping mound of pasta on my plate. "If Macy wants to starve to death for the sake of appearances, then so be it, right, Dad? As long as she looks good."

"That's not what I said."

It's what he meant. I can't bother myself to argue, though, I'm too hungry. My mother is a phenomenal chef. It's how she met my dad. He'd been at Haute, this five-star restaurant where she worked. He ordered overpriced beef Wellington that was so good, he'd insisted on delivering compliments to the chef, and the rest, as they say, is history. If you ask me, she could have done better.

"I'm not starving, Kyler," Macy says. "I'm just trying to stay slim. There are a lot of lifts in the performance, I'm going after the lead role."

I shake my head. Ridiculous.

Dad sips his wine. "At least one child has goals."

And there it is. I think about the lawn. "I have goals."

Dad shakes his head. "Music is a tough industry."

Proof he knows nothing about me. Do I like my band? Yeah. Do I like making music? Yep. Do I want to do it for a living, become rich and famous and end up one of his hipster clients? A colossal-sized no. I don't tell him this, though; let him think what he wants. I keep my head down and eat, hoping he'll shut up. But he doesn't.

"You're getting older now, son, it's time to take life more seriously."

"Fire to Dust is good, Dad," Macy says, coming to my defense. "They'd have a real chance if Kyler would stop being so scared."

"I'm not scared, Mae, but I'm not stupid, either." My stomach churned the second this conversation began, and now I've lost my appetite altogether. My focus darts to my mother. Her eyes are sad, like mine. "Mom, thanks for dinner. May I be excused?"

She swipes her napkin at the side of her mouth, taking special care with the corners of her lips before nodding.

I know what my dad thinks. Even if he entertains the idea that we're good enough, which he doesn't, he's spent enough time around famous people and their entourages to know full well I could never make it for one reason and one reason alone. Celebrity. Los Angeles is a crazy place that favors beauty, not the beast.

Lennon

FACT: 1.3 MILLION PEOPLE DIE IN CAR
WRECKS EVERY SINGLE YEAR.
THAT AVERAGES TO 3,287 DEATHS PER DAY.

LOS ANGELES. CITY OF ANGELS. **City of Eternal Damnation.** It's a matter of perspective, I suppose. Considering my life is cursed, I'm placing all my figurative chips on a solid bet that it is eternal damnation. Since the air is hot, sticky, and humid here, it's fair to say I'm surrounded by hellfire. It clings to my skin and smothers me like plastic wrap.

I'd rather be back in the mental hospital.

My father hails a taxi and holds the door open.

Miserable, I roll my eyes at him. I haven't seen him in almost three years. Not because he didn't try. He did. Every winter, spring, summer, and fall, he'd invite me to stay with him and his family in Los Angeles. And every winter, spring, summer, and fall, I'd refuse. I'd refuse because by then, every day of my life had become a nightmare. A constant, ruthless, and grueling battle I'll never be free of.

I've never felt safe in cars, but now that fear is paralyzing. I almost didn't make the twenty-minute drive to the airport in

Portland without a massive panic attack. Panic attacks lead to the part of myself I can't control, and my dad will do everything in his power to make sure that doesn't happen.

Watching me must be like having a front-row view to a ticking time bomb.

Tick.

Tock.

Boom.

His shoulders draw inward—burdened by the weight of having to deal with me. "I'm trying here. I have to get you from the airport to home, that means you must suffer for the next forty-eight minutes in this car, but you're free and clear after that." He looks at his watch. "It's three o'clock now, traffic might be light."

"I'd rather walk."

"Not an option. Sorry, Bug."

Bug. Ridiculous. Perhaps once upon a time it was cute, but now I could think of a million other nicknames I'd rather have, yet there's no escaping the one gifted by my father. Lennon Rae Davis, after none other than the most famous Lennon of all, who also was a Beatle. Clever. Thanks for the stellar nickname, John.

In fact, it seems kind of ominous now. Lennon died tragically. The statistic probability of dying in a car is staggering, *tragic*, almost. I've never been a fan of driving—or *passenger-ing*, to be more accurate—but since my sixteenth birthday, all I can see is a coffin with four wheels and a blinker. Like right now.

Circulating around a nauseating mental carousel is an image of my dad, the man standing next to me, the same man pleading with me to *be reasonable* as he lies on the pavement bloody and dying, because it's a fact:

People. Die. In. Cars.

His arms fanned above him, his body on display in a crumpled heap of steel and glass...

His limbs pretzeled and folded grotesquely... twisted, shredded metal.

His lungs ragged with each pull, desperate to cling to breath.

Even if it's his last.

And then.

It is.

A cold, lifeless stare shadows his face. Just like that, he simply ceases to exist.

My father will die if he gets in that car because people die in cars.

My heart rate quickens, pumping blood quicker, faster, until it careens straight through my veins in a race to the finish where my heart will surely seize or burst. The hammer of each pulse shatters my rib cage, as if my heart is screaming to escape. I struggle to catch the air, to hold on to it for more than a millisecond, and pull it deep and slow into my lungs. But my heart, the beast, hammers harder, determined to rip through my chest wall. That'll be it. It'll be over.

I reach two fingers into the pocket of my jeans, gathering the small sphere between my fingertips—the little magic pill that will help me survive this trip, or at the least, this *hour*.

Ativan. Breakfast of champions. My hands shake as I pop it underneath my tongue, close my eyes, and wait for it to dissolve.

My father reaches into the pocket of his worn jeans to retrieve the sheet of paper that's been his bible for the last week. It's a list, provided to him by the hospital when they released me, of my medications, what they do, when I should take them, and potential side effects. He doesn't need the list—I'm a far more valuable resource than his sheet of paper—but I think he feels empowered by it, as if facts on paper wrap around him like a security blanket. "Lennon, didn't you take a pill already, honey?"

I keep my eyes closed and hold my pointer finger up. *One minute. Give me one more minute.*

He speaks in hushed tones to the cabdriver as the two of them wrestle with my trunk and two suitcases. I'd tried convincing my dad to let me bring my mom's greatest treasure—her record collection. He said there were too many. He's right. There are hundreds of them, but now they aren't within my reach, and I'm scared they won't make the trip from Maine to Los Angeles unscathed. It's entered my mind no less than fifteen times so far.

I'd been trying to distract myself by reading from my own growing collection of trivia books, filled with the most useless information a person could hope to acquire. Unlike Mom's records, but much like my trunk, I wouldn't budge on the issue of my books remaining out of the truck. My life being uprooted was hard enough, but my life being uprooted without something to keep my shattered brain occupied is out of the question, and my father, it seems, was wise enough to pick and choose his battles about a small box of trivia books. Realistically, my nitpicking has been distracting me from the real situation I'm now faced with.

A situation where, unfortunately, no amount of obscure knowledge or fact-recollection will help.

When I feel like I can speak, I say, "I took an SSRI earlier. This is Ativan, so I can deal with what's happening without a panic attack. Because my brain is telling me if I get into that car with you, you'll die."

My dad's face turns ashen. He's been trying so hard, but he still has a lot to learn.

The cabbie watches in silent fascination as my body slides across the worn leather seat. Beads of sweat collect on the base of my neck and my hand shakes as I swipe at it. Gross. I stick the tips of my fingers underneath my thighs, sitting on my hands. They twitch in protest. I press against them with the weight of my legs and force myself to focus on the discarded gum wrapper on the floor. It's useless. My muscles tense. All 640 of them. I hate this.

My mouth is parched and dry, and I free one hand long enough to roll down the window before hiding it again.

Pinpricks on my skin go from bad to worse until pain explodes across my chest and tears at my insides because my dad's about to die. It hurts to breathe. I'm supposed to be stronger than the thoughts, but no one can be strong all the time. I recognize the shift in my brain, and I realize it's coming. The nerves on my fingers spark and spread like wildfire, licking at my veins, commanding me to move them, begging me to make it stop. By the time my dad flops in the seat beside me, I've already begun. A series of fast-paced, timed taps against my leg.

I like the number five. Truth is, I favor all single-digit odd numbers, but five is my sweet spot, always has been.

One. Two. Three. Four. Five.

One. Two. Three. Four. Five.

One. Two. Three. Four. Five.

One. Two. Three. Four. Five.

One. Two. Three. Four. Five.

We merge onto the interstate, and my tapping takes on a greater sense of urgency, like I'm trying to send Morse code signals into the hemisphere. *Help me. Emergency.* The taxi surges ahead, going seventy miles an hour only to come to abrupt stops inches from surrounding bumpers. I squeeze my eyes shut and *count* and *tap* and *count* and *tap* until I lose track of time. I can only imagine what must be going through the driver's mind. He probably thinks I've escaped from an asylum and he's now aiding and abetting a criminal.

By the time we arrive at my dad's house, my fingers have bloomed pink with all the blood I've sent rushing into them. The car stops and finally, so can I.

My lungs release the air I've been holding in as the knots in my muscles switch to a throbbing ache—just enough to remind me that I'm still alive.

Dad opens the door. He says, "See, Bug. Everything's okay."

Are any of us ever okay, really?

Since I've last visited, Dad and his new family have moved up in the world. *Way up.* There is no greater proof than the building in front of me, flanked by a forest full of palm trees and lush green hedges. The modest Craftsman I'd shared with my mom in Maine would fit inside this thing, three times or more.

It reminds me of a Jenga tower, rectangle pods stacked upon one another; some architectural masterpiece most people can't even fathom having enough money for. Part of the house is crafted from fine wood, other sections brick, and some from glass. There may be more windows than walls. It's at least three stories and jutting out from every glass wall is a balcony that accompanies the room.

I can't help but stare. Gape. It's so pretentious.

"Nice, huh?" Dad says.

Nice.

Sure.

I shake my head and move to take one suitcase, but Dad grabs it from me. "Go on. I'll get these."

I manage a single step before the large front door swings open to reveal Claire, my stepmother, behind it. Her hair falls down her back like mine; it's also blond, like mine. Only difference is my hair is part of my DNA. Homegrown. I'm certain Claire's is courtesy of too much time and money spent in a salon plus a few packs of hair extensions. Doesn't matter, the result is the same, and there is no denying that Claire is stunning. She should be, she plays none other than Katherine Gladstone on *Cascade,* one of the hottest, most popular soap operas on television.

Yep, Dad is married to a celebrity. She's not so bad. I'd love to have an evil stepmother story to spin, like poor sweet Cinderella, but Claire just doesn't fit the bill. Held in the crook of her arm is a small dog that resembles a mop, with two little beady eyes peering up at me. Claire rushes over and wraps me in her arms, squishing my face into her double Ds. "Lennon, welcome, sweet-pea. Your daddy treat you well on your way here?" Her Texan accent is still thick, despite having been a Los Angeles transplant for the last fifteen years.

I nod as the dog squirms between us.

She breaks the bear hug seconds before I wonder how long it would take to suffocate in those.

OBITUARY

Lennon Rae Davis, age 16, died of accidental asphyxiation by an enthusiastic hugger.

Predeceased by her mother, Anne Desmond, and survived by her biological father, her step-slash-half-family, and one real friend.

The demons won.

"This little rug rat is Oscar," she informs me. "He is a jealous thing sometimes, don't mind him. You make yourself right at home."

"Thanks." It's the right thing to say, even though we both know I don't want to be here. I reach my hand out to pet the top of Oscar's head. He growls at me, proving he takes his job guarding Claire seriously.

"Hush now, Oscar," Claire says. "That's enough from you." She returns her attention to me. "Lennon, baby, you need any-thing at all, you go on and tell me or your daddy. Anything."

"Thanks," I repeat.

I spot my stepsister, Andrea, standing behind Claire. Her long, thin figure leans against the massive door frame, her arms crossed over her chest, a cell phone clutched in her hand. Her chestnut hair is straight and cropped to her shoulders in a blunt line. The haircut is as sharp as the features on her face.

Andrea has never been my biggest fan. Not since we were kids, and I'd spend my summers here. Dad and Claire would make my stay completely over the top, trying to cram a year's worth of quality time into a couple of short months. My dad always said he needed to make up for lost time. It was impressive, really—that he and Claire could pull off birthday celebrations, Easter egg hunts, and Christmas in the middle of July. But rather than being excited to have double the holiday fun, Andrea always seemed resentful.

When I was ten, I returned home to Maine and told my mom about it. Andrea's dislike was clearer with each year that passed, and I just wanted to know why she hated me so much. Mom reasoned that she was probably a little jealous. I wondered what she'd had to be jealous of, but before I could ask, my mom was making me swear that I would be patient with my stepsister—a promise that to this day remains a hard one to keep. I force a tight smile. "Hey, Andrea."

She glances toward me, her nose wrinkling in disgust as if my greeting has offended her. "Hi."

Claire grimaces. "Andrea, maybe you could show Lennon around?"

"Hell would have to freeze over first, Mother."

Dad stops wheeling my luggage and shoots her a deadly warning with his eyes. "Cool it."

"Fine." Andrea looks at Claire. "Liam and Jess are waiting for me."

As she turns to leave, headed to her much more important place to be, my five-year-old half brother, Jacob, almost barrels her over as he comes racing out of the house.

"Watch it, minion," Andrea says sharply.

Jacob is wearing a white dress shirt with a black tie and a pair of 3-D movie glasses with the lenses cut out. He's in jeans and rubber boots. A camera is clutched in his grasp, and it swings upward to capture Andrea just in time for her to snap, "Get your camera out of my face, Jake!"

The camera pivots around and lands on me, but only for a moment—he squints because of the sun, and it drops to dangle from his wrist. He shields his eyes with his hand and declares, "Mommy said you're living with us now."

"Yep. She's right."

"She said your mommy—"

"Jacob Davis." Claire issues a stern warning. "Mind yourself."

His gaze sweeps to the ground and settles on his glorious rubber boots before he nods and kicks at nothing with the tip of his toes.

"It's okay, Jacob, we're cool."

His green eyes swing upward and he grins, revealing two missing front teeth. "I told Mommy that I was happy you were moving in because you're nicer than Andi."

I want to tell him that a burlap sack is nicer than Andi. That the microbe stuck to the gum affixed to the dirty sole of my shoe is nicer than Andi.

"That's enough, Jacob," Dad says. "Let's get Lennon settled in, yes?"

Jacob ignores our father and aims his camera at my luggage, zooming in on my large trunk. "What's that?"

"It has my costume design stuff." The records I parted with, but the trunk was equal to, if not more important than, my books. It holds my one true *passion* inside. Silly, but when I'm designing stuff, often it's the only time I feel normal. My attention to detail is meticulous.

"What's costume design?"

"You know how sometimes in TV shows like your mom works at or in movies people dress up as knights or princesses?"

"Yep."

"The outfits they wear are created and put together by people called costume designers."

"You wanna be one when you grow up?"

"Yeah."

Jacob holds up his camera. "I'm going to be a newspaper reporter."

I arch an eyebrow, impressed. "A newspaper reporter?"

He nods. "It's for cover, though."

"Cover?"

"Yeah, 'cause I'm going to be a superhero."

"Right," I say. "I should have known."

Dad drops the luggage at the doorstep before hoisting the trunk up. Since his hands are full, I grab the first piece of my luggage and wheel it in behind him. Jacob is at my heels, my little shadow.

"Lennon?"

I turn my head to see him. "Yeah, bud?"

"Can you make a cape? Like the ones superheroes wear?"

"Yeah, I think I could do that."

"I told Mommy you were nicer than Andi. Way nicer."

KYLER

CHOKING ON SILVER-
SPOON SECRETS...

Random Thoughts of a Random Mind

I HEAD STRAIGHT TO EMMETT'S, the closest place for refuge. At the end of the block, I'm putting in my earbuds when I spot Claire walking her mutt, Oscar. Yappy little dog that looks more like it belongs on the end of a scouring pad than in Bel Air. For an inexplicable, crazy second, I debate asking her who the new girl is, but I don't. Why should I care? Oscar's leash wraps around one of Claire's hands and the other presses her cell phone to her ear while the dog sniffs at a shrub.

That's what Bel Air is. Obscene mansions obscured by shrubs. A place where people and their material things shout *Listen to me, see my vapid display of money,* yet those same people remain unseen, free to give birth to skeleton after skeleton in closets, until those same closets are graveyards built on secrets. I pretend music is playing, keep my eyes fixed on my Vans, and listen to the one-sided conversation. Maybe I care a little.

"Yeah, Josh is helping her get settled now."

The new girl.

21

"Yes, that's so unfortunate."

A chill tickles my spine and makes me shudder at the word *unfortunate*. When I had my accident, people used that word so much, so *often*, that even the sound of it makes me want to vomit.

He was such a handsome boy, so unfortunate.

Dreadful. Such an unfortunate day for that family.

Yeah, we're all just living in one great big misfortune. A bona fide tragedy.

"Right. We've explained it to Jacob, had a chat with Andrea and told her she'd have to be welcoming."

I almost choke on my own spit. The idea of Andrea welcoming *anybody* is outrageous. The broomstick she rides is so well used, she could hold a title in the Quidditch championship. My feet drag against the pavement in protest. I feel sorry for the mystery girl. She's sharing space with Andrea. That's got to be rough. I tune in for a little too long because Claire's gaze settles on mine for a heartbeat. No need to get busted for listening to her phone call, so I continue walking, head down. But the new girl becomes more interesting.

Emmett's flopped in the living room when I arrive. The blinds cast eerie shadows that black out the already dark-colored room. He's sprawled out on a large black beanbag chair with an Xbox controller in his hand. His hair is long, but he's sporting a man bun, and if not for the mass of facial hair along his jaw, I'd tell him he has a reasonable chance against Macy for the lead of *Swan Lake*. Girls seem to enjoy this stupid trend, and who am I to say anything? Man bun and all, Emmett has me beat for looking good.

His gaze hits me for an eighth of a second before he focuses again on the screen in front of him. His fingers work the buttons and from the looks of things he's playing a war game.

"Hey," I say. "What's up?"

He shrugs. "Not much. Killing stuff. Blowing stuff up. What's up with you?"

I pick at my cuticle. "Not much. Needed to get out of there."

He nods. Emmett's our drummer. His brother, Austin, is our bassist. I've known him since we were four, in the years before the tree house, so we have a pretty good history. He doesn't ask me to elaborate. Doesn't need to.

I walk over to where Austin's bass is discarded. It's vintage. Mint condition. Classic. If he had half a brain, he'd keep it in a case whenever he wasn't using it, but he's just another spoiled rich kid who believes treasures like these are replaceable.

I turn on a lamp, flop on the couch, and check the strings. At least he keeps it tuned—most of the time. Emmett mutes the video game so I can hear myself play. He doesn't need to do that for me—I hear myself play all the time—but I guess he feels he's being courteous.

"Your dad?"

I stop strumming the strings, swing my gaze up, and grin. "Great guess, bro. You move on to the next round!"

Emmett shrugs.

I don't want to talk about it. So I play a melody, deep and moody on the bass, and sing, exaggerating each word so Emmett doesn't get the wrong impression. I will not discuss my father.

He dies in the video game, swears, and stands up to power down the Xbox. "You want a drink?"

"Water," I say, in between lyrics.

Emmett grabs two bottles of H_2O out of the fridge and tosses mine over so it lands on the cushion beside me. I'm still playing, singing, strumming, when he asks, "Have you considered the demo?"

"Nope. Don't need to."

He sits on the couch opposite me, cracks open his water, and takes a big swig. "Look, man, believe me when I say everyone is painfully aware of what your face looks like, but it's not as bad as you think."

That's because he doesn't live with it. I shoot him a glance that says he's senseless before resuming the song.

He shakes his head. "Kyler, it's not that bad."

My jaw tenses. Not a single thing irritates me more than people telling me it's not that bad. I motion to the mottled pink skin that flares across the left side of my cheek. "Really, Emmett? 'Cause this sure as shit looks bad. It doesn't look bad to you because you're not the one with alien skin."

He shakes his head again. I'm frustrating him. Good. It's mutual. "I appreciate you guys want to make something of yourselves with it, but if that's the case, count me out. Find another front man."

"You know that's off the table. We're in it together."

"Then understand that I can't sub a demo to a producer." We've had this same conversation endlessly, like some stupid cat video that keeps looping around. The band wants to send demos to anyone and everyone in the industry. I want to play music in a garage to relax. The problem, I guess, is we're pretty good. When we started, it was for fun. A way to keep us out of trouble, but now we have local fans at school who have convinced Emmett, Austin, and Silas that we're good enough to score a record deal.

I can't argue that, but if they think I want to be famous, they can think again. Since I'm the singer, and one of two guitar players, my stubbornness is affecting them.

"I get it. Just keep hoping you'll change your mind is all."

I stick my tongue out and make the *Let's rock* symbol with my hand. "Keep hope alive, bro."

Emmett downs the rest of his water. "I think you're making a big mistake."

I shake my head. "Think that all you want; it won't change anything. I'm not trying to be a buzzkill," I clarify. "It's not something I can do, though."

"You should reconsider it, but I won't try to change your mind again."

"If you could convince the other two to back off, I'd appreciate it." I don't want to talk about it anymore, so I switch the topic to something that has piqued my interest. "Some new girl showed up at the neighbor's house. Didn't get a good look, but she's superhot."

"How do you know if you didn't get a good look?"

"Just do."

"You didn't see her face?"

"Nope. Don't need to."

"You can't tell if a girl is hot without looking at her face."

"She's hot," I say again. "I know it."

Emmett is quiet for a few minutes, and I think I've won the

hot-or-not debate until he says, "I guess you'll find out for sure at school tomorrow. Hey, can I ask you something?"

"What?"

"Well, you haven't seen her up close and you think she's hot." He looks at me, waiting for confirmation, so I nod. "Wouldn't it kind of be the same thing with your face, if we were playing a show or something? Stage lights shining on you in a dark club would make it hard for anyone to get a good look at you."

"What? What does that have to do with anything we're talking about?"

"If you didn't get a good look and you still think she's hot, what are you really worried about then? People will never see your face."

"One, don't care. Two, I didn't say I wouldn't play a gig in some dark, dingy club. I said I don't want to sub demos to record producers. Big difference. Colossal sized. Three, I'm still right. She's still superhot," I say. "Four, you said you would drop it. I came here to escape harping, not to get back into it."

Emmett's shoulders fall. "Sorry."

"Don't mention it." I stand up and turn the TV and the Xbox back on before picking up one controller and tossing it at Emmett. "Let's blow things up."

Emmett accepts my peace offering, and without another word, we play.

Lennon

FACT: SOME BELIEVE THE PHOENIX
SYMBOLIZES LIFE AFTER DEATH.
QUESTION: WHAT IF THIS IS IT?

THE OUTSIDE OF DAD'S NEW house is pretentious. The inside is plain overambitious. Not a hair on the spit-shined floors. They're bamboo hardwood everywhere, including the massive entryway with an enormous staircase in the middle. One side leads into a living room, the other to a kitchen, bigger and whiter than any kitchen I've ever seen. The island in the middle is pure granite and stretches at least thirteen feet. Every cupboard is slick and shiny, made from reflective white glass rather than recycled wood, like the ones I'd spent the last sixteen years looking at.

Dad nudges me in the shoulder blades. "Look around later, let me show you to your room."

He moves past me and heads up the stairs, luggage trailing behind him. My trunk rests on the floor. If I felt I could wrestle it up the stairs by myself, I would, but I'd never make it. Jacob appears out of nowhere and flies up the stairs ahead of our father. "You're in the guest room," he says over his shoulder.

Dad turns his head and stops his ascent. "Claire is hiring a designer, Bug. You can decorate your room however you see fit."

"A designer?"

"Yes, to create a space to call your own. This is your home now, Lennon. I want to make sure you're comfortable here."

It will never be home. I don't say that, though. I nod, to indicate he should keep moving. He heads for a hallway at the top of the stairs and pauses, waiting for me. We haven't seen each other much over the past three years, but he's done some research, and to be fair, he *has* spent the last week with me in Maine. His eyes dart from me to the doorknob. He's waiting.

"I don't need to do it," I tell him. "I don't need to ritualize all the time."

Jacob's eyebrows draw together. "What's that mean?"

Dad pinches the bridge of his nose, stressed. "Jake..."

"It's okay," I say to Dad. "I can explain it to him."

"I tried," he says. "Jacob, remember when Mommy and Daddy and you talked about Lennon coming to live with us?"

Jacob nods. "Uh-huh."

"Remember we told you that Lennon might do some things that don't make sense?"

I've had to explain obsessive-compulsive disorder to little kids before, and it's obvious my father has not. I crouch down so I'm eye level with my half brother. "Hey, Jacob, do you ever catch a cold? And it doesn't matter what you do, you have that cold. And you know how sometimes you have to take medicine to feel normal and stuff?"

"Uh-huh."

"I have OCD. It's like my brain has a terrible cold that tells me all kinds of silly things."

"What silly things?"

"Well, things like, if I don't turn a doorknob five times, something terrible will happen."

"Can't you tell yourself nothing bad will happen?" He giggles. "Nothing bad will happen because you don't turn a doorknob five times. That's silly."

"I tell myself that, but it doesn't matter." I pause and tickle his back. "Have you ever had an itch, and the itch is so bad that you can't be comfortable, you're just going to go mad until you scratch it?"

His nod is more animated this time. "Yeah, I have a back scratcher in my bathroom."

"That's what it's like. It's like my brain has an itch. One that's so awful, I'll do anything to scratch it, including turning a doorknob five times even though I'm positive it's a silly thing to do. It's called ritualizing."

He looks at me and absorbs this information unfazed. "Okay."

"Okay?"

He shrugs. "Yep."

"Cool."

I bite back a small smile when I catch the expression on Dad's face.

"Can I come in your room?" Jacob asks.

The door swings open and I wave him inside. "Sure you can."

The room is basic. My guess is Claire didn't want to go over the top with her own personal tastes in a guest room, so everything is neutral. Gray walls, gray throw rug, gray bedding. I think of the white kitchen. Perhaps this is Claire's style.

"Sorry it's not bigger," Dad is saying.

"It's fine," I say. "It's great."

"Only temporary," he reminds me. He points to a plain white table. "Claire bought you a cabinet for your sewing machine. She says she ordered a nicer one, but it's out of stock and she wanted you to have something right away." He looks at Jacob. "Lennon's had a big day, Jake. Let her settle."

"She invited me in her room." He holds up the camera, slung over his wrist by a strap. "I need a picture, too, it's Lennon's first day with us."

"You're standing in her room," Dad points out. "Take a picture and go brush your teeth. It's almost bedtime."

The disappointment is written on his face. He's looking at me, his eyes pleading with me to save him from my father's unreasonable request. My chest tightens. "Hey, bud, if you listen to Dad now, tomorrow after school I can make your cape."

"Really?"

"Yeah, for sure."

"Can I take a photo?"

I stand up straight and smile for him. He snaps the image, says, "Thanks," and turns to make a hasty retreat from the room.

My dad puts his hands in his pockets. "Do you need anything, Bug?"

I shake my head. "No, I'm good. Thanks."

"If you do, you holler."

"Got it," I say. "Thanks."

"I'll be back up with your trunk." Before I can ask him if he needs help, he's gone. He returns a few minutes later, looking both worn out from the luggage haul and aged with worry. He swipes the back of his hand across his brow. "Are you sure you're okay?"

I hoist the first of my suitcases on the bed. "Dad, relax. I won't slit my wrists or anything."

This earns me the pointer finger and a stern expression. "Not funny, Lennon. Not even close."

"I'm sorry, but you're worried about something like that, aren't you? With me, I mean. Suicide is the second most common cause of death for people my age. It's a fact." I face him. "Dad. Relax. I get that you're worried, but I'm fine. You're old now. All this stressing out isn't good for you. I think you're getting gray hairs."

"Hardly a fossil," he says. "Get settled, call if you need anything. There's a bathroom behind that door." He points to a wooden door on the wall I missed because it, too, is gray. "Claire made sure there was toothpaste, a toothbrush, clean towels, and stuff for you to shower."

"Noted."

He drops an awkward kiss on my forehead. "Sorry, kid, I wish you weren't going through this."

My eyes sting with tears that threaten to spill over. "That makes two of us."

He leaves and I place my trivia books sideways, in five separate piles of even height on three of the built-in shelves so they're more like decor than a bunch of books. I analyze the top book on each pile to confirm they're lined up before I unpack my clothes. As with everything, unpacking my clothes involves uncompromising order. The darker items are first, followed by bright vibrant colors before pastels and whites. I sort first by color, then by season. It makes no sense to have cable-knit sweaters next to tank tops. I fold each item and place them in the drawers.

I move on to the trunk. Everything inside is meticulous, the fabric folded in small, perfect squares, army style. Spools of thread and ribbon sit in Tupperware containers while jars of beads stack together on the left side of the trunk. I lift the fabric, careful not to rustle it too much, but enough to retrieve the box hidden underneath it for weeks. It's covered in gift wrap, white, with huge blue stripes.

I love blue.

There's a card stuck to the front, my mom's elegant handwriting scrolling across it, wishing me the happiest of birthdays.

A knot lodges in my throat, and I head toward the bed to sit down. But before I do, the corner of my eye catches a shadow moving stealthily across the yard. As if the Universe has offered me a small escape from the heartbreak I'm about to inflict on myself. My pulse races, but only until the shadow pivots and heads toward the house next door. The person is male. No question. Tall and lean, he's in jeans and a black hoodie with a white phoenix stretched across the back. I'm not sure how anyone could wear a color that absorbs heat, let alone a hoodie, here.

My thoughts are interrupted by a knock. Jacob lets himself in. "I came to say good night."

"Night, buddy."

He walks over to the window, curious about what's captured my interest. "That's Kyler. He's scary."

"He doesn't look too scary. A little silly for wearing a black fleece in this heat, but not scary."

Jacob shakes his head in disagreement. "No. Andi told me he's a monster. He even looks like one." He looks down. "Is that a present?"

I nod, my focus still fixed on the hoodie-wearer-slash-monster. "It was from my mom."

Jacob's hand touches my upper arm. "It's okay to miss your mommy."

I cast a glance his way and see that his eyes are filled with sympathy. The pure, nonjudgmental kind only a child can deliver.

My gaze continues to follow the neighbor, who has retrieved something from inside the house and has turned, headed in this direction. My eyes are full of tears, though, courtesy of Jacob, and I can't see him. I swipe at them with the sleeves of my top, rubbing, trying to get a good glimpse.

Jacob's fingertips fall from my arm to my wrist, which he grasps with a shudder. "See. He *is* scary."

My vision is blurry but even so, I can tell something is different about his face. A reason that has Jacob convinced he's scary.

The left side shows mild discoloration, red. "She's trying to mess with you. He has a birthmark."

Jacob crosses his arms. "I've lived here a long time. He's mean."

It sounds as if he's repeating Andrea-level wisdom, word for word. "Jacob, don't worry, he's just a kid. Andi doesn't know what she's talking about. You should go to bed."

"Night, Lennon. I'm glad you're here."

I wish I could say the same.

Jacob leaves, and I'm exhausted and in desperate need of a shower. I stand under a steady stream of hot water until my skin feels clean, blow-dry my hair, brush my teeth, and put my pj's on.

I carry the weight of the world on my shoulders. My chest is tight, and a sour taste lingers in the back of my mouth. It sinks in. This is my new reality. My ever-evolving portal into hell. What if no one likes me? What if they're Andrea versions 2 and 2.0 and so on? What if something bad happens? The sour taste becomes a thing that morphs and twists, lodging itself somewhere along the pulse in my throat while hot tears still linger and the air in here becomes stagnant. I walk across the room and open the window before heading back to the light switch on the wall. With trembling fingers, I turn the light on, then off. On. Off. On. Off. Five times. Then five more. I can't stop until I perform the ritual fifty-five times.

By the time I'm finished, my head is going to explode from exhaustion. I ritualized more than normal today, even for me, so I flop onto the oversized bed. The linens are ultrathick and heavy, probably cost more than the bed itself, and in a strange place, surrounded by strange sounds and even stranger things, I try to fall asleep.

I wake the next morning with heavy eyes and a foggy mind. My sleep was both awful and broken, because truth be told, it doesn't matter how sorry my dad is, or how kind Claire is, or how sweet Jacob is, this isn't home. It doesn't smell like coffee and bacon in the morning. There aren't mismatched teacups hanging from hooks in the kitchen and knitted blankets thrown over the couches. It isn't filled with the things my mother loved, the things that *I* love.

I remember something Mom told me once, when I was first diagnosed with OCD: *The hardest things fall on the shoulders of the toughest people, Lennon. It will get better. I promise. It always does.*

It doesn't feel that way. I blink and tears fall, so I wipe them away with my sleeve, take a shaky breath, and head down the hallway toward the master bedroom. I pass one of the four bathrooms, the sound of a shower almost drowned out by my dad's terrible singing.

The door to Jacob's room is open with a lamp illuminating a small lump under a coverlet that is peppered with cartoon dinosaurs. I turn right and proceed down another hallway where Claire and Dad's room is located, but when I reach the door I stop.

Andrea stands in front of a frosted-glass shelf beneath a mirror. There's a curling iron in her grasp, and she's wrapping strands of her dark hair around its barrel, then releasing them in quick succession. Claire sits in an armchair, practically across the room, cell phone in her hand, her eyes fixed on its screen.

"Did you call your daddy about summer break?" she asks without looking up.

"Called him," Andrea replies flatly. "He says he'll have to check his schedule. He's not sure a visit with me is, and I quote, 'the best idea at this time.'"

I wince. Brutal.

"Maybe he's just busy." There's a desperation in Claire's voice. She's trying to give Andrea a reason. Some valid excuse as to why anyone wouldn't want to see his kid.

"Really, Mom? For sixteen years he's been busy. He's as good as dead to me, anyway."

Claire gasps. "Andrea, sweetpea, don't speak that way about your father. He's your family."

Andrea sets the curling iron down and turns to her mom. Scared of being discovered, I take a step back.

"Does he know that, Mother? Josh would never say that to Jake. Or his princess, Lennon."

"That's not fair, Andi. You know Josh loves you like you're his."

"But I'm not his," she says. "I'm not, and now that Lennon is here, it's really obvious."

"Mind your mouth, Andrea Lynn. You know full well that's simply not true," Claire says. "You're feeling overwhelmed right now. I know when something big happens, it takes some getting used to. I understand that Lennon living with us may require some adjusting—"

Andrea cuts her off. "I'm not adjusting, Mom. I'm tolerating it. Mostly because there is no other option. I can't go live with Dad, not that he'd want me, anyway, and I'm not old enough to move out, so there's not really a choice."

"Sure there is, but you're too hardheaded to hear it. You have the choice to make the best of the situation," Claire says. "The choice to be kind."

"Whatever. I'm going to school."

I hear Claire let out a frustrated sigh and the sound of the curling iron being set back onto the shelf. Crap! My heart hammers as I turn and sprint on the tips of my toes to the start of the hallway so when Andrea leaves Claire's room, she doesn't see me standing by the door listening in.

As we pass each other, I say nothing, holding my breath so she doesn't hear how hard I'm working to catch it. She doesn't speak, either, but she does roll her eyes at me.

I approach the bedroom a second time and tap lightly on the door frame.

Claire is putting combs away and turns. She smiles when she sees me. Mom always liked her. She said once that Claire smiled so big that the love would travel from her lips to her eyes.

"Good mornin', beautiful," she says. "How'd you sleep? I hope everything was all right."

"It was fine," I lie and look down at my feet sinking into the plush area rug like it's quicksand. "I just wanted to come and say thank you for the sewing table. Dad said you ordered another one. You didn't have to do that. The one that's in the room will work perfectly."

Claire dismisses me with a flick of her hand. "Nonsense. You just wait, kiddo. You're going to have a fabulous room and a sewing area fit for a master seamstress."

Heat flushes my cheeks. "Thank you," I say again. "You really didn't—"

She doesn't let me finish. "I don't ever do anything I don't want to do. Ask your daddy." Her eyes flick toward the clock. "You'd best be getting ready for school."

She's right.

"Yeah," I say. "Thanks again."

"You're welcome."

Much to the absolute horror of my father, we walk to school. That's how everyone wants to arrive on the first day at a fancy private school, right? Loser. Walks with parental unit. I *refuse* to get into the car. And my father *refuses* to send me out into the big bad streets of Bel Air, so we end up compromising. He's been staring at his phone the whole time.

"By tomorrow, I'll figure out the buses," I tell him. "Betcha didn't even know you have those things around here, huh? In the meantime, be grateful. It's a fact that walking twenty to twenty-five miles per week can extend your life."

He looks up. "I'm not sure that's the best idea."

"Extending your life isn't the best idea?" I arch an eyebrow.

"Funny, Bug. I mean the bus. I'm not sure the bus is a good idea."

"Why?"

"Are you being serious right now?"

I stop walking. "Are *you* being serious?"

"Lennon, this isn't some small town in Maine. You live in Los Angeles."

"Check my report cards, Dad, I'm slick in geography. You live in Bel Air. One of the richest neighborhoods on the planet, no one around here is suffering enough to mug me."

"I'm aware of that," he says. "I was referring to—"

I wait for him to continue but he looks at me.

"Referring to?"

"I mean someone in your condition."

My eyebrows dart upward. "My condition?"

"I'm not sure how well someone with OCD may do on a bus."

"Well, I can't speak for everyone, but this person with OCD will fare far better on a bus versus a car. Research has shown you're three times more likely to get injured in a car. Can we please not argue? I'm nervous."

He stops. "The doctor said we had to keep you to a routine as much as possible, otherwise I would have given you a few days to settle in."

"Doesn't matter." I had three months in the Riverview Psychiatric Center to settle in. Life doesn't stop because I lost everything. The world keeps spinning and people keep living and life goes on. That's the harsh truth of it all.

We spend the remainder of the walk in silence until we reach the school. Like everything I've seen here so far, it's a structure built with bricks of privilege in a striking display of grandiose gloating. It resembles a prestigious Ivy League university campus more than a high school. Tall, towering buildings created in a Gothic revival style sit encompassed by massive iron gates, paved walkways, and parking lots. A large marble sign is perched on the pristine lawn: BEL AIR LEARNING ACADEMY. I turn to him, hands in my pockets. "I can walk home by myself."

He's not paying attention. Instead his head turns to the side, and his hand issues a small wave. I look sideways to see who has captured his attention.

The phoenix kid. Kyler. Like yesterday, his black hoodie is hiding his face. He's standing next to a car that's worth more than most normal houses, a shade of royal blue, with flashy chrome. Despite it being my favorite color, it's still the ultimate douchemobile, but not much different from every other car in the parking lot.

The only facial features I can make out are strong and defined, but it's near impossible to see his eyes, because they're cast down. In a split second, though, I decide he's not a monster. I study him for a moment longer.

I'm so transfixed that when his head sweeps up, and those same eyes I wondered about seconds ago pin me frozen to the ground, I lose my breath. They're a steely, glacial blue.

They darken and shift, and his brow creases in frustration.

Are you the villain of someone's story?

I return my attention to my father. "So I'll see you later."

I pivot and begin a fast-paced walk to the school, head down. The doors to the building open, and I'm blasted with air-conditioning. Thank God, because that stare was the human equivalent of a fire-breathing dragon.

The woman behind the desk is busy sorting papers, and she only glances up when I clear my throat. "Can I help you?"

"I'm, uh, I'm new. I'm Lennon. Davis. Lennon Davis."

She picks up the phone and cradles it on her shoulder. "Jada Dempster, please report to the main office." She hangs up the phone, stands, and heads to a filing cabinet. Her fingers fly across the file folders until she retrieves one, opens it, and pulls out more paper. "Here's your locker assignment and your schedule. Jada will be along any minute to show you around. You can wait there." She points to a small leather chair. I sit, crossing one leg over the other, resisting every urge to get up and organize her papers.

A small girl enters the office. Her hair is black as midnight, her skin dark and flawless. It's intimidating, to be honest, and I'm self-conscious. She's beautiful.

When she smiles, like she's doing now, she's stunning. "Hi, I'm Jada. Welcome."

"Lennon," I say, clearing my throat. "Thanks."

Jada thanks the secretary before turning. "Lennon, huh? That's a cool name. Your mom or dad a Beatles fan?"

Most people never ask if my name is courtesy of a parent's loyalty to Mr. John Lennon himself. Maybe they don't know enough to ask or maybe they don't care to. Either way, I'm impressed. I nod. "Yeah, something like that."

She takes the folder and opens it to examine the contents.

While she's looking over the paper, I cross one arm over the other so my fingertips wrap around the wrist opposite them and pulse against my skin, counting in my head. *One. Two. Three. Four. Five.*

What if there's something confidential? What if my entire medical records are in that file? That's ridiculous. It's a schedule. That's it.

Before I can come up with a thousand different scenarios of the information available in that folder, Jada looks up. "We aren't in all the same classes, but I'll show you where your homeroom and your classes are. It won't take long to learn your way around."

I wind through the hallways, keeping my eyes fixed on the back of Jada's light pink sweater. She weaves through the crowd. "What about uniforms?" I ask. "I thought all schools like this had uniforms."

"Used to," Jada says, "but a few years ago some students threatened to sue the school for infringing on their rights to express themselves. It was a whole thing here, and by the next school year, the uniforms were gone. Most students are happier this way, at least you can be an individual."

I follow her down several long corridors filled with kids. By private school standards, it may be small, but an obscene number of people fill the space. When I think there is no end in sight, Jada stops walking and points to her left. "Mr. Martin's class."

I peek in while Jada leans closer. She smells like jasmine. "Are you all right? Want me to go in with you?"

I shake my head. "No. I'm good. Thank you."

"We have English together, second period," she says. "I'll be outside this door to get you."

My heart races, my palms sweaty. I clench them into fists to stop myself from turning the doorknob.

Jada senses my hesitation. "Everyone's pretty nice. Try not to worry."

Telling someone with OCD not to worry is like telling someone not to have blue eyes or five fingers. It's illogical and absurd. Jada doesn't know that.

She knows I was named after a Beatle.

KYLER

"MY SCARS ARE WRITTEN BY YOUR GUILT, THE PAST
WILL ALWAYS FIND YOU, THERE'S NO ESCAPE, EMBRACE
YOUR FATE, THE FIRE BURNS INSIDE YOU."

Fire to Dust, *Life-Defining Moments* EP, "Scarred"

I SPEND MOST OF THE first class distracted, but it doesn't really matter. Grades have always been important, so I stay on top of them. Academic success is imperative because life treats beautiful people differently, and since I don't have the luxury of looks, I sure as hell better have something smart to say. My father is hoping for a clone but expecting a failure, and I'm not into giving him the satisfaction of either.

By English class, second period, I'm wishing for a coffee and thinking I should have gone to Strings and Things, checked out records instead of coming to school. I'm bored and my only prospect of entertainment is our English teacher, Mr. Lowry himself, until I walk through the door and see Jada Dempster next to the new girl, whose eyes are large glassy orbs fixated on her shoes.

Jada is speaking, her finger extended to the row of desks. The blonde looks up and I freeze. First thing this morning, when I saw her with Josh, I knew I'd won bragging privileges with Emmett because I was right. She's hot. But up close and personal, she's beautiful. The extraordinary kind of beautiful that makes guys like me do stupid things. Her hair is long and tumbles down her shoulders in loose, bouncy waves. Her eyes are light and flecked with amber, her skin freckled slightly across the bridge of her nose, which along with her mouth, are both upturned. Sure, it could be mistaken for aloof, but it's not; it's cute. She bites her lip before tucking her hair behind her ear and scooting into a chair. First she retrieves a notebook from a brown canvas bag before placing it on the desk. She does the same with a pen and then sits on her fingers, like a kid scolded for being too rambunctious.

I stalk past, staring at my feet to avoid eye contact. In the parking lot when she looked at me, it made me nervous. An uneasy feeling flip-flopped in my gut, and my throat got dry. Zero chance I want to do that again.

The fabric of my trusty hoodie once again forms a barrier, a protective bubble between her scrutiny and me. I'm hoping that my casual walk-by will kill any interest she may have in me—because new people *always* have interest—but as I move past, she turns her body at her waist and I can feel her glancing at me over her shoulder. I sit down, praying she's had her fill, but when I shift my gaze up, she holds it, refusing to look away. Her head tilts. This minuscule change in expression catches me off guard. I'm not used to such fearless staring contests with girls. I feel like some freaking world wonder she's seeing for the first time; her, a curious spectator, eager for more. What is it? How does it work?

Irritated, I lean down and grab my tablet, open it, and swipe my finger across the screen. From my current perspective, I can see her feet, which are weirdly small, turn to face the front.

Mr. Lowry enters the classroom. He's wearing a long black robe with a white puffy collar, a fake mustache, even a wig that's bald on top with long gray hair rimmed around his skull. "Good morning, students," he says.

A girl named Whitney pops her gum. "Who are you supposed to be?"

"Welcome to the neighborhood, Willie," I say.

Mr. Lowry closes his hands and claps. "Bravo. Astute observation, Mr. Benton. Please share with your fellow classmates, who, like Whitney, may not be aware of who I am?"

"William Shakespeare," I say. "Willie for short, Bill if you prefer."

Mr. Lowry is the dorkiest person I've met in my life. He's always a little quirky and a lot outspoken. I appreciate it. The guy doesn't mince words. Short. Sweet. To the point.

His eyes settle on the blond girl and his face falls. "Oh right. A new student. Class, we have a new student. Tell us what your name is and where you come from. Stand. Project your voice. Be quick. We have things to do. It's the start of a new module today."

As she stands, the legs of the desk chair screech across the industrial tile floor. She cringes and then takes a deep breath. Her hand falls to her side, and she taps the top of her thigh with the tips of her fingers. She's creating a sporadic rhythm. *One. Two. Three. Four. Five.*

"I'm Lennon," she says.

Tap. Tap. Tap. Tap. Tap.

One. Two. Three. Four. Five.

"From Maine."

Tap. Tap. Tap. Tap. Tap.

One. Two. Three. Four. Five.

Weird thing to notice, right? Nope. I make music. Patterns or repetitive beats; it's all music. I bite back a smile. New kids aren't so often good at following directions—they'll give their entire life story. This girl answers the two questions and volunteers nothing else.

I can also appreciate that.

Lennon. Cool name. From Maine. Like most Stephen King novels.

She looks at me a second time before she settles in her desk, exhales, picks up her pen, and taps it alongside the coil of her notebook. The tapping quickens in speed and triples in ferocity, and pretty soon, Lennon's foot is tapping, too.

Andrea clears her throat. Her eyes cut into Lennon as if she's nothing more than an ant, ready to be crucified under a magnifying glass. "Do you have a nervous tic or something?"

Lennon's pale face blooms with color, tension rolling off her in waves.

Andrea is horrible. Two years ago, when she showed up as both my new neighbor and a school transfer, she hadn't known anybody. Still, somehow she got invited to a rager thrown by Abigail Belcourt, who guaranteed everyone it would be the party of a lifetime because Halloween was her *favorite* holiday. She wasn't exaggerating. Ghosts were projected onto the windows; waiters walked around serving brains and blood bags; a sketchy, twisted soundtrack played in some of the darkened rooms strewn with candles and various replicas of creepy things;

strobe lights and pop music blasted in the main room. Abby's father, a movie producer, had access to props, so everything was shockingly realistic. The macabre atmosphere supercharged the urges of sweaty teenage bodies entangled together in some lust fest of doom.

Andrea was dressed as a zombie nurse and yeah, she looked hot. Me, on the other hand, I didn't dress up. I went as myself, scary in its own right. I sat on a chair, minding my business, when Andrea sauntered over and fired up a conversation that included a very sincere compliment on the awesomeness of my mask (my actual face). Before I could tell her any different, she climbed on my lap and stuck her tongue down my throat. I'm a guy. The thought that I should tell her the truth vanished in a millisecond. Her mouth was on mine, and I kissed that girl like both our lives depended on it. And the way she started to move on top of me, it felt like hers did.

Her teeth bit down on my earlobe and she said, "If you kiss like that, I wonder what else you can do."

I had enough time to smirk at that little implanted thought before the lights flipped on, the music came to an abrupt halt, and the police declared our party over. Her head turned from the cops to me, her mouth dropping open in abject horror. Revulsion painted every line on her face. She swiped at her mouth, got up, and walked out silently, deciding in that very moment I was now her mortal enemy. She is both relentless and tenacious in her pursuit of her vendetta, and she makes no secret that she utterly loathes me. The feeling is mutual, so it's the one and only thing we will ever have in common.

I look at her victim. "Maybe you should run away before you catch Andrea's batshit-crazy-bitch syndrome. BCBS for short. I hear that stuff is fatal and all it takes is one exposure. Might be too late for you, though. She can really spew venom, like some demonic llama."

Andrea holds her hand up. I'm certain zero people do that anymore. Well, zero plus Andrea. "Stay out of it, freak."

Freak.

'Cause that's the worst thing I've ever been called. *Try again, pugnacious princess.*

I pick up my bag and pat the outside, my fingertips running along the seams and the pockets. "I can't believe it. I had them less than an hour ago, and now for the life of me"—I shake it around before proclaiming—"I can't find a fuck."

"Mr. Benton!" Lowry's voice barks loudly in warning.

But I'm having too much fun, and sometimes you gotta go for it. "Hold up." I reach into my bag, grinning the whole time before revealing my fingers. I wiggle them in a wave that morphs into a straight-up middle-finger salute. "There's one, and it's got your name on it. It's a fuck-you."

"Mr. Benton," Mr. Lowry bellows. "I will not ask again, so unless you'd like a one-way ticket to the office, I suggest you keep yourself in order!"

I lean back in the chair. "Sorry, Bill. My bad."

The tapping slows, then stops. Her hair falls down her back as she shifts, turning toward me. She smiles.

Mr. Lowry clears his throat. "Mr. Benton, perhaps since you've taken such a keen interest in your new classmate, you may wish to pair up with her for the term. You'll have an exciting task to complete that is worth a significant amount of your final grade."

There's a collective mutter of protest from the classroom. Lowry looks at me, waiting for my response.

"Sure thing, Bill. I only had a single fuck left anyway. Wasted it on Andrea."

Lennon

FACT: DIDASKALEINOPHOBIA IS A FEAR OF GOING TO SCHOOL.

THOUGHT: DISTINCT POSSIBILITY THAT I SUFFER FROM THIS, TOO.

THIS GUY MUST BE ANDREA'S ex-boyfriend. There is no other reason for the hostility between them. I want to tell him I don't need protection from her, but I'm silent. Her stupidness and his chivalry have rendered me speechless.

I think I smile for the briefest of moments before I hear Mr. Lowry say Kyler Benton is my partner for a class project. The smile evaporates.

Mr. Lowry gives me a questioning look. "I trust you have no objections, Miss Davis."

I shake my head despite every single instinct not to. I object! He's a hoodie-wearing, foul-mouthed, sulky guy. I can't be tethered to him! Not for an entire project, module, unit, term, or otherwise.

"Excellent. In that case, let's begin. As Mr. Benton so kindly pointed out before gracing us with his love of profane English language, I am Shakespeare. By the end of this unit, you will learn, love, and appreciate Shakespeare more than your little minds could ever conceive." He takes both of his hands, places them beside either temple, and mimics an explosion. "Mind blown. For now, get together with your partner and come up with five facts about Shakespeare."

People holler for their pairs, their *friends*. I cast a glance at Kyler, but he yanks his hoodie up farther and slouches in his chair. My heart speeds up. I freeze, waiting for it to take hold, but to my surprise, it doesn't. Moments like this, where I'm free from the OCD, are as fleeting as a shooting star exploding across the sky, so I try to enjoy it until Lowry's voice enters my thoughts: "We aren't waiting for Shakespeare's resurrection, Miss Davis. Off you go."

I drag my chair over to where Kyler sits. As soon as I place it beside him, he extends his legs in a single fluid movement to put distance between us.

A nervous laugh leaves my lips. I can't determine if he really *is* an asshole or if he's just an angry emo kid with a knight-in-shining-armor complex, so I attempt to make light of it. "I haven't caught Andrea's BCBS yet. Not contagious, I promise."

He acknowledges me with a tip of his chin. "Good to know. Not sure if I want to take the risk, Lennon. From Maine."

"Observant." Setting my notebook on the table, I reach for my pen, but before I even retrieve it, he rips a page from his and offers it to me. In penmanship neater than I'd expect is a list:

1. Shakespeare didn't go to university.

2. He started writing in the 1590s.

3. Shakespeare's phrases are used all the time without thought: good riddance, as luck would have it, break the ice...among others.

4. He also wrote poetry. Times were tough.

And my favorite:

5. Part of the epitaph on his tombstone reads: "Cursed be he that moves my bones."

A dire warning for anyone who considers robbing his grave.

I stare at the list, dumbfounded. "You know all of that?"

"I'm a slave to the great oracle Google, Lennon."

I see a tablet on his desk. "So you Googled it?"

"Indeed I did."

"In an eighth of a second?"

He shrugs. "What can I say? The school has good Wi-Fi."

"You can't believe everything you read on the internet."

He moves the side of his hoodie with his finger to reveal only his eyes. "You trying to say you've got facts about Shakespeare stored away in the back of your mind for immediate recall when it's necessary?"

"Not exactly." It's a lie. I could spew a fact or two, so I test one. "But three days after Shakespeare was born, the parish in which he lived recorded an outbreak of the plague."

The eyebrow not draped in his hair inches up his face. "Impressive. Anything else?"

He's already putting off an unwelcoming vibe, so I shake my head. "Not much directly relating to Shakespeare."

"A-plus for your efforts, but it seems the internet is our best option."

"Fine. You win."

Mr. Lowry is writing something on the board. *Romeo and Juliet*. He draws a line down the middle of the blackboard and adds, *for modern culture*.

Kyler grabs his paper back and scrawls on it.

6. Bonus fact: <u>Romeo and Juliet</u> was first published in 1597.

Damn. He's good. He grins and slides the paper across the table. He taps his temple. "That one was all from up here."

"Your assignment, should you choose to accept it—"

"I don't," Kyler mutters.

Lowry continues, "—is a modern-day retelling of *Romeo and Juliet*. Think of something that will have a contemporary, edgy twist that would appeal to the youth of today. And think hard, because this assignment will reflect thirty percent of your final grade."

Kyler's hands cover his face. "Oh my God," he says into them.

My gut twists. He hates me and now he's paired with me. Perfect way to start my student experience in Bel Air. I look at him apologetically as though I should feel bad that we're stuck on a project together. "Well, he didn't sell that as fun for me, either," I tell Kyler. "For what it's worth."

The hair is hanging over his left eye because his hood is pulled forward, but he still looks at me when he speaks. "Forget about it. Got any ideas?"

"For?"

His smirks. "The project. The shitty project we have to do about *Romeo and Juliet*."

"Well, if we wanted to do modern, we could have it set up like a dating app, only in essay form."

"No."

"I beg your pardon?"

"No," he repeats. "A dating app is romantic. The story of *Romeo and Juliet* is anything but."

"What? That's not true."

His eyebrows knit together. "Are you kidding me? It's goddamned tragic."

"Well, technically the play is a tragedy, but—"

He shakes his hoodie-covered head. "No. No *but*s. You're insane if you think *Romeo and Juliet* is a love story."

Now it's my brow that furrows. "So I can't have an opinion. You asked me for an idea, I gave you one."

"Yeah," he says, looking at the clock. "A bad one." He swipes his tablet, notebook, and pen into his backpack and holds out his hand. "Phone."

"Excuse me?"

"Your phone," he says, pronouncing the words carefully, in case I'm hard of hearing. "Give it to me, we can exchange numbers and discuss the project worth thirty percent of my final grade. Whether I want it to be or not, that makes it important."

No use praying that my hands don't shake, because they do as we exchange phones. I enter my number and hand it back. He snatches it from me, stands, slings his backpack over his shoulder. "Later, Lennon from Maine." With those words, he's gone.

Jada waits for me beside the door at the end of class. "That was weird."

It was such typical Andrea behavior; I'd almost forgotten about it...almost. Hoodie-boy's intervention seared my brain, despite being overshadowed by our pairing. I think I'm most interested in what makes him hate Andrea, because it gives us something in common right away. Might help with the animosity about the project.

"It's not that weird. She's my stepsister. She hates my guts because I woke up and took a breath this morning."

Jada frowns. "Oh my God, I'm so sorry. No wonder she was picking on you."

"Yeah, well, you get used to it."

Jada dismisses me with a wave of her hand. "No matter. That's not what I was talking about, anyway. It's no real surprise your stepsister is a bitch. I'm talking about Kyler."

Kyler.

"Did Andrea date him?"

Jada coughs. "Pardon me?"

"Did they date? My half brother says Andrea told him that guy's a monster."

Jada pauses thoughtfully. "Well, he isn't friendly, but I'll tell you this, he may be an angel, what with that voice of his...." She stops, as if she's forgotten a detail. "He has a singing voice that'll make you weep."

I have a hard time picturing him singing. "He seems more like the smoke-pot-and-wallow-in-life's-problems kind of guy. Is he in the choir?"

"No, like in a band. With three other guys. They're called something about Fire."

A student walking by turns. "Fire to Dust," he volunteers.

"Are they any good?"

Jada nods. "Amazing, but he doesn't like to play. He's done it twice. Once at a fund-raiser for a student here named Jenny Fischer. She got cancer, and we were trying to raise money. And once at the school pep rally last year because Principal Walsh offered him a reduced suspension to perform after half of the choir got strep throat. Kyler had been in three fights in less than a week, so he was in more than enough trouble to take the deal."

"Why be in a band if you don't want to perform?"

Jada shrugs. "No one blames him. I mean, he has to live with it."

"With what?"

"You know." She makes a motion with her hand around her face.

"What?"

"His face."

"What about his face?"

Her eyes narrow in disbelief. "You were sitting right across from him."

"Oh, his birthmark?"

She examines me as if she's not sure if I'm blind. "That's not a birthmark."

"What are you talking about?"

"His face. It's not a birthmark. He's tortured. Like the Phantom of the Opera. A reclusive musical genius with a burned-up face." She spins on her heel and I trail behind her, chasing after this piece of information and trying to grab on to it, to possess it.

"Wait. What did you say?"

Jada stops walking. "His face is scarred."

"Oh my God."

"He was in some house fire as a kid. The left side of his face has burns from chin to cheekbone and up across his temple, it even dips down on his neck and over his shoulder to God knows where. He tries to hide it, I've seen it once or twice, but never for long. Almost never see him without a hoodie or a beanie, and if you catch a glimpse, that hair of his is always hanging down in front of it, anyway."

It takes every ounce of resolve I have not to do a one-eighty in the middle of the hallway and return to him. Not to scrutinize, no, I would never do that. But I'm curious. I know these two things about him. Just two. His name is Kyler, and he was in a house fire as a little boy. And instantly, I am fascinated.

Not in some morbid fascination kind of way, either.

I mean I am truly captivated, enthralled, and utterly fascinated by him.

My scars are invisible, buried deep inside, guarded by the monster in my head.

Kyler who was in a house fire.

His scars are there, literally written on his face.

I pass the rest of the school day wondering about him. By the time I walk home, I only want to sew Jacob's cape. I don't want to be captured in the pages of Kyler's story. He'd be like a book I could never stop reading. I know it. It's possible I can convince Mr. Lowry to give me a new partner.

Jacob waits on the front porch when I return home. His knees fold up to his chest and he's got one arm resting over the other, his camera in his palm, and his chin resting on top.

I sit down beside him. "What's the matter? Rough day?"

"Andi told me I was a terrible reporter."

Nice.

"Andi is wrong." I smile. "You're a great reporter, and soon, you will have a cape like a real superhero."

"She's says there's no such thing as superheroes," he laments.

"You need to ignore her. She'll regret being mean one day."

"I don't know why she doesn't like me."

"She's afraid of your mad superhero moves."

"Andrea isn't scared of anything. 'Specially me."

"She's scared of something. Everyone is. And it's the bravest people who admit it."

"Really?"

"Yeah."

"What are you scared of?"

Everything.

I choose something safer. "I don't like heights."

"I'm not scared of heights," Jacob says, his voice heavy with pride. "We went to New York a few months ago. I went to the stake building."

"I'm not surprised you went to the Empire State Building. You're a superhero."

He smiles and stands. "I'm a hungry superhero. I got us snacks. I was waiting for you."

I cringe, imagining the various scenarios that may wait in the kitchen for us. "What did you get us?" I hope to God he doesn't answer with something like "pizza."

He reaches into his pocket and retrieves two small packs of fruit snacks. "I got us these," he says.

I take one from him. "I love fruit snacks. Who told you?"

He shakes his head and stands tall, proud. "No one."

KYLER

"WE HIDE BEHIND THESE PETTY LIES, WEARING MASKS
WITH HOLLOW FACES, WALLS WILL FALL AND ROADS
WILL CALL, THAT LEAD TO DIFFERENT PLACES."
Fire to Dust, *Life-Defining Moments* EP, "Impostor Syndrome"

AFTER SCHOOL, SILAS AND AUSTIN stand outside my car, flipping coins for who gets to ride shotgun. I drive an Aston Martin Vanquish, so space is limited. Yeah. I'm *that* guy. Wealthy parents with guilt complexes, born with a silver spoon, the works. The rich teenage douche of Instagram everyone loves to hate. Not going to lie, the car is sweet, but it's also unnecessary. I'm seventeen. My dad seems to forget that, or perhaps he can't bear the mental anguish he'd suffer at the wheel of a Honda. Only the best, and because of the blood that runs through my veins, it extends to me, too. Anything less is a blow to his ego he'd never recover from.

I'm pacing, hands buried deep in my pockets while I contemplate what will comprise the next few months of my life. "I should have kept my damned mouth shut. If I hadn't caused a scene, I wouldn't be in this situation."

Silas looks at me, a coin perched on the side of his hand, ready to be sent flipping into the air in a fate-changing battle. "Well, you are, so now what?"

"If I woke up this morning and told the Universe to screw me"—I point my arms to the sky—"please screw me over as much as possible." I let my hands fall to my sides. "I still couldn't have thought up a worse scenario."

Silas flips the coin and catches it before answering me. "Wanna know what I think? She's just a girl, bro. I don't know why you're getting all freaked out."

I shrug. "The only thing I like less than change is being forced to meet new people."

Austin waits for Silas to rest the coin on the back of his hand and reveal the results. Silas takes draped fingers off the quarter, and their eyes shift to the disc on the back of his hand. Austin groans and throws his arms up with frustration, much like I just did, at the same time Silas kisses the coin and shoves it back in his pocket. Given that he tops even me by at least two inches, he has to fold his body whenever he's in the back seat. Good thing he won, I guess.

Austin looks at me. "What's wrong? You afraid someone might actually get to know you?"

I glare at him. "Do I remember you saying something about how you're walking today?"

Proving he's wiser than he looks, he opens the door and lets himself into the back.

Silas gets into the passenger seat. "It won't be that bad. You're a little crusty around the edges, sure, but you're not a crappy person, either, so you got that going for you."

"What a glowing endorsement," I say.

Silas laughs.

"Dumbest thing I've ever heard."

Silas turns, disbelief registering on his face. "Really? No more stupid than being scared of doing an English project with some girl."

I get into the driver's seat and start the engine. It purrs smoothly as I pull out into traffic. "I'm not scared, genius. I'm not into making friends. You of all people should know that."

To say I took a while to warm up to Silas would be an understatement. Austin and Emmett and I go way back, but before Silas, our guitar player was a guy named Alex. He was older, and once he graduated he was out. Emmett found Silas, who had just transferred from a foster home to his aunt and uncle's place. Talk about rags to riches, Silas lives it.

Emmett swore on his life I could trust Silas with mine, but I didn't buy it. Time's been the only thing to prove me wrong.

"Regardless," Silas says. "You're overthinking. Chill out."

Yeah, easy for him to say.

Austin pokes his face between the driver and passenger seat. "Text her. Talk to her first, then maybe you won't feel so weird about it."

"She's irritating. She thinks *Romeo and Juliet* is a love story."

"So that makes her irritating." Silas laughs. "Text her something—break the ice. Because you are frosty as the arctic morning in January."

I don't tell either of them this, but it might be a good idea.

I drop Austin off at his place and turn to Silas. "You going home or do you want to come over?"

I remember that it's Tuesday, and I regret issuing the

invitation. I have to pick up Macy on Tuesdays. On the surface, that doesn't seem like much of a problem, but it is, because despite my explaining the bro code to Macy, she's got it bad for my bandmate.

I don't get it. Emmett rocks this surfer, man-bun-wearing vibe, but it doesn't even come close to the rough-around-the-edges vibe that emits from Silas like a heartbeat. He's like a walking, talking pheromone that pulls Macy like a magnet. She can get to the back of the line.

We get to her fifteen minutes late. As she saunters up to the car, dance bag slung over her shoulder and water bottle in her hand, she notices Silas in the front seat, and a smile pulls at her mouth.

Silas gets out and moves the seat enough for Macy to get in. She stops and grins at him before subtly (not at all) slipping past and into the back seat. She slides herself from behind him, to behind me, no doubt to make sure the back of his chair doesn't block her line of sight.

Silas gets in, looks over his shoulder, and flashes her a smile. "Hey, Mae."

I don't need to see her to know she's blushing like a fool. "Hey."

Silas turns to face the front. "So, are you going to text that girl or what?"

Macy squeals. Her pitch makes me cringe. "What? A girl? What girl?"

"No one."

"Your new neighbor," Silas volunteers. "Your brother has to

do an entire English project with her. Rewrite none other than *Romeo and Juliet.*"

"So why does he need to text her?" Macy asks.

"'Cause she's hot," Silas responds. "And he's an idiot."

Right. Because that explains everything.

"Aww, are you shy, big brother?"

Silas smirks. "Or a reclusive asshole. Depends who's asking."

"Neither, I work better solo. That's all. I don't do group projects. It's not because she's hot."

"So you admit she's hot," Macy says. "Text her."

"No."

"It's just a text message."

"No."

"Kyler, do it you must."

"Settle down, Yoda. Not your call."

"But why?" she persists.

"Mae, stop."

"Answer the question."

"No."

"Well, I mean, you have to have a—"

I slam my fist on the steering wheel. "Drop it."

Macy slinks back in the seat, and Silas stares straight ahead, silent.

We get home. Macy leaves the car but not before shooting me a nasty glare.

After a few hours, Silas leaves, so I shower, change into pajamas, and head to my room. I sit at my desk, intent to write. I put pen to paper until the words spill out in a ritualistic emptying of the overload of things inside my head. I grab my favorite pen and my notebook, and that's when I see her.

My desk provides a direct view into the room where the new girl has taken up residence. Figures. She's sitting on her bed, showered, too, from the looks of her. A box is in one hand, its lid on the bed. Her eyes are down, her hands shaking as she sifts through the box, stopping every so often to hold a picture closer to examine it before setting it back inside the box. I can only see her profile, but I can still recognize her expression. She's lost. I know, because I am, too.

I put my pen down and pick up my phone.

True or false, Lennon? Shakespeare invented the word "assassination."

I glance back up. Her focus has gone from the box to the phone on the bed beside her. She picks it up, tucks her hair behind her ear, and reads.

Lennon

FACT (MAYBE): ACCORDING TO THE INTERNET, IT
WOULD TAKE APPROXIMATELY 18 HOURS AND 14 MINUTES
TO GET FROM LOS ANGELES TO ANTARCTICA.

I'D SEWN JACOB'S CAPE AFTER school, eaten dinner with everyone except Andrea, listened to Claire and my father speak about people I don't know. I showered, even taking the time to deep-condition my hair. We watched an episode of a spy-based TV drama. It was mundane. It was so *normal*. Everything was going fine until I entered this room. I told my father it would do, but I hate it. Its walls are harsh, cold, and impersonal, yet somehow it ignites painful memories. It's as dead as I feel inside.

Tonight, after a particularly bad episode with my light switch, I tried to take the initiative, control my destiny. I even started small, with my best friend from Maine, Ashley. No pictures of my mother. Just Ashley. Who is alive and well and worried sick about how I'll fare in LA.

The box holds treasured photos of school dances, local fairs, going on the fishing boat with her dad, but it also holds concert tickets and friendship bracelets and things I'd always kept. I once thought they were treasures, but now I'm not so sure something that causes so much pain deserves the title.

My phone vibrates, dancing across the duvet and shaking me from my memories. A blessing in disguise...unless it's Ashley.

The screen comes to life, and I see Kyler's entered GOD_DAMNED_TRAGIC as a contact name.

True or false, Lennon? Shakespeare invented the word "assassination."

I type back.

Hang on. Let me GOOGLE it. Oh wait that's right I have a brain. The answer is true. Don't test me at trivia. Promise you'll lose a solid 99.999% of the time.

Whoa. Look out your window. I'm impressed.

I stand and see the top of a desk against the window facing into my room.

Great Kyler, thank you. I can sleep tonight now that I possess that information. It might make it a little less weird that you can see into my room.

I smirk as the dots appear again, and I close the blinds, even though I hate to block out the stars.

Ouch. She bites. Good night Lennon. Oh and tell Josh something in your electrical panel is shorting out. The light was flickering like crazy earlier. Better than fireworks.

I crawl underneath the covers and text back.

Good night Kyler. I'll make sure to tell him.

I set the phone on the nightstand. Oh my God. He saw. Unknowingly or not, Kyler witnessed my giving in to the pull of the compulsion. *Flip the switch. Flip the switch. Flip the switch.*

I close my eyes and entertain the idea of telling my dad about the electrical short. *Hey, Dad, I'm a few faulty wires away from total mechanical failure. My fuses are all shorting out. They're frayed. On fire.*

I get extra time the next morning due to a doctor's appointment. This turns out to be a good thing, because I'd been interrupted by Jacob and skipped flossing, which only meant I needed to start my morning routine from scratch. I shower, wrap myself in a fuzzy bathrobe, brush my teeth, floss, towel-dry, then blow-dry my hair, and apply makeup, which happens almost never.

Just like every other morning, I brush five times, floss once, and slip an Ativan under my tongue before I head out the door.

My dad's standing beside his vehicle, hands buried in his pockets. I grimace at the car as if it's a person, but I can't help it. It's like seeing your future and knowing it's about to suck. Then something catches my eye. I turn and see Kyler. He's in a different hoodie today, gray with a blue triangle on the front. I love blue because it's the color of the ocean and the sky. He's walking across the yard to his own car, I'd assume. He looks my way, nods, and keeps walking.

Thank God. Last thing I want is a witness to my potential meltdown.

By the time we arrive at the office building, I'm convinced there are traffic gods. I'd even be so bold as to name them—Mitsubishi and Lotus—because it takes us six minutes and forty-six seconds to arrive at Dr. Linderman's. Still, for six minutes and forty-six seconds, I tap like crazy and Dad drives with his shoulders tense and his mouth drawn in a line of painful silence.

It's not until I sit down and find myself relaxed that I realize I am in fact meeting my new shrink for the first time ever, while enjoying the calming effects of the Ativan. Perfect. Way to make a first impression, Lennon. If I'm being real, he's a psychiatrist. Medications are their bread and butter.

The receptionist types at the desk. The essence of furniture polish and leather lingers in the air. I've stacked the magazines and organized them alphabetically when the door swings open. A girl, somewhere near my age and with a shock of green hair, comes out. Her eyes dart to me before she turns all her focus to the ground.

What's your damage?

I'm watching her walk away when I hear a throat clearing. My attention snaps back to the door where a man leans against the frame, arms crossed over his chest. Dark green plastic glasses sit perched on his nose, but even so, he looks like someone who should star opposite Claire on *Cascade*, rather than sit behind a desk trying to shrink my broken brain.

He uncrosses his arms and smiles. "Lennon, I presume?"

I nod.

He sidesteps and gestures for me to come in. "I'm Dr. Linderman. Come in and have a seat."

Yep. I know the drill, Chief. Not my first psychiatric rodeo. His office is like my dad's house. Pristine. Reeking of money. I sit on the oversized black leather sofa, cross my legs, and stare at my fingernails.

"So, you're from Maine." He leans back in his chair, pen in hand.

"Yeah."

"You liking Los Angeles so far?"

He's watching me, studying how I will react. I sit up straighter, clasp my hands together, and lean forward. "You know something, there's this ridge in Antarctica where temperatures drop below minus one hundred thirty-three point six degrees Fahrenheit. It's literally the coldest place on Earth. I'd rather live there."

He tries and fails to contain a laugh. It's the last reaction I'd expect to see from a medical professional. "Such a scathing review," he says. "I will go ahead with a no on your behalf."

"By all means."

"So I understand that you have OCD?"

I nod.

"What's been done to date about that?"

I shrug. "Given that I spend at least three hours a day performing some kind of compulsion, I'm going to say not much has been done, Dr. Linderman. I did, however, just spend a solid three months at Riverview Psychiatric Center, where my meds have been adjusted and readjusted so I can function, or at least have a chance at pretending to."

"Just meds?" He arches an eyebrow.

"Basic behavioral therapy, too," I say. "I came to this melting pot of suck before they could do any real die-hard exposure therapy to combat the effects of..." I trail off. "Check the file."

He's checked the file. He knows about my mother. I'm also sure he doesn't want to pull the pin on my biggest trigger. We just met.

"Well, Lennon, here's what I hope will happen once we get to know each other. I like to think I have a pretty unique approach to treating patients, and I've had success with people who are dealing with some of the things you are."

He pauses, but I stay silent, waiting to hear about his vision.

"Medicine is great when it's used effectively," he says, "but just like a Band-Aid, in your case, it's a temporary measure. The root of the problem isn't currently addressed, so once we get to know each other, we'll aggressively address the root of the problem."

"Sounds like a blast."

He smiles again. "Are you aware of what category of OCD you have?"

"You wanna know if I'm a clean freak, a checker, a hoarder?"

"Yes. I'd be interested to know."

"Well, for one, I don't have hand sanitizer in my backpack, so strike the contaminator off your list. Germs exist. I exist. We coexist together."

"Are you a checker?"

"Who doesn't double-check things? Anyone who has common sense checks things."

"That's fair. So, what about intrusive thoughts?"

I shrug.

"Order," he says, flipping through notes.

I tap my toes on the ground. *One. Two. Three. Four. Five. One. Two. Three. Four. Five. One. Two. Three. Four. Five. One. Two. Three. Four. Five. One. Two. Three. Four. Five.*

"I like order, and yeah, I check things, and sometimes I worry about what people think of me, or hurting someone's feelings or hurting them by accident or that some horrible fate is about to come crashing down on someone I know."

"What happens when you can't control those things?"

I narrow my eyes. "C'mon. You're the shrink, you tell me. What happens? I have a panic attack that grips my throat and squeezes until I can't breathe. Every nerve ending catches fire and scorches me from the inside out while my skin tries to crawl off my body. My heart bursts with the power of a herd of wild animals while my ears ring. And the only thing, Dr. Linderman, that makes that agonizing sensation go away is to give in to the compulsion because at least I control *something*."

"What's your favorite compulsion?"

"Five," I say. "The number five. I love the sound of its name, how it rolls off of my tongue. Or at least...I used to."

A knot lodges itself in my throat.

Dr. Linderman glances at the clock. "You all right?"

"Debatable. Is anyone all right, really?"

"That's a reasonable question. What do you think, Lennon? Is anyone all right?"

I shake my head. "No. People pretend they are, but they're not. My friend Ashley, back home in Maine? Total control freak, type A personality. She's in every club at school, she never has so much as a hair out of place on her head. Everyone thinks she has it together, but she cuts herself sometimes. So, no, Dr. Linderman, I don't think anyone is all right."

"Interesting and rather unfortunate. Do you do that?"

"What?"

"Cut yourself."

I don't hide my offense. "Hell no. I think it's fair to say I have enough problems without having to deal with something like that."

"A smart and accurate statement."

Dr. Linderman spends the next forty-seven minutes grilling me about Maine, about my grades, about Dad and Claire and Jacob and Andrea, about my future hopes and dreams. I answer his questions as generically as possible because I haven't decided if I like him or not.

"Well, Lennon, it's been nice to talk with you, but I'm afraid our hour is up. I can't wait to see you next week, though, and talk more about this."

I stand and brush my hands off on my knees. "Nice to meet you." As I leave, I still don't know how I feel about Linderman. On the one hand, he seems laid-back, but I sense that he doesn't enable. My last doctor fed me meds like they were candy and left well enough alone. I'm almost at the door when his voice stops me.

"Hey, Lennon."

I stop.

"One more question."

"What's that?"

"First instinct to answer. What happens to you when you perform the compulsion?"

"Little drops of relief, so I make more, until the drops ripple and spread and then I can breathe."

"Good answer," he says. "You have a way with words. You should be a writer."

Dad is waiting outside the front door, hands in his pockets. He waves when he sees me. "How was it?"

"Five out of five stars," I say sarcastically. "He thinks I should be a writer." I search for the car and step to head toward it, but Dad stops me.

"A writer, huh?"

I nod.

Dad cracks a smile, and I find myself doing the same when he says, "We can walk to the school from here if you'd like. I took the morning off so I can leave my car here and walk back."

"Are you sure?"

Dad smiles again, but the expression on his face is heavy, shadowed in pity. "Yeah. I know this is rough, Bug, I do. I want to help you as much as I can."

"I know. Thanks."

I say good-bye a block from school, where my dad assures me there is a late slip waiting at the office and I should have no problems. In theory that's true, but by the time I gather the slip and get to the classroom, I'm thirty minutes late for English. The tables branch into pairs, and I spot Kyler, his hoodie-veiled head down, scrawling something in his notebook.

I drag the chair and fight my gag reflex as the chair legs mimic nails on a chalkboard. I stop where he's seated, but before I sit down, his eyes settle on mine. "Nice of you to show, Lennon from Maine."

Whoa. I can't tell if he's kidding or not. I swipe my hair behind my ear, and vibrations from my racing pulse tickle all the way in my throat. Kyler looks back down as I mutter, "I was at the doctor's."

His eyes seem bluer next to today's gray hood. They make me uneasy as he directs his attention to me a second time. "Anything broken?"

Yes. My mind. My fingers stiffen. One hand wraps around my wrist, like instinct, and my fingers ignite. *One. Two. Three. Four. Five.*

His focus drops to my hand for a millisecond before he's staring at me again. "Chill with the drum solo, Bonham. Sit down."

Every muscle freezes. How did he notice? I take a second to pull in a long breath and force a tight smile. Keeping my fingers wrapped around my opposite wrist, I slide into the chair. I search for something to prick a pin into the tension. "What did I miss? Fact: It wasn't your reference to Led Zeppelin's drummer."

Kyler's mouth drops in legitimate shock. That I'm the cause makes me smirk. He nods in appreciation. "Impressive, Davis." He slides his notebook across the table. There, on the lined paper, scribbled in heavy ink, are the words *Passion and Death.* From these words, inky branches stretch and reach, weaved intricately into each other on the page.

"That's super emo, Kyler. What did I miss in school?"

He laughs. His shoulders shake underneath the hoodie. "As much as I appreciate the incredible display of stereotyping you've just subjected me to, I'm not emo. Passion, *not love*, is the main theme of *Romeo and Juliet*. Meanwhile"—he points to the word *death*—"death is also a theme we may find in *Romeo and Juliet*. Look at the whiteboard." I turn my attention to Mr. Lowry's scrawl: *Name two themes we may find in* Romeo and Juliet.

Oh. Color blooms, igniting my face in a rush of heat, and if I'm not mistaken, Kyler Benton is smiling at me.

KYLER

PRACTICE LASTS LONGER THAN IT should. I'd written some new songs, and when we're all learning something for the first time, the hours slip away because everyone is stoked for bright and shiny ideas. When I get home, I want to crawl into bed, watch a crappy TV show, and go to sleep.

My stomach grumbles as I let myself in. My mom sits at the kitchen island, its surface littered with candles. She's in her pajamas drinking a glass of water and reading a book. She looks up, smiles when she sees me, and sets the book down. "Hi, sweetie. You're getting home late."

I open the fridge and get the items I need to make a sandwich. Sliding one of her candles over, I set out a plate and get to work. "Band practice," I say.

My mom nods. "Kyler, can I say something?"

I add mustard and mayo to the pile of lunch meat and tomatoes on bread and finish the top with another slice before I look at my mom, picking up my sandwich. "You can say whatever you want."

"I haven't seen you this happy in a long while."

I return the items to the fridge, grab my sandwich, and plant a kiss on her head. "It's solid, Mom, you should try it sometime. Being happy is all right, but don't get any wild ideas—I'm still your angst-ridden, brooding teenage boy."

She smiles, placing her hand on top of mine. "I can't imagine you any other way."

Somehow, my mother is the only person who can say this and have me believe it. "Good night," I tell her.

"Good night, darling."

As I head upstairs, my feet are bricks, heavy and cumbersome. Macy stands in her doorway wearing a face mask that looks like green puke. I cringe at her as I pass. "Looks like algae vomited onto your face."

She raises an eyebrow. "I would suggest you try it. It's supposed to minimize redness."

"Negative. I'm exhausted."

She spins around to head into her room. "Your loss."

I think about my bed. No. Not a loss.

I wolf down my sandwich, have a five-minute shower, put on pajama pants, and slide under the covers. I point the remote at the TV, and no sooner do I click the button than I'm on my feet.

A dim yellow glow comes from the room where I saw Lennon last night, but it comes fast, in spurts. Handmade lightning strikes, but far less ominous because they are soundless. I stalk over to the window, irritated at being torn from my comfort. The lights continue to flicker, so quickly that I need to rub my eyes to get the blur out. When I do this, I notice. *One. Two. Three. Four. Five.* Pause. *One. Two. Three. Four. Five.* Pause. *One. Two. Three. Four. Five.*

I pick up my phone.

Lennon. Tell Josh about the lights. It's like living next door to a disco.

I wait. The light show continues, and when it stops, my phone buzzes.

I forgot. I'll let him know. Sorry.

She didn't forget. Question is, why is she orchestrating a one-woman symphony with the light switch? I type it into my phone without thinking. If I were thinking, I'd ask myself why I keep texting this girl. She'll assume I want to get to know her. Zero chance I want that. Girls are a distraction. I've seen it firsthand. I attempt to salvage myself. I'll make it work related. How should we tackle the project?

With relentless vigor.

You're a smart-ass, Lennon. A musically adept smart-ass. Congratulations! A rare find.

Thanks.

Hey Lennon?

What?

Can I ask you something?

It's my experience that people ask even if you say no so go ahead.

Is it hard to be named after a musical legend so profoundly impactful? Must be a lot of pressure.

I try to reason with myself. I must at least attempt to get along with her if I'm forced to work with her for a term. I've grown up with my mother and Macy and know when to surrender. Maybe that's why I'm texting her like this, but why do I like it so much? Three dots appear. And they stay on the screen forever.

I don't know Kyler. Is it hard to be an asshole of monumental proportions?

I smirk. She thinks I'm an asshole. It was a simple question. What's in a name Lennon?

It's just a name.

I shake my head, even though she can't see me. It's not just a name though. That which we call a rose by any other name would smell as sweet.

Did you just pull some ridiculous Romeo and Juliet reference via text message?

In fact I did.

Good night Kyler.

Hold tight young grasshopper and listen. Reread what you just wrote. Romeo and Juliet told in text messages. Boom. That's how we ace English. Romeo and Juliet for the modern times. The world's love affair with technology. Lowry will eat it up. Trust me.

KYLER, THAT'S BRILLIANT UNLIKE MY HORRIBLE DATING APP IDEA WHICH HAS PRECISELY NOTHING TO DO WITH THE WORLD'S LOVE AFFAIR WITH TECHNOLOGY.

She's right.

Stop yelling at me. I'm sorry I said it was a bad idea. I don't like Andrea. She got under my skin and it made me hostile. We're stuck working together so let's not make it suck.

Fine. Apology accepted.

Great. Back to my awesome idea...

I see you have no problem patting yourself on the back.

Someone has to. Good night Lennon.

Good night Kyler.

I put my phone on the floor beside my bed and plug it into the charger. I want to sleep, but now I won't be able to. I bring my hands to my temples and squeeze, trying to find any trace of common sense. I wish she wasn't on my mind so much and reason that it must be a strange fascination with the first new arrival in a long time. It needs to end there.

There's a knock on my door. Macy pokes her now-clean face in. "Are you decent? Can I come in?"

"Yep."

She steps inside the room and instantly I'm assaulted by the scent of berries. She sits down on my bed, forcing me to slide over. "I heard Silas and Emmett talking at lunch today."

"'Bout what?" In this moment, I couldn't care less what it was about. For some stupid reason, I'm wondering if Lennon over-doses on perfume like my sister does.

"About the record demo."

"Out."

"Kyler," she protests.

"Not open for discussion."

"Just let me say one thing," she pleads.

I turn my head and look at her. "What, Mae?"

"When I look at you, I never see your scar. I know you're really messed up about it, but, Kyler, I swear, you're a beautiful person, inside and out. I wish you'd realize that."

I look at her for a minute. "You drunk or something? Was your puke face mask infused with vodka?"

"No."

"Then why the deep, introspective thoughts?"

"Because," Macy says, "I know you love music, more than you like to let on. You should do something you love."

I pull the blind back from the window and point to the lawn. "I was considering taking up gardening. Landscaping, if you will."

She rolls her eyes. "I'm being serious."

I sit up and grab my notebook, my pen, and a candle before returning to my bed. I set the candle on the bedside table and strike a match. The fire sparks, then settles into a slow burn down the stick. "Life's too short, Macy." I light the candle and blow out the match. "One day everything is fine, and the next your whole world is engulfed in flames."

Macy feigns shock before rolling her eyes a second time. "Enough with the drama. We get it. You're brooding and mysterious, but you're also talented, Kyler."

"Noted," I say. "Thanks."

"What about covering your face? Wearing a mask? Like that old band Mom and Dad used to listen to—the guy with the tongue."

I rub my face. "KISS, Macy. That's KISS. They're epic. Untouchable."

"Well, Fire to Dust should do that. Keeps everybody happy and lets you do what you love."

"It's not the worst idea you ever had, but I'm not sold on it."

She smiles, clasping her hands under her chin. "But it isn't a solid no?"

"Not solid. But it might still be a no. Don't get your hopes up."

She stands. "Good night, big brother."

"Good night. Oh, and, Mae?"

"What?"

"Silas didn't put you up to this, did he?"

She looks me dead in the eye. "No," she says, "I swear it."

Lennon

FACT (DEFINITELY): KYLER BENTON'S HANDS ARE SOFT, SLIGHTLY
CALLUSED, AND WARM. I KNOW BECAUSE I TOUCHED THEM.
DISCLAIMER: I LIKED IT.

JACOB SITS AT THE KITCHEN table the next morning, arms
crossed over his chest with an undeniable scowl on his face. He's
wearing black shorts, a T-shirt, his rubber boots, and his cape.
His camera is placed in front of him while Claire stands behind
the counter with her hand on her hip. She's flustered.

"I tried to tell your daddy it's not too early for margaritas,"
she says before turning to Jacob. "You can't wear the cape again
today, Jacob. It needs to see the inside of a washing machine.
There's peanut butter stuck to the bottom."

"I don't care," he says. "I want to wear it."

Claire's eyes dart to me and issue a silent plea. *Help.* It's funny
how beneath all the looks, fame, and good fortune, Claire is like
any other mom.

Clearing my throat, I slide into the seat across from Jacob.
His arms drape themselves protectively over his chest while he
observes his bowl of cereal getting soggy in front of him. "Hey,
bud, maybe you can let your mom wash your cape."

"I can't," he says. "I can't take it off."

"Why not?"

"What if someone is in trouble and needs a hero? Then what?" His face is deadpan. He's convinced this is in fact a problem he may have to deal with.

"You know what makes someone a true hero?"

He looks at me like I've asked him to tell me the first letter of the alphabet. "A cape, for one."

I shake my head and point to the left side of my chest. "A true hero comes from here."

"Your heart?"

"A true hero doesn't need a cape. Just a big heart and a little courage."

Jacob considers what I've said but still doesn't budge.

Time for bribery. "Listen, if you take off your cape and let your mom wash it, I think I have enough stuff here to make you another one."

He uncrosses his arms. "Two capes? I'd have two?"

I nod. "Sure. But you have to stop complaining, let your mom wash it, and listen to her all day. No matter what."

He looks at his mom, then me, before extending his hand in offering. "Sold." He unties the cape and hands it to Claire before running back to the table and throwing his arms around my neck. "Thank you, Lennon!"

Claire smiles. "Run along, Jacob, Lennon has to get to school."

Jacob releases his grip. "Bye. Have a good day, okay?"

"You too, buddy."

He races from the room, and Claire looks at me. "I didn't think he'd ever take this off," she says, holding it up. "He cherishes it.

"You're a wonderful person, Lennon," she continues. "A great sister to Jacob. I know you comin' here isn't what you'd planned, and I know losing your mama must be the fiercest pain you've ever felt in all of your life, but for what it's worth, you're a blessing to me, darlin'. You always have been such a sweet girl, and Andi, well, she's—" Claire stops, choosing not to finish her thought. "Never mind," she says, "you go on and have a good day. Oh, and before I forget, the moving company should have your stuff delivered this weekend."

"Okay." I stand and grab my backpack. "And, Claire?"

"Yeah, sugar?"

"Thanks. I mean, for saying that stuff."

Claire smiles, walks over to me, and throws her arms around me. "Every word is true. I forgot to tell you, I've called my friend Trixie, she's itchin' to get started."

I pull away. "Started?"

"On your room." Claire's hand flutters to her chest. "She's the designer friend I mentioned and my goodness, she is talented. All the celebrities use her, she's so in demand, girl's got a wait list as long as a football field. I wish she were available when we bought this place, it sure would look a whole lot different, but she was in Morocco finding herself. Andi was so disappointed." She shakes her head and looks around her gorgeous home. "But I told her you're going through a bit of a rough patch, and she was happy to make an exception."

"Thank you," I say. "That's very nice of you."

"Leave it to me," Claire says, "you'll feel at home in no time."

She's kind, but honestly, this will never be home. I don't tell her that. "I should go or I'll miss the bus."

"You go on and have a good day, sugar."

Claire's words ricochet in my brain like a pinball as I walk to the bus stop. I slip my earbuds in, select my rainy-day playlist, and take in my surroundings. The leaves of the palms, the sun shining in a bright blue sky dotted with marshmallow clouds above me. Could this place ever feel like home?

The trees in Maine were lush, thick foliage. In the fall, they would change colors and paint the landscape shades of red, auburns, and orange. The ocean was dark and mysterious, hiding secrets beneath its surface. It was beautiful. It *was* where I belonged.

Los Angeles holds a different beauty. A surreal concrete jungle melted into a real one. Everything is larger than life here. A metropolis sprawling far and wide, its edges clutched by the sea, hedged by tall, towering palm trees. Pillars of strength. Of power.

My head is tilted skyward with a certain awe when the toe of my sneaker catches on an uneven sidewalk paver. I snap to attention seconds before I fall, thank God, but it doesn't come without its share of dire humiliation. My arms flail to the sides and I stumble awkwardly before I catch my balance. To my absolute horror, all of this happens at the exact moment Kyler Benton's car dips into view and rumbles down the street.

My heart falls.

Maybe he saw nothing.

His car slows.

He saw everything.

The passenger window rolls down.

"Lennon from Maine, first day on your new feet or what?"

My cheeks bloom with color. "Something like that."

"Want a ride?"

"What?"

"Do you want a *ride*?" He stresses the word *ride*, as if I'm slow to catch on. "To school?"

I blink, unable to conjure up a scenario that could be worse. Getting into the douche-slash-death-mobile is the last thing I want to do. "Um, no."

Kyler's one visible eyebrow darts upward in surprise. "No?"

"I'm good," I manage. "Thanks."

He's still shocked. "You're good?"

"Yep." I hold my hands out to the sides. "As in marvelously okay with taking the bus."

He smirks. "Suit yourself." I keep walking, putting him and his car behind me, but he's not done. "Hey, Lennon?"

"Yeah?"

"Don't hurt yourself."

And there it is. The jab at my withering pride. My reaction is instinctive. I hold up my hand and extend my middle finger. Then I smile. Kyler laughs, turns his attention back to the road, and all I see are taillights.

By the time I make it to school, the hallways are buzzing with noise. In a place this size, considering I'm the new kid, no one seems to notice me. Perfect. I don't want to get close to anyone. Not Jada or Kyler—especially not him. At present a difficult task because no sooner do I think about him than he materializes. I'm at my locker, having opened and closed my lock four times, but when I reach the fifth rotation and open the door, there he is, hands jammed in his pockets. "You survived the mean streets of Bel Air unscathed," he says, grinning. He pulls his hands out of his pockets, crosses his arms over his chest, and leans against the locker next to mine.

"You sound disappointed."

"Not even a little bit, Davis. I'm just wondering about your ability to survive the jungle that is Hell Air Learning Academy."

He's wearing a blue hoodie today. He's so close, I can detect mint, I can almost *taste* it. I thought the gray brought out the icy color in his eyes, but the blue, God help me, makes his eyes liquid and fire all at the same time. It's unnerving. I shrug my backpack off my shoulder. "Good question, I guess we're about to find out."

He ignores the last part. "The weekend is coming. We need to work on the project."

I grab my books and shove them inside my backpack, quick to realize there are two coiled notebooks plus two textbooks. Four. The hair on the back of my neck stands up, so I grab a third coiled book and shove it beside the other ones. Five.

I turn my attention to Kyler but only hold his gaze for a moment because his eyes remind me of the business end of a hot poker. "Friday, after school?"

"Friday works," he says.

Jada's voice breaks through our conversation. "Are you guys talking about Abigail Belcourt's party?"

Kyler straightens. "What party?"

"I don't know," Jada says. "She's having some party this weekend while her parents are in Munich. The whole school is invited."

He pulls his phone from his pocket, his eyes cast to the screen. "That explains the random text I got last night."

"So, are you guys going?"

I take a moment to acknowledge how strange it is for Jada to use that term. *You guys.* It's like Kyler and I are a pair. Some dynamic duo. Sidekicks. Comrades. We are none of those things. One look at him tells me he didn't notice *you guys* the same way I did.

Jada waits for one of us to reply.

"I'm not really into parties," I say. It's a lie. Truth is, I've never been invited to one.

"I'm not really into people," Kyler adds.

To my surprise, she accepts this answer with no argument. "Well, you're both missing out." She turns. "There's an assembly this morning. I'm helping with the audio stuff, so you're on your own until lunch." The weight of her stare is heavy. She's trying to gauge how her absence will affect me.

"I guess I'll meet you in the cafeteria at lunch, then?"

"Sure." She faces Kyler. "Make sure she doesn't get lost."

He doesn't answer her with anything more than a cool nod. As she heads down the hallway, he looks at me, hitching his backpack up his shoulder. "Trust me," he says. "Solid decision not to go. Those parties are nothing but a bunch of rich kids with too much money and not enough basic regard for their livers."

I try not to show him how shocked I am. If we were sitting in the gymnasium packed to capacity, I'd have pinpointed him as the rebel, the badass partier, the kid out back behind the parking lot smoking cigarettes. So far, he's proving to be none of those things. I'm so lost in thought I don't notice how far ahead he's gotten until he turns. "Pick up the pace, Davis, the bleachers at the back fill up fast."

I will my feet to move, to keep time with his, but I end up looking like a crazed person chasing after an enigma. Before I can complain, I spot a girl with caramel-colored waves piled high on her head grinning at Kyler.

She runs up to him and puts her hand on his shoulder. I cringe because that's not something I'd dare to do. Ever. I don't even have time to consider who she might be before she speaks. "Hi, big brother."

"G'day, Mae."

She looks at me. "Aren't you going to introduce me to your friend?"

"Macy, this is Lennon Davis. She's from Maine. Lennon, this is my kid sister, Macy. She's from the fucking milkman because there is literally no other plausible explanation how we are related."

Macy crinkles her nose and sticks her tongue out at Kyler before she extends her hand. "Nice to meet you, Lennon. Ignore everything Kyler says. He wants everyone to think he's bad. He's not." She's smiling at me, so large, so wide, so warm, that I can only agree with Kyler. There's no way they are related. She lets go of our handshake and squeezes his shoulder. "He still loves his tree house."

Kyler removes Macy's hand from its resting place. "As much as Macy loves walking home," he says. "C'mon, Lennon, we're going to be late."

I smile at Macy. "It was nice to meet you."

"Yeah," she says. "See you around."

I follow Kyler to the gym, biting my tongue the entire time. A tree house? A tall, brooding, hoodie-wearing, mysterious, scarred boy who drives a fast car, doesn't like parties, plays music in a band, and has a tree house.

Why can't he be boring?

As we make our way up the steps of the bleachers, I see Andrea sitting with her groupies. The girls look like various incarnations of the Barbies I used to play with growing up, and the boys resemble stereotypical jocks from teenage TV dramas. There's one with bleached-blond hair in a football jersey with his arm thrown lazily over Andi's shoulders.

Kyler's strides are huge, and he doesn't so much as glance sideways as we pass, but my chest gets tight, as if my body knows that Andrea has spewed every hurtful thing about me to their eager ears and they've all passed judgment without ever speaking a word to me. I shouldn't care, but I do. Kyler heads to an empty space next to three other boys.

Two of them are identical. There isn't a strand of DNA that's different. Each has a mass of blond waves. The one on the left wears his pulled into a loose bun, while his brother's is sprouting every which way from his head. Both have a decent growth of facial hair shadowing their jawlines.

The third one is wearing dark jeans, black boots, and a Nirvana T-shirt. His hair is onyx, clipped short at the sides and longer at the top.

Kyler turns and points to the pair of blondes. "The one with the ballerina hair is Emmett," he informs me. "Sitting next to his twin, Austin." He motions to the dark-haired boy. "This is Silas." All of them look up at me. "This is Lennon. She's sitting with us."

Silas smiles. "Hey, Lennon."

The other two offer the same greeting, speaking in unison.

I lift my fingers to offer small wave. "Hi." My words exit my mouth in a near whisper, my brain consumed by thoughts of what Andrea may be saying about me at this precise moment in time. Warmth spreads across my limbs and flares like flames to my face. Shit. It's the first sign of panic. Panic leads to fear, fear leads to OCD me, OCD me leads to compulsion, compulsion leads to ritualizing, and ritualizing leads to the part of myself I would rather die than show. Too much has happened this morning. It's enough mental stimuli to last a lifetime, and it's overwhelming.

I slip a stealthy hand into the pocket of my jeans and retrieve an Ativan while the fingertips of my other hand begin their ritualistic dance across my thigh. Kyler turns his head around, as if he's gifted with supersonic hearing and knows what I'm doing. The way his vision strays to my hand for a second suggests that he does, which only makes me more nervous.

I stop tapping. Kyler motions for me to sit next to Silas and then slides in next to me. His leg touches the length of mine. I look down at our knees, connected.

I hunch down, rummaging for my water bottle. The pills dissolve, but it's an easy way to slip the Ativan underneath my tongue without attracting attention. I clutch the bottle in the hand I can control. I wish the Ativan would kick in. I can *feel* my heartbeat thrumming against my rib cage in time with my fingers drumming. *One. Two. Three. Four. Five.*

Andrea casts a backward glance to where we're sitting. Her gaze flutters to my hand. She glares at me, turns, and leans in to whisper to the blond Ken doll by her side. He sneers and twists his body so he, too, can investigate, his focus on my tapping.

"Hey." His voice is loud, drawing the attention of anyone on our side of the bleachers. "You didn't tell me your stepsister was hot as fuck, Andi. I mean, you said she was a bit mental, but who cares? She doesn't need to talk, so long as she can sit there, shut up, and look pretty."

Kyler sits up straighter.

The boy continues, "What I can't understand is what she's doing with Freddy Krueger over there. What are you doing with him, sweetheart? Come sit with us." He motions to one of the other boys. "Brady's lap is ready for you."

The expression on Andrea's face is a trifecta of amusement, boredom, and irritation. I look at her, wondering if she's going to put an end to things, but she doesn't bat an eyelash.

"Are you mute?"

My stomach churns.

Why is the stupid Ativan taking so long?

Tap. Tap. Tap. Tap. Tap.

One. Two. Three. Four. Five.

He looks at Andi. "Is she mute? Or is she slow?" He snaps his fingers in my direction. "Earth to Andi's stepsister. Are you stupid?"

Oh. My. God. I turn my head toward Kyler, who stiffens. His posture is rigid and unmoving, his voice deep, almost menacing. "Choose your next words wisely, Chase. I'm going to suggest you start with 'Sorry' to my friend here."

Tap. TapTapTapTap. One. TwoThreeFourFive.

TapTap. TapTapTap. OneTwo. ThreeFourFive.

TapTapTap. TapTap. OneTwoThree. FourFive.

TapTapTapTap. Tap. OneTwoThreeFour. Five.

TapTapTapTapTap. OneTwoThreeFourFive.

His hand comes down on top of my fingers. His skin is warm, a few degrees hotter than the temperature in my veins at his touch.

My brain, my body, my fingertips freeze all at once. Fire and ice collide.

"'Sorry'?" Chase says, half-laughing. "Nah, I don't really feel like it."

Kyler gives my hand a squeeze. It doesn't feel like one meant to reassure; rather to say, *Watch this.* He leans forward. "Listen, I'm in a good mood," he says. "I'll pretend you didn't ask a question that dumb. I'll pretend you remember in tenth grade when I nailed your scrawny ass so hard in rugby that you had to go to the emergency room *and* the dentist all in the same week. I'll pretend you remember last year when I gave you a black eye for disrespecting my sister. I'll pretend that you remember those things, and being the upstanding citizen that I am, I'll let you off with a warning instead of kicking your ass like we both know I can. But you need to shut your mouth. Now."

Silence falls over the crowd as so much tension fills the entire gymnasium that I forget to breathe.

Without a *sorry* in sight, Chase turns to face the front. Kyler's fingers lift from mine as his thumb strokes the top of my hand.

Exactly five times.

KYLER

LENNON WHO LOOKS LOST.

LENNON WHO IS LOST.

Random Thoughts of a Random Mind

I DON'T MENTION HER WEIRDNESS at the bus stop. I'd offered her a ride, but if the look on her face was any sign, one might have thought I'd asked her to come club baby seals instead. I don't mention Chase Maxwell and his dick move and I don't mention the mad drumming skills Lennon seems to possess or how that fascinates me and makes me want to know more. And I sure as hell don't mention my random caresses, yes, plural, of her hand. I don't mention it because I do not understand how or why it happened in the first place. It was obvious she was panicked and uncomfortable, and only a heartless person like my father could ignore that.

When I walk up to our fence, I realize I've been thinking about her for most of the day. Then I realize that it pisses me off. I like being in control of my thoughts, so when they wander, sneaking in uninvited and unwelcome, my mind gets a huge thumbs-down.

Silas's words echo in my head. *She's just a girl, bro.*

Yeah, she is just a girl. But she's a beautiful, charmingly strange girl who isn't afraid to dish my brand of comic relief back at me. She knows music. Real music. She's named after a legend. If I believed in fate, even a little, I'd reckon this could be it. But I'd have to believe in fate, which I don't, so she's just a girl, bro.

I watch TV for an hour until my mom hollers that dinner is ready. I deliver the silent treatment to Macy as punishment for trying to embarrass me about the tree house.

The sound of utensils hitting the china plates echoes through the dining room. My mom's eyes narrow on me. "You're quiet this evening."

"A lot on my mind," I mutter.

Macy pauses with her fork in the air. "The girl you were with today, maybe?"

She's walking home from dance class for two weeks straight.

My mom squeals in delight. "Oh! I knew there was something! What girl?"

I say nothing.

"Kyler," she presses, "is there a girl?"

"There's lots of girls, Mom."

"The girl next door," Macy volunteers. "Her name is Lennon."

When her name exits Macy's lips, my dad messes with his tie and clears his throat, shifting in his seat. "Josh's daughter," he says. "The one who just moved here from Maine?" *Pft.* Lawyer. Always prodding me for information.

"One and the same," I say. Now I'm curious to know what it is about the mention of her that makes him so uncomfortable.

"You'd best keep your distance," he warns.

Despite my better judgment, my interest level in Lennon was high, but now it's skyrocketed up the charts on account of my dad's apparent disapproval.

I cross my arms over my chest and lean back. "Oh yeah? Why's that?"

"It's my understanding that girl has issues."

"Everyone has issues, Dad. You should know that."

"Serious issues," he clarifies.

"What kind of serious issues?"

He shakes his head. "Josh didn't get into specifics. I was leaving for work. But I know he inherited her and her mile-long list of problems when the mother died." He says *the mother* as if Lennon's mom wasn't a living, breathing person. And everything suddenly clicks.

Lennon who looks so lost.

Lennon who *is* so lost.

I understand.

This makes what I'm about to say undeniably satisfying. "Well, she's my partner for our term project in English, so staying away from her will be hard."

"Ask for a new partner."

"Pass," I say. "I can manage with the one I've got."

"She's pretty," Macy volunteers.

My mom smiles.

My dad stands from the table, picks up his plate, and shoves the chair in. "Don't say I didn't warn you."

"Got it," I say. "Thanks for your concern, Greg, that's solid."

A few years ago, before I had what my mother has dubbed the

greatest growth spurt in history, I would never have spoken to him this way because he'd hand my ass to me, but now I'd like to see him try.

My mom, roused from her cheerfulness courtesy of my father, stands and clears dessert plates. I thank her and pretend to kiss the top of Macy's head. I barely whisper the words, "Thanks for that. You're walking from dance class. Two weeks."

She angles her head to look up at me, grinning. "Worth it," she says. "Totally."

Brat.

I go upstairs to my room and pick up my guitar. I strum a few chords, humming to myself. I don't know where it comes from, or why, but I'm inspired, so I set the guitar down and head to my desk, convinced that I'm doing it only to write lyrics, to ride the wave of creative inspiration. She might be there, too, and there's no point in denying it. I want to see Lennon from Maine with Serious Issues. This girl, whether I want to admit it or not, has caught my attention. I know better. Any kind of fascination with her will lead to epic disappointment. People like her aren't meant for guys like me. It's a shitty, simple truth, but it's just that—the truth.

I peek through the blinds, but the light in the guest room, where she sleeps, is off. The tinge of disappointment I feel doesn't go unnoticed.

I grab my notebook and a pen, somehow irritated that she's not there. Like she's got some damned job to do for my viewing pleasure. I scribble a few words on the paper. One of three things will happen.

1. The words will be lyrics (always the actual goal).

2. The pages will be coffee coasters (sometimes the result of not achieving the goal).

3. They will be filed under "random thoughts of a random mind" alongside many other useless, random things I scribble, draw, ponder, or creatively upchuck onto paper (neither a good nor a bad outcome; neutral).

> Stop hiding in the darkness,
> Step out into the light,
> The sky is filled with all these stars,
> So come and kiss the night.

Thoughts of her flood my brain. How she nervously tucks her hair behind her ear all the time, or how she bites her bottom lip when she's writing, the constant tapping of her fingers on her thigh or wrist.

> Infinity is waiting,
> Calling you by name,
> The world is yours for taking,
> So take it just the same.

Lyrics.
Not coasters.
Not random thoughts of a random mind.
Not creative upchuck.
Just. Lyrics.

The light flicks on in the window across the yard and my pen freezes.

Lennon comes into the room, black fabric slung over her shoulder. Jacob, the little kid next door—her half brother, I realize now—is on her heels with a square of yellow felt clutched in one hand and a camera in the other.

I squint and lean forward, trying to get a better look. She sets the pile of black material on the bed and moves to what looks like a desk, until she folds open the top, reaches inside, and pulls a sewing machine up and out of its guts. Jacob documents this with his camera.

She holds the fabric up against Jacob's back and nods, speaking to him as she cuts a large piece, setting the rest aside.

Shock and awe, surprise them,
Those who think you're weak,
Look to the sky and chase them,
Those answers that you seek.

I keep writing. And watching. Lennon is measuring, cutting, measuring, cutting, sewing. And I keep writing. I have no idea how much time passes before she stands, holding out her finished item for Jacob's inspection. It's a cape. Jacob clasps his hands together before hugging her, putting it on, and bolting from the room like his sneakers are on fire. She smiles after him and sits on the bed, pieces of scrap fabric and torn thread at her feet. She stays that way for a few minutes, and I wish to know her thoughts.

Because it's there you'll find me,
Talking to the moon,
Telling him my secrets,
Asking about you.

The stars will light the sky for us,
They'll illuminate the way,
They show you how to find me,
They'll make you want to stay.

I gaze at the paper and back at her. She hasn't moved. Her hair is pulled into a high bun, and she's seated on her bed, wearing sweatpants and a black T-shirt. Her hands are folded in her lap. Letters on my page are still wet from where the ink has yet to dry. I turn my focus back to her.

Lennon from Maine with Serious Issues Who Sews, you're something unexpected.

By Friday, I'm edgy as hell. When I see her in the hallway at school, I can barely bring myself to say hello, and by the time I get home, I'm like a kid waiting to see if anyone will show up for his birthday. Mom is cooking over the stove, making a red wine reduction, while Macy is seated at the kitchen table, a science textbook open in front of her, her hand sailing across paper in a mad rush of note taking.

The front door slams closed, and I hear the thump of my dad's briefcase hitting the floor. Mom's eyes land on mine. She says nothing. She doesn't need to. I know.

Lennon

Lennon from Maine

Lennon from Maine with Serious Issues

Lennon from Maine with Serious Issues
Who Sews

unravel me

By the time my dad makes it to the living room, his suit coat is gone, his tie is loosened, and he's rolling up the sleeves on his shirt. He doesn't speak to anyone, heading straight for the bar by the dining table, removing a bottle of scotch from one shelf before pouring it over ice. Scotch. He's angry.

I pick up my phone, debating whether to cancel or not, but I've been thinking about her all week, and seeing her tonight, one-on-one, is like my reward for not losing my mind to thoughts of her any more than I have already. I can't cancel.

I text Lennon.

Change of plans, Davis. Meet at the side gate. We're working in the tree house. Inside's not safe.

Not safe?

My dad + bad mood = great jackass. Tree house. 7 PM.

We can study here.

Andrea + the fact that she exists = greater jackass, which trust me, is really saying something. Tree house.

Haha. Truth. Tree house it is.

By ten to seven, I'm at the side gate waiting for Lennon. At 7:00 p.m. sharp, she exits her house and comes along the side of the fence that borders the two properties. Clutched in her grasp are a single notebook and four pens. I smile like an idiot the second I see her. I'm pathetic.

"Very punctual," I tell her. "Much respect."

"Time shouldn't be wasted," she says. "I don't believe in being late."

"Neither do I, unless I don't want to go, which is most of the time."

She laughs. "So it's true, you have a tree house?"

I point toward the east side of the yard where my tree is. "It's true."

She nods in quiet appreciation. "Well, I think it's kind of cool."

I think it's kind of cool that she thinks it's kind of cool, but I don't say that. Instead, I open the latch on the gate and swing my arm across it so she can get by. She moves past me, but only far enough to turn and wait, to allow me to lead the way. I stop at the ladder and motion for her to climb.

"Ladies first. Here, let me take your notebook."

"I got it," she says. "Thanks, though." She shoves her pens in her pocket and places the notebook in her waistband. Straightening, her hands make quick work of resecuring her mass of blond hair into that high bun that Emmett would die to have. She hauls herself up each rung with no problem, and I'm quick to follow behind. Her body is folded at the waist so she's half in the tree house, half still on the ladder when she says, "Holy crap. This is an apartment, Kyler, not a tree house."

"It's sweet," I agree. "Go on in. You're holding up traffic."

Her shoes clear the last two rungs as she hoists herself through the door.

I climb in myself and rise to my feet as she's looking around in wonder. Reminds me of when Macy was a toddler and saw the ocean for the first time. "This place is yours?"

"Since I was six. Make yourself at home." Feels weird to say that, because I can count on one hand the number of people who have been permitted to enter the sacred ground of the inside of the tree house. Lennon doesn't realize this is a big deal for me.

She sets her notebook down on a small end table that sits in the back corner before I spot one of my own notebooks. The thing is practically held together by stickers at this point. I'd been searching through it for one of the random thoughts of a random mind I'd remembered writing. Thought it would make for good song lyrics. But I've searched three full notebooks so far and keep coming up short. I eye the book, trying to figure out a way to get it without being obvious, but I don't get the chance—she's already reaching for it. I move fast enough to snatch it out from right beneath her fingertips.

Her eyes widen with surprise. I get it. It was an innocent gesture on her part, and I've startled her. "Sorry," she blurts. Her hand pulls back, and she intertwines her fingers. As if by lacing them together, she'll be able to keep them in check.

"It's okay." I hold the book up. "Song lyrics. It's like showing someone my diary, Lennon."

She nods. "Fair enough."

There's a long, awkward silence between us. "Let's get started, yeah?"

"Sure."

"Sure? I mean, I know the subject is boring, but don't sound so excited."

"I'm fine with the project," she says curtly. She sits down on one side of the mattress, cross-legged, before opening her notebook and uncapping her pen, flipping it, and placing the cap on the other end. Oh God, she's pissed.

I try to redeem myself. "Listen, I'm sorry I snatched the notebook away like that—"

She cuts me off. "It's not that. It's your hoodie."

I arch a brow. "My hoodie offends you?"

"It's not offensive," she says, "it's distracting."

"How is my choice of clothing distracting? That doesn't even make sense."

"Sure it does. I've seen your face precisely once: the first night I moved here. Fifty-five percent of communication is nonverbal. It's hard to read people who stay hidden."

"I'll ignore the fact that you're a Peeping Tom and I'll tell you this: You don't want to read me, anyway. Flat character arc."

She laughs. "Somehow I doubt that."

"It's true."

"No one is perfect," she says.

Now it's me who laughs. "Says the perfect-looking girl."

"Looks are deceiving." Her hands shake and her eyes close. She breathes deeply. *Tap. Tap. Tap. Tap. Tap.* The edge of her pen is making a series of inky dots as it hits the paper again and again. *Tap. Tap. Tap. Tap. Tap.* It's as if calling me out is physically paining her.

I gesture to her hand. "You all right?"

She nods.

Tap. Tap. Tap. Tap. Tap.

"Five has to be your lucky number," I tell her.

She freezes for a moment before resuming. *Tap. Tap. Tap. Tap. Tap.* Pause. *Tap. Tap. Tap. Tap. Tap.* "What?"

"You tap everything in intervals of five. Or did you think I didn't notice?" I consider this for a second. "Wait. Do *you* even notice?"

She stops tapping and captures her bottom lip between her teeth. I don't know if she's nervous or just plain irritated. "You're changing the subject."

She's right. I am.

"Please," she says. "I'd like to look at you while I'm talking to you. It feels weird, otherwise."

She's probably right. And if I'm being honest, it's hot as hell up here. A virtual inferno. All of that aside, I can't say I'm looking forward to it, because this always ends up being awkward. Every. Single. Time. Historically, when people get a look at my face, one of four things happen:

1. Women, mostly mothers or older women, will let out the smallest gasp and look away before their eyes flood with tears. As if seeing my face, something that could be decent if not for the burn, is the most heart-wrenching thing they've ever been forced to endure.

2. Men, like my dad's friends, look at me with the worst kind of pity. The pity that seeps through all your pores and weighs you down. *Poor bastard*, they say without words, *hopeless*. Odds stacked against me like a Tetris game.

3. The guys. Ninety percent of the time they're too self-involved to care what I look like. The other 10 percent live in some polar-opposite parallel universe where my face gives them permission to tell me where I stand in the land of jerks and jocks. My fists usually speak first in those cases and I end up suspended or in trouble. Don't worry, though, my dad's a lawyer. He's got it covered.

4. The girls, the ones my age, the ones like Lennon, they're

the worst. Studying their facial expressions when they first see me is like registering symbols on a slot machine. Shock. Horror. Sadness. Fascination. Sympathy. Friend zone. Over.

I sigh. She's sitting too far away, so I lean forward and place my hands on the sides of her thighs. There's a sharp intake of breath, but she's not scared of me. She should be. I tug her closer until her knees are touching mine and place my fingers underneath the hem of my hoodie. *Get ready to see what's behind door number four, Lennon.* I pull the hoodie up and over my head. Her eyes are wide, and her gaze narrows as it flutters across my face.

"Just breathe," I say, and I can't be sure if I'm talking to her or myself.

Her mouth forms the words, but they don't come out.

Just breathe.

Lennon

FACT (DEFINITELY): KYLER BENTON IS A BREATH STEALER.

HE'S THAT BEAUTIFUL. I KNOW BECAUSE I SAW HIM.

KYLER'S LEGS TOUCH MINE. Body heat radiates from them. That's the first thing I notice. Second, I observe his hoodie, discarded on the mattress beside us. It looks warm, cozy, and worn. Last, I see his face. Unhidden by darkened car windows or shadowed in fabric. He's exposed. It's all I can do to take his advice and just breathe.

Just. Breathe.

His hair is the color of sand, thick and wavy, hanging cropped to a clean, square jawline. His eyes are deep, different shades of blue, like the ocean in Maine and the one in Los Angeles collided. They're fringed with a set of midnight lashes and hooded slightly. His cheeks are strong and defined, his skin practically flawless. Practically. The right side of his face has clear, smooth skin, a perfect painting of porcelain. But the left...

My eyes dart to his, seeking permission.

He doesn't speak.

He doesn't move.

He doesn't blink.

Kyler's scar begins somewhere underneath the neckline of his T-shirt and brushes the edge of his mouth with a hardly visible crescent-moon-shaped line of discolored, slightly marred skin. From there, it extends upward, straight across his jaw, and flares to spread over his cheekbone before it finally settles on the temple directly beside his eye.

The damaged skin pulls taut, pink and waxy in texture. It looks painful, even though I'm sure after all this time, it's not. It'd be a shame for someone so beautiful to hurt at all.

And his knees are touching mine.

I inhale, slow and deep.

Physically, he is strong. A force to reckon with. He's sitting up straight, his stare, unflinching, projecting an air of confidence I can't be sure he feels.

My hands shake as I reach for his face. He looks surprised, but he doesn't stop me. Using the tip of my finger, I trace the scar. His eyes don't leave mine for a moment. This is so damned intense. Like he sees through my armor into my soul and all its dark corners. Something in every single cell, each molecule, tells me this is a one-in-a-million event. I can guarantee Kyler rarely lets random girls next door touch him. I owe him a token of myself in return. Something real.

"So, Lennon from Maine, do I scare you?" he whispers.

I pull my hand away, pausing at his cheek to show that he doesn't. "Not even a little."

It's true.

Those eyes. They mirror my own.

He's been judged before. He's different.

So have I. So am I.

"I'm broken, too," I tell him.

"I know." His voice is hoarse.

"You don't," I say, shaking my head. "Not really."

"Tell me."

I suck in a breath, holding it a little too long before I utter some of the bravest words to ever leave my mouth. "I have OCD."

He doesn't bat an eyelash.

"As in obsessive-compulsive disorder," I continue.

His eyebrows knit together. Surprise registers on his face, but he says nothing.

"That's why I tap things. Five. It's my favored compulsion."

"Your what?"

It's easy to forget that not everyone knows about OCD. Not everyone is cursed enough to have to learn the lingo. "I get anxious. I think about terrible things. Awful things. Things that no person should ever think about, or at least *admit* to thinking about. And once I think them..." I pause nervously. "Once I think about them, it consumes my brain and eats at it like some kind of cancer. The thought dominates every single waking moment, over and over and over again. Like being forced to watch a gruesome movie in your head with your eyes wide open. The only way to make it stop, to get relief, to silence the goddamned thought, is to do things in patterns of five or whatever stupid, irrational, illogical idea my mind has in store."

He considers what I've told him before he leans forward,

breaking even farther into my personal space. He smells of mint and dryer sheets. Ocean breeze.

"What kind of things do you think about?"

"Dying, or someone dying because of me. My dad dying because of me." I look down at my hands and pick at my fingernails. "Or what if someone I know gets kidnapped, raped, murdered, maimed, tortured? I'm certain that something I said or something I did was stupid or offensive. Like right now. I'm going to obsess later over what I should have said and should not have said in this conversation. Guaranteed." I pause, short of breath.

Kyler's ice-blue stare remains glued on mine.

"I have thoughts like that, and the only way to make them stop is to give into whatever compulsion," I say. "Sometimes I tap things, mess with switches or door handles, whatever it is, it has to be in five. Everything has to be in five."

My heart surges with such force, I'm positive it may break straight through my chest. I'd read once that hearts are wild animals, that's why they're kept in cages, but mine is determined to free itself in this moment. In the tree house of a boy who was burned in a house fire, whom I barely know, yet somehow he feels like everything I never knew I was missing.

"Lennon?" His voice is low, quiet.

"What?"

"Normal is boring."

"What?"

"So what, you have a thing. Doesn't everybody?"

"I'm not sure I'd classify OCD as a *thing*," I say. "It's a mental illness. A poison."

"It's a label," he says.

"Right, a label that exists for a reason."

"Your shrink tell you that or what?"

"Excuse me?"

"I mean, they wanna convince you something is wrong with you, right?"

"Kyler, there *is* something wrong with me."

"You're a little weird, Davis, I wouldn't say something is wrong with you. I mean, yeah, you may have some horror-movie-level thoughts. And yeah, I can see how that's some scary shit to deal with on the daily, but it's not like you've ever killed anyone." He looks up at me, a satisfied grin on his face.

But that's where he's wrong.

Tears rim my eyes. My throat burns with a massive, solid knot. *I can't cry in front of him.* I open my mouth to speak, to say *No, I've never killed anyone*, but I can't. It's a lie.

"I killed my mother."

His smile evaporates. I begin to tap my toes on the floorboards.

"It was my birthday. And I *needed* ice cream cake. My mom offered to bake an angel food cake, but I needed ice cream. I insisted. They got the wrong color of icing. Red. I hate red. As if that weren't bad enough, they epically failed at the decor and put just four flowers when she specifically asked for five." I take a deep breath and continue. "A normal kid could have laughed it off, but not me. All that wrongness, the even-numbered crimson flowers—it would have felt like pinpricks on my skin. She knew this, so instead of leaving it, she went to have it replaced. Blue icing. Five flowers."

The tears spring from my eyes and begin to fall down my face. His hands reach for me, and I didn't think it was possible, but he pulls me even closer, envelops me in his space. He moves his hands up and pauses for a moment midair before bringing them to my face, which he frames with his fingertips. His eyes fill with unspoken comprehension of what it's like to feel this sad and still be alive.

My feet tap harder. I don't even have to count anymore. I know the pattern, I know how it feels, and I know every single time I mess it up and have to start over. "I mean, who the hell cares about a bunch of stupid icing and flowers? But I do. The last time I saw her, I was irritated with her. On my birthday, every year, she'd measure me, ticking off my growth on a door frame. I'd been on the phone with my friend Ashley, we were talking about this guy who asked her out, and my mom interrupted my phone call and I was pissed. She measured me anyway, kissed my head, and told me she loved me and she'd see me later."

His thumbs move and swipe the tears from my cheeks, which sting with heat.

"They said the guy was drunk. That his car came reeling across the median and killed her. I never saw her later, I never told her I loved her back, and now I'm scared she didn't know. I can't close my eyes at night without seeing her face, I'm terrified I'll forget what her voice sounded like or that she smelled like oranges, and I'm so weak, so *broken* inside I can't even ride in a car anymore without being certain someone I love will die because of me. Just like she did."

The words leave my lips and I fall apart.

The silent tears become dry, racking sobs that consume my whole body.

There isn't enough medication, money, or therapy to fill the empty space inside me. The gaping mass of hollowness that chews at my soul is permanent.

I want to die and pretend this conversation didn't just happen.

Because every time I have it I remember that this is permanent. This is real.

I cry harder.

My mother is dead. I never said I loved her back.

Kyler's eyes soften.

I squirm from his grasp and move, determined to flee. I'm embarrassed and ashamed. I can never look him in the face again. But before I can go anywhere, he's got me caged between his knees on the mattress and he stands, towering over me. He grips my hands and pulls me to stand in front of him, and his arms wrap around me with the force of a boa constrictor. He pulls me into him, and I bury my face in his chest and let the tears continue to fall. I can't remember the last time someone held me this way, this close, this tight. I don't think anyone ever has, and for one tiny second it feels like everything might be okay again.

He frees a hand and rubs circles on my back.

"No," he says softly. "No. It's not your fault, Lennon. This is not on you. I'm sure she knew you loved her. I'd bet my life on it."

I shake my head in disagreement. Up close, the smell of mint-and-ocean-breeze Bounce sheets is overpowering. "It's all my fault," I say. "If it weren't for me, she wouldn't have been driving, all because of a stupid cake."

"Listen. It's horrible and awful and shitty and I'm so sorry that happened to you, but it isn't your fault. Not one bit."

"She's dead because of me."

"She's dead because of some dick who drove drunk, Lennon. Not because of you."

KYLER

SLEEP IS FOR THE WEAK

UNITED INSOMNIACS

Random Thoughts of a Random Mind

SHE'S JUST A GIRL, BRO.

I came up here to do a school project, and now we're in the midst of an emotional hurricane filled with all the issues Lennon from Maine with Serious Issues Who Sews has. The storm of feelings I'm immersed in is maximum-force, category-five brand of bullshit.

Bullshit because we're sharing.

Not my strongest point.

I showed her my scars.

She showed me hers.

And now we're connected on some weird level that part of me wanted to avoid while another part of me wanted to see bloom. She's shaking in my arms like crazy, sobbing, falling apart at the seams, and I'm just trying to hold on tight, to keep all the broken pieces of her together. She smells like rain. I love when it rains.

My hand cups her head, the strands of that caramel-and-vanilla hair winding around my fingertips like ribbons. "It's not your fault," I tell her for the third time. I could tell her that ten times a day for the rest of her life and she may never believe me.

I can't imagine the guilt she's pinned on herself. I wouldn't want to.

My dad is right.

Yeah, I'll say that twice because it's so freaking surreal. My dad is right. Lennon from Maine with Serious Issues Who Sews has issues. Pretty serious ones.

I don't know how long we stay that way, but I hold her until her body stops shaking, until the horrible sobs stop retching through her, until her breathing slows and stills, and then, even though it's the last thing I want to do, I let her go.

"You okay?"

She wipes at moisture that lingers on her face with the edge of her sleeve. "As okay as I ever am. Sorry," she says, looking down at her feet.

"For what?"

"For having an absolute meltdown."

"Don't feel sorry for feeling things."

Her brows knit together. "What?"

"I mean apologize if you step on someone's foot, not for having a heart, a soul that bleeds."

She just stares, so I continue. "I realize we've only met recently," I tell her. "And I'm a lot of things, including hard to get to know, but that's because I'm real and I don't show that part of myself to many people." I point to my face. "Rarely goes too well for me, so I can appreciate what just happened for the raw and unfiltered moment that it was."

As I speak, I realize how full of shit I am. I appreciate it, but it scares the hell out of me. Raw moments lead to more feelings and that's an area where I have little to no experience. But Lennon from Maine with Serious Issues Who Sews and Is Broken is broken. Just. Like. Me.

"Thanks," she says under her breath.

I touch her arm. "You okay?"

She nods, swiping at her eyes, which are now both black as the night sky, rimmed in makeup that is most definitely *not* the waterproof kind. "Want to work on the project?"

I smile. "Sure. I love distractions from the elephant in the room."

"Me too." She picks up her notebook with shaky hands and offers it to me.

Her handwriting looks like some font used in fancy script. I look up at her. "I thought I had nice handwriting. Yours is unreal."

The words *Romeo and Juliet: Act One, Scene One* are written in elegant script across the top of the page, followed by a CliffsNotes version of the first act. "Simple," I say. "Benvolio texts Romeo. Tells him about the stuff that went down with the Capulets, with Tybalt and whatnot. Romeo replies with a broken-heart emoji and rants about Rosaline and his unrequited love for her ethereal beauty. Act one. Scene one. Finished."

Lennon from Maine with Serious Issues Who Sews and Is Broken is grinning. A huge, wide smile stretched right across her face. She looks moderately absurd with the dark-angel-eye thing she's got going on, but she's cute as hell.

"You're hilarious," she says.

Now I'm the one smiling. "Well, I mean, that's pretty much it, right? Romeo is a slut. He's all into Rosaline until he sees Juliet. Then he gets tunnel vision. That's why it's about passion, not love."

"It is about love," she argues. "He loves Juliet so fiercely that he would die for her." She takes the book back and holds it to her chest, and her eyes close for a moment. She's trying to savor the hope of a love that grand.

"No one should be that consumed by another person that they'd want to die for them. That's messed up. Tragic."

"It's tragic, but it's also a little romantic."

"There's nothing romantic in basing your whole identity on someone else," I say. "But for the sake of the project, let's agree to disagree, shall we, Davis? Because aside from your gross misunderstanding of *Romeo and Juliet*, you're sort of cool."

She laughs, shakes her head, and opens her notebook again, placing pen to paper. "Fine. Agree to disagree, then. Ready for act one, scene two?"

"Hit me," I say.

We get to act 1, scene 5. There are no more emotional meltdowns. This is both good and bad, because I don't want her feeling sad, but when she was, it gave me an excuse to be close to her. I'd enjoyed that so much, I forgot I wasn't wearing my hoodie.

Time passes too quickly. Reminds me of waiting in a massive line in an amusement park for the best ride. You know it will rock your world, but it's over in a flash. It's like that.

She closes her notebook, sticking all four of her pens in her back pocket. "I should go." Looking down, she brushes stray hairs behind her ear and stares at her feet before her gaze swings up again. "I think we're going to do well on this," she says.

"Me too."

She looks like she's thinking about walking, but she pauses. "Sorry if it was weird or anything like that."

"It was weird, Lennon. Weird is beautiful."

She says nothing, but she holds my gaze long enough for my gut to somersault. She's leaving, taking the first real feelings I've had in a long time with her in her tap-happy little hands. She finally speaks. "I guess I'll see you on Monday."

"Let me get out of the tree house first. It's dark."

I use my phone as a flashlight for her to see where she's putting her feet. Her notebook is tucked into the band of her jeans again, sticking out from the small of her back. When she says good-bye, I turn and rake my hands through my hair. What am I getting myself into?

I sneak into the house, hoping I see no one. For an introverted guy, I've had a dose of real moments long enough to buy me a solid two weeks of avoiding human interaction. My wish is granted, and I make it to my room without Macy or my mom knowing I'm back inside.

I shower and change into my pajamas. The lights are off. It's pitch-black, but I still make my way to the window without tripping over anything. Her room is dark, too, but only for a moment. The light switch turns on. I wait for it to flicker, but it doesn't.

She enters the room, pauses, and gazes into the mirror before her face drops in horror. She holds something out in front of her, which I realize is her phone the same second mine buzzes.

You could have told me I looked like a raccoon that fell victim to the undead and then rose to walk again amidst a terrible zombie apocalypse.

I smile. That's a lot of self-loathing in one text message Lennon. You look fine.

The reply pops up on my screen in a flash. I LOOK like a zombie raccoon. I'm going to wash my face.

Good night Lennon.

Good night Kyler. Sleep well.

Never do but thanks for the sentiment. Oh and Lennon?

Yeah?

Thanks for not giving me an epileptic seizure with the light switch tonight. That's solid.

Thanks for making jokes about my worst secret.

It's what I live for. ;)

Glad I give you a reason to live. Good night.

Good night.

I'd probably wait to see if she has anything else to say, but she sets her phone down, so when she heads into her bathroom, I climb into bed and put on a TV show. I'm about halfway through when my phone chimes again, and I nearly fall out of bed trying to get it.

Kyler?

Yeah?

I don't really sleep much either.

United Insomniacs. Could be a band name. Think about it.

LOL

Will you ever show me your lyrics?

Maybe.

Maybe?

Better than no right?

Yeah I guess that's better.

Then maybe.

Good night Kyler.

Good night Lennon. Think about the band. Could be rad. Could have potential.

I'll think about it. United Insomniacs.

Exactly. Our slogan could be "Sleep is for the weak."

Something possesses me to stand. I get up and head to the window a second time. Hers is wide open, revealing her bed. She's stretched across it, on her side, facing the window. The phone sticks out from under the covers, closer to where her face rests on a pillow.

She's got the biggest smile I've ever seen.

My phone lights up.

I can see the band merch in my head! Now I should go to sleep and dream about becoming a rock star.

You've learned nothing, I type back. Sleep is for the weak.

Or those with doctor's appointments in the morning.

Good night Lennon. For real this time.

She sends me an emoji of the moon while I watch her face being illuminated by the real thing.

Lennon

FACT: SOMETHING INSIDE OF ME IS CHANGING....
THOUGHT: MAYBE THAT'S NOT A BAD THING.

EVERY SO OFTEN, SOMETHING HAPPENS that's so surreal, something inside of you changes. Closeness with a stranger becomes a sacrificial moment where, in a blink, in a breath, you lose a piece of yourself to them. Forever altered, an exchange of damaged, spliced shards of soul. Maybe when that happens, time isn't a true reflection of the connection you share. Like, it doesn't matter how long you've known them; you find yourself breaking for someone who has never seen all the moving parts that make you tick.

Yesterday was one of those moments. As I go through my morning routine, which hasn't changed at all for the last two and a half years, an eerie sense of calm settles over me.

It's as though Kyler's laid-back attitude has transferred to me. I entertain the notion of me getting his personality and him getting mine in that strange moment we shared. If there were any truth to that, God help him. I'd win the mental lottery in comparison to the fate he'd find.

I floss my teeth and brush for five minutes and I'm done. According to my watch, I am also early. Jacob is cocooned in a blanket sound asleep on the couch, so I tiptoe past him and into the kitchen. When I peer around the corner, my dad is sitting at the kitchen table with a cup of coffee, toast, and a pile of papers in front of him while Claire is perched on a barstool at the island, eating oatmeal that looks more like wood chips.

"I'm not sure what that charge on my card is for," Claire says. "Could be a mistake."

Dad looks up from the papers, his reading glasses slip to the base of his nose. "Sweetie, I'm not sure how two thousand dollars at Orchid is a mistake. Did you and Mel have spa day? Things have been hectic around here—perhaps you forgot."

Claire points two fingers to my dad before she turns them around and points to her eyes. "Joshua, look at me. I'd remember, busy or not, if I spent two thousand dollars at the spa. I'm not sure how you think something of that magnitude can slip someone's mind."

Dad's brow furrows. "Well, one of us needs to call and get it sorted."

"I'll do that today," Claire replies. She spoons oatmeal in her mouth again, so I clear my throat. She smiles when she sees me. "Mornin', Lennon."

"Morning."

"You're up early."

"Doctor's appointment, remember?" I direct my question to my dad, who is still in his pajama bottoms.

"How could I forget?"

Dr. Linderman's office is mellow first thing Saturday morning. The blinds are open, and sunlight filters through the windows and cast shadows on the floor. The receptionist, rather than entering data into a machine or answering a phone, is lost in a book with a male torso on the cover. The only sound in the place is the occasional gulp of air bubbles in the water cooler and the *ticktock* of the clock that I've been watching with eagle eyes.

The second hand on it shifts, marking the hour at the exact moment the door to his office swings open. I have no idea if that's coincidence or if he planned it that way, but I appreciate the punctuality.

Dr. Linderman has a takeout coffee cup in his hand. He's in jeans and a lightweight gray sweater, and he's got skate shoes on his feet. His glasses have different frames, a vibrant cobalt blue. I wasn't entirely convinced the first time, but this time I'm certain I like him.

He resembles an older college friend more than a doctor. Especially when he smiles. "Lennon, how are you this fine morning?"

"I'm alive," I say. "So that's a plus."

"Definite plus to be on the right side of the dirt," he says. "Wanna go for a walk?"

I laugh. "What?"

"A walk," he says. "I realize it's not quite the same view as the Arctic tundra in all its glory, but it's nice just the same. There's a park about ten minutes down the road."

I stare, dumbfounded for the second time this morning. "Like leave the office?"

The corners of his mouth pull skyward in amusement. "Well, I suppose we could walk circles in here, but Stacy is trying to read and I don't like this place much. It's pretentious."

The receptionist, who I now know is Stacy, looks up from

her book and smiles. Somehow that gives me validation that his request is not all that unusual.

I stand, brushing my fingertips over my thighs. "Yeah, okay."

I follow him outside and down a large block of winding, smooth concrete. As we walk, Dr. Linderman tells me as much as he appreciates my homesickness for Maine, he's lived here his entire life, so he has little to compare it to. As the park comes into view, he gestures toward it. "See for yourself," he says. "Los Angeles isn't all that bad."

The path we started on expands into huge cobblestoned walkways surrounded by plant life that branches out in all directions from a large fountain of a cherub.

"It's beautiful." I don't know if it's due to Claire and her kindness, or Kyler and the way he seems to understand me more than anyone ever has, but suddenly Los Angeles isn't so bad, and standing here in this park, surrounded by scenery that resembles a postcard, it's hard not to see the beauty all around me.

Dr. Linderman's voice interrupts my thoughts. "How has the first week been? Still longing for frostbite?"

I surprise myself by shaking my head. "It would seem ungrateful to be somewhere like this and wish to be anywhere else."

"It gets your seal of approval, then?"

I nod. "Yeah. Definitely. I mean, I'd still rather be at home in Maine with my mom, but that isn't happening."

"How's the OCD been since you moved?"

I glare at him, and he holds his hands up, coffee still clutched in the left one. "I'm asking because a traumatic event often spikes behavior in—well—most mental illnesses."

"Well, if you already know the answer, why do you need to ask?"

He wants to hear me say it. Clever Dr. Linderman. Gets me out of the office only to attempt to make me slice open my figurative veins and bleed for him.

What he doesn't know is that I'm embalmed. My soul, each fiber of my being was spilled out in Kyler's tree house yesterday. The entire endeavor has left me almost too exhausted to let the good doctor pull my trigger. Besides, this morning has been decent so far.

"What's the worst thing you've had to do since you've been here?"

"Get into cars," I say. "No question. Hands down."

"What happens?"

I know he's getting to know me. He's charging a lot of money for it, too, but I wish he'd stop firing questions.

"I'm afraid getting into a car means someone will die because of me."

We both know it's as ridiculous as it sounds and that's one of the killer parts about OCD. I'm aware that it's absurd to think the things I do. They're ludicrous, and the chances of any of them happening are pretty much zero. I know this without an ounce of doubt or any question in my mind, yet that doesn't stop the thought, and it doesn't stop my brain from believing that thought to be true. Over and over again. It's as if I'm painfully and constantly aware of the fact that I am insane.

He says nothing, just sips his coffee and nods. I offer nothing else, having grown accustomed to silence. That's what happens when you live in your head. Dr. Linderman, it seems, is not down with silence, because he doesn't stay quiet for long.

It's a shame.

"How's school?"

"Decent."

"Make any friends yet?"

"A couple."

"Nice," he says. "Everyone needs a good friend they can be honest with. It's a great place to start when your life is uprooted."

I think about Kyler. Yesterday was the start of something... I'm just not sure what.

KYLER

"CAGE ME UP AND KILL ME, SAVE ME FROM THE PAST,
THIS HOLLOW IS A DEATH IN ME, LET'S MAKE EACH MOMENT LAST."
Fire to Dust, *Life-Defining Moments* EP, "Solitary Confinement"

I NEVER SLEEP FOR LONG, and when I do, it's never well, so even on Saturday, I'm awake before sunrise. I prefer it this way because there is a certain kind of beauty in darkness. I check for a text from Lennon, but there's nothing. Disappointed, I nurse a cup of coffee, eat two bowls of cereal, and watch Netflix for two hours before I go to work.

Earlier in the week, my father brought home an obscene mass of paperwork and deposited it in the garage. My former practice space now looks as if it belongs to some criminal investigation show. I assume it's research for a case; what I can't decide on is *why* he put it in there. There is a sophisticated and empty pool house. A whole damned apartment, which I proposed to use for my practice space, but no, I was banished to this place. My father didn't want us wrecking the pool house. Then, instead of putting his papers inside an unoccupied building, he buried my band equipment beneath his crates.

It's a safety hazard. If I don't move it, there is a good chance someone will get hurt, so that's how I spend my morning. Hauling box after box from the garage to the pool house. I'm looking at the proverbial light at the end of the tunnel, a few boxes shy of being finished, when I turn to see Macy standing in front of me, one hand on her hip, the other clutching the twisted paper stick of a lollipop, her mouth shut around it.

I arch a brow. "Doesn't that have ten thousand calories?"

She shrugs, gripping it between her teeth. "It's sugar free."

I make a face. "That's revolting, it's like having Coke without the fizz."

"It's like having a Diet Coke. What are you doing?"

"What does it look like? I'm moving boxes."

"Why are you moving boxes?"

"Band."

"You're such a Neanderthal, Kyler. Speak in sentences, not just words."

"Fine." I pick the box back up, but Macy stops me.

"Sorry about yesterday."

"About sticking your nose where it doesn't belong?"

"Something like that. For what it's worth, I like her."

"You met her for ten seconds in the hallway."

"I know," Macy says, "but you're happy lately."

"I'm a regular ray of sunshine all the time, Mae, what are you chattering about?"

"You know what I mean," she presses. "You like seeing her."

She's right. I do. I exit the garage, two boxes in my arms, ignoring Macy's comment. "Anything else?"

"Yeah, I need a ride to dance rehearsal later."

I set the boxes down. "Is that why you apologized? Trying to make nice so I'll taxi you around town?"

"No," she says. "I'm trying to make nice because you're my brother and I love you."

I nod, considering what she's said. "Fine. I'll drive you, but you're going to earn it. Pick up a box, Twinkletoes."

She stops twirling the lollipop and rolls her eyes. "This is a blue job."

"A what?"

"Heavy lifting is for boys."

"Nice try, Macy. But apart from just having said one of the most dogmatic statements expressed in the history of ever, you're forgetting I know you. You're a ballerina with the discipline of a workhorse. If you actually set your mind to it, I'd bet you could bench-press your own weight, so quit bitching and pick up a box or start walking and howl all you want."

She places the lollipop down on a scrap of paper and marches to a box, making a tremendous to-do of the fact that I've ordered her to help me.

We finish, and I drop Macy off and pick Silas up on the way home. Austin and Emmett are supposed to meet us here. We pull into the drive, and I spot Lennon, sitting down on her front doorstep with her knees pulled up, fiddling with her phone.

I park the car, get out, and look at Silas. "There's root beer in the mini fridge. I'll be right there."

His eyes flicker to Lennon. He nods in understanding and heads to the garage. I enter the gate on the side of the house and come out directly parallel to where she's established herself on the porch.

My shadow blocks the sun from her, alerting her to my arrival in seconds. She stares up from the phone and grins. I hope that smile is for me. Some tiny part of me thinks I should feel strange about yesterday, but I don't. I can't. Scars come out and links of understanding, of acceptance, are born. Besides, she's just a girl, bro.

"You doing anything, Lennon? Or did you just decide to chill on a doorstep on Saturday morning?"

"Trixie, the interior designer, is coming," she says. "Claire wants me to choose the stuff for my room, and Jacob had a nightmare last night and didn't sleep, so he's catching up now. I'm here to make sure she doesn't ring the doorbell."

"Sounds captivating," I say. "Do you want to work on the project later?"

She peers down at her toes. "I'm not sure. Can I let you know?"

"Yeah," I answer. "Of course."

"Thanks." She points to the garage, where Silas has the door ajar and is hunched over changing the dials on his amp. "Band practice?"

"Something like that."

"That's cool."

I wait. I ready myself to hear her say something else. I wait to feel uncomfortable. I wait to feel rejected, but it doesn't come. I jam my hands in my pockets. "Hey, Lennon?"

"Yeah?"

"No listening to my lyrics." I give her a half laugh, turn, and wander away.

When I return to the garage, Emmett and Austin have joined Silas. Everything, with the notable exception of my guitar, is set up. Silas is to the right of my mic stand, guitar slung around him. His fingers sweep across the frets while the other hand strums in his very own interpretation of a classic Nirvana tune.

Austin stares reverently at his phone, and Emmett is positioned behind the drums, chewing gum and looking bored to death.

I grab my guitar and step up to my pedal board and mic. "Sorry. I got distracted."

"How's that working?" Emmett prods.

"How's what working?"

"Your distraction."

"None of your business," I say flatly and seek to change the topic. "I'm writing a couple of new songs. Should be good to learn by next week."

Emmett chuckles. "That couldn't be more perfect. Tell him, Austin."

Austin clears his throat nervously. "Well, my buddy knows this guy at Shade, it's, like, a minor club where people go to eat, listen to music and stuff."

I stop him from wasting any more of his breath. "I know what Shade is."

"They want us to play a gig at the summer solstice party."

"As in two months from now?"

"Yeah. In front of people. Like a live gig. Not some high school dance or anything." He's smiling but struggling not to be excited. It's not working.

"Listen." Silas steps in. "We can all appreciate that you don't want to sub demos. But it's a gig, a *real* one. Shade is gothic. Everything is pitch-black, no one will see you, it'll be perfect."

He's right. I've been there. Someone would literally need to be using night vision goggles to have a clear look at my face, and even then, I'd be a suspicious green blotch on a digital display.

It's quiet in here. Too peaceful. The movement of air, the art of breathing, seems conditional on my response. My decision. Every single one of my band mates looks positively hopeful, and as much as I want to refuse them for selfish reasons, I can't. "I guess we'd better practice then."

Lennon

FACT: MUSIC TRIGGERS THE RELEASE OF DOPAMINE
IN THE BRAIN. LITERALLY A NATURAL HIGH.
BONUS FACT: NONPERISHABLES CAN PERISH.

KYLER WALKED AWAY, AND I stared after him, wishing he didn't have to go. Logic says I should be mortified to look him in the eyes, but when I do, I feel nothing but comfortable. I love talking to him. Maybe working on our project again isn't such a bad idea.

I rise to my feet, about to head inside to check if Jacob has woken, when a silver convertible comes up the drive.

The door behind me opens, and Claire's standing there, beaming.

The car parks and a woman exits. She has silver-platinum blond hair cropped closely to her scalp. She's wearing a white suit and strappy white sandals, and she clutches a bulky portfolio in her hand.

"Trixie!" Claire proclaims.

Trixie wraps her arms around my stepmother. "Claire-bear." Her voice is nasally and high-pitched. She releases Claire and grasps my hands. If I were a contaminator, I would be petrified.

"And you must be Miss Lennon." She drops my hands and clasps hers together underneath her chin. "You will have a splendid room by the time we're done, Lennon. A dream come true."

I force a smile. "I can't wait."

I start to head back inside a second time when, without warning, a wailing guitar riff sails through the air, accompanied in mere seconds by the steady pound of drums, and the deep notes of a bass.

I stiffen.

Fire to Dust.

Kyler's band.

Jada's words ricochet through the pathways of my brain: *He may be an angel, what with that voice of his.* Precisely in that moment in time, it's as if the Universe is in the habit of granting me what I ask for, because he sings.

"Cage me up and kill me,
Murder my affliction,
This hollow is a death in me,
The pain is my addiction."

I take pause. Both at the timbre of his voice, disciplined, dark, and raspy, and at the lyrics themselves.

"Loneliness is creeping in,
A poison in my veins,
The monster in my mind, it grows,
So meet me where I'm sane."

I remember Kyler's words when he'd snatched that notebook away from me in the tree house. *It's like reading my diary, Lennon.*

No.

It's like reading mine.

Trixie's portfolio is like a magic trunk, and, once inside the house, she unloads a shocking number of small square fabric samples and paint chip shards across the color spectrum. She shows me some illustrations of her vision, which are just rough, and she advises me to virtually ignore them for now. Then she obtains some measurements and vows she'll return to select my paints, accent colors, and textiles. Most of my life is still stashed away in crates in our garage at the back of the house, waiting for my room to be finished, so I hope the process happens sooner rather than later.

Inside, I spot Jacob in the living room, staring at the TV, which isn't even on, his eyes still heavy with sleep. He brings his fingers up and rubs them. "Where's Mommy?"

"She's just outside saying good-bye to her friend Trixie. Want a snack?"

He nods.

We walk into the kitchen, and Jacob points to a large pantry door. "I want pretzels, please. They're in there."

I open the pantry and unleash my personal hell. I don't know if Claire does the shopping, but the space looks as if she's bought items in bulk, opened the door, and tossed said items inside with little regard for general order.

I empty the entire thing out, piling the countertops with cans, boxes, bag of chips, and pasta.

Jacob watches in horror. Only rather than shock directed at the disorder, it's directed at me. "The pretzels are on the bottom shelf," he remarks. "I coulda got 'em."

I pace and rummage through the items I've removed until I locate a half-full bag of pretzels and give them to Jacob.

His eyes are wide and full of wonder. "Is it your brain cold again?"

I stop, recognizing how nuts this must look, but if I'm anything, it's honest. "Yeah," I tell Jacob. "I like things neat and organized. They have to make sense."

He faces away. "Can you find peanut butter for me to dip my pretzels?"

"Yeah, buddy, I can do that." I locate the peanut butter and unscrew the top. As Jacob watches me intently, I ask him, "Did you know there's about five hundred and forty peanuts used for twelve ounces of peanut butter?"

He shakes his head. "No. That's *a lot* of peanuts."

"It is."

"Lennon?"

"Yeah, bud?"

"Why do you know so many things?"

"I like to read facts."

"I like to read about heroes." He pauses for a moment before adding, "Mommy is teaching me how to read. She says it means I will be a well-spoken young man. I can read up to grade-two books."

"Wow, bud, that's awesome!" I high-five Jacob and get him set up with his snack and a glass of milk in the living room, I return my attention to the pantry and place everything neatly back on the shelves. I use logic, ordering the less used items, flour, sugar, vegetable oil, all near the back. Near the front, within easy reach, I place cans and boxes of nonperishables. I arrange them in alphabetical order in their category and turn each one so the labels face out.

When I first got diagnosed, they gave me infographics, lengthy articles, directed me to support groups, help lines, every conceivable resource they could find about obsessive-compulsive disorder.

It was overwhelming and satisfying all at the same time.

Overwhelming because duh, *your brain is sick, so dreadfully sorry.* . . . Satisfying because if they'd collected that much information about it, clearly I wasn't the sole person struggling to drown the ever-present demons.

I read them all. I went to the support groups and met countless other *quirky* individuals, people who, like me, had a penchant for numbers, or who carried the same terrifying burden of being convinced you're going to kill someone. There were hand washers, existing in fear of microorganisms or contamination, but there is a modest side that exists to OCD. For every light-switch-turning, leg-tapping moment, there was a far subtler one, like spending three and a half hours organizing cans by their spelling and expiration dates.

Andrea arrives, examines what I've been doing, jeers, and trudges upstairs. I wash my hands, pleased with the pantry, and head to my room. She squints as I pass by, seated on her bed, door wide open as she thumbs through a magazine.

"Lennon." She can't even say my name without sounding like she's going to choke on the syllables.

I stop. "Yeah?"

"Why would you even bother with the cupboard? It'll be total chaos inside in a week, anyway. Guaranteed."

I feel like this is a test that I'm destined to fail because I have no idea what she wants me to say. "I did it because I have to." Walking away from that pantry wasn't an option. Not once I saw the disorder hidden behind its door.

"Oh please," she mutters. "You don't *have* to do anything."

"You don't have to hate me, either, Andrea, but you do. You wouldn't understand, anyway, so I'm not sure why you're asking."

"Is that why you hang out with Kyler? You think he understands you?"

This is a trap. I'm sure of it. "Kind of, I guess. At least he makes the effort. Why do you care so much?"

"As someone who is forcibly related to you, what you do reflects on me. People talk, Lennon, and I don't know if you understand this yet or not, but you're not in Maine anymore. Word travels fast."

"Maybe you should be more concerned with grades and personal relationships than you are with what people think of you."

"My grades are fine, thanks," she says. "I'm looking out for you. It's bad enough that you're crazy, but no one likes Kyler. *No one*. It's like you're walking around school with a target painted on your forehead."

"Thanks for the warning," I tell her, "but I think I'll take my chances."

I head to the guest room feeling as if I've rolled in conversational dirt and text Kyler.

Want to work on the project?

His reply is prompt.

Nope.

Ouch.

Oh. Okay...

I want to eat.

Eat?

Yes as in consume food to sustain life.

Right. I got it.

Wanna come?

To eat?

You're pretty sharp there Davis. Yes, I am inviting you to eat. ☺

First of all shut up and second anywhere we can walk to?

Depends. Do you wanna eat before breakfast tomorrow?

I'm not up to going out. It's been a long week, and I already went to the doctor's this morning and spent my entire afternoon cleaning.

I wait for him to tell me it's my loss, or how much it sucks to be me, but he doesn't.

The three small circles that tell me he's typing appear.

What do you like on your pizza?

Hawaiian?

Fruit on pizza. There's a name for people who like fruit on pizza.

Oh yeah? What's that?

Demented. Lucky for you I'm tolerant of dementia. Tree house. 1 hour.

KYLER

"YOU CAME RIGHT OUT OF NOWHERE, A COMET RACING
ACROSS THE SKY, WITH JUST ONE VIEW I SAW RIGHT
THROUGH, THOSE SECRETS THAT YOU HIDE."

Fire to Dust, *Life-Defining Moments* EP, "My Silence"

I ORDER THE PIZZA, HAM and pineapple for her and a meat supreme for myself because try as I might, I can't be excited about her choice. A real pizza—a *man's* pizza, if you ask my dad—now that's something to be enthusiastic about.

When the delivery kid shows up, I take the food, give him a decent tip because I'm in a great mood, and head to the tree house. It's been about fifty-eight minutes since I ordered, and if I recognize anything about Lennon from Maine with Serious Issues Who Sews and Is Broken, it's that she's punctual.

She proves me right when she wanders out the door exactly one hour after I sent her the text. She strides across the grass, shoos the dog, Oscar, from her feet, and makes her way to the gate. I hold it open, extending my pizza-free arm across to let her by.

She pauses beside me and takes in an enormous breath of air. "Oh my God, smells amazing."

I smirk. "I assume you must be speaking about the pizza and not me."

"Won't you always wonder," she mutters as she squeezes past. I laugh as we stroll to the tree house and stop short at the base. I turn and hand her the boxes. "Hold these for a second. Okay?"

She nods.

I'm not ashamed to confess that I can scale the tree like a chimpanzee. If you ask my sister, she'd probably say it's because I'm so intimately related to primates. If you ask me, it's because I've had eleven years of practice.

I make it up in record time and slide the tray anchored by a cable down to where she's standing, transfixed.

"I've only ever seen those on TV."

"Well, now you can cross it off your bucket list," I tell her. "Put the pizza down, set your notebooks on top, and come on up."

She climbs up. I pull the rope until the basket with the goods reaches the top and retrieve her notebook and the pizzas.

"One Inedible and one Meat Lovers," I say, handing them to her.

The corner of her lip pulls up. "Inedible?"

"Listen, Davis, the truth hurts sometimes, and let's be real, you're the one with a pineapple on your pizza. It registers as something that's pretty Inedible."

She laughs, opens the box, and selects a slice. I watch in fascination as she brings the pizza to her mouth and takes a bite. As she chews, she smiles in delight. Once she's finished, she says, "You don't know what you're missing. A Greek Canadian invented Hawaiian pizza. Weird, right?"

I pick up my piece of pie and grin. "Well, regarding your endless amount of obscure knowledge, I'm impressed. I can assure you, though, that I do know what I'm missing and you can keep it."

She giggles. "You're crazy."

"You sure I'm the crazy one, Lennon?"

She peers down and, for a beat, I'm worried I've hurt her feelings, until she surprises me. Her gaze swings upward, and with conviction, she stares at me square in the eyes and says, "I may be stark raving mad, but talk about living in glass houses and throwing stones, Kyler Benton. You hide away from the entire world and everybody in it. Literally. Like some tortured emo kid. That's also kind of insane. Maybe more insane than OCD. Life isn't intended to be spent alone."

My eyebrow inches skyward, and I abandon the notion of pretending I'm not surprised. "A girl who calls it like it is. I like that."

"Do you ever wish you were normal?" she wants to know.

"Well, I'd like it if my face weren't fucked up, but otherwise not a chance. How about you?" I ask, even though I can predict her answer.

"Every single day."

"First let me point out that average can never attain greatness, Lennon."

"Is that what you're after? Greatness?"

I shake my head. "Not quite. I'm after a life I don't wake up to fifteen years from now wishing it was different." I tap my temple. "Thinking ahead."

"What do you see?"

"A place somewhere away from here, a dog who is fiercely loyal and, if I'm lucky, a hot girlfriend. After graduation, I hope to take something that'll make my dad rage, maybe a trade of some kind instead of law school, like he's hoping, so I can make sure I'm the epic disappointment he's expecting."

"A tradesperson is an asset," she says. "How is that disappointing?"

"Ah," I say, "an asset. The standard individual has the intellect to recognize that without tradespeople, laborers, all those skyscrapers built on the foundation of the American dream, where rich people get richer, would not be possible. But to people like my father, who believe in some utopian creation of social elitists, seeing your only son become a laborer is a worse fate than you can imagine. To him, I'd be better off dead."

Her nose screws up as if my words leave offensive traces in the air. "That's both a super grim and bold statement, but allow me to point out the obvious. If you really wanted to piss him off, wouldn't aspiring to be in a band and travel the world doing drugs and playing rock and roll be a surefire win?"

"Not only pretty, but you're smart. That seems like the obvious way to go on the surface, doesn't it? But between you and me, I'm not into showing off my face. If I was even marginally famous, can you imagine the media coverage? I'd be the biggest sob story on the planet. Pass."

"I disagree," she says. "You'd be inspirational."

I don't much care for talking about this anymore, so I put a stop to it. "Not hoping to inspire anyone. Just looking to make it out alive. Speaking of which, want hand sanitizer, Davis? To wash off your Inedible? That's a thing for you, right? Clean hands, no germs." I smile, hoping my delivery can issue a small salve for the sting I've inflicted and put the aspirational bullshit conversation to an end.

She doesn't seem to notice because when I grin at her, her entire face lights up. She can't quite trust we're half-insult-flirting with each other, but she loves it. "No thanks. If we're going to hang out, you'll need to brush up on your OCD knowledge base." She wipes her greasy hands on her jeans, looks up at me, and says, "There. Perfect."

I think I just fell in love.

"So bring me up to speed. I get you're into the number five and tapping so much that I bet you'd slay Emmett at the drums, I get that crappy thoughts infect your brain and what makes it worse is that you're aware they're crappy and ridiculous, but you can't help but give in to the pull of the mad drumming skills you possess, and you hate riding in cars. Am I right?"

She looks down at her notebook. "So far, so good. What else do you have?"

"You said you hated red, and judging from your backpack and almost always polished appearance, minus that mass of hair on your head, I'm guessing you like things organized."

"Also correct. Got anything else?"

"I don't," I say, shrugging. "To be honest, I assumed OCD meant people were clean freaks or germophobes."

Her eyes dart up from her pizza, her tone clipped. "I hate that."

My hands fly up, palms forward. I surrender. "Don't hate, Davis. I'm sorry. I'm not trying to make it less than it is. I guess it was a shameful belief I held on to. I blame modern pop culture for its alarmingly inaccurate portrayal of OCD."

"That's not entirely unfair. It's a sad representation of what it's like."

"Curious minds," I say. "What's it like?"

"Truthfully?"

"Well, I'm not asking you to lie." I take a huge bite of my pizza and wait.

"Imagine constantly battling a demon that controls every single aspect of your day-to-day life. Where you're trapped in a prison alone, a place where nothing makes any sense and you're uncertain about everything except being scared. I don't mean a little on edge, I mean genuine, terrifying fear. The kind that melts into your pores until it runs through your veins. It makes your heart pound, your ears ring, it takes away your breath. And it's all because of some stupid, morbid, horrible idea your brain is trying to convince you is your truth and the whole time, you know it's not. It's like the cartoon angel on one shoulder and devil on the other."

I'm at a loss for what to say, but I search for something. "That sucks." *No, that response sucked.* "Obviously. So can you be cured? I mean, is there a cure?"

She shakes her head. "It's chronic," she says. "I'll always have it. It gets better with treatment and with medicine. Back in Maine, I was doing fine. I mean, it was okay. I still had it, but it wasn't so bad. But then my mom died, and trauma triggers the illness. It went from zero to one hundred really fast. I was in a hospital back home called Riverview. But only for a little while until I came here."

"You doing okay here?"

She shrugs. "More or less. I still ritualize. I mean, the tapping you see me do. But I try to convince myself more and more that I'm in control. That's what they tell you to do in the hospital. To sit there. Be with the panic, because it always goes away, but you have to make it through the dread, the part of your brain telling you something catastrophic will happen if you don't ritualize."

Well, fuck. That's horrible. I don't tell her that. Instead I say, "For what it's worth, Davis. You don't need to be afraid, you can do your weird shit around me whenever you want. You're the most interesting person I've ever met."

The pout in her lips turns upward. "You're not exactly boring, either."

We finish eating and Lennon grabs her notebook and pen. "We were on act one, scene five, but I finished that. I got us to act two, scene two." Her chin tips in a display of pride.

I lean back and cross my arms over my chest. "Nicely done. I trust you, Lennon. So what scene is that? Refresh my memory."

"Romeo texts Juliet that he saw her on his way home, suntanning on her balcony."

"Suntanning?"

"We're in LA," she points out, as if I will forget.

"Okay." I motion with my hand. "Continue."

"So then he says to her: 'You are the sun.'" She pauses and brings a finger to her lips. "Or is it something about the east?"

Her face scrunches in concentration, her nose wrinkling as she looks through her notebook.

"Watch and learn," I say, clearing my throat. "'Juliet, you were outside today. I know because the world was brighter, but not as bright as my world was, my love. Because you are my sun, sweet Juliet. You're brighter than the sun, more mysterious than the moon, and more infinitely beautiful than the stars themselves. You shine more than a hundred suns, a thousand moons, a million stars.'" I pause, for effect. "'And God, I want to touch you.'"

I look up, expecting to see her smirking. Instead, her cheeks are red as tomatoes, her bottom lip is between her teeth, and she's writing, pretending she isn't turning over the same thing I am.

I want to touch you.

Later that night, I stand in front of the sink in my en suite bathroom, eyes narrowed in fierce concentration, casting a careful glance at my reflection. I lean in closer, tracing the tip of my finger along the outline of my scar. The sensation is odd. Feeling without feeling. Aware of the touch to my face, a numb trail left behind by the pads of my fingers, but no sense of weight, pressure, body heat. The nerves under the burned skin have no real sensory function. Still, I look different.

My eyes are brighter. My posture is straighter. My mouth curls with some kind of contentment I haven't felt in a long time.

Shit.

I'm displaying all the classic signs and symptoms.

I'm catching feelings for her.

Lennon from Maine with Serious Issues Who Sews and Is Broken, get out of my head.

After school on Monday, we jam at Silas's house. It's his aunt Lena's house, technically, a far cry from anything recognizable to him a few short years ago. Silas doesn't talk about it much, but I'd be willing to bet my life that Bel Air is the last place he'd ever expected to be. I suspect for a while he thought he'd be in prison somewhere or dead.

I do know he grew up dirt-poor with an addict for a mother. At age eight, he was removed from his home and bounced around in foster care until his mother's sister, Lena, and her husband, Patrick, took him.

Now he's a quiet guy who expects nothing from anyone. Makes sense considering he learned from a young age that expectation only leads to disappointment.

So rather than throw a huge house party when his aunt Lena and uncle Patrick leave for the weekend, we end up practicing at their lavish estate and grilling burgers by the pool. Perfect way to spend the afternoon, if you ask me.

Austin and Emmett are already there when I pull up the long circular cobblestoned drive. When I let myself in the monstrous entryway, I spot our band equipment set up to the left, and Silas, Emmett, and Austin seated on the couch.

The large maroon wall behind them is covered in masks from all over the world. A small piece of a place in the Universe or a part of history brought home to remind Lena and Patrick that they are loaded and love to travel. I have hundreds of eyes on me instead of three sets.

I look at my watch. "Am I late?"

Austin stands and rubs his hands together. "No. We were early. Everyone's excited about the gig."

Right. The gig.

What Austin meant was *Everyone's excited about the gig except you.*

Silas raises an eyebrow as if he can read my mind. "You're still cool about it, right?"

"Yeah," I say.

But I'm not. I've never been cool with the gig and it's hard to pretend otherwise, but all three remind me of kids waiting on Santa Claus, and contrary to what my father might think, I'm not a grade A jerk. So here goes nothing. I force a laugh and point toward the wall, as if looking at it somehow reminded me. "Macy thinks we should wear masks like Slipknot." I say it like it's absurd. As if it's the most ridiculous idea on the planet. As though it is the worst idea in the entire Milky Way.

And I wait.

Three...

Two...

One...

Emmett's spine stiffens.

It's registered.

I said it.

Slipknot.

One word.

But Emmett hears *Legends*.

Gods among music.

That which we aspire to be.

Something changes in his eyes. Something that tells me Emmett considers this the best idea within both the Milky Way and the Andromeda Galaxy combined.

Maybe we can play the gig.

"That's kind of a cool idea."

Austin nods to support his twin. "That's an awesome idea."

Silas rises to his feet and walks to the sitting room, picking up his guitar, which was resting against one wall. He slings it around his shoulder. "Would that make you more comfortable?"

Buzzkill. I shrug. "I don't know. Would it be stupid?"

Emmett clears his throat, and his mouth hangs open in offense. "The only thing that's stupid is you. For asking that question. For the love of all things Slipknot, I'm going to pretend that you didn't even ask that question. You can thank me later."

"I'll keep that in mind," I say.

Austin laughs.

Silas plugs the guitar into the amp, cranks the dial, and plays a riff. "I couldn't care less if we came out wearing masks of our dead presidents so long as people can hear us. That's how the magic will happen."

Emmett takes his place behind the drums, turning the cap he's wearing backward, and picks up his drumsticks. "Macy got the looks and the brains in your family, Kyler." He nods, unable to wipe the smirk off his face at the prospect of being anywhere near as cool as Slipknot. I don't have the heart to tell him it'll be a cold day in hell before we're even on the subpar level of hundreds of levels below Slipknot. Who am I to crush his dreams?

Austin grabs his bass, so I get one of Silas's extra guitars and plug it in.

Austin twists the pegs on the neck of his bass. If he kept his instrument in a case where it belongs, he'd be less likely to have to tune it every time we practice. His head tilts to the side and his fingers slide along the frets. "We can go to that store in Hollywood..."

I cut him off. "No," I say. "If I have to wear a mask, I want it to be one of a kind." *Lennon from Maine with Serious Issues Who Sews and Is Broken, I told you to get out of my head.* "I think I might ask someone to make mine."

Lennon

FACT: PEOPLE IN LOVE ACT FANATICAL BECAUSE OF A DECREASE IN SEROTONIN, PROVEN IN OCD SUFFERERS. PEOPLE IN LOVE EXPERIENCE SYMPTOMS SIMILAR TO THOSE WITH OCD. QUESTION: WHAT DOES THAT MEAN FOR ME?

I COULD TELL YOU IT'S been a little over four months since my mother died. I could even say it's been six weeks, six days, seven hours, and forty-three minutes since I arrived in Los Angeles to live with my father, but I can't tell you what day it happens to be when I realize I've fallen in love with the night.

After dinner, I often stare out the colossal windows waiting for the sun to dip its brush and paint the sky tangerine and apricot before the sky turns inky and the stars come out to play. I tap my fingers, not on my thighs, and not in patterns of five, but in a steady drumming motion along the surface of a table. I do this as an ordinary person would while they wait hungrily for the moon to rise and eclipse any remnants of the day.

Nighttime is when the uninhibited and very real version of Kyler comes out. Something in him is born in darkness and I get to experience it in all of its raw magic. He's fascinating.

We talk of big things that are little things. We talk of little things that are huge things. We talk about things that shouldn't even be things yet somehow are.

I go to bed each night with my tummy in vibrating coils. The twists and pulls that stem from nervous anticipation of pleasure to come. The kind that casts smiles on faces where there were none before.

I like him.

More than I should.

Way more than I should.

Every molecule of my DNA wants to overthink that. I want to analyze it, pick it apart, measure it, and put it back together in some semblance, some kind of order I may be able to recognize, but I can't. I can't because it counters my survival instinct. The place somewhere deep inside of me where I understand that speaking to him, *with* him, about important things, trivial things, or shouldn't-be things, fires each piston in my brain, and for the first time in recent memory, I get deliverance from the storm that forever brews inside my head.

It's calm.

It's quiet.

It's settled.

And it never lasts long enough.

Tonight we've just had a lengthy discussion about the likelihood of dreams being a portal to some external, alternate reality.

All signs point to yes. They could be. Inceptions of inceptions and so forth.

I'm in oversized pj pants, lying in my bed with my phone held close to my face as I type.

Kyler?

Yeah?

This is the best part of my day.

Bed? Geez Davis you're OLD.

I mean talking to you.

I see you every day in English.

I mean really talking to you.

Why?

Dunno. Just is. Hey. Have you thought about it?

What?

Your lyrics. Can I see them?

Depends, will you tell me every shitty thought you have?

What? No.

Well you're basically asking me to do the same thing.

It's not the same thing at all! You know my worst secret. A secret that trumps lyrics, even if they are sacred and personal. You choose those thoughts. I don't.

Fair. I'm a man known to bargain, Lennon, and you have something I need.

I do? I bite my lip. What could I possibly have that you need? I won't give you my Ativan or any other mind altering narcotics.

Hmmm. Tempting. But no. I need somebody with an artistic eye and some serious skill.

Want me to make your prom dress, Kyler?

Funny. I need a mask.

Like for your face?

Uh yeah, Davis. Where else do you wear a mask?

Why?

Rule one. Don't ask questions.

Are you trying to make yourself sound way more badass by making like I'm crafting a disguise for a bank robbery?

Totally. Is it working?

Not even close. Why the mask?

I'm starting a trend...

Kyler!

Fine. It's for a gig.

A gig?

Refer to rule number one and stop asking questions.

Fine. In exchange for?

Three small dots appear on the screen and last far too long; long enough for me to hold my breath. The words pop up and immediately snatch away the air I so desperately tried to keep in my lungs.

You're broken and you're beautiful,

Shattered till you're jaded,

Drink the bitter with the pain,

Withered, wilted, faded.

The dots appear again.

My.

Heart.

Stops.

Until he types: There. Song lyrics that equal a virtual handshake. G'night Davis.

My fingers fly across the keyboard in protest. What? Wait. Where's the rest? That can't be it!

The dots don't appear.

Silence.

I type faster.

Kyler?

A song can't be four lines.

Hello?

The dots return and I pull my phone closer, just to make sure it's real.

You only get four lines.

What? No! Why? Why on earth would you do that? That's unkind! Unjust! And a slew of other words to describe the horrific nature of what you're doing. Deal's off.

Horrific nature? That's some kind of accolade, Lennon.

Tell me the rest of the song!

Good night, Lennon. Deal's on. You can thank me later when you wake up with something to look forward to in a world that is unkind and unjust.

Will you ever send a full song?

Circumstances are uncertain. Will the mask be a piece of art? Sleep well fangirl.

I plug my phone in and reach for the string to draw the blinds because if he's looking, I don't want him to see the smile that's taking over my face.

Sunday. It's a thing around here. On the third Sunday of every month, it's a *big* thing around here. Unless otherwise scheduled,

Claire, my father, Jacob, Andrea, and now me host a Bel Air brunch for all of Claire's socialite friends and their families. With all the fuss everyone is making, it's as though we're lunching with the queen.

Jacob is seated on my bed playing with building blocks while I stand in front of my closet, nervous. What if no one likes me? What if I say or do something stupid? What if OCD me comes to the party uninvited like that uncle no one wants to talk about?

"Jake?"

"Yeah?"

"What do Andrea and your mom usually wear to brunch? Jeans? A dress?" I wasn't up to attending Claire's last brunch, so I'm looking to him for guidance.

He thinks for a moment. "Mama is always in a dress, sometimes with pearls. Andi wears jeans most of the time except when the Lawsons come. She has a crush on Michael, I heard her telling one of her friends that once. When Michael comes she wears a dress."

Let's hope Michael isn't coming. I select a pair of jeans from the hanger with a plain black T-shirt and head to the bathroom to shower and get ready.

An hour later, Jacob stands next to me dutifully plucking sliced strawberries from my cutting board and putting them in a bowl. I'm not sure why Claire doesn't have help for things like chopping berries for fruit salad, or brewing coffee, or folding napkins around the rose-gold cutlery. I thought all celebrities had household staff, but I was wrong. Dad said Claire prefers it this way, that she likes to keep things real.

"Mommy loves Sunday brunch. She says it reminds her of when she was a little girl."

I cast a glance toward Claire, who has her back to the counter. She's wearing a black-and-white polka-dot apron with neon pink accents and piping, and she holds a whisk in one hand, a bowl in the other.

"Mmm-hmm," she says, whisking her batter. "Granny always said as long as you had good breakfast, good friends, and a good family, then you could do anything in life, and I'm inclined to agree. She was a tough one, my gran. Every Sunday we were expected for brunch, rain or shine. Unless you had a flu or an injury that rendered you immobile, you were going. The world could be comin' down around us, and Gran thought a stack of pancakes could fix it all."

"My mom made eggs, bacon, and pancakes every Sunday." My voice comes out small and unsure, as if it's testing out the memory of my mother, to see if it will make me break.

Jacob doesn't even look up from his task as he once again reminds me, "It's okay to miss your mommy."

Claire's whisk slows. "Jacob, mind yourself."

I finish the strawberries, wipe the cutting board with a paper towel, and get the cantaloupe from the pile of groceries on the table. "It's okay for us to talk about my mom." Truth is, I'm not sure it is. I don't know that it won't make this room shrink and my chest hurt, but somehow allowing myself to remember her helps to keep her alive.

"I don't want Jacob to accidentally say something that could bring pain to your heart," Claire states. She looks at Jacob. "If

Lennon wants to talk about her mama, Jacob, then she can bring it up. Otherwise, hush."

Jacob looks up at me for confirmation, so I give him my best smile. "It's okay."

He eats one of the strawberries from the bowl and with it stuffed in the side of his cheek, he asks, "Lennon, can I ask a question about your mommy?"

"Sure you can, buddy."

"What was she like?"

"She was awesome," I say. "She liked to bake cookies and knit blankets and play the guitar. She loved music so much. I'm pretty sure the only thing she loved more than music was me."

"My mommy loves me more than anything else, too," he says.

I smile at him. "Of course she does."

"Do you look like her? I bet she was pretty."

"She was, and it depends who you ask, but some people think so."

My dad enters the kitchen. "Some people think what?"

"That Lennon looks like her mommy," Jacob offers.

Dad ruffles Jacob's hair. "She does." His head tilts slightly to the side and his eyes soften. "My God," he says under his breath. "You really do look *just* like her. With your hair down like that, it's hard to tell the difference." He focuses on Jacob again. "When Lennon was a little girl, she used to love to hear the story about how her mom and I met."

Jacob hops down from the stool and looks up at our dad, then at me. "Can he tell us, Lennon, please?"

"Sure." I've heard the story hundreds of times, maybe more.

Both his version and hers. I don't know why things didn't work out between my parents, because I was only two when they separated, but I never asked. They were best friends for as long as I can remember. If Dad was driving me to school, he'd come over and drink coffee with Mom for an hour before I'd even be ready. He'd steal bacon from the frying pan and Mom would slap his shoulder and laugh. If it was my birthday, they'd go shopping for my gift together. Dad would sleep in the guest room on Christmas Eve to be there when I woke in the morning, and when he got this amazing opportunity out here in Los Angeles, my mother was the one who convinced him to go.

She moped around for weeks afterward but told me that things only came around once in a lifetime, and we both loved my father enough to support his dreams.

I must look lost in thought, because my dad clears his throat. When I look up he asks, "Are you sure, Bug?"

I nod.

He pours Jacob a glass of orange juice and himself a coffee before they both sit down at the table. Jacob sets crossed arms on its surface and rests his chin on top, ready to be enthralled by the impending tale. I keep chopping the cantaloupe and brace myself for one of the best memories my father held of my mother, long before I knew her.

"I was at a concert in Tennessee," he begins. "It was Fourth of July weekend and already it was hot as Satan's underpants. My clothes stuck to me like I'd run through a sprinkler. In fact I'm pretty sure I had pit stains all the way to my wrists."

Jacob and I both laugh. Claire flips a pancake and places a

finished one next to it in the warming drawer. She giggles, too. "Good Lord, Joshua, always such a charmer."

"So there I am, sweat dripping from me in buckets, when I see her. She was sitting cross-legged on the ground with a group of friends. Her hair was long, down to her waist like Lennon's, and she wore it in these two huge braids. There was a flower crown around her head, and she had a guitar across her lap that she was strumming while she hummed a tune. She must have felt me watching her, because next thing I knew, she looked my way and without missing a single note on her guitar, she gave me the brightest smile I'd ever seen."

I wait for the next portion of the story, because it's always been my favorite part. I look at Claire, hoping it won't offend her, but she looks at me warmly and I know she can tell how much this means to me.

"I knew from that moment, Jacob, that I had to know this girl. I had to meet her and talk to her and find out everything I could about her, because that smile changed my whole world. Like as soon as she gave it to me, everything was brighter and more alive. It was like she hid the sun behind those lips. She kept singing and I walked over. The whole time I wondered what on earth I was doing. I knew for a fact this girl was out of my league. Not even light-years out of my league, entire galaxies out of my league."

Jacob shifts in his seat, looks at me, and grins, so I smile back.

"But you know what I said to myself?"

"What?" Jacob asks.

"I said to myself, 'If you don't talk to her, Josh, if you don't say hello, you'll regret it every single day of your life.' So I picked a wildflower nearby, the same ones that made the crown on her head, and I walked up to her and said"—he pauses for dramatic effect—"'Excuse me, but I wanted to show this flower how beautiful you are.'"

"You did not," Claire says, her mouth curling at the edges. She looks at me. "Lennon, sugar, tell me he's lying. Tell me the man I married was not that cheesy."

"It only gets worse," I reply. "Just wait."

"And then," Dad continues, "I was worried I wasn't smooth enough, so do you know what I said next?"

Jacob shakes his head while Claire mumbles, "I'm afraid to ask."

"I said to her, 'I was also wondering if you could give me directions?' And she said, 'Sure, where are you headed?' So I said, 'Hopefully straight to your heart.'" Dad looks painfully proud of himself, as if he's just told the best punch line in history.

It works, though, because with those words, none of us can keep it in, not even for a second, and the whole kitchen erupts with laughter. Claire's laughing so hard that tears start to stream down her cheeks, which only makes everyone laugh harder.

When she can finally catch her breath, she says, "Your mama must have been an angel to even give your daddy the time of day after that. For the love of all things holy, Joshua. Directions to her heart?"

Claire echoing Dad's pick-up line prompts another fit of uncontrollable laughter. I have to put the knife down because my body is shaking. "Dad, your game was terrible. Actually you had no game. Zero. None. Like if it's possible to have less than no game, that's what you had."

"In all fairness," Dad says between chuckles, "I was eighteen and stupid. But it worked. So you see, Jacob, Lennon is a total miracle from a beautiful woman that I didn't deserve back then." He stands up and kisses Claire's forehead. "I learned a lot from her, though, she made me a better man and gave me Lennon. Just like your mom did when she gave me you."

A loud thump interrupts any reply Jacob may have to this, and everyone turns to see Andrea, who has just dropped her cell phone on the floor. "Shit," she mutters as she picks it up, inspecting it for damage.

"Andi," Claire says brightly, "you just missed the most ridiculous story about Josh."

"Total ladies' man," Jacob adds.

I laugh again, this time at such a grown-up statement coming from the mouth of a little boy.

"Sounds captivating," Andrea says drily. She doesn't care at all about anything Claire, my dad, Jacob, or I have to say. "I won't be here for brunch, Mother."

Claire's hands go to her hips. "Pardon me, but yes you will, young lady."

Andrea has sucked the happiness from the air with her arrival, and everything feels tense.

"No," she says firmly, "I won't. It's Liam's birthday. Jess and I are taking him for lunch in Beverly Hills."

She heads to the front door, puts her hand on the knob, and turns to shoot all four of us a deadly glare. "Besides, I wouldn't want to ruin your happy family moment."

"Andi." Claire moves to step forward, but my dad puts a hand on her shoulder to stop her.

"Let her go," he says softly. "Forcing her to stay will only make her angry."

Jacob's smile is gone, too, and as Andi gets in her car to leave, I wonder if she will ever allow herself to be happy, even for a second.

KYLER

WHAT IS SHE LISTENING TO?

Random Thoughts of a Random Mind

I SIT WAITING FOR LENNON at the bus stop the next morning. She's got headphones on, the bulky kind, and she looks like she's enjoying whatever it is she's jamming to, until she sees me. She stops dead in her tracks, and her mouth hangs open in shock.

Her hands flutter to remove the headphones. "Is your car broken?"

I reach for the brown paper bag beside me, retrieve a muffin, and grab one of the takeout coffees, handing both to her. "Good morning to you, too, Davis."

She sits next to me and pulls a piece off the muffin, shoving it in her mouth. She chews and then smiles. "Why the breakfast?"

"Call me a concerned friend," I tell her. "Trying to start your day off on a positive note."

Her smile grows wider. "With breakfast at the bus stop?"

"With *me*, at the bus stop," I say. "But yeah, breakfast comes in a close second."

"I already ate breakfast." She looks at the sky before turning her attention back to me. "But they do say it's the most important meal of the day. So you can't really have enough breakfast, can you?"

"You can't. And you already ate breakfast but haven't seen me yet."

"Where's your car?"

"At my house. The one next door to yours."

"Why?"

"Why not?"

She tilts her head to the side and gives me a stern look that reminds me of a childhood scolding. I slump my shoulders. "Because you have a doctor's appointment you're taking the bus to, since you don't do cars. I can appreciate that, but I also know you'll miss English, and whether you will admit to it or not, you'll miss me, so I'm kinda saving you the trouble," I tell her. "You're welcome."

"You're coming over later, remember?"

How could I forget? We're starting the mask. "Yeah, but then I couldn't give you these." I reach into my pocket and pull out a piece of folded notepaper. I rise to my feet, grab my paper bag and my coffee, and say, "See you after school." We have no other classes together today. There's a good chance I won't see her till then.

She holds the paper up. "What's this?"

I shove my hands in my pockets. "It's the first installment of my payment plan. Read it on the bus." It's not the song I've been writing for her. That's way too much, way too soon. But it's a song. Something she's been trying to get her eyes on.

Lennon from Maine with Serious Issues Who Sews and Is Broken has officially taken up residence inside my head. Damn.

Lennon

FACT: IT TAKES A MONARCH BUTTERFLY 28-38
DAYS TO COMPLETE ITS METAMORPHOSIS.
THOUGHT: IT TAKES A TEENAGE GIRL SIX WEEKS.

HE'S IN A PALE BLUE hoodie today, the color that makes his eyes look surreal. They remind me of postcards of those Caribbean islands, oceans painted by the hand of Mother Nature in devastating shades of blues and greens.

As I watch him walk away, I realize he's right. I will miss him.

I look down at my coffee cup, and there on the sleeve, in Kyler's handwriting, it says, sleep is for the weak. think about it.

I laugh and bring the drink to my lips for a sip, then shake my head. The bus pulls to the curb and rumbles to a stop. I keep the square of paper between my fingers until I'm seated and then, my hands shaking, I read it.

> You're broken and you're beautiful,
> Shattered till you're jaded,
> Drink the bitter with the pain,
> Withered, wilted, faded.

Hide among the walking dead,
Fill empty cups with hollow lies,
Silence the screams beneath your skin,
Or look through different eyes.

See the world just like me,
You'll never be the same,
The planet and its mystery,
Its pleasure, and its pain.

More later...
Kyler.

I think I'm still smiling when the bus drops me off in front of Dr. Linderman's office. I hope we go for a walk today, because it's a lot easier to think with the sun beating down on your skin than it is in some stuffy room. I wave to Stacy, who waves back, her fingers moving one after another in a manicured hello. She picks up the phone and tells Dr. Linderman I'm here.

I don't even sit before the door swings open.

Dr. Linderman is wearing obnoxiously orange glasses that remind me of a traffic pylon, and a suit. Probably Versace. I smirk at him. "I realize I'm cause to celebrate, but you're a little overdressed."

He gives me an impish grin. "Clever. I've had an important business meeting this morning, but now I need a walk. Too much coffee, too much breakfast."

I spin on my heel. "No such thing as too much breakfast. It's the best meal of the day. And you say I'm the crazy one."

By now I know the way to the park we are beginning to frequent. I know the good Dr. Linderman has been to Thailand and Bali to study alternative medicines and natural approaches. I know he likes to order food from a restaurant in Pasadena, close to where he grew up. I know his first name is Levi and his middle name is James.

I also know Levi James Linderman is a cool shrink.

"You look happy today, Lennon," he remarks. He walks with his hands clasped behind his back, his posture impeccable.

"I am," I say.

"Los Angeles isn't the cesspool you once feared it was?" he guesses.

"Not exactly."

"Good school?"

"Not exactly." I pause. "Do you think it's weird if you meet someone but feel like you know them, and they know you? Like your soul has perpetually danced with chaos until you met them?"

Dr. Linderman arches an eyebrow. "Perpetually dancing with chaos." He's impressed. "The plot thickens. Did you meet someone like that?"

"I don't know," I say. "I think so. But maybe it's not that. Maybe I'm so sad, so shattered, that I'm using the distraction as a way to deal with my grief and none of it means anything."

When it feels like everything.

He pauses. "Why would you think that?"

"I don't know, you're the doctor. Am I just dealing with loss?"

"When we lose people, Lennon, especially those closest to us, we all deal with our grief differently. Some lash out and become angry, some become reclusive and introverted, depressed, hopeless. Yet there are those who are resilient, and somehow the heartbreak of loss changes them."

"So what you're saying is you have no idea if I'm randomly attaching myself to this person?"

"I really don't. Only you can answer that. What is it about this person you like?"

Everything.

I don't answer. A small blond girl races past us, in pursuit of a bright green balloon, her young mother chasing after her. She steals Dr. Linderman's focus long enough to provide me the opportunity to change the direction of the conversation.

I can't walk outside on a warm spring day with a beautiful boy on my mind, surrounded by flowers that stretch toward the sun just trying to feel alive, and be forced to justify the reasons *why* he's there. I turn to Dr. Linderman, point to the green balloon that is now chasing the clouds, and ask, "What do you think it's like to fly?" I spread my arms out and tilt my head to the sun like those flowers, just trying to feel alive.

"What do *you* think it's like?" he asks.

"Do you always answer questions with questions, Levi?"

"You mean like the question you answered my question with?"

"Is it a shrink thing?"

He laughs. "This could go on forever, couldn't it?"

"I think flying would be terrifying," I tell him. "Think about it, you're up there at the mercy of the wind, one miscalculation or one simple shift in the air can send your entire trajectory off."

"Pretty accurate comparison to life itself, Lennon. Anyone could be a step away from everything they know in life changing forever, but you can't let that stop you from living it.

"But since you're asking, it's freeing," he continues. "It's my experience that the sensation of flying is liberating. Free-falling into oblivion, your heart hammering, your mind living for that exact moment in time. Like nothing from your past matters, and your future is coming at you so hard, so fast, there's nothing you can do but hold on for the ride."

I stop walking. "You have a literal answer for that?"

"I'm an avid fan of skydiving," he explains. "Been hang gliding a time or two."

"Of course you have."

"I try not to wonder what things are like. I do them, so I know firsthand."

"Don't you get scared? What if you die?"

"Everybody dies sometime, Lennon."

"But why would you put yourself at risk?"

"I guess because I want to feel everything there is about living."

"You're one in a million," I tell him. "People do everything they can to numb their pain."

He considers this before saying, "They should strive to understand it. Pain can be transformative."

I walk again, staring down at my shoes.

If pain is transformative, falling in love must be a complete metamorphosis.

KYLER

"YOU'RE THE STRENGTH INSIDE MY WEAKNESS, THE
KEEPER OF MY PAIN, YOU MAKE THE DARKNESS
DISAPPEAR, LIKE SUN RIGHT AFTER RAIN."

Fire to Dust, *Life-Defining Moments* EP, "My Sweetest Sin"

LENNON HAS MY LYRICS. I've never let a girl read any of my
lyrics before. They are a brief look inside a cluttered mind. Once
they've been glossed over, joined with music, and formed into a
song, it's kind of remarkable, but when they're notes scrawled on
ripped pages, they are raw and unfiltered and it's like standing
naked in front of a crowd. Exposed. Vulnerable.

I don't do vulnerable.

Or at least I didn't . . . until now.

I've never met someone whose wounds run as deep as mine.
Buried in layers of flesh, embedded deep into every cell. Small
nicks and cuts from life that split open your soul and rot, fester-
ing until nothing means anything and everything is numb.

Lennon knows. I know she knows.

It's written in the fire behind her golden eyes that withers to a
slow burn when she looks at me. It's painted in the shape of her
mouth when she tries to keep her smiles trapped inside because
she doesn't trust them, and it's sketched in the way she pauses

every so often to stare into nothingness, trying to catch a glimpse of the answer to whether life ever stops hurting.

This tells me when she reads those words, she will understand.

She's lost. I'm lost. Together, we're somehow found.

Thoughts of Lennon distract me for a while. Too long, because when I come back down to earth, I witness a particular brand of horror unfolding in front of my eyes. There, a few yards down the hallway, I spot my sister—in Silas's arms. I take a calming breath, which feels utterly useless in this case, but it manages to dull the anger threatening to bubble up from under my skin. I surge forward before realizing I have to slow my approach. Last thing I want to do is remind Macy of my dad and his temper, barreling down on them like a bat out of hell.

When I reach them I clear my throat, and Silas pulls away, his face shocked like he's spotted an alien spacecraft. "Kyler, what's up?"

I tilt my head. "Why don't you tell me?" But before Silas can say anything, I turn my attention to Macy, whose eyes are swollen and red. I immediately soften, forgetting for a millisecond how one of my best friends is holding my sister. "Mae, what's wrong?"

Macy is silent.

My spine stiffens. "Did someone hurt you?"

"No one hurt me, Kyler, I didn't get it."

"Get what?"

My question offends her. "The stupid part! The lead role. They gave it to Elena Windham."

Swan Lake.

I look at my shoes. Mae has been busting her ass for months for that role. My gaze darts back to Silas, and my entire perception of the situation shifts, but only slightly. To be fair, it seems he was offering comfort to my distressed sister. I can appreciate the honor in that. But it's not his job. I look at Silas. "Thanks, but I can take it from here."

He completely ignores me and rests his hand on Macy's shoulder. "You gonna be okay, Mae?"

She nods and rubs underneath her eyes with the tips of her fingers, sniffling. "Yeah. Thank you."

"Text me if you need anything," Silas offers.

On instinct, my teeth clench together so hard that my jawbone feels like it might break. But the stabbing pain in my chest, courtesy of a knife forged from sympathy for my little sister, hurts more, so I insert myself between them and do what any good brother would. I wrap my arms around Macy and pull her to me. I'm sure it's the familiarity—the bond we share from growing up under my father's rule. Because Macy and I don't have to hide anything from each other—especially not our weaknesses—so now, in the hallway of Hell Air Learning Academy, she really starts to sob.

There's nothing I can say to make it better, although there are a million curse words dancing on the tip of my tongue, ready to come out in a conga line, because damn it, I just don't like Silas touching my sister.

Yeah, maybe I'm a jackass to think this way because I should want Macy to be happy, and it's not that I don't, but the thing is, someone has to look out for her and that someone has been me since I can remember. Macy is close to perfect and Silas is anything but, so I can't help but think she'd end up getting hurt. I can't accept it, no matter how much Mae wishes I would. That's why Silas and I are good friends. He's broken like me. Like Lennon. Macy isn't.

Her tiny body is heaving, breaths coming in short spurts, and it reminds me of when Lennon told me about her mom. Macy's situation is obviously less traumatic, but that dumb part in that stupid show meant everything to her.

"I tried so hard." Her voice is muffled by the fabric of my shirt, and I feel warm, wet heat on my chest and know her tears have soaked through.

"Everyone knows you busted your ass, Mae. Everyone."

"It's not fair."

"I know. Whoever is in charge is too blind to see what's right in front of them. I know it's not what you want to hear, but it's the best I've got."

"Dad is going to be disappointed."

Another stab to my chest. Macy seeks his approval often whereas I gave up a long time ago. "Who cares? And look at it this way, you'll never be even close to the epic disappointment I am to him, so there's always that." She cries for a while longer until she settles, standing in the hallway of our school, her head on my chest and her arms wrapped around my back. I don't let her go until her breathing evens out completely. "They're ridiculous not to choose you," I tell her. "You're the best ballerina I know." I tilt my head. "To be fair, you're also the only ballerina I know, but that's beside the point."

This earns me a sliver of a smile, so I continue. "Oh, and Mae? You might want to fix your face, kid. You're redder than me. Massive accomplishment there."

She looks up at me, better, but still sad. "You're a good brother."

"By 'good' I'm sure you meant 'the best,' but I'll forgive you for the oversight."

I'm rewarded this time with a laugh. Hardly a good one, but it's a start. "Text me if you need anything. Like a getaway driver so you don't have to look at Elena."

"She doesn't even go to our school."

"Well, text if you want to skip and go get greasy diner food." The second coming of Jesus is more realistic than Macy skipping a class, so I don't expect to hear from her. As she walks away, I think that maybe it's time Silas and I had a talk.

I don't see him or Macy for the rest of the day, but I do see Lennon that afternoon. Her backpack is slung over her shoulder, and she's walking with Jada. She gives me a ghost of a smile, flickering so fast I understand it was only meant for me to see, and after this morning's incident with my sister, I appreciate it.

When I'm leaving the school, Macy is in the parking lot talking to Violet, her best friend.

"Want a ride home, Mae?"

"Hi, Kyler," Violet says, waving.

"What's up, Vi?"

"The sophomore who saw more than he bargained for when he caught me using the janitor's closet to change."

I roll my eyes.

Violet hugs Macy. "See you tomorrow."

Macy flips the seat and tosses her book bag in the back before climbing into the passenger side. She buckles her seat belt, then adjusts the visor, making it lower because Silas was the last person to sit there.

I start the engine. "How are you? Better?"

She shrugs.

"Listen, I know you have a thing for Silas and I think he's kind of feeling the same vibe."

She smiles bigger than she would have if I had just told her that she got the lead role in her ballet. "What?"

"He's too old for you."

"Age is just a number."

We spend the rest of the ride in silence, and I'm driving up our street in record time when I spot Lennon, walking from the bus stop.

"Does she always take the bus?" Macy asks. "You'd figure Josh would get her a car."

"I don't know. It's not my business."

"Are you serious?"

"Deadly," I reply.

"The two of you are insta-inseparable. Everybody sees it. You think I haven't noticed that you check your phone as soon as dinner is done every night, or that you're constantly sitting on your bed or at your desk, scrawling in that notebook or typing on your phone? A guy is only like that when he's into a girl. You're coming out of your hermit land, and being the Kyler I know again," she says. "It's obvious. You're totally comfortable around her."

I don't know if I even have a valid argument to give. It's obvious. It's obvious to me, for God's sake, surely my family—my sister, of all people—would notice that somehow I hate the world less. "Macy, I don't know why you're making such a big deal out of it. I'm a teenage guy. I like a girl. It's simple."

"Because," Macy says. "You're you, but ... different."

"Different good or different bad?"

"Good," she says quickly. "You smile more. You smile lots. Usually when you're looking at your phone."

"She makes me smile. Hardly a miracle."

"Ha!" Macy says. "It's more than a miracle. It's unparalleled."

"You're stretching," I tell her.

"For years you've been, like, this introvert, but I know when I'm around you, and you're just yourself, you're funny and charming and kind. And you're being you, but with more confidence than you show anyone but us. Mom and me. So I'm guessing she must think a lot like you do."

"Yeah." I nod. "You could say that."

"Are you together?"

I shake my head. "No."

"Why not?"

I grab my bag from the back and shut the door. "Fear."

Macy slings her own bag over her shoulder. "Everything you've ever wanted is on the other side of fear."

"Deep, Mae. Quoting George Addair."

"That's right," Macy says. "Smart man."

Lennon

FACT: FOR A FEW MOMENTS IN TIME, A SINGLE SUPERNOVA
CAN TRANSCEND AN ENTIRE GALAXY OF STARS,
UNLEASHING AS MUCH ENERGY IN A SOLITARY BURST
AS THE SUN WILL IN ITS 10-BILLION-YEAR LIFE SPAN.

I SPOT KYLER IN PASSING in the corridor, but he's blocked by a sea of heads. He shares a glance with me across the mob, and I wish I could break through them and tell him his song lyrics are unbelievable. But I'll wait. He's coming over later to start the mask. It'll be the first time he's seen my room and the first time we'll be doing anything other than English work together.

The clock plays tricks on my eyes all afternoon, and I'm constantly feeling like it's later than it is. When the dismissal bell rings, I power walk to the bus stop, determined not to miss my ride.

The house is silent. I drop my keys into the basket on the table near the front door and notice a mountain of crisp white envelopes. Each one is addressed in dense black strokes of ink, handcrafted into exquisite works of art. I pause a moment to marvel at their perfection. I flip to the second card in the pile, and interest takes hold as I riffle through them.

SunStar Records
Attention: William Wallen

Dream Chaser Records
Attention: Burke Madison

Electrified Music
Attention: Michael D. Trevanni

I run my fingers along the lettering as if I can somehow absorb its flawless loops and arches. I've never seen anything so beautiful. Lost in reflection, enthralled by the writing, I don't hear Jacob sneak up behind me.

"What are you doing, Lennon?"

Startled, I jump and lay my hand across my chest, whirling around to see him aiming his camera at me. "God, Jacob. You scared me."

He points the camera at the floor. "Sorry," he says sadly. He's positioned in front of me with the blue cape on. Instead of his suit and faux glasses, or his rubber boots, he's wearing jeans, a T-shirt, and green-and-white-striped socks. The tip of his tongue dances across the ridges of his teeth before it lands on the blank space. He nods at the pile of envelopes in my hand. "Daddy and Mommy have a big party every year when summer starts. Mommy always makes real nice invitations. Nicer than the ones she makes for my birthday."

"Yeah, they're nice," I admit.

He nods and repeats his question. "What are you doing?"

I set the stack of envelopes down and shrug. "Just got home. Figured I'd get a drink and do homework."

He smiles. "Mom's on her way home. We're going to take Oscar for a walk. Andi's supposed to be watching me, but she's in her room."

I'm about to ask him if he holds Oscar's leash when the doorbell rings.

"That'll be Kyler."

He winces.

I kneel so I'm eye level with Jacob. "Don't pay attention to what Andi told you, Jacob. Kyler isn't scary."

He peers at his socks, so I put my hand on his shoulder and his eyes rise to meet mine. "Kyler is cool, Jacob. If he wasn't, I wouldn't have asked him over, and I sure wouldn't let him come anywhere near you."

He still seems skeptical. "Are you sure?"

"Positive," I tell him. "I promise."

I move toward the door, but Jacob holds out his hand to stop me. He sucks in a breath, as if this is the bravest thing he's ever done, walks to the door, and opens it.

Kyler stands with his hands jammed into his pockets, his hair worn in a low ponytail at the nape of his neck with stubborn pieces spilling from the sides. He's wearing a white T-shirt and shorts with sandals. It's the least amount of clothing I've ever seen on Kyler and the first time, aside from the tree house, that he seems unbothered by exposing his face.

Jacob's wide eyes start at Kyler's feet, which are huge, and his gaze does a slow sweep upward to his face. And his scar. Jacob blinks.

"What happened to your face?"

"Jake," I say. His name is accompanied by an uneasy laugh because I'm mortified.

"Freak accident. I got burned."

"Did it hurt?"

"Like you couldn't imagine," Kyler says.

"Does it hurt now?"

"Nah," he says. "Not at all."

Jacob squints. "Do you like superheroes?"

"Who doesn't?"

Jacob steps aside, pleased with Kyler's answers to his interrogation.

Kyler smiles warmly. "That's a wicked cape there, little man."

"I know. Lennon made it."

"That's cool. My sister, Macy, doesn't make anything like that."

"Have you asked her?" Jacob inquires.

The sides of Kyler's mouth pull into a smirk. "Now that you mention it, I haven't. I should, huh?"

"You never know unless you ask. Besides, if your sister can't do it, I'm sure Lennon will make you one."

The smirk intensifies as he fixes me with his burning gaze. "Lennon's making me a mask."

Jacob's eyes grow wide in fascination. "What?" He turns. "You can make masks? Is he a superhero, too? Is that why Andi doesn't like him?" He faces Kyler again, expecting an answer.

Kyler shrugs, as if he's telling Jacob, *Who knows? I could be.*

The door swings open and Claire steps in, a large square leather bag dangling from her wrist. "Mommy!" Jacob runs to her, forgetting about his inquisition as he throws his arms around her waist. "Are you ready?"

"I'm ready, sugar," Claire says. "I need a minute to change my clothes." She looks at Kyler, then at me. "You didn't tell me you were having a friend over."

"Yeah," I say. "We're working on a project."

"Okay. Well, your daddy is workin' late." She pulls her wallet out and whips out a credit card. "You, Andi, and your friend here can order takeout. Jacob and I are takin' Oscar up the street to Mel's place."

"Okay, thank you."

"Let's go!" Jacob pleads.

"All right, all right." She smiles once more and stalks down the hallway toward her bedroom, Jacob at her heels.

I look at Kyler. "Sorry about that. I mean, Jacob, he's—"

"—five," Kyler offers. "Don't sweat it. He's a curious kid."

"My room is this way." Duh. He knows which way my room is. When we enter, his eyes do a quick sweep of the space. "A minimalist, huh?"

"My stuff is in storage while the interior designer is working," I explain.

He walks over to the bookshelves and sees the twenty-five or so books detailing random facts. "A trivia junkie? No wonder you're so smart," he says, casually walking around the room, scanning, observing. "It's so clean," he says, "like no one lives in it."

"I live in it," I tell him.

"You could never see my room," he says decisively. "It would freak you out."

"You're messy?" I guess.

"I like to think of it more as an environment of creative chaos. It's a mess, kind of like my head."

"Preaching to the choir," I tell him. "I hold the undisputed title for messes in heads."

He nods. "I'm not even sure I could hold a decent argument to that point, Lennon. But like I keep telling you, normal is boring."

I'd precut the sheets of bandage plaster into small, moldable strips. I set down the strips on the table beside the bed and slip into the bathroom to grab petroleum jelly, towels, and a basin of warm water and a cloth to wash his face clean afterward. I spread the towels across the pillow and point to the bed. "Lie down."

He issues a deadly grin. "I realize I bought you dinner the other night, but we should get to know each other more."

"Lie down or the only thing you'll know is the effect of gravity when I'm trying to capture the shape of your face. The plaster will pull, and the mask will look like something from a horror movie."

"Not the worst idea," he says.

I cross my arms over my chest and arch my eyebrow.

He shakes his head and lies down in the middle of the bed, leaving me enough room to sit beside him. Heat radiates from his skin, like the burn of his eyes is just as intense all over his body. I dip my fingers in the jelly and bring the tips to his face, lingering a moment longer than I should because he's looking at me.

No, he's looking *inside* me.

I swallow down the lump in my throat and make small, slow circles on his face with my fingers. His eyelashes flutter closed when skin touches skin, and his breath hitches. I keep moving until I've got the scarred portion of his face covered and wipe my hands on the towel beside the table.

I place a few of the plaster strips into the water and lay two on the spot beside him, then bring one to his face. I press it down, tracing my fingers gingerly down the length of it, until I get to the biggest part of his scar. I leave my finger there.

"Jada told me, but I didn't know if it was true." I worry I'm overstepping my boundaries, until he responds.

"Yeah, when I was six."

I get more plaster ribbons and continue to stroke his face, along the ridge of his jaw, his cheekbone. "You were probably so scared."

"I was terrified," he says.

I try to picture a tiny Kyler, Jacob-sized, engulfed by the flames of a fire. His sandy hair, those bright blue eyes. Stinging tears prickle, and I refuse to blink for fear they'll fall. I work faster, setting one strip over the others, smoothing and building them until they lie flush with the planes of his face, encased in plaster.

"I'm sorry you went through that," I say. My voice is on the verge of breaking, though, so I go silent. I turn a fan to face the side of him with the mask, but sit down and touch his arm.

His eyes are still closed, his hands clasped together over his stomach.

"My mom went to France for two weeks. She was training with

some superstar chef or something, so it was me, Macy, and my dad. I remember my mom's face when she left. She was excited, hopeful, like she felt she'd experience something magical."

He continues: "Mae was tiny, so she'd gone to bed, but I was always kind of a little shit and I'd stayed up long after my dad had put me to sleep for the night. For weeks before that, I'd been obsessed with secret spies and collecting information. I even dressed the part, like a robber in the night. Black sweatpants, a black sweater, a beanie, the whole badass getup. My imagination was wild, and I was pretending I was on this top secret mission to gather enemy files. I was going to go into his office, grab papers with his law office logo, and pretend they were documents containing classified information."

My heart tightens, and I trace my hand along the length of his arm. "You sound like you were such a sweet little kid."

"I wouldn't call me that." He smiles, but it disappears. "Anyway, to get to my dad's office, I had to cut through the living room and when I came down the hallway, there he was, with a black-haired woman who I promise you was most definitely not my mother. They were surrounded by candles and slow-dancing to some crappy jazz song. Like his wife leaves town, so now he's a real Casanova. I stood there for a second, not quite believing what I was seeing, and then he kissed her and I screamed.

"He turned and came after me so fast, I thought the vein was going to pop clear out of his forehead. He dragged me down the hallway and back to my room, shoved me down on the bed. He pointed his finger at me and said—"

He stops speaking and I freeze. I bring my fingertips to touch the tackiness of the plaster and remove the mask, setting it on the towel beside the bed to dry. I grab the washcloth and follow the same pattern, stroking away remnants of plaster and Vaseline. He opens his eyes. "I'll never forget what he said. He told me not to move a muscle. Told me that bad things happened when kids didn't listen. Kids like me. Then he warned me one more time that I better not move, and he left."

The knot in my throat becomes harder to swallow back down. His eyes flutter closed again.

"Next thing I woke up and my fucking room was on fire. My dad was across the hall, with Macy in his arms, and he's screaming at me again, and he's telling me to move. And I'm confused because I was asleep, and he'd told me *not* to move. Not a muscle. And now he's hysterical. Screaming at me to move. When I came to, became aware, there was a two-foot-high wall of flames between us. Flames were everywhere, spreading faster than it seems possible." He pauses. "I've always wondered if when you're about to die, time just morphs into overdrive, because that fire consumed everything. It devoured everything in its path in seconds, milliseconds, even. So I snap up and Dad's yelling at me to get to the window. To get out the window and jump. I stand, but my knees barely hold me and I think I fall, I stumble on the way there. I don't remember tripping, but I could have, or maybe the curtains were on fire, but then boom, like an object left in its path, it consumes *me* and suddenly *I'm* on fire. I'm on fire and I'm elbowing the window because it's stuck, and I pry it open and crawl out onto the roof and my face is on fire, my side is on fire. I don't jump. I fall."

His eyes open. "Wanna hear the worst part?"

How could it be any worse? "If you want to tell me," I say.

"For the longest time afterward, I thought it happened because I didn't listen to my dad. It was one of his candles lit to impress the woman he was cheating on my mother with that started the fire, but I blamed myself. Thought it was my fault because he said bad things happen to kids who don't listen and he'd told me to go to bed and I didn't. He never told me any different. Never told me it wasn't my fault. And my mom, when she came home from that trip, her eyes had gone from hopeful to anguished, and they've been that way ever since. How messed up is that?"

His words are not without a cost. Silent tears pour down my face, hot and steady. A charge, a penance to pay for the story of a boy named Kyler who was burned in a house fire.

His arms uncross, and he grabs my wrist without sitting up, to pull me on top of him so we are stomach to stomach, face-to-face. I'm sure he is aware of my heart hammering against his chest. I can hear it racing.

His hands slide across the underside of my jaw. "Don't cry for me."

"I'm crying for the little boy who was you," I say. My arms are shaking like mad, trying to keep myself upright.

Kyler closes his eyes and pulls me forward. He doesn't hesitate. He kisses me.

And the minute his mouth touches mine, I'm a supernova.

KYLER

NAME: *KYLER DEAN BENTON*

AGE: *17*

SEX: *UH, YEAH, PLEASE.*

RELIGIOUS AFFLIATION: *LENNONISM*

Random Thoughts of a Random Mind

I'VE NEVER BEEN A BIG believer in God. It's kind of like supporting the idea of a mythological creature. Never been confident some entity that controls every aspect of my life exists. She could change my mind. Lennon could be my religion, because there was something in that kiss that was ethereal. Divine. My personal nirvana. As though years of suffering have earned me a single blissful moment with this beautiful blond girl I've just kissed. She tasted like the human equivalent of rapture, and damn if I don't want to devour that taste, again and again.

Her forehead is pressed to mine, my hands are still framing her face, and wetness runs down her cheeks, her tears rolling over my fingers. It's an odd thing to have someone cry for me. She has enough problems of her own, and she's tormented over mine. I move my lips and press a kiss to her forehead. "Stop crying," I whisper. "I'm fine. I'm okay."

Her voice is laced with sadness that loves to bloom through quiet tears. "Are any of us ever okay, really?"

I stroke her hair with my fingers. "No. No one is okay in a literal sense. Everyone is screwed up, and they're either screwed up enough to admit it, or too blinded by ego to see it. But I think we can be okay for moments, Lennon. Sometimes for hours, days, even weeks. And I don't know about you, but in this moment, I'm pretty okay."

Her arms wrap around my neck.

It's the best feeling in the entire world. In the Milky Way and Andromeda galaxies combined.

"Yeah," she says, "I'm pretty okay, too."

I move my hand to the small of her back and she squeezes me. We stay that way in comfortable silence for a moment before she scoots off the bed and slowly stands, a smile stretched across her face. I feel decent about being the one who put it there.

I stand, too, and walk over to her and pull her back. Instinct. As if my body wasn't ready to let her go.

"This is crazy," she says.

"So are you. So am I."

"What happened just now?"

"I told you a terrible tale and then I kissed you."

"Yeah."

"Did you like it?"

She smiles. "The terrible tale, no, but the kiss, very much."

I smirk. "So I can kiss you again, so long as I don't pair it with a nightmare?"

She blushes. "Yes. I think I'd like that."

I take a moment to acknowledge how much I want to kiss this girl. I want to kiss her and hold her and tell her everything will be fine. That days can be hard and life can be shitty, but there's something to be said for little things that are big things and big things that are little things and things like whatever it is we are.

She's staring up at me, her golden eyes filled with questions but also a certain hope. I've been searching for a glimpse of that hope since I was six. It's the kind that believes in magic. This time, I use my thumb to hold her chin in place and I move slowly. I brush my lips against hers before I urge her to open her mouth for me. Her lips are soft like rose petals, her hair smells of something sweet, tropical. Her body melts into my arms while I explore her mouth.

When we separate, she looks at me, shades of pink flaring across her face. "You're really good at that."

"I'm a tortured musician, Davis, what do you expect?"

"I can't believe I forgot to tell you." She moves and sits on the edge of the bed, looking up at me. Her hair's messy, her mouth swollen.

I'm in so much trouble.

Religious Affiliation: Lennonism

"Do you understand how amazing those song lyrics are?"

Oh. That.

"Glad one of us thinks so."

"Kyler, it's true. They're unbelievably good. You have a gift and—"

I hold my hand out to stop her and narrow my eyes. "Don't be clichéd enough to tell me I have a gift. Besides, I just kissed you, Davis. There's a million endorphins running though both of us. You're not thinking straight."

"I thought they were good before the kiss."

"Now you're fluffing my ego."

She shrugs. "Or just speaking the truth."

I move to the bed and give her shoulder a small squeeze. "You're sweet. I've gotta go to band practice, but I'd way rather stay here with you. I'll see myself out."

"Text me later?"

"What kind of guy would I be if I let you miss out on your favorite part of the day? Of course I'll text you later."

"Kyler?"

"Yeah?"

"You don't need the mask."

"That's where you're wrong," I say. "I do."

"Okay," she whispers. She looks a little sad.

"You okay?"

She nods.

"Don't look so glum. We had a weird moment. A perfectly weird moment—and remember, weird is beautiful." I pause at the door and look over my shoulder. "Lennon?"

She smiles. "Yeah?"

"You're the weirdest person I've ever met."

With that, I walk out the door, leaving Lennon from Maine with Serious Issues Who Sews and Is Broken and Beautiful behind.

As I come down the hallway, I spot the sharp lines of Andrea's haircut. Her back is to me, but she's hovering over the island in the kitchen. Her arms are stretched out in front of her as though she's taking a picture. I clear my throat and watch as she jumps, slamming her hand over a file folder on the counter and trying to slide it inconspicuously underneath a small pile of paperwork.

"Must be interesting," I say.

She turns. "Ew. Gross. What are you doing in my house?"

"Witnessing a crime," I say. "What's the paperwork? Your parents' bank account information? School records? A script from your mom's TV show?"

She glares at me. "Get. Out. Now I have to disinfect everything."

"Start with your soul. I'll leave you to it."

"Thank God for small blessings," she mutters.

If anyone should cry for anyone else, I should sob for Lennon. Positively mourning the fact that she's forced to live with such a vile human.

As I walk across the yard, I open my phone and go to the notes app to copy the lyrics I'd typed on there. I'd been saving it for later, but I don't want to spend the rest of the night remembering the melancholy look on her face. I pull up Lennon's contact and type:

> I'm certain you're a fairy or something because you taste like unicorn tears. Thus, I'm inspired to share the rest of the song with you. Talk later.

> Let me take your breath away,
> Make your body shake,

Hold on to me forevermore,
My heart is yours to take.

See the world just like me,
You'll never be the same,
The planet and its mysteries,
Its pleasure, and its pain.

Explore my world with your mind,
Paint it with your soul,
Your eyes can see the lies I hide,
I'll never let you go.

I'll be your greatest pleasure,
I'll drown your deepest pain,
Walk with me through flames, my love,
You'll never be the same.

Lucky for me, I don't have to walk very far to make it to practice. It takes time to process kissing a girl like Lennon, so I'm not in a hurry.

I'm grinning, walking along the fence, when something stops me dead in my tracks and wipes the smile from my face. Macy. She's talking. She's laughing. Only it's not her regular voice. It's her *I'm so into you I feel like I could die* voice, which she reserves for Silas.

Neither of my parents' cars are here, Austin and Emmett's SUV isn't here, but Silas is. And he's alone. With my sister.

I strain against the privacy provided through the high fence to hear them.

"Slide your fingers down two frets," Silas says. A moment later, he says, "Atta girl. Now strum down and then back up, with your thumb."

"I'm so bad at this," I hear Macy say.

"Nah," Silas says. "You're doing good, you're—"

"—just a beginner," I say, coming around the fence and cutting him off. "What's going on?"

"Silas is showing me how to play a few chords on the guitar."

"I see that." I narrow my gaze at Silas, issuing a warning with my eyes so he knows I don't approve.

He disregards me. Again. "She's actually really good, Kyler. Why haven't you shown her anything before?"

This catches me off guard. Not because I'm surprised Macy is good—she's good at everything she does—but at Silas calling me out for not sharing with my sister, something I've always been into. "Dunno. She never asked, I guess. You really want to learn the guitar, Mae?"

She looks up at me, a smile on her face. After what happened with her *Swan Lake* audition, I don't have the heart to take this from her, too. Fuck. I don't have the heart to take her wish for Silas away, either, as much as I want to.

I look at Silas again, so he by no means mistakes what I'm about to say as my blessing for anything to happen between them. "Silas is a good teacher. I'm sure he'll show you some stuff."

Her face lights up brighter than the sun on a California

summer day before she looks at him questioningly, *longingly*. I have to clench my fists at my sides to make sure they don't get me into trouble. It takes a lot of work to swallow the instinct inside of me to be the protective older brother.

He doesn't say anything for a beat, and now I'm swinging on an emotional pendulum between wanting to kick his ass if he agrees, and wanting to kick his ass for not agreeing right away. We both wait until Silas breaks the silence.

"Yeah, sure, Mae. I'd love to."

She sets the guitar down and springs up from the chair to hug me first, then him.

"Get the black-and-white Fender out of my room. You can start with that one, it's been broken in."

"You're the best!" she says. She bolts toward the house but turns around to look back at us. "Thank you, Silas."

"Yeah," he says, picking his guitar back up. "No problem."

When Macy's out of earshot, I turn to him and glare. "Hurt her and I will kill you with my bare hands. I swear to God—" Even the mention of him hurting my sister makes rage boil inside of me.

His voice is calm and even. "Relax, I'm showing her some stuff on guitar, not taking her to prom."

I point my finger at him. "I mean it. Don't fuck around. If you feel something for Macy, I'll stop standing in your way, but don't screw with her, because you screw with her, you screw with me."

"Your sister is an awesome person, Kyler. I'm not going to hurt her. You're overthinking this. I'm showing her some stuff on guitar," he repeats again. "That's it."

"Good," I say.

"We done?"

I nod.

"Come on, then," Silas says, "we have a gig to practice for."

Lennon

FACT: KISSING RELEASES OXYTOCIN IN THE BRAIN.
IT'S A HORMONE THAT STRENGTHENS THE BOND
BETWEEN TWO PEOPLE. SO DOES SHARING SECRETS.

KYLER STANDS BESIDE MY LOCKER, leaning against it, as if his weight is responsible for holding up the wall. "If it isn't the Mad Hatter herself. Hi." He grins.

I slide my backpack down my shoulder and enter my locker combo: 5, 15, 55. "Why, hello, tortured-artist-slash-amazing-kisser." I open the lock, close the lock, and enter the combination again.

"'Tortured artist' is cringeworthy. I'll take the 'amazing kisser' part, though."

I stick out my tongue, open the lock, and close the lock. "Both are true."

"True," he agrees. "What are you imagining?"

"About your kissing?"

"About that, but you're . . ." He nods to my lock. "You're doing your ritual or whatever. What are you imagining right now?"

"Doesn't matter." I open the lock. I close the lock. I turn the dial back to five.

"It does. Tell me."

"No."

"C'mon."

"No."

"Tell me and I'll do something just as epic."

I don't meet his gaze. I can't stop at three. I must do five. "Trust me, you don't want to know." I open the lock. Close the lock. And enter the combo for the last time.

"I do."

"You don't. Besides," I say, "I can't tell you. You won't see me the same way again."

"Right, what if you get more interesting?"

"I won't."

"Can I guess?"

"Probably not."

"Would you tell me even if I guessed right?"

"I'd rather die."

"You're dying inside anyway, Lennon. Every time you let those thoughts hijack your brain, even for a second, you're dying. Live a little, yeah? What if I did something completely out of character and sacrificial? I'll lose the hoodie for the whole day. Let us have some strange life-defining moment." He leans closer, dropping his voice. "C'mon. I really wanna understand this one thing about you."

Then, to my total shock, he reaches for the bottom of his hoodie and pulls it up and over his head, then extends it to me. I glance back up at him, standing in the middle of the school hallway doing something that is uncomfortable for him. And he's doing it to discover something about *me*. "I didn't think you'd do it," I say.

"I know. That's why I did it." He lets out the ponytail that's secured at the nape of his neck, and his sand-colored hair falls against his jaw. Oh my God. He looks incredible. "Now tell me what is going on inside your beautiful mind. Please."

I don't understand why, but I feel like I owe him.

"That if I don't turn the lock right now, something bad will happen to Jacob. He could fall down the stairs, slip on the patio where the pool is, and knock himself out. What if he got kidnapped? Or tortured or sold into some child sex-trafficking ring? Claire is famous, so that's not entirely unrealistic."

Speaking the words makes me turn to begin the ritual again, Kyler's hoodie tucked into the crook of my arm. When I finish my round of five, it still doesn't feel right, so I do it again. Three sets of five. Can't be an even number. Ever. When I'm finished, I slip his hoodie up and over until I'm wrapped in its fabric. It's the kind that stays supersoft even after it's been washed a hundred times, and right now it smells like Bounce sheets again.

Kyler observes my entire ritual, consideration etched into his features. He smiles. "You are cuter than me in that. Wasn't so hard, was it, Davis?"

I regard him. He's made his point. "Do you want your hoodie back?" I don't really want to give it back, but it's something I should offer. I can keep my insecurities inside, most of the time. Kyler's are there for the world to see.

He shakes his head. "Fair is fair. A deal is a deal. I said if you told me what you were thinking, I'd be just as brave as you. You're into all that inspirational garbage, right?"

"I'm serious. You can have it back."

"Return it later. I'm a lot of things. But when I say I'll do something, I do it."

"That's something pretty admirable."

He looks at his watch. "Ego fluffing to commence in three, two…"

"Shut up," I tell him. I retrieve five notebooks and five pens from my locker and place them in my backpack. "Last chance, want it back? No English today. What are you going to tell people?"

He shrugs. "That I lost a bet with a cute girl. Once-in-a-lifetime things happen once in a lifetime, Lennon. Gotta catch those things while you can."

As he walks away, everybody has turned to stare past him. They're gloating, their California glows shadowed by fascination. When he disappears from sight, all eyes turn to me, and Jada comes barreling down the hallway, gawking.

"Did I miss something?"

I look at my shoes. "No."

Her eyebrow darts upward. "No? It sure looks like I missed something." She reaches out and tugs on the hoodie. "Really trying not to lick you right now. Could that hoodie smell any better?"

I fight against a grin. "We made a bet. He lost. I offered him the hoodie back, but he said a deal is a deal."

Jada's mask of shock wears away to reveal a smile stretched across her face. "Girl, what did you do to Kyler Benton?"

"I did nothing," I say. "He's a really cool guy."

"Yeah," she says, "like, four people are aware of that. Kyler is friends with no one, except his band and his sister."

"And now me."

"And now you."

"We'll be late," I say, hitching my bag up my shoulder.

"There's something you're not telling me."

Kyler, the real Kyler, floods my mind, and I can't fight it anymore. The smile wins. Worse, it's a huge smile—the kind that permanently sticks on the faces of lovesick teenage girls. Pathetic. I'm one of them. I say nothing. Kyler is my secret, and I don't want to share him. Not even a little. Because if anyone knew how different he was—I wouldn't stand a chance.

At the end of the day, I spot Kyler in the parking lot, standing beside his car. He's talking to his friend Silas when he sees me approach. Silas gives me a small wave, says, "Hi, Lennon, bye, Lennon."

"Bye." I walk up to Kyler and take off his hoodie, holding it out to him.

"You like it?"

I nod.

"Keep it."

"Really?"

He doesn't answer me. Instead he smiles wide, his hair falling over his eye. "What are the chances I can convince you to let me give you a ride home?"

"Almost nonexistent."

"Is there still a percentage of said existence? Like would you say I have a point-zero-zero-zero-one percent chance of convincing you to get in the car with me?"

I shake my head. "I wouldn't even say the odds are that high."

He removes his hand from his pocket and points his key chain toward his car. The headlights flash and an alarm sounds to show that it's armed. "Let's walk, then."

"Really?"

"Sure. I'll come back for my car later."

I put his hoodie back on and sling my backpack over my shoulders. It's only then I realize that after my ritual with the locker this morning, I made it a full day without giving in. I can't remember the last time that happened.

I look at my shoes as I walk. He keeps pace beside me, and I hazard a glance at his face.

"What was it like?"

"Eye-opening," he says. "Weird. Scary as hell."

"I'm proud of you," I say.

"Thanks, Mom."

"I'm serious."

"It was incredible, Lennon. I feel like for once I wasn't letting the world control me. I didn't care what they thought."

"That's what I try to do with the OCD," I tell him. "Sometimes I win. Sometimes the thoughts don't control me."

"One day, you'll be able to ride in a car," he says. "I want it to be with me. I want to witness the day you kick that fucker to the curb once and for all. It'll be a pivotal, soul-changing kind of moment to call your own, Lennon."

"So are you done with the hoodies? I don't need to finish the mask?"

Kyler stops dead in his tracks, his head turning sideways. "Don't get any wild ideas. I've got an entire closet of them. My hoodies and I have a history, and we're not ready to part ways just yet. And yes, I still need the mask."

"Maybe the day you decide you don't need to hide yourself from the world, I'll decide that I can conquer my biggest demon."

Kyler extends his hand. "Deal."

KYLER

"AND THEN YOU CAME TO PULL ME UP, MY
SWEETEST LITTLE SIN, IT'S HARD TO SEE THE PART
OF ME, THAT ENDS WHERE YOU BEGIN."

Fire to Dust, *Life-Defining Moments* EP, "My Sweetest Sin"

I WALK THROUGH THE PATIO door and spot Macy seated at the kitchen table. She's reading a book, a lemonade on a coaster in front of her. The coolness of the liquid and humidity from the house have produced small droplets of water on the surface of her glass. She glances up when she hears me before she looks back down at her book and says, "Fresh lemon—" She stops, her gaze snapping up at me from the pages. "Where's your hoodie?" In seconds she's on her feet. "What happened?"

I can't answer her because I don't know.

"Are you okay?" Her hand trembles, as if she wants to reach out and touch my face like our mom does. Macy never has, but I'd probably let her if she tried.

"I took it off," I tell her. "To prove a point."

"To prove what point?"

I look at my sister, more serious than I ever have in my entire life. "That I'll do anything for her, I guess."

"Are you in love with the girl next door?"

"You know something, Mae? I'm beginning to think I am."

As I leave a shocked Macy behind, it hits me. I realized it a while ago. I'm in love with the girl next door. How utterly clichéd. I climb the stairs two at a time until I get to my room. I lie across my bed and rake my hands through my hair.

What the fuck happened today? Why did I do that? Their gazes burned into me exactly like the flames of the fire that gave them a reason to stare. Hushed whispers told a thousand different stories inside their heads of my untimely transformation into a monster. And for the first time in my entire life, I didn't care. The snickers, the whispers, the smirks, they didn't bother me, because Lennon knows I'm not a monster. That's the only thing that mattered. It's the only thing that matters.

I'm not sure how I let that happen.

But I'm sure I have to tell her.

Later that night, I'm in the tree house. The window to the guest bedroom has been dark and I'm growing impatient, waiting to hear from her. I text her.

Come to the tree house.

It only takes a few moments for her to respond.

Now?

Now. Yes.

Why?

Because I need to see you, Lennon. Deep thoughts. That's why.

I'll be there in five.

You'll be here in like 4 minutes and 37 seconds. Not sure who you're kidding.

She doesn't reply, so I set my phone on the mattress beside me and close my eyes. I keep them closed while I hear her scale the ladder, and when she comes in and spins around, her arms make fast work of the rope attached to the tree house's pulley. It reaches the top, and she grabs a basket from it as I open my eyes. She turns to face me, grinning. Her hair is in what I can only say is the messiest ponytail I've ever laid eyes on, she's in cutoffs and a black T-shirt, and she has a huge smear of what I'm guessing is either cocaine or flour across her cheek. Since she doesn't really strike me as an addict, and I can smell something intoxicatingly sweet coming from that basket, I'm going to take an educated guess that it's flour. "You brought gifts."

She showcases her basket. "Jacob and I baked cookies."

I sit up, wrapping my hand around her wrist and pulling her to me. "Is that why you look like you've waged war against the Pillsbury Doughboy?"

She nods, smiles, and pushes the basket toward me. "Try one."

I take a cookie. It's still warm, and as I split it, melted chocolate chips ooze from the gooey middle. I eat half of it before devouring the second part. "Best cookie I've ever had," I tell her.

She rolls her eyes and laughs. "Your mom is, like, a Michelin-star chef. I somehow doubt it. But Jacob and I did a decent job with them." She sets the basket on the floor before sitting down next to me, her hands folded in her lap. "So, another important epiphany, huh? For someone who doesn't believe in inspirational garbage, that's inspirational."

"I know," I say. "Can't quite believe it, either."

"So what's the big moment? The second experience in one day that will define your life?"

I cover my hand with my sleeve and swipe away the flour on her face before I slide my hand to her jaw and underneath her ear, cupping the side of her face. I smile first and then I kiss her. *"You* are my life-defining moment, Lennon. For all the shit you've been through, for all the shit you're still going through, and for the weird things you do that I'll never understand. And for this moment, right here." I brush her lips with mine a second time and she shivers. "This memory in the making, right now, when everything is perfectly okay, and I tell you that I'm falling in love with you. Since it feels pretty big, and it's never happened to me before, I think classification as a life-defining moment is fair, don't you?"

I freeze, unable to believe I said those words. My breath sticks until her smile sends the air rushing back into the space between us. Maybe I should take some of Lennon's drugs and chill out, because this is the last thing I expected. I'm not that guy. I don't do romantic things, I don't bare my soul for anyone.

Why her?

"That's fair," she says. "I feel like I'm supposed to know you."

"Yeah," I tell her. "I get that. Me too."

"I'm falling in love with you, too."

I hear nothing else. The sound those words make is far greater, so much more exceptional, than any piece of music I could ever make.

Lennon

FACT: PANIC ATTACKS SPARK THOUGHTS OF
CATASTROPHIC EVENTS AND AN OVERWHELMING
BELIEF THAT DEATH IS ABOUT TO TAKE YOU.

I HAVE A THERAPY APPOINTMENT this morning. The bus is empty, and it doesn't take me long to get to Dr. Linderman's office. To my surprise, he's sitting outside, on the steps of the large building.

He's wearing khakis, a golf shirt, and Vans. Purple spectacles today.

"How many pairs of glasses do you own?"

He considers this. "Thirty. Maybe thirty-five."

I nod to the door of the office. "Carbon monoxide leak?" I guess.

"Well, isn't that an OCD state of mind," he says, rising to his feet.

"Guilty as charged, Levi."

"Come with me," he says, his hands dipping into his pockets.

I follow quietly, at first assuming we're headed to the park, but at the side of the building, Dr. Linderman takes a sharp turn and veers off toward the back. As I move to catch up with him, he holds up a set of keys, pressing a button on a key chain. A car chirps, its headlights flickering to life.

"A BMW. Believe it or not, I've seen a more douchey car than that lately."

"Douche-y," Linderman repeats slowly.

"Read: 'pretentious,'" I say, holding up my hands to make air quotes. "And if you think I'm going anywhere near that silver death trap, think again."

"We're just going to get into the car," he says. "I won't so much as turn the ignition over. I just want you to sit in the seat, Lennon. Can you do that?"

I shake my head.

"Well, for the sake of arguing that it's kind of my job to help you, I'm going to need you to dig deep and be able to sit in the car. I'll be with you the whole time, and we will talk about it."

"You sure know how to destroy a perfectly good day."

"You'll be stronger for it in the end." He smiles warmly. "You got this, Lennon. I wouldn't ask you to do it if I didn't believe you were ready."

"It's a waste of time," I tell him. "I'll never be normal."

"You don't need to be. We're not trying to change you. You don't have to be normal."

Kyler's sentiment exits my mouth. "Ordinary can never achieve greatness."

"Good thing you'll never be ordinary," he says. "And like I told you, no one says you need to be normal. The objective is to focus and take back your control."

He stops and looks at me. Dr. Linderman may be a Beverly

Hills doctor, but he cares. I can tell he does. "I promise you, Lennon. I only want to help you become stronger, more independent. I hope to see you take back your life, even if it's hard."

I nod, then look at my shoes, because I may not travel in this car, but what if I can sit in it? What if I can lay the first brick in a staircase of life-defining moments right here, right now, today? I remember Kyler and how brave he was. How brave he is. "I'll try it...."

I make it to the car door and rest my fingers on its handle. The second they do, an image of Jacob, bloody and dead, flashes in my brain. A lump solidifies in my throat, and I gulp at the air.

Jacob could die. People die in cars.

My dad, arms and legs twisted in a tangled, distorted mess.

I can't breathe.

People die in cars.

I open the door and gaze across the car's hood. Dr. Linderman is directly across from me. "How is the anxiety on a scale of one to ten?" he asks.

"A hundred."

He looks at me.

"Fine, like a nine point five."

"What are you thinking?"

"That everyone is going to die."

He nods. "They might."

I can't breathe.

Dr. Linderman taps the hood of the car. "Eyes over here, Lennon. Maybe something bad *will* happen."

How is this supposed to be helping?

"Can you say that?" he says. "Maybe something bad will happen."

"Maybe something bad will happen." I hardly choke the words out.

"Let's sit in the car."

I fold like a lawn chair and sit. Not because it's easy, but because I'm about to pass out.

"Maybe something bad will happen."

He says it again, and I think of my dad. I think of how hard he's trying. He's the only family I have left. And Jacob and Claire. I think of Kyler. What if something bad happened to him? Tears spring from my eyes and fall down my face, so I close them. My entire body is trembling.

"Just breathe," he says. "Breathe and focus. Remember it's the disease controlling your thoughts and you do have the power to ignore them," he says. "Even when it seems like you don't."

His words sink in.

And my hands twitch as if they're trying to argue his point, to prove that they are in control.

"Just breathe, Lennon. What's the anxiety at?"

"Seven," I mutter. My heart is slowing, my breaths coming easier.

It's the OCD. Nothing will happen to Jacob, Dad, Claire, or Kyler because I'm sitting in this car. Nothing is going to happen to them because of me.

He makes me sit there, sweating bullets, being afraid, for the full session. When he says we're done for the day, I cannot get out of there fast enough.

As I'm walking three steps ahead of him, he hollers, "Lennon?"

"Yeah?"

"Be proud of yourself. It's a big deal."

"Yeah," I say. "It is."

KYLER

LENNON HAD AN APPOINTMENT THIS morning, so instead of being in Chemistry—studying matter—I'm here, soaking up the sun on the east side of the school, thinking about a different kind of chemistry. The Lennon and Kyler kind. A handful of rebels stand fifteen feet or so away, smoking pot or cigarettes and drinking Vitaminwater spiked with vodka.

The bus's air brakes hiss, and when she steps off, her focus is on the tips of her sneakers. It's so unbreakable that she doesn't even see me. Her hair cascades down, making a curtain for her face, and her shoulders slump so she's almost hunched over, arms wrapped around her middle as if she can hang on tight enough to keep herself stitched together. My hand shoots to the side to stop her. Her gaze darts up, a wary look painted in her eyes before relief registers on her face.

"Shouldn't you be in class?"

"Maybe. Shouldn't the weekend be, like, four days instead of two? Life is full of questions, Lennon."

"Dr. Linderman made me sit in his car this morning."

So she *is* trying to keep herself stitched together. She's wearing the face of fear.

I reach for the belt loop of her jeans and pull her close, then wrap my arms around her. Her body is rigid at first, but then she exhales and relaxes a bit. "You okay?"

"Been better. It wasn't exactly how I wanted to spend my morning."

I squeeze her and kiss the top of her head. "But you did it, and that is pretty badass."

She gives me a small, proud smile. "I did, and you're right, it is."

"You're a hero," I say. "You should tell Jacob."

She pretends to look at a watch that isn't on her wrist. "Ego fluffing to commence in three, two..."

"Touché, Davis." I release her but slide my fingers through hers. "Let's go inside, get something to eat. I'm starving."

Lennon from Maine with Serious Issues Who Sews and Is Broken and Beautiful and Badass is on my arm. She's proud to be there, and for one infinitesimal speck of time, I hold on to the feeling of a beautiful girl on my arm who is proud to be there, because I know I'm going to lose it. Before I drop her hand, I close my eyes to savor the moment, even just for one infinitesimal speck of time.

Lennon

FACT: F*&% CAN BE USED AS A NOUN, VERB,
ADVERB, ADJECTIVE, AND INTERJECTION.
THOUGHT: I SHOULD SWEAR MORE OFTEN.

IT'S A STRANGE THING HAVING the most repulsive start to what turns out to be a beautiful day. A cosmic paradox, if you will. Kyler releases my hand the second we breeze through the school doors. His fingers clench into a fist before raking through his hair, his brows drawing down into a pained expression. No part of him *wants* to let go. I don't want him to let go, either. He moves to pull away from me, but I grasp the tips of his fingers with mine and bring him back to me. "What's wrong? Scared of being seen with the crazy girl?"

He's stunned for a moment before he links our fingers together, a cautious smile flittering across his face. "As if, Davis. Being the nice guy that I am, I was simply doing what's right and thinking about what this means for you. You're about to walk headfirst into a hot iron. The most damaging branding on your high school reputation for being with the number one social reject of Hell Air Learning Academy. There might not be any coming back from that. A situation like this is less like testing the waters, more like diving into a typhoon headfirst. Seems only fair to give you the chance to back out while you can." He pauses for a breath. "I'd also like to discredit your theory I'd be the one afraid to be seen with you by adding that no one but me knows you're doing battle with those OCD terrorists all the time. Your secret's safe with me, kid. Just trying to give you options."

"For a social reject, you're kind of adorable, too."

As predicted, everybody stares.

Unexpected: Neither of us cares.

We walk through the doors of the cafeteria; I lean in close to him. "I feel liberated."

"From?"

"A demon."

Kyler gives me a sideways glance and squeezes my hand. "Could be a band name. Liberated Demons. Think about it."

"Our slogan could be 'No Fucks Left to Give.'"

Kyler freezes, his feet glued to the floor as the weight of every single person with cautious glances presses down on us. Spectators who have no idea they're about to witness a miracle. A look of understanding flashes across his face and he turns, the corners of his beautiful mouth curl into a mischievous grin. "Did you just swear, Lennon?"

I nod. "I believe I did swear, yes."

He lowers his hoodie to expose his face, reaches out, snakes an arm around my waist, and pulls me in so hard, he almost flattens me against his chest. "I love it when you talk dirty," he says, and before I realize what's happening, Kyler Benton's tongue is down my throat.

The air in the entire cafeteria is sucked out in a vacuum. One silent moment where this is a big thing that *feels* like a big thing because it's never happened before. A spot in time where there is nothing but him and me and the electric currents that fire through our cells. A single second that changes everything until it's stolen by the students who begin to clap and cheer.

My heart grows so big, it's going to burst.

Heat surges through me like wildfire, and I bite my lower lip to stop my foolish grin from spreading. "We should eat."

"Eating is a fine idea." Kyler sweeps his arm in the direction of the lunch lineup.

I order a turkey burger with salad, Kyler orders an old-fashioned cheeseburger with fries, and ten minutes later we are standing at a table where Austin, Emmett, and Silas are seated and avoiding eye contact as if watching Kyler and me kiss is the most uncomfortable thing they've ever done.

Silas stands and switches chairs to make sure the two empty ones are side by side. I sit and say, "Thanks."

He nods. "Don't mention it."

Kyler sits, too, and takes a huge bite of his burger at the same time that Emmett asks, "So, Lennon, are you coming to our gig?"

I hadn't thought of that. I look at Kyler because he hasn't exactly invited me. His eyes go wide and he finishes chewing his food and swallows. "Whatcha looking at me for, Davis? I'd like to know, too. Are you coming?"

"Am I invited?"

"We just sucked face in the cafeteria, what do you think?"

I turn to look at Emmett. "Yes," I say. "I'd love to come."

The rest of the afternoon, anywhere Kyler and I go, people look, they whisper, they speculate. I think someone tags Kyler in a picture of our kiss on Instagram, but none of that matters because this, *this* is my normal, and it's not normal at all. And that's okay.

I can't rid myself of the grin for the entire day, and when he walks home from school with me, his fingers still tangled in mine, I can't remember the last time I ever felt this happy. Maybe there wasn't a last time. . . .

"We should walk together in the mornings," he says. "Until you're ready to drive, that is. I know you don't believe it, but one day you will be."

"Just like one day you won't need your hoodies, or masks."

He nods. "Maybe. But today, it was huge, Lennon. Huge things have been happening to me a lot lately."

"Yeah," I say, "me too."

"I think it's time to celebrate. Agree?"

"Agree."

"Tree house. After dinner," he says. "You can bring your notebook. We'll work on English to make sure our project is ready next week, and then we'll do whatever the hell we feel like because we earned it."

"I'm almost done—the mask," I say.

"Is it dark and gothic?"

"Depends on how you feel about bedazzling."

He laughs. "I was going for something harder, more mysterious, but I trust you."

"Back to square one," I tease. I think about the mask. It's

almost complete. It's a little dark, a little twisted, but beautiful. Like him.

I'm proud of the mask, but he doesn't need it. I wish he could see himself the way I do—the truth I see reflected in an old soul that has too much wisdom for a seventeen-year-old kid, the smile on his lips when he's observing me and doesn't think I notice, the waters of his eyes, calm as a glass sea yet harboring the constant threat of a riptide. What I don't notice are the burns on his face. I am blind to the story he wears on his skin—yet I love them, those terrible scars I cannot see—because without them, he wouldn't be Kyler. And some days, even though I know my own happiness is up to me, Kyler is the reason I remember how to smile.

After promising to meet in the tree house at seven, we part ways at the stretch of fence between our houses. As I come through the door, Oscar races out from behind a kitchen cupboard and offers a sad bark accompanied by a wagging tail. I crouch down and pat his head. He happily accepts my greeting, jumping up on his hind legs to hold his paws up in an effortless display of cuteness.

"Pretty quiet around here," I tell him. I scoop him up in my arms and head straight for my room. I set Oscar down on the end of the bed, on top of a plaid throw. I've unpacked a handful of things from one of my many Maine boxes in an effort to make my room less generic and more inviting while Trixie works her magic, which I have yet to see any real evidence of. After placing my bag on the left side of my desk, I pick up the mask to examine it.

It will cover approximately one half of his face. I used the plaster mold as a base and have built up layer after layer of papier-mâché and latex. I follow the curvature of the scales, crafted to resemble those of a beast.

Kyler is seventeen. He was not born in the year of the dragon, but he sure reminds me of one, and I used that for inspiration. The most powerful figure of the zodiac and rumored to be an intellectual hothead. In some cultures, dragons are said to represent strength, courage, balance, and magic. And to me, he is all of these things: strong, brave, and able to make an ordinary world seem extraordinary. My fingers extend to touch the piece I've fashioned into a replica of one of the two deadly horns seen on a ram or an ibex.

I gather the paint I need, turn on the overhead light, and begin to finish the small, delicate strokes that will bring the mask to life so it can keep hidden the face of someone whose thoughts and ideas could change the world.

There's a knock at my door. I don't stop painting. Hyperfocused on making it perfect. "Come in."

Claire peeks her head in. "Lennon, we're going to a dinner party, sugar."

KYLER

NO FUCKS LEFT TO GIVE

Random Thoughts of a Random Mind

THE BAND PRACTICES FOR AN hour before supper, and after everybody leaves, I head to the kitchen. It's 6:00 p.m. Every night since I can remember, we eat promptly at 6:15, so I'm surprised to find my mother standing at the counter, chopping herbs, looking pleased, and humming to herself while pots steam and bubble on the stove behind her. Normally she'd be setting the table or plating the food, but dinner isn't even close to ready. I glance at my phone to check the time to make sure I'm not early.

"Everything okay, Mom?"

She stops chopping the pile of green in front of her. "Hi, honey," she says. "How was your day?"

I gesture toward the herbs on her chopping block and fetch a Coke from the fridge. "Day was great. Are we having company?" It's the best guess I've got. If we don't eat at 6:15, it's because my dad is bringing home some work associate or a grateful client. The other option is worse, which says a lot. My aunt Betty and uncle Robert sometimes materialize for surprise visits, bringing with them my cousin, Solomon. The forced conversation that always takes place ends with me pondering how many IQ points I've been robbed of in the hour of my life I'll never get back.

She nods and resumes chopping. "I told your sister to tell you."

God, please not Solomon. "Tell me what?" I crack the can of Coke and take a sip.

"I've invited Claire and her family over for dinner."

I almost spit out my drink. *God, please not Claire and family, I'll trade three hours with Sol.* "What? Why? Why would you do that, Mom?"

"Something wrong, honey?"

"Well, yeah, something's wrong. Are you kidding me?"

She stops cutting and looks up. "Your father will be on his best behavior, Kyler, I've warned him. Claire's family has been through a rough time. It's a good thing to do, have them for a night where everyone can relax and enjoy good food and some company. Besides, if you're getting close with this girl, meeting her isn't the strangest request. I *am* your mother, Kyler."

I roll my eyes, but she arches an eyebrow and uses the giant knife in her hand as an extension of her pointer finger. "Go change, please. I need your help to set up the patio."

I pinpoint the inflection in her speech. It's the mom voice. The linguistic equivalent of a clarion call only heard by reckless teenagers who recognize when they're teetering on the brink of an outbreak of Momzilla. This is not a request; it's an order, and we're not discussing the possible ramifications of having everyone in the same space, so here we are about to have dinner on the patio with my family, including my dad and hers. So much for celebrating.

An hour and fifteen minutes later, I've switched the place settings twice to make sure there isn't so much as a hint of red showing, and there's a knock at the door. Macy is in the kitchen with Mom, who is putting finishing touches on what will be a masterpiece, and Dad is seated at the dining room table reading something on his laptop, so I go and open the door.

Jacob pushes himself past my legs and steps inside, proudly wearing his cape. "I can't wait to see your room," he blurts out.

Poor kid doesn't know what he's about to walk into. "Hey, Jake."

Claire steps forward, too, and reins him in with a firm hand on his shoulder. "Jacob, baby," she says, "y'all wait to be invited into someone's house, otherwise it's vulgar."

"He's fine," I say to Claire. "Jacob and I are friends." I step to the side. "My mother is in the kitchen, we're eating poolside."

Andrea, standing to the left of Josh, rolls her eyes, and Lennon, to his right, looks up from her shoes and gives me a shy smile.

"Is that the Davises?" Mom asks from the kitchen.

No, Mom, it's a Girl Scout selling cookies. I raise my voice so she can hear me. "Yeah."

"Come in, Claire. We're in here."

"Can I see your room?" Jacob inquires again.

"How about I show you after dinner? That way we can hang out there and not have to come down to eat in ten minutes."

He nods, satisfied with my answer.

Fifteen minutes later, we are all seated at the poolside patio set underneath the giant pergola that sits on the west side of our swimming pool. The sun is dipping in the sky, and Mom has firefly lights strung across the top of the trellis, so it appears as if we're dining a few feet under the stars instead of a million miles away from them.

We're eating the first course, the appetizer, garlic lime shrimp for everyone except Jacob, who has a homemade chicken strip served with carrot sticks.

"How's work?" Dad asks Josh.

Josh finishes chewing his shrimp and takes a sip of water to wash it down before he clears his throat. "It's going really well, thanks. Some exciting projects coming up, which is good timing coinciding with Claire's and my annual event."

The *annual event* he's referring to is a party that Claire and Josh throw every year. Always happens at the end of June. A slew of music industry people show up for what starts off as a formal affair, but after a few years of observing from my tree house, I can tell you things turn wild once the guests who show up only out of courtesy leave. I recall one year involving tequila shots, a limbo bar, and a few pairs of breasts from women who'd obviously shed inhibitions. I was fifteen. And until Lennon came around, it was literally the greatest day of my life.

Josh continues. "I'm trying to set up a few bands this year to play. We need to find new talent for some of our clients who are seeking original work for some online streaming shows and a few movies. It's been a challenge, but I think we're almost there."

Claire smiles stiffly. "Honey, I thought we agreed on my idea for that."

"We didn't. I'm not sure I want to book one single band, Claire. Putting all your eggs in one basket never seems like a wise idea."

"It's a favor for a friend," Claire says. She scowls, then, realizing everyone is looking at her, seems to conclude there's a better time and place for this conversation. She turns to my father. "How about you, Greg? Living the dream at the law firm?"

Dad picks up his red wine and takes a sip. "You have no idea," he replies.

We sit through five courses of almost painful small talk from everyone except Andrea, who has said only two words, repeatedly and only directed at my mother, who has been serving her food: "Thank you."

It's the quietest Andrea's ever been and a refreshing change.

We finish off our dessert trio, bite-size servings of mango yuzu brûlée, some German chocolate mousse with an edible flower, and a side of mixed berry crumble. I'm the first to set my napkin down, rise, and pick up my plate. I gather the plates from my mom, Claire, Lennon, and Jacob, but everyone else is still eating. "Thanks for dinner, Mom. Can we be excused?"

By *we*, I mean Lennon and me, but Jacob is shifting around his chair like the thing is made of nails. "Can I see your room?"

I look from Jacob to my mom, then back to Jacob. "Waiting for my mom to excuse us from the table, bro. It's a rule around here."

"I want to see his room," Jacob says excitedly. Just in case my mom didn't hear him the fifteen times he's mentioned it over dinner.

"Lennon and I have homework," I tell my mom. "Project is due in two weeks."

"How's that coming?" my dad asks. He's asking to look like a more invested parent than he is.

"Good," I say. "Mom?"

Mom waves her hand. "Go on. You're excused."

Andrea uncrosses her arms and slumps in relief. "Can I go home? Please."

Claire glares at her, so she forces a smile. "I mean, thank you so much for having me, Mr. and Mrs. Benton, dinner was delicious." She looks at Claire again desperately. "Liam and Jess are coming over, Mom. Please."

"Run along," Claire says. She looks at my mom. "I can help with dishes."

Macy stands and waves her hand. "You're a guest." She looks at our mother. "You cooked all afternoon, sit. Lennon and I can do the dishes."

I glare at Macy, determined to put the brakes on her volunteering Lennon to do dishes. "Lennon is a guest, too," I point out. "Besides, she has homework. With me."

"Relax, Romeo. Jacob wants to see your room. Show him. Lennon can come do homework when we've finished the dishes. You don't mind, do you, Lennon?"

I wish she did mind, but she shakes her head. "Happy to help." She smiles warmly at me. "Go on," she says, "I'll be up soon."

I mind, but Macy won't care about that. I issue a silent stern look of warning to Macy not to cross any lines, then I bend down so I'm eye level with Jacob. "Ready, little man?"

"Yep." His head bobs up and down.

"Cool. Follow me."

I open the door to my room, and Jacob shoots through it like a balloon that's been let go, free to fly crazily through the world when it loses its air. Once he does a full lap, he stops at my bed, his hand dragging across the blankets. "Your room is huge."

"I know."

"Like ten times huger than mine."

"It's too big," I say. "More space for things to feel empty."

He looks at the shelves that line two full walls and are filled with records. "You collect those?" he asks.

"Yeah," I say. "Kinda."

"Lennon has lots of them, too," he says.

I don't recall seeing a single record. "She does?"

He walks around my room, surveying first, then inspecting everything closely. He'll select an object, pluck it from the shelf, and turn it over in his hands curiously, a sense of wonder clear on his face. I wish I'd enjoyed being five more, but I guess there was no way for me to know back then that age five would be the last year of my life without a curse on my skin. "Yep," he says. "Lots of boxes of them. In storage till her room is done. She said they're her mommy's."

He laps the room again, his hand settling on my acoustic guitar. It's propped in one corner on a guitar stand. "Can you play?"

I nod. "Yeah."

"Are you good?"

"Better than some."

He continues examining my room. "What else do you like to do? You have lots of stuff."

"I write a lot." I gesture to my desk. Jacob saunters over to it and looks down at my notebook. It's closed, but to be honest, I'm not exactly concerned with a five-year-old reading my words and looking for the deeper meaning in them, *if* he can even read yet. I try to recall how old I was, or even Macy, but I blank.

"You have so much paper," he observes.

"I do."

"You must write a lot. Do you want to be a writer when you grow up?"

"No," I say, walking over to stand beside him. "I do it for fun. Want to know what else I do for fun?" I reach into the bottom drawer of my desk to pull out a letter-sized sheet of paper that's a higher stock and heavier weight than average. "I make paper airplanes, too."

Amazed, he looks at the paper in my hands. "Can we make one?"

"Yeah," I say, grabbing a few more sheets of paper. "We can make as many as you want."

I don't have to tell him twice. He sits down at the desk and waits patiently. I put a piece of paper in front of him and sit on my knees so we're the same height. I fold creases into the paper. "The trick is folding the tail of the plane," I tell him. "Or sometimes, adding weight to its nose. I'll show you."

Jacob and I make twenty-three airplanes in an hour.

Lennon

ON FIRST IMPRESSION, MACY COULDN'T be more different from her brother. As I follow her into the kitchen, she spins to face me and beams. Her teeth are perfect, her eyes the same intense blue as her brother's, which I now know they've both inherited from their mom. "Thanks for helping," she says. "My mom has been cooking for most of the afternoon. I figured dishes were the least I could do."

I nod and try to smile back. I don't know what, if anything, Kyler has told his sister about me, so I assume she thinks I'm boring-slash-normal. "It's no problem at all. I'm happy to help."

She opens the dishwasher and loads plates while the sink fills with hot, soapy water to wash pots and pans. She hands me a dish towel and pauses. "Wait. I didn't ask, do you want to wash or dry?"

I hold up the dish towel. "Drying is fine."

We get to work. I think what she says next is meant to be casual, but it's obvious she loves her brother and is trying to determine if I'm good enough for him. "Kyler seems different since he met you."

"Oh?"

"Yeah," she says, "I mean, I've only seen him walk around school without his hoodie a few times before in all of his life. Last week, he did it twice. That's incredible."

I remember Kyler's excuse for anyone curious enough to ask. "He lost a bet," I say.

"He loses bets to Silas all the time," she says. "He'd never lose the hoodie for Silas. I guess my point is, I've never seen him so settled in his own skin before. He can be himself with you. I love seeing him this way."

I'm not sure what to say, so I continue drying a pan while she keeps talking. "We both know it's because of you, and I want to say one thing." She pauses, waiting for me to acknowledge that what she's about to say is important.

"Go ahead."

"My brother, he pretends to be a lot tougher than he is, you know. I worry."

Understandable. If anyone knows what it's like to worry, it's me. "That I'll hurt him," I supply.

She cringes when I say the words out loud. "Yeah. And I'm sorry if that's unwarranted or silly, I mean, you seem nice, but he's the only brother I have, and I feel some need to protect him. He's a good guy, Lennon."

I nod and set the clean pan down on the island before retrieving another. "I know he's a good guy," I tell her. "He's a great guy. I'd do nothing to hurt him. I promise." What Macy doesn't know is I would do *anything* if it meant I'd protect him from pain or hurt. Like flipping a light switch, tapping the floorboards, door jams, walls, windows, my thigh, or my wrist, or entering a locker combination fifty-five times. I'd do all those things on an endless cycle if it meant he would be safe and happy. I don't tell Macy that. Instead I look at her as sincerely as I can. "I like your brother," I tell her. "I swear I do."

Relief flares across her features. "Thank you, Lennon. He deserves it."

"Yeah," I say, "he does."

We finish up and Claire tells me it's time for Jacob to go to bed and asks if I'd mind sending him down when I go up to start homework. Truth be told, I'm not confident homework is on the agenda anymore, but I tell her I'll do that and head up the stairs to Kyler's room.

I pause at the door, bracing myself for his creative chaos. I have a general idea of the layout, but I've never fully seen inside; he's usually at his desk or standing by the window. When I swing it open, it's worse than I thought. His room is massive. The huge window where Kyler can see into my room is right behind a long, sleek black desk entombed in papers. Mammoth panes of glass stretch along the walls, flanked by shelves. Tons of them. They begin to the left side of his desk and extend in an L shape down another fifteen feet of shelving filled with records.

The wall opposite is covered with framed pictures and artwork of musicians, album covers, vinyl records encased in shadow boxes, and the last wall, maybe the most impressive of them all, showcases guitars. *Five.* It's my favorite wall.

"Holy crap," I mutter. I knew he liked music. I never knew how much.

Kyler and Jacob are seated on the bed while Kyler tries to explain aerodynamics. At my words, they both look up. Kyler rises from the bed and hurries to his dresser drawer, pulling out a couple of handfuls of fabric. He moves fast and drapes them over some of the music memorabilia that decorate his walls. I realize what his objective is, because he's covering anything that has a hint of red with his T-shirts.

"You don't have to do that for me," I mumble.

"I know," he replies. "I want to."

Jacob is still seated on the bed, so I turn my focus to him. "Jake," I say.

"I don't want to go," Jacob says.

"Your mom says it's time to go to bed."

His head hangs down and his shoulders fall. "But I'm having fun."

Kyler touches Jacob's arm. "You know what? I don't have band practice or anything next Wednesday, maybe you can come over and we'll make more cool stuff."

Jacob blinks. "Really?"

"Yeah," Kyler says. "I had fun, too. Macy doesn't appreciate the skill in building paper airplanes." He walks to his wardrobe and retrieves a box. He removes something, puts it back in the bureau, and returns to Jacob with the box. "Here. Put the planes in this, you can fly them outside tomorrow if you take them home."

Jacob loads the planes into the box before pausing, grabbing one in each hand, and racing to the desk. He picks up one of Kyler's pens, writes something on the wing of each, caps the pen, and returns, proudly offering his gift.

The wing of one plane says *K*, while the other is marked with an *L*.

"These are for you two. So you can have your own planes."

Kyler grins and takes his plane. "Thanks, that's cool."

I ruffle Jacob's hair. "Thanks, buddy."

He grabs the box and turns. "See you at home, Lennon. Thank you for making airplanes with me, Kyler."

"It was awesome," Kyler says. "Good night, Jacob."

"Night," he says, and leaves. I can hear him hollering at my Dad and Claire, asking them to guess what he made, before he's even down the stairs.

"You're great to him," I say.

Kyler shrugs and sits on the bed, leaning against his headboard. "He's a cool kid. Makes it easy. How was doing dishes with Mae? I'm sorry she volunteered you. She worries about me."

"I know. And it was nice. Your sister is sweet."

He laughs. "That's only because you've never pissed her off."

I grab an acoustic guitar from its stand and sit beside him, the guitar across my lap. I position my hands, one underneath to reach the frets on its neck, and one slung over the top. "My mom used to play guitar." A knot forms in my throat. "She's the reason I know a lot about music. I remember watching her while she played, thinking she was the prettiest woman on the planet. She was so beautiful."

"You must look exactly like her, then," he says. "Because you're beautiful."

I press down on the frets to make a C chord and shake my head. "I can't play. Not really. Just notes. A few things I remember from watching her play."

"Do you *want* to know how to play?"

I nod. "One day."

Kyler sits up and slides closer to me. He lifts one leg over and behind my body, so I'm between his legs, my back pressed to his chest. His breath is in my ear, his words, spoken so low, so deep, they vibrate my eardrum. "Today."

His arms slide through the space between the guitar and me as an electric current pulses through every nerve in my body. His fingers glide on top of mine on both hands, and he positions them on the frets. "I'll push, you strum."

I nod. Unable to speak.

He applies pressure on two of the fingers of our left hands, and as I move my right one to strum the set of strings, I feel his right hand slip to my side and underneath the fabric of my T-shirt. He rests it there, just above the waistline of my jeans, and even though his hand is frozen in place, the tips of his fingers trace fire into the skin near my belly button. I inhale sharply and try to focus on strumming.

"Go," he says. "Do it."

I strum. He slides our fingers both horizontally and vertically down and presses again. "Again."

We repeat this a couple more times. The hand he has resting

on my belly slides more boldly in exploration with every note we play until it feels as if he's strumming *me*, making music with his hands on my skin. My body and mind both betray me, because as he touches me, I let out these uncontrolled breaths and utter little whimpers that have no business escaping from my mouth. It's accompanied by chills, tingles, and an ache that's so foreign to me I have no idea how to react.

Kyler seems unaffected, his focus on the chords of the song. "We're going to do it faster this time, the transitions from one note to the next."

Easy for him to say. He's not the one being tortured at the moment. I pause and listen for a change in his breathing, anything to indicate he's as on edge as I am, but I get nothing.

We repeat the chords at a faster pace until suddenly, we're playing something beautiful.

He rests his chin on my shoulder as he glides my fingers seamlessly across the frets, and I strum in the same rhythm. He sings, each word soft, his tone curving seamlessly around them.

"A girl like you, untouchable,
You're haunting all my dreams,
I wish you could be mine somehow,
But that's hard for me to see."

Our fingers continue to dance from fret to fret. My breath continues to tremble, my body continues to buzz, and my brain starts to fire as it processes the words he's singing.

"I have no faith in fateful things,
I'll always be alone,

You could change my life, and make it right,
Show my heart it's home."

The tension in his words soaks into my pores and seeps through me. The tenor of his voice, the closeness of our bodies consumes me, and when Kyler pauses long enough to play a few extra notes and says, "Lennon's song," I come unglued.

My hand falls from the guitar and he squeezes my side. "Don't you want to hear the rest of it?"

I shake my head. I spin to face him and wonder if the look on his face reflects my own. Vulnerable. Having reached that point of a relationship there is no coming back from. When you look at the other person and know, without question, that your hearts beat in sync, that your minds are connected, even if they're broken, and that you will never be the same person again no matter what happens. "That song's a bit tragic," I say, sucking in a breath. "Show me that we aren't a tragedy."

I climb on top of him, lock my fingers through his hair, and I kiss him.

He grabs the sides of my face with his hands. "You're beautiful."

I kiss him again.

And again.

And again.

I kiss him until it feels right.

Fifty-five times.

And like any good OCD girl would do, I repeat the process.

KYLER

LUST Я US

Random Thoughts of a Random Mind

LAST NIGHT. LAST NIGHT. LAST NIGHT.

I cannot stop thinking about it and I wonder if this is a small taste of what Lennon's mind is like *all the time*. My brain is flooded with memories of how she smelled, the taste of fruit on her mouth, the way she reacted to my touch. I don't know which one of us was more surprised: me or her.

She comes to the end of her driveway, in her sneakers, with huge, messy hair and a backpack slung over her shoulders. Her skin is glowing, her face flushed hues of pink. She doesn't even try to hide her massive smile when I approach.

"Good morning, sunshine. I realize we had a pretty wicked make-out session, Davis, but you're sparkling like I did utterly unspeakable and indecent things to you last night."

Her blush goes from pink to scarlet.

"I feel like a make-out junkie," she says.

I bring my hand to her face. "Could be a band name, Lennon.

Make-Out Junkies." I lean in and kiss her before saying, "Think about it."

She giggles. "We'd need a slogan."

"Make-Out Junkies. Lust Я Us." I kiss her a second time and pull away. "As much as I'd rather stand right here in this spot with my mouth on top of yours, we should get to school. There's a mandatory assembly on cyberbullying this afternoon. Can't miss that, now can we?"

She grabs my hand. "No, definitely not."

I spend the entire first part of the day attending classes, but really my brain is a million miles away. Imagining and replaying various scenarios of the make-out session with Lennon. I've kissed girls, sure, but it was never like that. A tornado of feelings and secret thoughts spilled out through lips and hands, and it's all I can do to make it through the morning without trying for a repeat performance in the janitor's closet.

Lennon is getting extra help with math at lunchtime, so by the time the announcement comes on about the quarterly "awareness assembly" I'm itching to see her. Four times a year we're forced to attend them and acknowledge whatever cause some committee has in mind. Whether it's saving villages in need of clean drinking water or arming the students with information about drug use and the serious risks associated with sexual promiscuity. Today, we get cyberbullying.

I can hardly contain my excitement.

The assembly is in the gym. The lifeblood of high school.

Home to pep rallies, basketball games, and school dances. Right now students are spread out everywhere, mumbling about math tests and who is going out with whom. Some are shouting, yelling loudly across the gym at their peers, occupying the bleachers in large groups.

I put my hand on the small of Lennon's back to help her up the first step toward the top of the bleachers. There's less chance of being called on, or made an example of this way. Silas, Austin, and Emmett are all seated.

Students continue to pour in for a few moments before Principal Walsh takes his place at the podium erected in the middle of the gym. The microphone on the podium gives feedback for a moment, but then the buzzing stops, and the room falls silent save for a couple of students coughing and a soul or two daring enough to finish their thoughts to their friends in hushed whispers.

"I'd like to welcome you to our assembly on cyberbullying. Thank you all for coming."

'Cause we had a choice.

Lennon leans down to root in her backpack for something. She locates a bottle of water and takes a sip before screwing the lid shut, smiling at me, and setting it down.

"... and that is why it's important to take a stand," Principal Walsh is saying. "We'll watch a short film and then hold an open-forum discussion. I'd like to encourage conversation and participation."

The lights dim, and a video comes on the three big screens

placed throughout the gym. *Bel Air Learning Academy Awareness Assemblies Presents: Cyberbullying. Take a Stand.*

The music that accompanies the slides is off; it doesn't transition in time with the images being presented. Something about that prompts an irritating tic in my brain. Maybe that's what the color red is like for Lennon. The video starts by listing facts about cyberbullying. Statistics about the number of kids who are victims, different mediums where cyberbullying can occur, how the law is starting to change regarding cyberbullying. The video introduction cuts to a group of kids. The footage is clearly pre-internet era, maybe the '70s or the '80s. The children on screen talk about being bullied. From name calling to laughing, the schoolyard brute, stuff that parents were told can be chalked up to "kids being kids."

It then cuts to a news story dated last year about a fourteen-year-old girl who'd committed suicide because of the extent she was bullied online. Everyone is tuned into the screens, horrified expressions on their faces, while the camera shows a pretty girl smiling, living the American dream, and then it shows her heartbroken mother, and then her headstone.

The next image in the documentary makes no sense. It's a screen cap with my name, KYLER BENTON, displayed on what appears to be my Facebook account.

I whip my phone from my pocket and open the app, but a screen pops up to request that I sign in. I enter my log-in information, but it flashes and tells me I don't have the correct username and password combination.

I try it a second time and the same message appears.

Horrified, I look back to the screen to digest what is currently displayed for all to see. My status reads: *I LOVE my crazy girlfriend...she really is...crazy...*

Directly underneath the text is a picture of a letter, shot as close as possible to blur the background yet still produce a clear image of the words scrawled on the paper. There's a logo at the top from Riverview Psychiatric Center, in Maine.

My eyes scan the picture.

To Whom It May Concern:

   Please find all documentation related to patient Lennon Davis, age 16, enclosed. A broad overview is below; however, you will find detailed reports and recommendations contained within the attached documents. Please don't hesitate to contact me should you have any questions or concerns.

Davis, Lennon. 16.

   Patient displays symptoms of identified obsessive-compulsive disorder and generalized anxiety disorder. Patient speaks of being plagued by intrusive thoughts, dominated by thoughts or disturbing images of harm to loved ones. Patient's compulsions vary; however, repetitive behaviors in patterns of five are predominant. Patient displays a

```
need for logic and order. Having undergone
a recent trauma with the death of her mother,
the patient's symptoms worsened, and she was
subsequently placed in our facility.
```

The room comes to life. Phones hum and buzz, ding and vibrate in every direction. People begin to talk. The lights in the gym flash on and Principal Walsh rushes to the laptop, demanding that everyone remain calm, but it's no use. Every student in Bel Air Learning Academy has pictures of Lennon's medical records on their phone right now.

My eyes dart to Lennon, and hers are wide with terror, with shock, and they're filling fast with tears of humiliation. My hand shoots out to cover hers. "I didn't do this, you know that, right?"

She nods, blinks, and silent tears pour down her face. I stand up and make my voice as loud as I can. "Shut the fuck up. You closed-minded rejects of society. You walk around here like you're something else, but everyone knows the truth. You." I direct my speech to Elizabeth Ronan, for no other reason than she's the first one I see. "Think no one knows you snort your brother's Ritalin in the bathroom at lunch? I hope the minuscule amount of brain matter you have bleeds from your nose." I look at Chase and his buddies. "And, Chase, my friend, if you don't think we all know your dad is boning Cynthia Lancaster's much younger mother, think again. And you." I point to Ally Winters, who was so engrossed in the drama of Lennon moments ago, and is now staring at me, her mouth open in horror. My words exit with the force of fire from a dragon's mouth in the heated silence. "We all know your sister is away at rehab because she was addicted to coke. She's not at the school for athletes you told everyone she had a scholarship to."

I grab Lennon's hand, but she's stiff. I squeeze it, but she's still staring at the screen, her eyes huge and rimmed red, her body shaking.

"Is she okay?" Silas asks.

I stand up and wrap my arm around her waist to pull her up. It gets her attention. "Walk out of here with me. We don't need to stay here."

She nods robotically. I take her hand and together we talk down the stairs, and as I get to the door of the gymnasium, I don't bother saying anything but I do extend my middle finger and hope like hell they all see it.

Lennon

FACT: AS FAR AS DAYS OF THE WEEK GO, FRIDAY HOLDS
THE RECORD FOR MOST AUTOMOTIVE ACCIDENTS,
CYBERATTACKS, AND DECLARATIONS OF WAR.

TEARS SCORCH MY EYES AND blur the gym, the students, the teachers. Everything is covered in a dense fog. Dark, vast emptiness stretches out in front of me and extends to either side. I attempt to focus on my shoes, but my brain flips to a spin cycle that hurls a million feelings into the pit of my belly at the exact same time. Humiliation. Anger. Rage. Betrayal. Embarrassment. Loneliness. Heartache. Loss. Grief. I'm completely exposed.

Topsy. Turvy.

Round and round and round she goes, where she stops, nobody knows.

My heart strikes my chest, punishing my airway, and for every gulp of oxygen I'm desperate to take in, an inferno spreads in my lungs. I've ingested poison and it hurts to breathe. I gulp hard and fast as Kyler's arms hold me tight. He helps me to the gym door and outside where the air is just as thick, maybe even thicker, and he leads me to the *parking lot*, steering me in the direction of his bright blue car. I dig my feet into the pavement and my nails into the skin on his arm. "No."

His breath warms my ear, but his voice is a million miles away. "You've got to trust me," he says, releasing his grip. "Lennon, please, I'm trying to help you."

"No." The taste of salt drips onto my tongue as the tears that put it there fall. I shake my head quickly—too quickly—and make myself dizzy. Kyler spins to face me. "Please, we don't have a lot of time. They're gonna come out of that school with their cell phones up and you'll be all over YouTube in a matter of minutes." His voice drops. "Listen to me, I know how scared you must be. I know every single cell in your body, every instinct inside of you is telling you not to get into that car with me. I know how much you're fucking hurting, but please, trust me. You can do this, Lennon." He rests his forehead on mine. "You can be whatever you need to be with me, just get in the car. I'm trying to protect you." His eyes dart to the doors of the school, clouding with the kind of desperation I've seen only a handful of times.

The hot fingers of fear grip my throat and squeeze. I inhale sharply, but it's still a blaze in my lungs and makes me gasp instead.

Kyler will die in the car.

Don't you see, Kyler? I'm trying to protect you.

I shake my head a second time. The liquid fire on my cheeks and the California air fuse together, and I'm in flames. Like the boy standing in front me. Kyler Benton who was burned in a house fire, who is everything I never knew I was missing. Kyler Benton who will die if I get into his car.

"You'll die." My voice doesn't sound like it belongs to me. It trembles and cracks in a million fractured pieces.

Kyler's hands reach out for my face and I glower, afraid I'll burn them, too. "I won't die, Lennon. I promise you I will not die, not in this car, on this day. Please, I am begging you to get in this car."

Kyler will die in the car.

Kyler. Will. Die. In. The. Car.

"No," I say more firmly. "I can't."

"You can do this. You can do anything. More than anyone I've ever met in my life." The familiar prickle that I hate tickles the tips of my fingers as they, too, ignite. I sob again.

Kyler opens the car door. "Please. It'll be okay. You'll be okay. I promise you, I'll be okay."

He'll be okay.

The dismissal bell rings.

How long have we been standing here?

I settle into the car and pull my legs in. He shuts the door, and I tap before he's even seated. *One. Two. Three. Four. Five. One. Two. Three. Four. Five. One. Two. Three. Four. Five. One. Two. Three. Four. Five. One. Two. Three. Four. Five.*

He fires the ignition at the precise moment hundreds of curious students are expelled from the school doors—a swarm of teenage locusts.

"Shit," he mutters. He slams the car into reverse, swings his arm around the back side of my chair, and looks behind him. Once he's out of the stall, he hammers into drive and doesn't even stop at the stop sign before we are gone.

The movement of the vehicle makes me ill, so I squeeze my

eyes shut and mutter something under my breath about breathing, and I tap. I tap, I tap, I tap, I tap, I tap. Faster, harder, and with more vigor than I've ever committed to doing anything. Because if I tap enough times, at the proper speed, with the proper pressure, Kyler will not die. And I'll do anything to save him. Me? I'm already dead.

One. Two. Three. Four. Five. One. Two. Three. Four. Five. One. Two. Three. Four. Five. One. Two. Three. Four. Five. One. Two. Three. Four. Five. One. Two. Three. Four. Five. One. Two. Three. Four. Five. One. Two. Three. Four. Five. One. Two. Three. Four. Five. One. Two. Three. Four. Five. One. Two. Three. Four. Five. One. Two. Three. Four. Five. One. Two. Three. Four. Five. One. Two. Three. Four. Five. One. Two. Three. Four. Five.

One. Two. Three. Four. Five. One. Two. Three. Four. Five. One. Two. Three. Four. Five. One. Two. Three. Four. Five. One. Two. Three. Four. Five. One. Two. Three. Four. Five. One. Two. Three. Four. Five. One. Two. Three. Four. Five. One. Two. Three. Four. Five. One. Two. Three. Four. Five. One. Two. Three. Four. Five. One. Two. Three. Four. Five. One. Two. Three. Four. Five. One. Two. Three. Four. Five.

I don't know what streets he's navigating. I don't know how long we've been driving, but I recognize when we stop. There's a click as the door opens, and Kyler extends his hand to tug at mine. "C'mon, Lennon, let's get out of the car."

I stand and grab hold of his hand, unsure of my legs' ability to perform their function of keeping me upright. Kyler holds on to the tips of my fingers with one hand while he shuts the door with the other. I drop his hand as soon as the alarm signals that it's locked so I can grasp the door handle. Tears continue to burn at my eyes, my nose is plugged, and there is a knot in my throat the size of a grapefruit.

Pull. Release. Pull. Release. Pull. Release. Pull. Release. Pull. Release. Repeat. *Pull. Release. Pull. Release. Pull. Release. Pull. Release. Pull. Release.* Repeat. *Pull. Release. Pull. Release. Pull. Release. Pull. Release. Pull. Release.* Repeat. *Pull. Release. Pull. Release. Pull. Release. Pull. Release.* Repeat. *Pull. Release. Pull. Release. Pull. Release. Pull. Release. Pull. Release.* Repeat. *Pull. Release. Pull. Release. Pull. Release. Pull. Release. Pull. Release.* Repeat. *Pull. Release. Pull. Release. Pull. Release. Pull. Release.* Repeat. *Pull. Release. Pull. Release. Pull. Release. Pull. Release.* Repeat. *Pull. Release. Pull. Release. Pull. Release. Pull. Release.* Repeat.

Kyler remains dutifully silent at my side as I direct all my focus to the door. *Pull. Release. Pull. Release. Pull. Release. Pull. Release. Pull. Release.* Repeat. *Pull. Release. Pull. Release. Pull. Release. Pull. Release. Pull. Release.* Repeat. *Pull. Release. Pull. Release. Pull. Release. Pull. Release.* Repeat.

Everyone knows. Everyone at Bel Air Learning Academy knows. I will never live it down; they will never let me. Kyler could die. Jacob could die. My dad could die.

Pull. Release. Pull. Release. Pull. Release. Pull. Release. Pull. Release. Repeat. *Pull. Release. Pull. Release. Pull. Release. Pull. Release. Pull. Release.* Repeat. *Pull. Release. Pull. Release. Pull. Release. Pull. Release. Pull. Release.*

He touches my shoulders, and for some reason I turn to face him and scream, "Don't touch me!"

He raises his hands in an instant, palms forward. His eyes are wide, watching the true horror of OCD me unfolding before him. He's helpless to stop the spiral, and so am I.

Pull. Release. Pull. Release. Pull. Release. Pull. Release. Pull. Release. Repeat. *Pull. Release. Pull. Release. Pull. Release. Pull. Release. Pull. Release.* Repeat. *Pull. Release. Pull. Release. Pull. Release. Pull. Release. Pull. Release.* Repeat. *Pull. Release. Pull. Release. Pull. Release. Pull. Release. Pull. Release. Pull. Release.* Repeat. *Pull. Release. Pull. Release. Pull. Release. Pull. Release. Pull. Release.* Repeat.

Pull. Release. Pull. Release. Pull. Release. Pull. Release. Pull. Release. Repeat. *Pull. Release. Pull. Release. Pull. Release. Pull. Release. Pull. Release.* Repeat. *Pull. Release. Pull. Release. Pull. Release. Pull. Release.* Release. *Pull. Release.* Repeat. *Pull. Release. Pull. Release. Pull. Release. Pull. Release.* Repeat. *Pull. Release. Pull. Release. Pull. Release. Pull. Release.* Repeat.

Pull. Release. Pull. Release. Pull. Release. Pull. Release. Pull. Release. Repeat. *Pull. Release. Pull. Release. Pull. Release. Pull. Release. Pull. Release.* Repeat. *Pull. Release. Pull. Release. Pull. Release. Pull. Release. Pull. Release. Pull. Release.* Repeat. *Pull. Release. Pull. Release. Pull. Release. Pull. Release. Pull. Release.* Repeat. *Pull. Release. Pull. Release. Pull. Release. Pull. Release.* Repeat.

A car comes barreling into the driveway, its engine's purring quieted by the slamming of its door.

"Josh," Kyler says frantically. "Please ... I don't know what to do."

KYLER

DESPERATE TIMES CALL FOR DESPERATE MEASURES

Random Thoughts of a Random Mind

I LOATHE THE DESPERATION LACED through my voice. I despise the helplessness that put it there. And I abominate the beast hijacking Lennon's thoughts right now, but most of all I vehemently detest Andrea for doing this.

Josh glares at me, as though *I'm* the reason Lennon is falling apart. He doesn't acknowledge that I kept her together—at least enough to get home—but instead he rushes over to where his daughter continues to pull at the door handle of my car while I stand there and watch in stunned horror. "What happened?" he demands.

"I—I—" Shit. How am I supposed to explain this? "Lennon." I gesture toward her. "She—We were at an assembly and—"

Lennon stops pulling the door handle, spins, and demands, "Don't tell him!"

Her sudden order catches me off guard, making me pause long enough for Josh to slaughter me with his eyes. "Tell me what happened."

My gaze falls to Lennon. She asked me not to tell him, but as I watch her, yanking the door handle with her forehead pressed to the frame of the door and her eyes closed, I know I have to. Her cheeks are wet, her mouth forming silent words. She's counting.

Back to Josh. He's watching Lennon and his expression has softened. His voice is now desperate and pleading. "She's my *daughter*, Kyler. Please, you need to tell me what happened."

What Josh is about to find out is that I'm desperate, too. She doesn't want me to say a word, but I can't bear to watch this a second longer. I can't stand here and witness her coming undone and not try to help. Problem is, I don't know how to fix it. I don't know how to make it better. Maybe he does. Maybe he can help her. "We were at an assembly and someone had pictures of Lennon's medical records displayed on the projector. The whole school knows."

Lennon stands up straight, turns like a soldier, and marches toward the door of the house. She doesn't speak to me. She doesn't look at me. She just walks away.

Lennon

THOUGHTS: MY MOTHER DIED IN A CAR
GOING SOMEWHERE. BUT AT LEAST SHE HAD A
DESTINATION. I DIE INSIDE STANDING STILL.

ONE. TWO. THREE. FOUR. FIVE. One. Two. Three. Four. Five. One. Two. Three. Four. Five. One. Two. Three. Four. Five. One. Two. Three. Four. Five. One. Two. Three. Four. Five. One. Two. Three. Four. Five. One. Two. Three. Four. Five. One. Two. Three. Four. Five. One. Two. Three. Four. Five. One. Two. Three. Four. Five. One. Two. Three. Four. Five. One. Two. Three. Four. Five.

One. Two. Three. Four. Five. One. Two. Three. Four. Five. One. Two. Three. Four. Five. One. Two. Three. Four. Five. One. Two. Three. Four. Five. One. Two. Three. Four. Five. One. Two. Three. Four. Five. One. Two. Three. Four. Five. One. Two. Three. Four. Five. One. Two. Three. Four. Five. One. Two. Three. Four. Five. One. Two. Three. Four. Five.

Off. On. Off. On. Off. On. Off. On. Off. On. Off. On. Off. On. Off. On. Off. On. Off. On. Off. On. Off. On. Off. On. Off. On. Off. On. Off. On. Off. On. Off. On. Off. On. Off.

On. Off. On.

Off. On. Off. On.

Pull. Release. Pull. Release. Pull. Release. Pull. Release. Pull. Release. Repeat. *Pull. Release. Pull. Release. Pull. Release. Pull. Release. Pull. Release.* Repeat. *Pull. Release. Pull. Release. Pull. Release. Pull. Release. Pull. Release.* Repeat. *Pull. Release. Pull. Release. Pull. Release. Pull. Release. Pull. Release. Pull. Release. Pull. Release.* Repeat. *Pull. Release. Pull. Release. Pull. Release. Pull. Release. Pull. Release.* Repeat.

Pull. Release. Pull. Release. Pull. Release. Pull. Release. Pull. Release. Repeat. *Pull. Release. Pull. Release. Pull. Release. Pull. Release. Pull. Release.* Repeat. *Pull. Release. Pull. Release. Pull. Release. Pull. Release.* Repeat. *Pull. Release. Pull. Release. Pull. Release. Pull. Release. Pull. Release.* Repeat. *Pull. Release. Pull. Release. Pull. Release. Pull. Release.* Repeat.

KYLER

EVEN THE BIGGEST DREAMS CAN SHATTER...

Random Thoughts of a Random Mind

IT'S BEEN THREE HOURS SINCE she walked away without a backward glance. I've texted her seventeen times, and now I'm bordering on stalker. Josh won't answer the door. A silver BMW I've never seen before takes up real estate on the driveway at their house and I'm going to vomit. I can't stop pacing. Her pieces are breaking—all of them—and there's nothing I can do.

Lennon

THOUGHTS: ONE. TWO. THREE. FOUR. FIVE. ONE. TWO. THREE. FOUR. FIVE. ONE. TWO. THREE. FOUR. FIVE. ONE. TWO. THREE. FOUR. FIVE. ONE. TWO. THREE. FOUR. FIVE.

ONE. TWO. THREE. FOUR. FIVE. One. Two. Three. Four. Five. One. Two. Three. Four. Five. One. Two. Three. Four. Five. One. Two. Three. Four. Five. One. Two. Three. Four. Five. One. Two. Three. Four. Five. One. Two. Three. Four. Five. One. Two. Three. Four. Five. One. Two. Three. Four. Five. One. Two. Three. Four. Five. One. Two. Three. Four. Five. One. Two. Three. Four. Five.

One. Two. Three. Four. Five. One. Two. Three. Four. Five. One. Two. Three. Four. Five. One. Two. Three. Four. Five. One. Two. Three. Four. Five. One. Two. Three. Four. Five. One. Two. Three. Four. Five. One. Two. Three. Four. Five. One. Two. Three. Four. Five. One. Two. Three. Four. Five. One. Two. Three. Four. Five. One. Two. Three. Four. Five.

Off. On. Off.

On. Off. On. Off. On. Off. On. Off. On. Off. On. Off. On. Off. On.
Off. On. Off. On. Off. On. Off. On. Off. On. Off. On. Off. On. Off.
On. Off. On. Off. On. Off. On. Off. On. Off. On. Off. On. Off. On.
Off. On. Off. On. Off. On. Off. On. Off. On. Off. On. Off. On. Off.
On. Off. On. Off. On.

Off. On. Off. On. Off. On. Off. On. Off. On. Off. On. Off. On. Off.
On. Off. On. Off. On. Off. On. Off. On. Off. On. Off. On. Off. On.
Off. On. Off. On. Off. On. Off. On. Off. On. Off. On. Off. On. Off.
On. Off. On. Off. On. Off. On. Off. On. Off. On. Off. On. Off. On.
Off. On. Off. On. Off. On. Off. On. Off. On. Off. On. Off. On. Off.
On. Off. On. Off. On. Off. On. Off. On. Off. On. Off. On. Off. On.
Off. On. Off. On. Off. On. Off. On. Off. On. Off. On. Off. On. Off.
On. Off. On. Off. On.

Pull. Release. Pull. Release. Pull. Release. Pull. Release. Pull. Release.
Repeat. *Pull. Release. Pull. Release. Pull. Release. Pull. Release. Pull.*
Release. Repeat. *Pull. Release. Pull. Release. Pull. Release. Pull.*
Release. Pull. Release. Repeat. *Pull. Release. Pull. Release. Pull.*
Release. Pull. Release. Pull. Release. Repeat. *Pull. Release. Pull.*
Release. Pull. Release. Pull. Release. Pull. Release. Repeat.

Pull. Release. Pull. Release. Pull. Release. Pull. Release. Pull. Release.
Repeat. *Pull. Release. Pull. Release. Pull. Release. Pull. Release. Pull.*
Release. Repeat. *Pull. Release. Pull. Release. Pull. Release. Pull.*
Release. Pull. Release. Repeat. *Pull. Release. Pull. Release. Pull.*
Release. Pull. Release. Pull. Release. Repeat. *Pull. Release. Pull.*
Release. Pull. Release. Pull. Release. Pull. Release. Repeat.

KYLER

JUST TRY TO STOP ME...

Random Thoughts of a Random Mind

SILAS SENDS ME A TEXT. **Is Lennon okay? Am I okay? And what about our gig next week?** But I don't have the answers for any of those questions. I'm texting him back, telling him I don't know if she's okay and I don't know if I'm okay and I don't know about the gig, when I spot Jacob walking across the yard. His camera is clutched in his hands, and he's examining something on its display.

I toss my phone on the bed and fly down the stairs, through the kitchen and out the patio doors. Hurdling the corner of the pool, I holler, "Jacob! Jake!"

He stops, turns his head, smiles, and jogs toward the fence. "Hi, Kyler."

"Hey, bud, listen, I need your help."

His spine straightens. "What's wrong?"

"You wanna be a reporter, right?"

His head bobs. "And a superhero," he reminds me.

"Right. Well, I need you to do a little investigating," I say,

266

trying to catch my breath. Damn, it's been a minute since I've exerted this much physical effort on anything. "Just like a reporter."

He considers what I've put forth. "I'm good at that, but should I get you a water first?"

I'm huffing and puffing and wheezing something fierce.

"No thanks. I need you to go inside and make sure Lennon's okay."

Jacob shakes his head. "Daddy told me to go outside and wait for him."

"Did you see Lennon? Do you know what she's doing?"

"No."

"Can you go back inside, pretend you need a drink or something, and try to find out?" I can't believe I'm asking a kid to lie, but I'm desperate.

"Daddy might get mad, but I can try to sneak in. I'm good at sneaking."

"Can you come back here and tell me?"

"Sure," he says.

"Be as quick as you can, okay?"

He nods, turns, and runs toward the house.

He doesn't return, so I head back inside. I spend the next hour pacing back and forth. A caged animal with a deep sense of unease and constant demand for motion. *Where's Jacob? What's taking him so long? What is going on with Lennon?* My thoughts are silenced, the spell broken by a knock at the door.

It's about time. I spring to my feet and head toward the stairs, but before I can descend them, the knocking gets progressively louder, more forceful. There's a small, thinning patch of my father's hair that—to his horror—is spreading. It shines as he walks, reflecting the light as he grabs the door handle.

The frantic knocking continues growing in intensity until an indignant fist pounds at the door. No way that's Jacob. I stop, freeze, and wait to see who the owner of the rage is. Dad's voice booms. "All right already. I'm coming." He swings the door open, irritated.

Josh stands behind it. He reminds me of a computer-generated image enhanced to show a person how they will age. In four hours, he looks ten years older. I'm about to rush down the stairs and ask if she's okay until he brandishes a cell phone. "Do you have any idea what your son has done?"

I don't move a muscle.

"I beg your pardon?" My dad may be an asshole, but his pride extends to me, my sister, and my mom. We all reflect him, so when someone comes blasting accusations, he isn't one to receive them calmly.

"Your son has single-handedly destroyed my daughter," Josh says. "He posted a picture on Facebook and revealed Lennon's mental illness to the entire student population."

My dad grabs the phone from Josh's hand. "Kyler would do no such thing," he says. At least he's right about that.

"I'd argue that there's evidence right in front of your eyes that he did."

No. He can't possibly believe that. I bolt down the stairs. "I didn't do it, Dad! I saw Andrea taking snapshots of something when I was at your house, Josh, a yellow folder—"

Josh's eyes narrow in revulsion. He lowers his chin and speaks in a menacing tone. "And now you have the nerve to blame my stepdaughter. Andrea is a lot of things, but she would not do this." He holds the cell phone up and wags it at me.

"You're wrong," I start to say. "I saw her—"

My words fall on deaf ears. Josh looks through me and glares at my dad. "I want your son to stay the hell away from my daughter." He points at me. "If he doesn't, I'll get a restraining order."

My dad gives a curt nod. "It won't be a problem."

He can't be talking about me. Me? Stay away from Lennon? That will be a cold day in hell. "Oh yes, it will, Dad," I offer. I look at Josh. "You can't keep me away from her. Besides, a restraining order is stupid as fuck. You live next door."

"Watch your goddamned mouth," my dad snarls.

"Well, c'mon, Dad. What do you expect? Andrea framed me!"

I turn to Josh, not for forgiveness but maybe just an ounce of understanding. "Why would I rat myself out? *I'm* the one who brought her home, *I'm* the one who told you what happened. Doesn't make any sense that I'd do all that if I were guilty. Josh, you have to believe me, I'd never hurt Lennon, I'm in love with her—"

Dad's fingers grasp the fabric of the back of my shirt. "Kyler! Get out of here. Shut up before you get yourself into more trouble!"

I move away and Dad says to Josh, "My son won't come anywhere near your daughter. I'll make sure of it." He slams the door shut and turns to face me.

"I didn't do it," I say emphatically. "That stupid bitch Andrea—"

"Kyler!" he yells. The vein in his forehead looks like it's about to pop. Just like it did the night of the fire. "Enough. So help me God, if you only listen to one thing I say—if one thing sinks into that thick and stubborn skull of yours—let it be this: You will not be seeing that girl under any circumstance."

"Did you miss everything I just said?"

"Heard it loud and clear, son."

"Then you probably heard that I'm in love with her. I hate to tell you this, old man, but there are two things on earth you don't fight against. Mother Nature and love. Follow that law and life will be incredible, but if you try to fight either one of them, *boom*." I make an explosion with my hands. "Game over."

Lennon

FACT: KYLER BENTON IS NOT A MONSTER AND MY FATHER HAS
GONE BLIND IN HIS OLD AGE BECAUSE HE CAN'T SEE IT.

WHEN I WAKE, JACOB'S CAPE acts as a makeshift pillow, wedged between the side of my face and a cold pane of glass. Fog floats in my brain, so it takes a moment to gather my bearings, but I'm in a car. We're *parked* in a car. Dr. Linderman sits beside me, eyes cast down to his phone screen until I move the cape, bunch it up, and set it on my lap.

"Hi, kid," he says. "How are you doing? We gave you a little something to make you sleepy."

My eyes are weighed down by clouded thoughts. I press my palm to my temple, hoping to clear them.

Dr. Linderman gestures to the pile of fabric on my legs. "Jacob was concerned that you might need to be a hero, so he sent his cape with you."

"With me where?"

He points to the building we're parked alongside. It's a gigantic mansion, three or four stories tall, supported by huge white columns. For a structure that towers so high, it's remarkably well hidden behind shrubs with incredible gardens that stretch out on either side. "Willow Recovery Center," he says.

"You brought me to a hospital?"

He shakes his head. "It's not a hospital, Lennon, it's a private residential treatment facility where you can focus on meeting your challenges head-on."

"Where's my dad?"

"He should be right behind us. He was waiting for Claire to arrive home so he wouldn't have to bring your brother. We don't want to scare young Jake."

"Where's Kyler?" I want to stay angry about Kyler's full disclosure to my dad, but I can't. His face is the only one I want to see.

"Who?"

"Kyler? Where's Kyler?" I feel panic grip me again, and I cannot breathe. "Please, Levi. Tell me."

"Isn't he the reason you're here?" he asks. "Your father showed me the Facebook post, Lennon."

I shake my head, tears filling my eyes. "He wouldn't, he didn't do that. There's no way, please, you have to tell my dad—"

"What I *have* to do, Lennon, is get you on the road to recovery. We need to tackle this issue with a vengeance, and this stay at Willow Recovery Center is the first step."

I inhale, slow and long through my nose, and exhale through my mouth, trying to find one ounce of resolve to avoid verbally tearing him to shreds. "You're a shrink. Is it a fair statement to say that you get paid to listen to people's concerns?"

Dr. Linderman pushes his glasses up the bridge of his nose and nods. "That is a fair statement, yes."

"Good," I say, "then hear mine. I need to know he's okay . . . that he'll be okay. He was set up. He wouldn't do this. Please, Levi, you have to trust me."

He looks momentarily sympathetic but seems to shake himself out of it. "You need to be concerned with you, Lennon."

I look at him and point to the building and make my voice firm. Begging and pleading didn't work, so I'll resort to threats. "I *am* concerned with me. The same me who is not going in there until I know he's okay."

"I'm sure he's fine."

"I'll kick and scream and make the next hour of your life a lot more trouble than it needs to be. How easily you forget. I spent three months in the psych ward, and I've seen meltdowns that could rival anything you can imagine." I hold out my hand. "I know the drill. You have my phone, I'm sure of it. Let me call him."

He narrows his eyes in caution, so I try one more appeal. "Levi, *please.* He'll be worried. *Please.* If you let me call him, I'll get out of this car with you and walk through the front doors of that building as a willing participant."

He reaches into the pocket of his jacket and pulls out my iPhone. "Five minutes," he says. He opens the door and steps out. "I'll give you five minutes to say what you need to say."

I hit Kyler's contact and pray that he answers. It takes two rings. "Lennon!"

I almost cry at the sound of his voice. "Hi, I'm sorry."

"Nothing to be sorry for," he says. "Tell me you're okay."

I shake my head even though he can't see me. "Are any of us ever okay, really?"

"We can be okay for moments, Lennon." Silence, and then he whispers, "Please be okay in this moment."

"I feel so stupid," I say quietly. "I had this idyllic wish. And when I met you, it kind of came true. Like suddenly it didn't matter that I wasn't normal, because neither are you and that was okay, and finally that feeling of constant trepidation might learn how to take a back seat to life, but it always seems to catch up with me."

"Idyllic Trepidations," he whispers. "Could be a band name, Davis. Think about it. Our slogan could be 'Make Peace with Your Fears.'"

I half sob, half laugh in return.

"That's what you need to do," he whispers. "Make peace with your fears. You know that, right? I get that it's a big ask. Making peace with the enemy requires digging deep, but that's something I guess both of us have in common, huh?"

The glass of the passenger-side window presses against my temple. The salt of my own tears drips into my mouth, and I can taste them. "I know."

"You got this," he says. "You can do it."

I don't feel as confident as he seems to about that, so I change the subject. "My dad refuses to believe you didn't do it."

"I know," he says. "You believe me, right? That's the only thing that matters."

"Yes," I say. "He's putting me in a recovery program."

"What?"

"I'm at Willow Recovery Center." My eyes flick toward the building beside me before settling back on Dr. Linderman, who is pacing next to the car, hands shoved deep into his pockets. "It's some private treatment place."

"For how long?"

"I don't know."

From the driver's side Dr. Linderman's body folds down, and he holds up three fingers. Three minutes.

"Don't forget about our project." I shouldn't be thinking about our project at a time like this, but I am.

"I won't."

"I'll try to get Jacob to get you the mask so you don't miss the gig."

"Fuck the gig," he says.

"You want me to make peace with my fears, you should do the same, don't you think?"

"You won't be there," he says. "I can't."

"You can," I say, swallowing hard. "Once-in-a-lifetime things happen once in a lifetime and all that, right?"

"Stop talking like that, Davis."

"Like what?"

"Like you're leaving." Three words that make his voice crack.

I put my palm over my mouth to muffle the sob that tries to escape. Linderman's finger gives me the one-minute warning from outside the window. "I have to go. They'll take my phone. I'll miss your texts. Kyler?"

"What?"

"You're the weirdest person I know."

"You don't get to do that," he declares. "You don't get to make me fall in love with the wonder of you and walk away. You can't expect me to give up that easily."

"I have to go," I say again.

His voice is desperate. "Wait!"

"What?"

"I love you. I'm not giving up on us, Lennon. I fucking love you and I don't care who is trying to keep us apart, I won't let it happen. I promise."

"I love you, too," I say and before he hears the sob that escapes, I hang up the phone.

KYLER

MAKE PEACE WITH YOUR FEARS.

Random Thoughts of a Random Mind

MY CELL PHONE HITS THE space of drywall between two of my guitars, denting the plaster before it rebounds and slams to the floor face-first. I broke the screen, guaranteed. The solid wood flooring is hard as rock, plus, I chucked the phone like I was pitching in the major leagues.

She's in recovery. They took her away from me.

Andrea took her away from me.

I press my fingers to my temples to try to make my brain stop throbbing. I need to expose her. But I'm the only person who saw her with the folder. Andrea may be a grade A bitch, but she's involved in several school clubs, eager to maintain a persona of do-gooder among those she deems important enough to know her.

Me, I'm the so-called troublemaker at school. The kid who pushes boundaries, questions authority, and is considered a thorn in everybody's side. And now it's my word against hers, so my situation is definitely desperate, bordering on hopeless.

I'm haunted by the image of Lennon's face when her deepest secret was exposed. I let her wounds seep underneath my skin until they're my own. They join the burden of the stares, the speculation that I'm capable of something so deplorable.

I pick up my phone from the ground, seeing that I did shatter the screen, but I text her anyway. It's her favorite part of the day, and it makes her smile and that's all I want to do: Erase the image branded into my mind of her undoing and replace it with my memory of her smile.

I'll make things right with Josh, I promise. I told him I loved you. Don't worry, I didn't mention the inception of Make-Out Junkies: LustRUs. ☺ XOXO Kyler

I don't sleep at all. The nightmare of my reality keeps my brain firing at überspeeds. Life without Lennon is not something I'd prepared for.

The next day, school is unbearable. I've been here for half an hour, each second under careful scrutiny of the student body. I can tell some of them have already decided I'm guilty. I'm in a foul mood, and I want to run my fist through something, but instead I'm determined to find Andrea and tell her I know she's the one responsible. I'm headed toward the hallway where Andrea's locker is when Jada steps in my path, a near miss to being bowled over. "Watch where you're going," I grumble.

She ignores my comment, her eyes drifting to meet mine. "Is Lennon okay?"

I don't focus on Jada, instead surveying the hallway for

spectators. "You sure you want to be seen with the big bad wolf, Jada? Might tarnish your reputation."

"Oh please, Kyler, we both know you pretend to be bad. You're not."

I'm too tired to argue.

"Lennon. Is she okay? I tried calling, but it goes to voice mail."

"She's fine," I say, unsure of how much information I'm supposed to volunteer.

"I had no idea she had OCD, I hope she's okay. I'm worried about her."

"I'm worried about her, too."

"Who do you think did it?"

I'll be honest. It's nice to know Jada at least assumes that I'd never do such a thing. Nicer to know she's more concerned about Lennon's well-being than the actual fact that she has OCD. As for everyone else, I try to ignore them and focus on clearing my name.

"Andrea did it," I say. "I saw her."

Jada looks shocked, although I have no idea why. "What?"

"I saw her taking pictures of a folder at Lennon's place," I say. "Somehow she hacked into my Facebook account. It's shut down pending further investigation from their security team."

"When is Lennon coming back?" Jada asks, hiking her backpack up her shoulder.

"I don't know. Listen, I have to go. I'm going to interrogate Andrea."

Jada's gaze drifts to the side. "Where's Lennon?"

"Not here," I say, because her whereabouts aren't my business to share. "Listen, she won't get your texts, but I'll tell her you're worried about her."

This appeases her. "If you hear anything, please let me know."

"I will. Later, Jada."

"Okay. Good luck."

"Thanks." I leave her behind and travel south down the corridor. They stare, they murmur, they gossip. I find Andrea standing at her locker, talking to her friend Liam. "We need to talk."

Liam glances at me for a moment before turning to Andrea. "I'll see you at lunch."

"See you." She smiles at Liam and turns, rolling her eyes at me before she faces away and slams her locker shut. As she spins back around, she probably thinks I'm going to let her pass me, because she takes a step forward. I don't touch her, but I stand directly in front of her so when she moves, she hits me like a brick wall. She stumbles, her back hitting the locker.

"You're not going to get away with this," I tell her.

Her eyes are disgusted, dragging from my head to my feet and back again in a slow dance. Reminds me of the night we first met. "I have no idea what you're talking about," she says. "We both know you did it."

"You know something, Andrea, I'm not a big believer in redemption, but maybe you are. You have a chance to do the right thing, to tell the truth."

She crosses her arms over her chest and arches an eyebrow. "My my," she says, "how valiant are you? I'd say Lennon is lucky to have you, but she isn't and she doesn't."

"You're fucking psycho."

She shrugs and continues, "You're guilty. May as well stop denying it, Kyler."

My teeth clench so hard, pressure grips my skull. "What does this accomplish for you, Andrea? What do you get out of ruining someone's life? You're so messed up."

"Me? You and Looney Tunes there are like the epitome of messed up. How unfortunate it is that you'll never see Lennon again, the two of you were perfect for each other."

Never see Lennon again. That thought never crossed my mind, and it feels like a blow to the gut, but it doesn't last long. Anyone who tries to keep her from me permanently will have to kill me first. My heart wallops inside my ears, blood coursing through my veins, making them burn and pulse. My vision clouds and I lurch forward and slam my fist into the metal locker beside her head.

Andrea's eyes go wide. She's scared.

"You know what? We are perfect for each other. And your sorry ass is going to die alone."

I remove my fist from the locker, turn, and stalk away, knowing I'm going to regret that move later.

Later comes in ten minutes when I'm beckoned to the principal's office. It's a new record. My dad is standing outside already. Also a record. His fingers are at his throat, loosening his overpriced silk tie. Truth is, I think the veins in his neck get bigger when he's pissed with me.

Andrea sits on one of the chairs inside the office, eyes cast down to her phone texting frantically. She's telling everyone she knows she was right—I'm a monster.

My dad's face is red. "What the hell is wrong with you, Kyler? You punched a girl?"

"What? No! I didn't punch a girl."

"I heard you punched a girl."

I stare at him blankly, dumbfounded. "And you actually believed that? I punched a locker. Near a girl."

My dad throws his hands up in the air in frustration. "Right, because that's much better than actually punching a girl."

"It's significantly better than punching a girl. I shouldn't have to tell you this, you're a damned lawyer. Destroying public property is a far lesser crime than assault. I won't even try and explain to you the other reason I'd never hit a girl, since I'm pretty sure human decency is beyond your scope of understanding."

He points his finger at me. Looks like he's going to have a coronary. "Human decency, Kyler? Really? Cut the bullshit. Punching a locker isn't civil. It's barbaric much in the same sense as a caveman would clobber his woman over the head and toss her over his shoulder."

"Wow, Greg, that's an impressive comparison. Angsty teen turned stunted homo sapien on the evolutionary scale."

He shakes his head. "You're an imbecile. How about uttering threats? Did you ever think of that?"

"Nope. Didn't have to. I didn't threaten her."

His shoulders slump with short-lived relief until Josh comes strolling through the front door, shoving his keys in his pocket.

My dad accosts him. Wastes no time. "Josh, I am so sorry. I don't know what's gotten into him."

I look at Josh. "With all due respect, your stepdaughter is a liar. She sabotaged Lennon. She planted evidence to implicate me. I think if you just ask Lennon, I mean, I would never do that to her. I swear it."

Josh completely ignores me and looks at my dad. "Sure can tell he's the child of a lawyer."

He walks through the door of the office and Andrea stands. She begins to speak animatedly to her stepfather, pointing the odd finger through the window in my direction. My dad joins them, then Principal Walsh comes out, Andrea sits, and the three men disappear behind a closed door.

I lean against the wall outside the office door, cross my arms over my chest, and close my eyes. I try to decide if I'm remorseful or not. Not—at least not *yet*. Fifteen minutes must pass before Josh and my dad emerge.

"You're out for the rest of the day." As I follow my dad to the car, he speaks. "You're lucky, Kyler. I was able to talk to Principal Walsh. You aren't suspended. You can return to school tomorrow."

"But?"

"But you're doing community service at the school for a month and you are positively prohibited from seeing Lennon."

Yeah, we'll see about that.

Lennon

FACT: 20% OF YOUTH BETWEEN THE AGES OF
13 AND 18 LIVE WITH MENTAL ILLNESS.

WILLOW RECOVERY CENTER. **Psychiatric luxury at its finest.** Rich people converge on this place in pursuit of exorcising their mental demons, all the while never straying too far from the perks to which they are accustomed. Every comfort conceivable is offered to anyone with adequate money, sufficient courage, and the fierce resolution to step into the ring and conquer the beasts inside their heads.

Sterile white corridors and cold tile floors won't be found here. No imposing steel tables supplied with restraints for patients who've had psychotic breaks. No padded rooms and straitjackets. I'm not sure those things would even have a place here.

A sign near the front shows that Willow Recovery Center is home to several wings, named after flowers: Wild Rose, Morning Lily, Country Orchid. They sound more like essential oils than they do psychiatric wings. I assume they keep the anxiety disorders in one wing, psychotic disorders in another, and so on.

Maine was different. The hospital there was short on funding; it was a mishmash of people filling overcrowded spaces. A human chain of lost souls struggling to stay alive by attending group therapy sessions and sipping on cocktails of Zoloft, Prozac, chlorpromazine, and my personal preference, my dear friend, clozapine.

The Wild Rose wing is one opulent private room after the next. They line long hallways that span massive distances, seemingly too large for a house. The dining room resembles a five-star restaurant; I count three separate lounges equipped with televisions, a game room, even a bowling alley for guests who are rewarded for good behavior.

Dr. Linderman answers all the questions the staff have about me. He keeps assuring me that my dad will be around shortly with my belongings, as if that's a real treat. I don't want to see my dad any more than I want to see Andrea. I squeeze my eyes shut, unable to fathom what transpired today.

Upon admission, while Dr. Linderman makes fast work of filling my dad's absentee shoes, I'm outfitted with a bracelet displaying my first name and an allergy warning. Penicillin. The bracelet is the only thing even remotely similar to an actual hospital.

We follow Libby, the woman who admitted me, down one of the long hallways, which is agony. I must stop every few feet to ritualize. New people. New situation. No Kyler. Everyone knows. The potential for dreadful events is infinite.

Libby and Dr. Linderman pause and wait each time I do. Neither seeks to stop me from carrying out my ritual. This comprises tapping every third door jamb with my fingers five times on the top, five times on the middle, and five times with my foot on the bottom. Because the hallways are so long, we could have been at my new home away from home twenty minutes ago if I didn't have to keep stopping. I wonder how many people inside those rooms heard my tapping on their doors. Only one had their door open, the room belonging to a young guy who had his face buried in a book. He looked up, watched for the briefest of moments, and then returned his attention to his book without a word.

By some small miracle we make it to my room. Libby shows me where the help button is, where the bathroom is, and where I can find pajamas in case I brought none.

She smiles warmly and clasps her hands together. "You try to get your rest tonight, sweetie. Big day tomorrow. You'll be meeting with Dr. Earl Waxman, who will be your attending doctor here at Willow."

I look at Dr. Linderman. "What about you?"

"You'll still see me way more than you'd like to, Lennon. Dr. Waxman is here to keep an eye on things while I can't."

"Do you need anything before I leave?" Libby asks.

"No thanks," I mumble. "I'm good."

"Perfect. I'll tell Dr. Waxman you're looking forward to meeting with him."

I force a smile. "Great. I can't wait."

The room, like the one at my dad's house, is bare. But unlike the gray industrial walls of home, this room is warm. Everything is in soft earth tones and creams. There's a large bed and a dresser with a television. The bedding is a warm color that reminds me of the golden-brown streaks in Kyler's hair. There's a duvet and four pillows. I point to it, irritated that I hadn't noticed before, when Libby asked if I needed anything. "I need another pillow."

"I'll go get you one," Dr. Linderman says. Placing his hands in his pockets, he turns and leaves the room.

Even with the wrong number of pillows, it's light-years ahead of my room at the hospital in Maine.

Levi returns with a pillow. "Your father just texted. He's leaving in about fifteen minutes to come and deliver your stuff."

"Tell him not to come, please. I don't want to see him."

"He has your belongings."

"I'll deal with the hospital pajamas."

"Lennon, I think—"

I plead with him. "Dr. Linderman. I don't want to see anyone. I want to sleep and forget about this day. Please."

He nods. Whether this means he'll tell my father to stay home or not, I don't know.

"This is a great place," he says. "I'll let you settle in, but I'll be back in a few days to check on you. You know you can call if you need anything."

"Thanks."

"Try to get some sleep." He issues one more sympathetic glance before he leaves, closing the door behind him. When he does, I perform my bedtime routine five times despite the fact that I'm exhausted. I want to pretend the last forty-eight hours didn't happen. I want to go back to life-defining moments where big things are little things and little things are big things and we were happy for a moment.

My head rests on the pillow. I close my eyes, my chest in a vise as my stomach pulls and twists because I miss him so much it hurts. I tell myself to remember what it felt like to be happy for that moment, to hold on to it for when I need it the most.

KYLER

EVERYTHING IS GONE.

Random Thoughts of a Random Mind

I FINISHED OUR ASSIGNMENT AND handed it in. It's been a week since they took her away. Lennon from Maine with Serious Issues Who Sews and Is Broken and Beautiful and Badass is gone. The sun is gone. The moon is gone. The stars are gone. I'm dying inside. I need to get her back.

Lennon

FACT: WRITING BY HAND HELPS RETAIN
KNOWLEDGE OR ENHANCE MEMORY.

I HAVEN'T SEEN MY FATHER. Levi stayed faithful to his word, and when I woke the next morning, on my big day, it was to discover my dad had left a jumble of my belongings. I spent until noon organizing things how I liked them in the room. I think they let me do this rather than attending classes on my first day *because* of my diagnosis. It would have been physcially impossible to walk away without organizing my belongings. I talked to Claire once on the phone and made her promise me the mask would be given to Kyler and told her that, for a few days at least, I didn't wish to see my dad. That was a week ago.

Since then, Kyler consumes most of my thoughts. During class, when I'm outside playing basketball, or inside doing some kind of art therapy, he is still at the forefront of my mind. And when I'm not reflecting on Kyler himself and the way he makes me feel inside, I'm conjuring up awful details about his demise.

He shares this coveted spot in my brain with Claire, Jacob, and my dad, whom I am still not happy with.

When I was home, whether it was with my mother in Maine or my father here, I ritualized at my leisure because I could. Here, the doctors (and there are so many) enthusiastically encourage me to outlast the fear, for as long as I can bear it. Sometimes it's a win, sometimes it's a loss.

Trauma turns a spark, a small fire of anxiety, into a raging inferno. It's a spiral effect. I've learned it firsthand two different times. It's as if unfortunate incidents kick-start the mental illness, cranking its voltage to dangerous levels that are hard to control.

What I didn't tell Levi was, even if he hadn't granted my phone call with Kyler, I would have come willingly, because maybe I'll never be typical, but maybe that's not the worst idea, if I could learn how to handle it. Normal *is* boring.

Kyler's words give me strength. *Make peace with your fears.* I'm not certain I'll ever reconcile my fears, but I'm sure I'm done letting them control me.

Dr. Earl Waxman is standing with me today. He's more like what I'd expected Levi to be. Old. We don't have the same close relationship that Levi and I do, but he's all right for a psychiatrist. He has blue eyes that remind me of the great impostor Santas from shopping malls.

I've just bested the door frame in a scenario strikingly akin to sitting in that car with Dr. Linderman. *Maybe something bad will happen if I don't do it, but maybe it won't.* Dr. Waxman praises me for my progress. He's passionate about that, too. He dismisses me for free time because it's four o'clock, and every third day we don't have group therapy, so I'm off for the night. Lights out at 10:00 p.m., which gives me six hours to obsess over Kyler, worry if he's okay, ache to talk to him, while I try to keep my shattered mind occupied with sports and painting.

The temperature here is regulated. Designed to be the perfect ambience for comfort. It's never too hot, never too cold, invariably perfect. My room is cozy, so far as rooms go, and although I'm missing some of my things, like my trivia books and my costume design material, it's okay. Because it's warm here. It's safe. Not to mention the dim lamps throughout the room to provide atmosphere, and *all* the fabrics—the sheets, blankets, and towels—hold the sweet scent of vanilla.

I hang my hoodie on the hook behind the door, sit at the desk, and fetch a piece of paper and a pencil. Dr. Linderman had to clear both items before I was allowed to have them.

~~Dear Dad~~,

This is the third time I've tried to write my father a letter. I should say something to him, but I don't know where to begin. He struggles to understand me. I know he thinks it's right—and maybe it is—to lock me up in this place without access to the outside world, but that doesn't make it any easier. I struggle to understand why he thinks Kyler would do something so despicable or why I was so far beyond help that he had to send me here. If I'm honest with myself, there's a good chance I'd have ended up here anyway, but it would have been nice to have more of a choice in the matter.

On the fresh paper, I start again, printing in small, neat letters.

Dear Kyler,

I'm alive but not living and am therefore just a girl who is dying to live. I'm working on the living part, but it's hard without you. I've only been here a week but it feels like a month. I'm doing my best to make peace with my fears. It's going marginally well, not yet an A-plus student in the art of governing myself, so the progress is slow.

Let me tell you about this place. The wonder of it all. Willow Recovery Center could be the next big idea for reality television, where we're all mere spectators to the madness. There's school (of course), art therapy, support groups where we do nothing but talk about our feelings, and all kinds of outdoor activities, like basketball and even a small tennis court. I'm guessing lawn darts is a hard pass for Willow.

The wings (parts of the house) are named after flowers. I live in Wild Rose, but there are many, even one for the really strange people. There's a bowling alley on the property. The blankets smell like vanilla, and the dining room serves eggs Benedict for breakfast and prime rib for dinner. On my wing we have about five subsets of OCD (five, I know, ironic), generalized anxiety disorders, body dysmorphic disorders, bipolar disorder, and disturbances that have names I'll never remember. So we have all these mental cases in a setting like a five-star therapeutic resort.

The list of potential band names skyrockets in here. Those classic, single-word band names are limitless: Straitjacket or Purplepill, Morphine, Sedated. Alternately, you could go with Chaotic Disorder. The possibilities are endless, but here's my favorite, Fuck with Fear.

Think about it, Kyler.

What's our slogan?

Also, please notice I swore again. I wish you were here to shove your tongue down my throat in response.

Yours in madness (and passion),

Lennon

I let myself miss him. It hurts. And even though it destroys me a thousand times more, I let myself miss my mom, too.

If I close my eyes and wish it hard enough, I can almost smell the scent of chicken and dumplings simmering on our stove on the nights when winter's icy chill blanketed the city. I see her grinning at me while she played the guitar. She had a single rogue curl near her forehead that refused to twist any way but straight to the sky. The memory of her voice, of her smile, of those nights, of her, eats away at my insides and for what might be the first time since she died, I let it happen.

I award myself the time to have a decent cry, then fold the paper into an airplane. I do this because it reminds me of Jacob and Jacob reminds me of heroes and sometimes we can all use one of those.

I shower, change into sweats and a T-shirt, and head to one of the lounge rooms. Cecilia Prescott is sprawled on one of the paisley couches, her legs perched over the top, her body coiled, so her head hangs upside down where her legs and feet would normally be. She's wearing shorts that cover a third of her butt and a sports jersey.

Cecilia is sixteen and bipolar. Her father is a huge director in Hollywood, and her mother is an A-list actress named Penelope Prescott. Cecilia looks just like her. Tall with chocolate-brown eyes and a head full of raven-colored tresses. One look at this girl and anyone can tell she's at the top of the food chain in terms of wealth. She has never, and will never, want for anything... except maybe to be normal-slash-boring.

This is her third stay at Willow in three years, so she knows the ropes. I'd been here for only two days when she'd accosted me in the dining room. I was picking at something that was presumably oatmeal when she came over, wrapped up in a kimono and heels, and sat across from me, advised me to never eat the oatmeal again and opt for the French toast or the eggs Benedict instead.

I clear my throat when I get into the lounge—a courtesy to let her know she's no longer watching TV alone. Her long legs swing up and over until she rights herself on the couch.

"Hey," she says. She picks up the remote and shuts the TV off.

"You don't need to do that for me," I say.

"Wasn't," Cecilia replies. "Turned it off for me. It's boring."

I nod and take a seat on the armchair across from her. I'm silent. I'm not sure why I came to the lounge rather than staying in my room. At least there I could miss Kyler fiercely in solitude.

"You look like you have something on your mind," she says.

"You could say that."

"Well, if there's one thing you learn at Willow, it's how to be a good listener. Wanna talk about it?"

"Yeah, I miss people, you know?"

Cecilia nods. "I miss sex."

"Not what I meant, but sure. Same thing, I guess."

She leans forward and pats my knee. "Who are you missing?"

I can't be sure I can trust Cecilia, but I give her the benefit of the doubt because I have nothing to lose. "My boyfriend."

She perks up immediately. "Boyfriends are my specialty," she says. "Is he a cheating slimeball? Sometimes I feel like we miss those jerks the worst of them all, 'cause the rejection is so bad."

"Drastic that you'd start there, but no. Not at all."

She looks disappointed before she holds up a finger. "Wait, let me guess—he didn't know about the OCD and he found out and dumped you?"

"Still off," I say.

I open my mouth to volunteer information, but she interrupts. "You found out another girl was after him?"

"No. My father thinks he did something terrible, and now he won't let us see each other."

"The parental intervention. That's the goddamned worst."

She leans forward, her elbows on her knees. "What does your dad think he did?"

I consider what I should tell her. The truth? "My dad thinks he leaked my medical records all over social media and then broadcast them to our entire school at an assembly."

Cecilia's face drops in horror. "What?"

"Yeah," I say. "He didn't, but now he's accusing my stepsister, who has an attitude but a perfect reputation she doesn't want tarnished, and he's kind of a loner, so it's his word against hers."

"You've got to be kidding me," she says. "That's better than fiction."

I nod. "The worst part is, Kyler made things feel right. Everything felt right. I miss him. I almost felt like it was okay to be—"

"Yourself," she volunteers. "I can tell by the look on your face. He's the first guy who makes you feel like it's okay you are the way you are. Then your dad is fighting an uphill battle," she decides. "You can't keep two people who are meant to be together apart for long."

"Since I'm locked up with no computer access, no phone, and he's out there doing God knows what, it doesn't really seem that way."

"Willow is hardly a prison," Cecilia says. "Relax. The first two weeks are stiff with rules and whatnot, but you're an ideal patient. You do what they tell you to do when they tell you to do it. You'll get your privileges next week. Visitors, your phone, the wondrous internet. All of that."

I read about the review policy in the handbook titled *Welcome to Willow Recovery Center*. Every Sunday patients are reviewed.

If you had a satisfactory week, you're awarded personal perks, or the removal of those same perks if you'd previously earned them and were now being unmanageable.

"They monitor your phone. My dad has forbidden me from texting him."

Cecilia looks at the door, reaches into her pocket—which should not have room to disguise a cell phone—and retrieves one, handing it to me. "They don't check my phone anymore. Here. Text him."

I could kiss her.

I punch in Kyler's number at lightning speed. Being this close to getting perks of my own, I don't want to blow any chances I may have, so I type fast.

Borrowing a phone so don't reply, just to be safe, I type. I miss you. Play the gig and you can show me videos when I bust out of here. You can do it, Kyler. . . . XOXO, Lennon

KYLER

AS LENNON WOULD SAY, FACT: DYING STARS CREATE
STELLAR BLACK HOLES. I'M A BLACK HOLE. A DEAD STAR.

Random Thoughts of a Random Mind

LIFE'S FULL OF SURPRISES. Welcome ones. Unwelcome ones.
Regardless of which they are, both create a small tear in the
patchwork of the universe, a blip in time that swallows a person
whole and spits them out to point them in a different direction.

When Lennon came into my galaxy, it was a welcome surprise. I didn't see it coming, hence the surprise part, but then
she was there. Beside me. In a different direction. It felt as if she
belonged there, like she was always there and would always be
there, so now that Josh has removed her from my orbit, the tear
in my patchwork will spread until it's a gaping black hole.

If I had known it was his intention to take her away from
me, I would have stayed silent. I never would have said a word.
I would have kept my eyes down and my mouth shut. If I had,
I wouldn't be sitting here missing her nightly disco, or the way
my hands get tangled and knotted in the hair that's way too big
for her head, or how her nose crinkles when I make her laugh.

My patchwork would be stitched together with late-night text sessions about bad band names or making *Romeo and Juliet* moderately comprehensible. Pivotal moments, I like to tell her, but minus my declaration of being in love with her, I've kept the mention of life-defining people to myself. Lennon was my life-defining person. And now she's gone.

I'm sprawled on the bed, facing the lamp, debating turning it on, then off a few times like she does. Maybe I'd feel connected to her, because she could be doing the exact same thing. She could be giving the light switch at Willow Recovery Center the royal treatment of fifty-five rituals of five. I brush the thought off as ridiculous, though, and as soon as I do that, the screen of my phone illuminates with a gentle vibration.

There's a message from an unknown number.

Borrowing a phone so don't reply, just to be safe. I miss you. Play the gig and you can show me videos when I bust out of here. You can do it, Kyler. . . . XOXO, Lennon

Don't reply.

Telling me not to reply equates to torture, but I don't want to risk getting her in trouble.

To obey, I'm forced to either sit on my fingers or find something else to do, so I set the phone down and head to my desk. I used to write every day, all the time, but since she left, my muse is gone, or maybe it's hibernating. Some of the thick paper remains from Jacob and me building airplanes, so I grab a sheet and place my pen on its surface.

The words come fast, so rushed, that the sides of my hands and fingers get stained with blue ink that has no chance to dry before I drag my fingers to form the next sentence.

The night is blinded by your wonder,
So it steals you from my grasp,
These walls we've built came tumbling down,
Our wills were caving fast.
So wash away the world we've built,
But please don't let them break you,
Brace yourself, you gotta fight,
Don't let the thoughts control you.

There's a knock at my door followed by a swoosh of air as my mother, who doesn't wait for a response, enters the room. In her hands, an offering: peanut butter cookies and milk. My favorite. My vision grazes the paper, which I slide underneath a stack. I'll decide later if they'll make the lyrical cut or if they're hipster coffee coasters.

My mom comes closer, sets the plate of cookies and the mug of milk next to me. "Mind if I stay for a minute?"

I nod. "Be my guest."

She smooths her hands over her jeans and turns to sit on the edge of my bed. I take a cookie and dip it into the milk. She brought it in a mug, which is perfect because the cookies always fit.

Before I take another bite, I hold up my half cookie. "Thank you for the baked goods."

"I'm a little worried about you, sunshine."

Sunshine. Her nickname for me since childhood and a surefire indicator we're about to embark on a journey of serious conversation. The cookies were bribery, so I'd allow our talk to happen.

"Don't worry about me," I assure her. "I'm fine."

"You're not fine," she says, shaking her head.

Any resolve I had to argue that I am, in fact, fine dissipates. It's exhausting to pretend, anyway, so I look at my mom. "Fine. I'm not fine. Josh thinks I'm an asshole capable of doing something like that to Lennon. I don't know how to prove I didn't."

"Well, maybe it's best you leave it alone, Kyler, at least for the time being. Josh is navigating unfamiliar waters, and he's only doing what he thinks is right for his child." Her face softens, but she doesn't pause. "I'd do the same for you, sunshine. Believe me, you're young, and so full of questions about life, about yourself, about this girl. I know sometimes it must feel to you like she's the only person in the world, and that's fine, but I'm not sure it's worth poking an angry bear over."

"It's worth being mauled by an angry bear over." My appetite for the cookies is waning. I'd better eat fast. "We're talking about my upstanding reputation," I add, trying to crack a joke. "I hate that anyone thinks I'd do that to her."

"Anyone who thinks you'd do such a thing isn't someone you want on your side, anyway."

She's right with one major exception. Josh. I want Josh on my side.

"I know you're feeling out of sorts, sunshine. I remember my first love, Thomas. He was a linebacker on the high school football team, a real charmer, and when we broke up, I wasn't so sure the pain would ever end. I cried myself to sleep for weeks."

"Not to lessen your experience, Mom, but remember who you're talking to. I'm not Mae," I point out. "Zero chance I'm crying myself to sleep. But I miss her." I find myself clenching my jaw. "I miss her and I won't apologize for it and we didn't break up," I say flatly. "Her wicked stepsister framed me for a crime I did not commit, then her father whisked her away to some treatment facility and cut off any contact with her."

She speaks quickly to oblige me. "I know you didn't break up per se, but you're still apart." She stops and folds her hands together. "When I went to Paris, when you were little, I learned this. When the French miss someone they say, '*Tu me manques*,' which translates to 'You are missing from me.' That kind of pain runs far deeper than we all want to recognize."

I smirk at her. "You sure you didn't see that on Facebook, Mom? I've seen that on Facebook."

She rolls her eyes, but there's a smile behind it. "It's on Facebook because it's true."

"Totally. Must be."

"I'm glad to see you're still you. My point is, when someone is taken from you with no justification or reasonable cause, it's worse. But there is a justification here, sweetie, and that's what I'm trying to make you see."

"Nothing justifies keeping two people apart who want to be together."

"Can I ask you something?"

I shove the last morsel of my cookie in my mouth and nod. "Go for it."

"You love her? Do you really love her?"

I nod.

"Then I want you to think about that girl, your Lennon. Bless her heart. She lost everything. Poor thing must be traumatized, and I want you to be careful."

"We're all traumatized, Mom. There's no need for me to be careful with Lennon. She's a lot less fragile and a lot more awesome than you're giving her credit for."

She rises to her feet, her socks shuffling across the bamboo floors. When she gets close enough, she extends her hand to the left side of my face. Mom only does this when I'm upset or she's had a glass of wine and is taking a walk down memory lane. I don't mean to, but I grimace. "I have to worry about you, because we both know you won't worry about yourself."

"If you're so worried, then help me," I plead. "Can't you talk to Josh or something? Tell him to be reasonable?"

"I know right now being away from her feels unbearable. I know that. But sometimes, the best thing you can do is give things time. You care about this girl. Give her the time she needs to recover. She's smart enough to love you. I believe she'll find her way back to you. Be patient. Try not to create unnecessary tension." She pats my knee. "Take my word for it."

Be patient.

Two words that feel impossible.

Lennon

FACT: TRYING TO REASON WITH A MIDDLE-AGED MAN IS
VERY SIMILAR TO TRYING TO DEAL WITH A PETULANT TODDLER.

MY PERKS COME WITH ONE ultimate, cruel caveat. Whereas, every *other* patient at Willow Recovery Center is offered family visits, cell phones, and internet access, I'm afforded but one. Courtesy of my father. Petra, the liaison between the doctors and patients—sorry, *clients,* as Willow likes to say—in our wing advised me yesterday that my dad thinks it's best for me not to have access to social media. I informed Petra that I think it's best for me not to have access to my dad. But Jacob, he was another story. Dr. Linderman mentioned he was upset when I left, which was why he wanted to send his cape. I owed him a visit, so here I sit, with Jacob's cape folded on my nightstand.

I can't say there's any special interest in seeing my dad, because the only person I want to see more than Jacob is Kyler, but he's better equipped for my absence than Jake and I can't ignore that, so after Cecilia and I had breakfast this morning, I showered and even put makeup on. I want to show my dad this is unnecessary. I don't need to be here. I want to show him I can function again. As long as I never have to return to Bel Air Learning Academy.

I'm resting on my bed, gazing at my paper plane, when Jacob races into the room, his black cape sailing behind him, clutching an airplane of his own instead of his camera. Held high above his head, it swerves and dives through the air.

This is accompanied by airplane noises that come to an abrupt halt a foot away from me. "Lennon!" Jacob exclaims. "I miss you!"

"I miss you, too, bud."

He sets the plane down on my bed and races to throw his arms around me. I hug him back and wish I could just keep him tucked away with me. "How's being a hero coming along?" I ask him.

Claire and my dad enter the room, and even with Jacob's little arms around my neck, I feel a twinge of anger when I see my father's face.

Jacob unlatches his limbs from my neck and peers at me intently. "It's going okay, but I need a sidekick and Andi isn't great."

I bite back a laugh. "Right. That makes sense."

"Is this your room?" he wants to know.

"Yep. Not as nice as my room at home," I lie, "but it does the trick."

Claire smiles. Her heels click on the tile floor as she takes a seat on one of the two small armchairs. She reaches in her large purse and pulls out a Ziploc bag filled with Lego pieces. "Jacob, here you go." Jacob eagerly retrieves the Lego pieces and makes himself comfortable on my bed.

"I'm going to build you something, Lennon."

I smile. "Thanks, Jake."

Claire clears her throat. "Lennon, sweetie, there's something your daddy and I wanted to talk to you about."

My dad stiffens his spine.

Uh-oh.

My stomach flips before Claire comprehends the expression on my face and hurries over to touch my shoulder. "Oh no! It's nothing bad."

I shake my head and look fixedly at my father.

Claire sucks in a breath. "You are under no obligation, but my agent thought it may be a valuable idea if we could use my platform to raise awareness about OCD when you're back home. Kind of like damage control, I suppose."

I raise an eyebrow. "What?"

This is what Claire says to me when she repeats herself:

"My agent, Dan, he thinks having you move in with us, despite the dire circumstances, could work to our advantage. I mean, it's a wonderful opportunity to promote awareness. Help people like you. Perhaps an interview or an event like that. You shouldn't be ashamed of yourself, Lennon."

I can't, knowing Claire, imagine she doesn't believe what she's saying. She's not hurtful by any measure, and I think she *thinks* it would help. Yet I gawk at her. Speechless. She doesn't understand what it's like to be me. A nightmare that was wholly mine for so long. Only a handful of people knew of my OCD until the incident at school. It was a secret I struggled every day to keep, because more and more it defined me, so it's not something I want to go on national television to talk about after being torn up and humiliated at school.

People fear things they don't know, and I'm a human version of some complex mathematical equation that only a few people ever truly understand.

Kyler was the first new person, medical professionals aside, that I'd spoken to about my OCD in ages. He's good at the math of me.

"I'm not sure I'd want to do that," I tell Claire honestly. I decide not to tell her that I'm sure I don't.

She seems disappointed, picking at her cuticles, but she forces a tender look. "Well, it's not anything you need to decide now. But it's an option. It may help bring understanding to your peers. Maybe we can talk about it with Dr. Waxman at our family therapy session next week."

"I don't want understanding from them," I cut in. "I'm absolutely not going back to that school."

My dad blinks. "Excuse me?"

"Never again," I say in case he didn't hear me the first time. "I don't care if I need home schooling or a two-hour bus ride to attend a different school. I'd rather die than go back to Bel Air Learning Academy."

Dad's face falls. "That's extreme, Bug. We were talking to some of the officials at the school, they mentioned putting you on an individualized plan, making sure there was someone you could talk to once a week. A school of such caliber can offer you better resources."

"By making me more of an outcast than I am already?"

"Lennon," he says, pinching the bridge of his nose, "that's not what I meant. We're trying to help you."

Jacob finishes his Lego masterpiece, which looks like a large tower. He holds it out proudly. "It's a trophy."

I force a grin, despite my irritation with my father. "It's perfect, Jake, thanks."

The bed shifts as he leaves it. He has the Lego tower in one hand and his plane in the other, and he marches to my desk to place them both down. "Jacob," I warn, my eyes darting to the side. "Don't mess up my stuff."

His finger dances along the edges of my folded plane. "I won't," he says. "I know the cold in your brain makes you need things a certain way. I really like your plane. You did a great job."

I return my attention to my father, gritting my teeth because I want to scream at him. "Forget learning plans and school counselors. I'm not going back there. You can't make me."

This is absurd. He could *make* me. But he won't. "We can talk about this later."

"Let's talk about it now, Dad," I say. "I mean, you want me to feel normal, but you've taken away the first person I've ever felt normal with, and now this. They told me you decided I couldn't have my phone or internet access." I glare at him. "I can't even text him."

Jacob is staring out the window, probably wishing he could

escape the conversation. My dad scowls. "We're not having this discussion, Lennon."

"We're not *not* speaking about it, Dad. If you feel that strongly about it, you should be prepared to defend your actions."

"There's a more appropriate time to have this talk. This isn't it."

"Well, in case you haven't noticed, time is in short supply. Since you had me locked up, there are certain times for visitors, so when would be a good time to talk about it?"

Claire looks uneasy. She's chewing her lower lip, running through her options. Does she defuse the situation, or does she remove Jacob before this heated conversation turns into full-on war? Maternal instincts must kick in, because she grabs Jacob by the elbow. "Jake, your mama is hungry. Why don't we go get something to eat real fast so Lennon and your daddy can talk? I saw a taco place not far from here."

Jacob looks at me. "I don't want to go."

"I'll be here when you get back," I say.

Wordlessly, he rises to his feet and grabs Claire's hand, leaving his paper airplane behind.

I wait long enough for the door to swing shut behind them before I look at my dad to deliver what I hope will be an Oscar-winning speech.

"Dad, please don't do this. Don't keep him from me."

I'm not presented the opportunity to say more than that before he interrupts. "Lennon. You have a lot on your plate. You're young, you lost your mother, you struggle with this"—he pauses—"this thing in your mind I'm trying to understand. You're my daughter. You're so much like your mom and I feel the need to protect you, bug. I'm sorry if that includes telling you things you don't want to hear, but I don't think access to social media, or quite frankly your cell phone, is a positive option for you right now."

"He didn't do what you think he did," I say.

Dad rises from the bed and shoves his hands in his pockets. "You claim he isn't the one who shared your confidential medical records with your entire school," he says. "Who do you propose did something like that?"

I give him a look like he's a fool. "Is that a trick question?"

Dad's eyebrows draw together, pointing into a V at the bridge of his nose. "You can't honestly be asking me to believe Andrea did this."

"You can't honestly not believe it. She *hates* me, Dad."

"Andrea is a lot of things," my dad says. "She's uptight and spoiled and entitled, but she is not a terrible person, Lennon. She has issues of her own, and I'd like to think I've known her long enough that I can say she wouldn't do that to someone. Her exterior is hard, but she has a heart."

I. Am. Speechless. This can't be happening. I refuse to believe my dad is that blind to something so obvious.

He's looking at me, and I know he must register the expression of shock on my face, because I can feel my mouth gaping open, and I'm sure my eyes are giant orbs shooting lasers of disbelief.

"I—I—I don't even know what to say. I can't believe you think he did this."

"That kid, Lennon, is nothing but trouble. His father is a

first-class prick who I tolerate for Claire's sake. His son is the kind who struggles with authority. He's an angry, damaged young man."

I feel my bottom lip tremble. My eyes well with tears. "He's not like that at all," I tell my dad. "You're not even close. He's smart and funny and talented and kind, and he may be a lot of things, Dad, but he's not a monster. News flash: Everyone is damaged. And if they're not, it's because they don't have a pulse."

My father's shoulders heave. "I'm doing this for your own good," he says.

"I can handle no social media. I just want to talk to him. There's a lot of schools." My mind is spinning, unable to keep thoughts in any comprehensible order, so they're tumbling out in mumbled chaos. My heart rate is accelerating. I'm gripped with fear. If I can't talk to him... "Why can't you send me to a different school? There's public school, I can go there."

My father grimaces at the suggestion.

"Look, I'll do the treatment or whatever, but don't take away the only person who makes me feel right. Please."

My dad holds out his hands to stop me. "Lennon. This isn't open for discussion."

"What if I go back to the stupid school? If I promise to do that, will you let me have my phone?"

"Lennon," he says, his voice firm. "Listen to yourself! This isn't healthy. This has nothing to do with the school, and everything to do with the fact that you need to focus on yourself and getting well, not on some boy."

"I love him!" I blurt out. "I love him and you aren't going to change that."

"You're sixteen," he says.

"Two years younger than you when you met Mom! Don't even try to tell me I don't know what love is." I start picking at my cuticles because I want to get up and flip the light switch or tap the door frame or do just about anything to stop this from happening.

"It's different," he says.

"Why? It's different because you think I'm sick," I accuse. "You think I'm so messed up that I couldn't possibly know what being in love is like? You think I can't make a grown-up decision about where I want to attend school? I'm not hopeless!"

Shadows cross his face and paint a definite scowl there. "Then *prove* it," he says. "Show me you're adult enough to be in the situation that you're in and face your struggles. We can talk about the school. You are not getting your cell phone. It's not a debate. Listen, Bug, I'm doing my best, and in this particular circumstance I'm doing what I think is the best thing I can do for you. One day, maybe, you'll have a child of your own. Maybe you can understand."

I'm not going to win. Frustrated, I rise to my feet to open the door, which swings open just as I say, "I want you to leave, please get out."

Jacob is standing there. His face falls. I feel terrible, but I can't stand to look at my father for a second longer.

"Fine," Dad says, rising to his feet. "C'mon, Jacob. We'll go to a movie."

Jacob's face is solemn as he assesses the situation. My eyes are burning and blurry. Jacob runs over to me and throws his arms around my neck. "I hope this place makes your head cold go away," he proclaims. "It's not fun at home without you." His arms unlatch themselves, and he races to where his paper airplane and mine are side by side. He grabs his and returns to Claire. Claire touches my arm to bid me good-bye while my dad positions himself in the door frame of my room, waiting for her to finish.

I mutter the mandatory good-bye, and when they leave, the tears really start to fall.

KYLER

COULD BE A BAND NAME...THINK ABOUT IT

Random Thoughts of a Random Mind

THE TREE HOUSE IS SO lonely without Lennon. I'm on my back on the mattress, staring up at the curtains, thinking of the night she ate pizza, wiped her greasy paws on her pants, and schooled me on OCD. It was then that I decided she would forever be the sort of girl you fight for.

I resent that she's not with me; I resent that I can't talk to her. I debate texting the number she'd texted me from, but she expressly directed me not to.

I still have no idea how I'm going to prove my innocence to her father, but I know somehow I'll have to if I ever want the chance to love her. And I do, unequivocally, want the chance to love her.

I'm so focused on this that when I hear the rope from the pulley system scratching across the wooden platform, it takes more than a minute to register what the sound means. I jump up and poke my head out of the doorway. Jacob stares up in awe. "I put something in the basket," he declares, pointing.

"Hey, Jake, wanna come up?"

His eyes dart warily to the side. "I do, but I can't. I'm 'posed to stay away from you, my dad said."

I nod.

"But pull up the basket, okay?"

I pull the rope. "Yeah, okay." When the tray reaches the top, I see a paper airplane. I grab it. "Did you do this?"

He shakes his head. "Lennon did. She made you a letter. I know 'cause I can read. I saw it on her table while Daddy and her were arguing and brought it to you." Just then, the massive door to their house swings wide, and Jacob's eyes grow large. "I gotta go," he says. "See you later." With that, he takes off running.

Lennon.

A paper airplane from Lennon. A letter in a paper airplane from Lennon.

I reach into the basket and recover the plane, unfolding it, mindful not to rip any of the paper.

I read it a hundred times, fold it, and put it in my pocket.

Later, in my room, I get out a piece of paper and grab my pen.

Dear Lennon,

Jacob delivered your letter. He tells me he can read already and saw it on your table. Crafty little guy for sure. As for being a girl dying to live, live, Lennon, live. Live for me. Live for you, because you, Juliet, are brighter than the stars! Pat yourself on the back, Lennon. We aced it. #EnglishWhut

Making peace with your fears is no simple task. I'm

glad you're doing it, even if it's slow. It seems like you've been gone for a year, but I'd wait a lifetime only to see you again, so please take your time.

You'll find me here, trying to do the same. Stay tuned for an epic video link to Fire to Dust's debut performance at Shade, where I'll attempt to practice all the bullshit I preach. Photographic evidence of colossal failure is possible but not guaranteed, and hey, if you can find the strength to go head to head with the demons in your mind, who is to say I can't do the same?

As for the limitless band names that exist within the walls of the unparalleled luxury of the Willow Recovery Center, yours is my favorite. Hands down the best choice. Fuck with Fear is a perfect band name, Davis. Your game is strong. A slogan for that needs thought behind it, but I'll let you know soon, I promise.

My favorite part of your correspondence, apart from the correspondence itself, was the tongue-in-throat reference regarding your sailor mouth. Poetically worded, if I may say so. I too wish my tongue was taking its rightful place down your throat, because when I kiss you, it takes me away somewhere else. A place where nothing but you, me, and that kiss even matters.

So hurry and take your time, Lennon, and get better so you can take me someplace else.

XOXO,

Kyler

I fold it up into a perfect airplane and wait for the moment to give it to Jacob, an opportunity that arrives faster than I'd anticipated. After my letter writing, I go into the kitchen to get an iced tea and spot a flash of blue in the darkness. A figure in a cape. Jacob sneaks into the backyard and tiptoes across the patio as I rush to slide the door open. There's something clutched in his hands. When he puts it down I see it's the mask. The one Lennon made. "Lennon wants you to have this," he says. "Mama said I could bring it over."

"Thanks," I say, and take his offering. "Hey, if I give you a paper airplane, can you bring it back to Lennon?"

He nods. "Yes. Mommy promised we can visit Lennon again, for longer next time."

I hold up a pointer finger. "Wait right here." Understanding the kid is on a time crunch, I race up the stairs and hurdle over my bed to grab the plane. I return to Jacob in a minute, out of breath, but holding the plane. "Thanks, Jacob. You're a good wingman."

"I don't have wings," he says pointedly.

I chuckle. "A wingman is someone who is always there for his friends, kind of like the superhero of friendship."

"Oh yeah, I'm a great wingman," he agrees.

Jacob leaves, and I pick up the mask from the counter, tracing my fingers across its surface. The textured scales, individually painted by Lennon's hand, bump along my skin. It's a muted shade of royal blue, with traces of forest green and narrow, even strokes of gold. The eye socket comes up like a dragon's, and there's a small horn that's painted gold on the side. She made me a dragon. Exceptionally badass.

I stare at the mask for a while longer, unable to comprehend how she saw this in her mind and then created it. Maybe that's how she feels about my song lyrics.

Of one thing I'm certain. Her hands made this. Her mind saw it. And it's now the most meaningful thing I own.

A week later, the most meaningful thing I own is serving as a headband, keeping my hair out of my face while I pace backstage at Shade. It was a unanimous decision as our own ode to Lennon that I would be the only one in a mask. Her mask for our first legitimate job. The band is doing me a solid, but I still feel guilty for taking that from Emmett, who worships Slipknot and aspired to wear a mask, too. But I owed this to her.

Emmett's neck cracks audibly as he rolls it. Tension oozes from even his bones. Austin knocks back his second bottle of water as Silas approaches me.

"You okay?"

I echo Lennon's words. "Are any of us ever okay, really?" When Silas glares at me, I glare back and slip my fingers between my neck and the collar of my T-shirt to swipe at the sweat there. The thing is, I'm not confident I'm fine. It's stuffy and hard to breathe.

"Seriously, are you okay?" he asks again. "I know this is a big deal to you, and I'm happy you agreed to do it, because I can appreciate it's not at the top of your bucket list, but if you're legit not okay, speak up." He gestures to Austin and Emmett. "We'll understand."

"It's not at the top of my bucket list, but it's at the top of all three of yours, so quit worrying. It's not like I've never performed before. I'll be fine. How many times are we going to have the chance to play our first real gig?"

Silas jabs me in the arm. "Lennon has a good effect on you."

Before I can issue a retort or Silas can interrogate me further on my current psychological state, a guy with a clipboard and a headset approaches. "You're up."

Silas, Emmett, and Austin all smile.

I don't. I slip the mask over my face, and the three of them form a line behind me. As we walk up the stairs, I hear the voice of a man introducing us. Half of Bel Air Learning Academy is here to watch us. To judge me. I pull in a long, deep breath.

"Please put your hands together and welcome Fire to Dust."

There's a round of cheering and applause and a skin-crawling, sharp whistle, which I can almost guarantee is coming straight from Macy, who somehow convinced my mother to let her come and watch the show. It's a good thing she did, though. I promised Lennon a video, and I'm a man of my word.

Silas, Emmett, and Austin take the stage first, and the shrieking gets louder. Emmett starts with a heavy, deep drumbeat. His twin joins in with the bass, then Silas with a few guitar riffs. I close my eyes and count it out before I move.

The second I'm in front of the mic stand and pedal board, I look out at the crowd. The place is packed and I have no idea why. I freeze for a moment, gripped by a horrible tight feeling in the pit of my stomach. I think of Lennon and how brave she is. I think about how she makes me want to be a better, stronger person.

My eyes dart to my sister, who is front and center, her entire body looking like it's about to burst with pride. She's angling her camera, Violet is at her side, and they're both screaming like lunatics.

I open my mouth and pray the words come out.

They do, but halfway through our set, my face, the covered side, is drenched in sweat. The mask is incredible, but underneath the lights of the stage, I'm an ant under a magnifying glass, being seared underneath the surface of the mask.

I clear my mind and try to focus. I stop for a minute and turn to find water. Silas plays a blues song on the guitar to give me some time. When I return to the mic, the crowd goes crazy again. Last thing I expected.

I decide to give them what they came for and step up as the front man.

"Thanks for coming to Shade to watch us play," I say. "Awesome crowd for our first gig."

A distant shout of "I love you" comes from the back and I try not to laugh. "Silas," I say, "they're talking to you."

"I'm talking to you," the voice says. "In the trippy mask."

The laugh escapes, because seriously, how else can I respond?

"I appreciate that," I say into the mic, "but I'm kind of in love with this girl—"

The crowd *awwww*s.

"Yeah," I continue. "Her name is Lennon. Named after a legend. She's a little weird." I pause and smile wide. "Actually, no, she's *a lot* weird. And I love every quirky, strange, weird, flummoxing, inexplicable thing she does."

Things get quieter.

"I wrote this song for her. This is its second incarnation because I played it for her once, and she said it was tragic and that she didn't want us to be a tragedy, but, uh, yeah, I guess you'll hear the new and improved version of Lennon's song."

My fingers slide along the guitar to play the opening riffs of the song. I've attempted to rewrite it since she said it was sad, because she's right. We aren't too late. No tragedies here. Silas, Austin, and Emmett don't miss a beat. We play four more songs after that before thanking the crowd and walking offstage.

The moment we're behind the curtain, I use the sleeve of my shirt to wipe away the sweat on my face. The applause from the crowd is constant, without a break. I strain to hear, but it sounds like they're chanting, "Fire to Dust."

"Dude," Austin says, "I think they want an encore."

And just like that, a major, big, *huge*, life-defining moment arrives. I look at my bandmates, take the mask off my face, and set it on one of the large pieces of audio equipment before I adjust my guitar. "Then let's give them one."

I don't know what I expect when I step back onstage, but this isn't it. It's *roasting* up here. Somehow, I can feel beads of sweat collecting at my temples and dripping down the ridges of my face. The crowd—who moments ago screamed at the top of their lungs—all roll together into a solid mass of questioning faces. They see me. It's registered. There's a monster in their village. A few of them blink, but most of them stare as silence fills every void in this room.

My heart wallops inside of my ribs, and suddenly it skips to a dead stop right before a redheaded girl with braids in her hair breaks the awful silence. She begins to jump up and down with her arms stretched toward the sky, yelling, "You're so hot!" And then—she *screams*. They *all* scream.

Those screams turn to chants of "Fire to Dust" over and over again like we're something to be celebrated. Something special. Their voices nail my feet to the ground. The air in here is electric. I can breathe it in. Inhale it. Absorb it. Ignite in it. I will never feel this way again for the rest of my existence, so I take a moment to relish in it, to cherish it, even for one infinitesimal speck of time.

After the performance, Macy is waiting. When I come around from backstage, she stands on the tips of her toes and throws her arms around my neck. "I'm so proud of you, big brother. You were amazing. Wait until you see yourself."

I squeeze her, careful not to break her. "Thanks, Mae."

She flattens her feet to the floor. Austin is out next and she hugs him, congratulating him. When she hugs Austin, he tells her how smart her idea about the mask was.

Silas is next, and the hairs rise on the back of my neck because Macy approaches him slower, her smile wider. She slips her arms around his neck, but if she thinks I didn't notice her fingers sliding up his arms first, well, I did.

Silas's head tilts to the left; his hand is like a giant paw at the base of Macy's spine. My teeth grind together and my jaw tics, but I'm too horrified to move. This is an undeniable stroke of luck for Silas, because if I could, I might just break his fingers.

Lennon

FACT: BABIES CRY, ON AVERAGE, 1-3 HOURS
PER DAY. HEARTBROKEN TEENAGE GIRLS CRY,
ON AVERAGE, 8-10 HOURS PER DAY.

MY TEARS ARE ENDLESS. A spring of pent-up sadness where a small leak turned into a raging river of salt and is now running down my cheeks, frantically trying to escape the loneliness in my brain. Worse, I'm not sure what the tears are for, because it's as if each tear falls for a different reason. Feelings of loss, despair, those of love, of hope, self-pity for what feels like a life sentence of war with my own mind.

I let myself cry until tears refuse to fall any longer and I've run dry as bone.

The world took my mother away, and then it gave me Kyler. Then my father took Kyler away, and I'm left with nobody but myself, and sometimes that's the scariest company of all.

I return to my desk and grab a paper and a pen, prepared to write another letter to Kyler, when I notice something. The edges of the wings on the paper airplane are double folded, with a strange tail on the back. I swipe at my eyes with my sleeves, because they're still blurry from my tears, but the moment I pick it up and bring it to my face, I know it's not mine . . . which means Jacob has my airplane.

KYLER

Random Thoughts of a Random Mind

MACY LEAVES WITH VIOLET, and we're loading our equipment up when I mention it. "Let me ask you something."

Silas lets out a deep sigh. "Go ahead, bro."

"Do you have feelings for Macy?" Saying the words makes me want to spit. I can't help it.

"I care about her," he says, "of course I care about her."

"I'm not talking the 'I care about this person' kind of bullshit. Do you want to be with Macy?"

Silas shoves one of the amps into the back of the truck. "I have no idea, to be honest, because every time I try and talk to her, her overprotective older brother cockblocks me."

"Don't ever use the word 'cockblock' in a sentence referring to my sister."

"Fair," Silas says. "Sorry. Bad choice of words."

"The worst. Answer my question."

"Yeah, Kyler, I like your sister more than as a friend. If you

326

stopped playing the enforcer, maybe you'd see that she's pretty awesome."

"I know she's awesome. She's my sister."

"I know that, too." He shuts the trunk and turns to face me. "I have nothing but respect for the fact that she's your sister, and I know you aren't too crazy about the idea of me being with her. So if you truly forbid it, I'll back off, but you're the one who suggested I teach her guitar, so you can explain why I won't be doing that anymore. I'm not going to be the one to make her sad. I'd rather die a slow and agonizing death than be the reason behind one of Macy's tears."

"Do you mean that?"

"A hundred percent. Your sister is smart and funny, not to mention beautiful. I know the type of guy she deserves, but what I can't understand is why you seem to think it impossible that it could be me. I'm not an epic douchebag."

"You're two years older than her."

He laughs. "If that's your only reason, it's a bad one."

He's right. It is.

A sixth-sense intuition strikes me that my very own words will come back to bite me in the ass here. *There are two things on earth you don't fight against. Mother Nature and love. Follow that law and life will be incredible, but if you try to fight either one of them,* boom. *Game over.*

"Take her out, then," I say. Then I point my finger at him and remind him one last time: "You better treat her like a goddamned princess. You shouldn't date your friend's sister, but if you're going to break the cardinal rule, remember the bro code. I will be forced to hurt you badly if you mess with her."

Silas smiles. "I won't mess with her. Does this mean I have your blessing?"

"No," I say, "you don't have that. I give you a hint of acceptance. That's as generous as it gets."

"That's fine," he says, "I'll take it."

School has always sucked. With Lennon it sucked less, but she's gone, and the tension between Silas and me is heavy; even worse, the weight hangs overhead like an ominous veil on a day where the air around us vibrates with excitement.

We're the center of attention, something I have very mixed feelings about. I spot Andrea in the hallway, and her face looks like she's spent the morning sucking on lemons. I'm guessing my little Lennon speech last night has pissed her off something fierce, because anyone who has half a brain would argue that I'd never do what she framed me for. I want to say something to her but I don't, choosing instead to let the school and its student body's newfound adoration of Fire to Dust do the talking.

I'm irritated with Silas, no doubt, but life hasn't exactly been handing me nice things lately, and irritated or not, I still don't mind seeing my friends living the dream, yet it's requiring a lot of socializing that I'm not used to.

This is the third time we've been stopped in fifteen minutes. People are smiling, saying they either heard it was awesome, or they were there and saw for themselves. Two girls ask for my phone number, and Blake Chandler, whom I've never spoken with before, has just spent ten minutes telling me about his band, looking at me the whole time like I'm a hero for playing in an underage club.

People I've never even noticed before are stopping me in the hallways to tell me what an epic performance that was. It's cool to be recognized for music, but being a people person is hard.

When Blake leaves, Emmett turns, unable to keep the grin from his face any longer. "This is awesome."

I wouldn't call it that. This is madness.

Proof of that comes that same afternoon in the cafeteria. I've seen various versions of my proclamation to Lennon followed by my song all over the social media circles of our high school and its known associates. We have a hashtag on Instagram and Twitter, and my phone's battery is about to bite it because of notifications from every single app and platform conceivable. This is the exact opposite of what I wanted to happen, but if there is one outstanding positive thing about it, it's that for the time being, Lennon is no longer Hell Air Learning Academy's hottest topic.

Lennon

FACT: LEVI JAMES LINDERMAN IS THE BRINGER OF
THE BEST EGG ROLLS ON PLANET EARTH.

LEVI JAMES LINDERMAN VISITS TUESDAYS, Thursdays, and once a weekend. It's almost guaranteed my father is paying good money for this privilege, but I like to believe Dr. Linderman has become invested in me as a person and not only a paycheck. He's like an older, wiser friend most of the time rather than a doctor seeking to pick apart my brain.

Lemon-yellow eyeglass frames circle his eyes today; he's wearing a white shirt, rolled up to the elbows, and jeans. A shoe box is tucked under his arm, and a plastic bag near-bursting with cartons of Chinese food is looped around the other.

I grin as soon as he enters the room. "It's like you know me."

He holds up the takeout bag. "Well, I can't promise it's the fine dining you're accustomed to, but the egg rolls are spectacular." With his free hand, he grabs the shoe box and holds it out. "I stopped by your place on my way over so I could talk to your dad. Jacob was insistent that I bring you this. Its contents have passed the vetting process at the check-in desk."

I take the shoe box and open its lid. Inside are four paper airplanes. Dr. Linderman raises an eyebrow, so I shut the lid and try to explain. "It's his new thing, paper airplanes." I point to the one he swapped for mine that sits on my desk.

"Ah yes," he says. "I noticed. Young Jacob was proud of the large selection he'd made." He nods toward the box. "That's but a sampling."

I wonder if one of the planes is mine. If that's Jake's way of returning it when he realized his mistake. I set the shoe box on the bed and rub my hands together. "Now, down to more serious matters, I believe you spoke of spectacular egg rolls."

He moves to the small table nestled between two armchairs, sets the food down, and sits in one of the chairs. I take a seat across from him and pull apart the chopsticks while he unpacks the food. I snatch a carton at random, and when I open it I'm pleased to have chicken chow mein. My mom and I used to have these lazy rainy-day weekends where we'd lie in her bed all day watching documentaries and emerging only when pizza, chicken, or Chinese food was delivered.

Dr. Linderman appears to have scored ginger beef. He chews, swallows, and says, "I was chatting with Dr. Waxman. He's deeply impressed with your progress. He's reporting that you're doing remarkably well, Lennon."

"Yeah. I can't lie, it's a nice place. But I want to get out of here."

"You're well on your way."

"We'll see about that. I have a horrible feeling my dad's gauge on whether I'm mentally fit to come back home is centered around a return to school, which will never happen."

"Never say never, Lennon. Maybe you'll feel otherwise."

"Doubtful," I say. "Nothing can ever fix what happened."

"Maybe," he allows, "but you can resolve to own it or choose to run from it."

"Says the guy who—wait for it—doesn't have OCD."

He smirks. "Right you are, but I know a thing or two about it."

"I bet."

He switches cartons, and his face lights up as he proudly displays an egg roll between his chopsticks before handing the carton to me. "Try one," he says. "You're welcome."

"You're talking up these egg rolls so much, I'm scared to try one. What if they don't live up to the hype you've diligently created?"

"They will," he answers without a moment's hesitation. "So, tell me something—let's assume your father doesn't base his decision on your willingness to return to school, and you get out of here. What are you looking forward to the most?"

I almost choke on my egg roll. "Egg rolls that taste like this."

"I told you: spectacular," he says. "Now the truth. What will make you happiest?"

"Kyler, obviously."

He reaches into the carton for a second egg roll. "I notice you're deeply connected to this young man."

I grin. "You got that, did you?"

"I think perhaps you should stop and think about that."

I take another egg roll. "Are you serious right now, Levi? Are you suggesting I'm obsessing over him, as an individual with obsessive-compulsive disorder may be predisposed to do?

There's a reason it's called obsessive-compulsive disorder. I can promise you, although I appreciate your concern, it is not an obsession with a human being. It's an obsession with who I can be with that person. Aside from with my mom, I've never felt okay with being myself, I've never been comfortable in my skin that way with anybody except her, until him. I didn't have to hide behind some lie to keep up appearances. I didn't have to pretend to be ordinary, I could just *be*."

He sets his chopsticks down and brings his hands to his jaw thoughtfully; it's a total clichéd shrink move, but I'll allow it. "That's fascinating you would say that."

"Not sure I follow."

"Well, you mentioned you could be yourself around him—that's what you like. Yet the door has only just opened for you to own this, Lennon, and be yourself, but you refuse to walk back through it and face your peers. Did you ever stop to consider they might accept this about you, too?"

"Hasn't even crossed my mind," I say, "because that sounds like some fantastical idea a guy who knows zilch about OCD would say." I pause. "Wanna try again, Levi?"

His answer surprises me. "I'll pass," he says. "As tempting as the offer is, if you don't adjust your attitude, there's nothing I can say or do that will change it. But I am curious about one more thing."

"What's that?"

"What do you hate most about OCD?"

I set the carton of noodles down. "What don't I hate most about OCD? That it's work to be who everybody believes I should be, it controls me, it killed my mom. That is what I detest the most about it. It killed my mother. She's dead because I'm this way."

Levi sets his carton down, too, and joins his hands together, leaning back into the armchair, assuming a secondary proper shrink position. "It didn't kill your mother, Lennon. An intoxicated driver did."

"She wouldn't have been driving if I didn't have OCD."

He shakes his head. "You are convinced you know that to be true, but who is to say she wouldn't have been out gathering up dry cleaning, or going to the hair salon? There are circumstances in life that are a matter of crappy coincidence. You did not cause your mother's death."

I stay silent.

"Can you believe me when I say that?" he asks.

"Maybe. One day."

Levi nods. "Not before you're ready."

"My turn to ask you something."

"Shoot. I'm an open book."

"Do you think my dad keeping me away from my friends, my *life*, is the right choice?"

"I think he thinks it's what's right for you. He doesn't wish you to see hurtful or harmful things on social media."

"He won't even let me text Kyler. He doesn't believe me that Kyler wouldn't do it."

"Give it time," he advises. "Besides, when true love is offered to us, Lennon, time or distance won't matter."

"Ever been in love, Levi?"

"Yes," he says, "I have. Her name was Melanie and she was"—he pauses, in search of the right word—"extraordinary. Unlike anyone I've ever met. I met her on a trip to Bali, we hit it off right away, found out we both lived in LA. When we had returned home and settled, we dated."

"So, was it true love?"

"Yes, Lennon, I have no doubt it was."

"Why aren't you with her?"

"Ovarian cancer," he replies.

My stomach knots. Not the answer I was expecting. My hands tremble as I set the carton down. "I'm sorry."

"It's quite all right," he says. "It was a long time ago."

"Can I ask you something else?"

"Sure."

"How did you know? That what you felt was real?"

"I stopped searching for proof. I quieted my mind when it questioned me. I listened to my heart."

"My heart tells me it wants to go home. Where he is."

"At this point in your treatment, you can leave when you feel you're ready, assuming you have your father's support, but I urge you to wait until that's truly the case. Like I said before, you're making tremendous progress—and please let me remind you, this isn't a mandated institution, Lennon. You aren't committed here like one may be in a psychiatric hospital. You can leave, but know everyone around you right now is trying to help you get your life back. Everyone has your best interests in mind. Even your dad."

We finish our Chinese food in a comfortable silence, and when

I bid the good doctor good-bye, I apologize for bringing up his pain. "I bet she was a total babe."

He smirks. "She was. Have a good night, Lennon. I'll see you Thursday."

"Can you bring pizza?"

"Your wish is my command."

Dr. Linderman leaves and I perform my bedtime ritual fifteen times. I don't even know why I'm doing it—I'm currently in control of my thoughts—but my anxiety spiked after talking about Kyler and my mother, and Dr. Linderman's Melanie.

Just as I'm ready to crawl into bed and end the day, I spot the shoe box I'd forgotten about. I grab it, sit down, lift the lid, and peer inside. None of them look like the plane I'd made, but one has a musical note on its wing.

My heart stops.

My hand shakes as I reach into the box to get it, picking it up before unfolding it. As Kyler's handwriting reveals itself, my heart accelerates. It's just as excited as I am.

And Jacob. What a mastermind. I'd underestimated him.

Plans for sleep are foiled by the adrenaline I feel from reading the letter. I read it five times, then fold it back into an airplane and set it on the bedside table. I grab my notebook and my pen and head to one of the lounges.

Cecilia is in there with another patient, Aubrey. Aubrey has a different subset of OCD than me, one that it could be argued is worse. She's a germophobe and spends a large percentage of her life doing things to ensure she or members of her family do not get sick. Cecilia is sprawled across the couch while Aubrey is perched on a single cushion as if the sofa is ground zero for the bubonic plague, her spine ramrod straight. They're talking about makeup and plastic surgery. Cecilia is checking her phone intermittently, and she bolts to her feet when I enter. "You look happy," she says.

"I am."

"I would be, too."

That makes little sense. My feet stop moving and I look at her. "You don't even know what I'm happy about."

"Hell yes, I do. It's everywhere. Even with them blocking your social media, I can't believe you haven't heard."

She's frustrating me. "Heard what?"

"About your boyfriend."

My feet unglue themselves from the floor as I dash to where she's standing. "What about my boyfriend?"

Germophobe Aubrey smiles.

"Your boyfriend, Kyler. That's his name, right? Kyler? You said he was in a band."

"Yeah, he's in a band."

She flops on the couch and pats the cushion. I take a seat next to her, and Aubrey scoots across the cushions to Cecilia's other side. Cecilia swipes her finger across the screen of the phone, mumbling, "I'm only guessing, but with names like Lennon and Kyler, I mean, it's hard to think it's anyone else." She taps the screen again and holds her phone resting on her lap so the three of us can get a good view. And there he is. Kyler, on someone named Lisbeth Beauchamp's Instagram. Lisbeth had checked into Shade, and in a small, perfect square a video is displayed.

"Everyone is talking about it," Cecilia says. "It's spreading like wildfire."

I'm about to reach out and click the small triangle to play the video, but Cecilia does it first.

Kyler's voice, which I haven't heard in so long, comes from the speakers of her phone. "Actually, no, she's *a lot* weird. And I love every quirky, strange, weird, flummoxing, inexplicable thing she does."

The crowd quiets.

"I wrote this song for her. This is its second incarnation because I played it for her once, and she said it was tragic and that she didn't want us to be a tragedy, but, uh, yeah, I guess you'll hear the new and improved version of Lennon's song."

He sings the first few lines of my song, and my body decides now is a good time to recall what happened the last time I heard it. I lean closer to the screen, forgetting for a moment that I'm not viewing it alone, and the smile on my face is impossibly wide.

"That's him, right?" Cecilia asks. She's proud, like she's cracked some great code in the mystery of Lennon and Kyler.

I nod. "That's him."

"You are so lucky. What I wouldn't do to have a guy like that write a song for me."

"Me too," Aubrey offers.

I ask Cecilia if we can watch it again, and we do four more times to total five. I want to steal her phone and bring it to bed with me, so I can watch him, hear him, over and over and over. Instead, I take my notebook to my room and pen my letter back.

Dear Kyler,

First off, may I take a moment to say Jacob is a little mastermind—the kind of kid who will take over the world someday with his ingenious brain. Talk about resourceful!

As for the performance at Shade, would you believe me if I told you I've seen it? Cecilia Prescott (yes, the one you're thinking of) is here at Willow. Since she's the child of a megacelebrity, she has everything. Including her cell phone.

My dad refuses to let me have mine, even if I earn it on the points system. He figures I'll be too traumatized by the evils of social media to continue, plus, well, you, but I digress. Since Cecilia's father isn't a dictator, she has her phone and has seen Fire to Dust on social media. I told her you were in a band, I told her your name, and just like that she put it all together. The Instagram post had more likes than I can fathom, I hope you're proud.

I didn't get to fully hear the lyrics because it was a clipped video, but everything sounded amazing. You changed the words a little bit! I'm fighting the urge to bust out of here all on my own and make my way to you because all I can think about is what happened last time I heard that song.

For the record, I don't think I will ever be able to give you such an outstanding display of my affection because you're setting the bar too high, frankly, but know that seeing you, hearing your voice, gives me the strength to get well enough to come home.

Dr. Linderman was just here. All reports indicate that I'm not a total basket case, and I've been advised that I can leave soon. I can't wait.

Sure, I'll miss the madness and the fine dining, but at least I'll get to see you. It's a fair trade. I want you to know that your talent extends far beyond singing, playing the guitar, or even the way you kiss, because somehow, because of you, I have the strength to believe in me. I know I need to get better before I can come home, but for the first time, in a long time, I believe I can.

With love,

Lennon

Dear Lennon,

I think it's fair to say we owe Jacob something epic when you break free from the literal chains of Willow Recovery Center, and the figurative chains of your mind. As for the Instagram fiasco, I know. It's unreal. People I don't know are stopping me at school, acting like I'm something special. It's ridiculous. Austin and Emmett are eating up the attention and Silas would be, too, if he could work a phone. (Insert a laughing tears emoji here to reminisce about our lost texting.) I'll practice and be ready with a solo performance when you bust out of the institution, Lennon. Promise.

You don't get your phone, huh? That's rough, but hey, we have Jacob. Part of me feels like we're abusing the kindness of that little dude's heart, but I like to think he's rooting for us. I'm glad you like the song. By the time you get out of that place, there is a good chance that I'll have an entire collection waiting for you. I eat, sleep, go to school, and make or write music. Not a lot different from what I did pre-Lennon, but insanely lonely given the Lennon era that followed, and the post-Lennon solitude that haunts me.

For the record, we already talked about this. The only thing I want is your lips on mine so I can have my Nirvana. And don't lie, you're a total basket case but not so out of touch with reality that you can't get better.

Oh, and before I forget to tell you, Fuck with Fear, our slogan is "Expand Your Mind." Think about it, Davis, taking on your fears is soul food for the brain. #truth

You should believe in yourself. I swear to God; your DNA is composed of 97% awesome and 3% whacked. If anyone can kick OCD's ass, it's you. I love you, and I can't wait to tell you that face-to-face every day at school until you're sick of hearing it, but until then, paper airplanes must do.

Tell me something I don't know about you yet.

Me: my favorite book growing up was <u>The Monster at</u>

the End of This Book. My mom used to read it to me all the time. I loved how Grover would warn you not to turn the pages, and I felt like such a little rebel when I kept going, even though he was pleading with me not to.

XOXO,

Kyler

Dear Kyler,

You're right. I am a total basket case. But I'm a basket case in the throes of mind expansion. (Perfect tagline.) Today, however, I took a step back. During our group session, one girl talked about her mom always being there for her, and I lost it. Sobbed like a wreck. A flood of snot and tears and tissues later, I made it out alive, and without OCDing the situation, but now I'm feeling sorry for myself.

On a happier note, Cecilia Prescott displays valiant attempts to rouse me from my pits of sorrow by offering the Instagram video of you at least a hundred and one times. If you're reading this, I've seen Claire, my dad, and Jacob. Things are still tense with my dad. I get he's trying to protect me, but he's protecting me from the wrong people. He doesn't know about OCD me and I think I confuse him. He treats me like a china doll, breakable and fragile.

I have cut my ritualizing down by almost 65%. Yay

me! Technically I can leave whenever I want, assuming my dad will let me come home. All indicatons at family therapy point to yes, but I'm waiting, because as nice as Willow is, and as much as I want to see you, I need to make sure I don't come back here. I need to make sure I can control it. I feel better every day, though, and today's crying episode proved to me that maybe I can, so I'm aiming for release into the wild in three weeks. A personal goal I've set for myself. That's not so bad, right? A week before summer break. Works out perfect, almost, because I don't have to go to school. I don't think I ever want to go back to that school, to be honest.

Doesn't matter, I suppose, but I don't think I will change my mind, even if I make it out of here somewhat more sane.

I'm determined. Nothing like the love of a boy to make me want to succeed. How disgusting is that sentiment, truly? Yuck. Anyway, I can't wait to see you, I promise it will be soon.

As for something you don't know about me. I used to climb fences when I was a little kid. Scaled them all the time in our neighborhood in Maine. I was trying to parkour or something insane like that, and I broke my femur. Like full-blown-surgery broke it. You can still see a tiny scar on my thigh.

Much love,

Lennon

Dear Mind-Expanding Lennon,

I'm sorry you felt sad about your mom. But you can be sad when you need to be, there's no law against it. Try to remember that and not be so hard on yourself.

I can't believe in a couple of weeks I'll get to be with you again. It's like I'm being reunited with my long-lost arm. The downside is, I gotta admit, paper airplane letters have grown on me.

Now let me say what is on my mind aside from the scar on your thigh and how much I'd like to see it. I don't think you should let them scare you away from school. Fuck them. I'm not you, but I can tell you I know what it's like to feel different. Running from them is telling them it's not okay to be different, when it is. Just my humble thoughts on the matter.

As for the love of a boy to make you want to succeed, I'm flattered. Even if you find it revolting. I'll leave you with this. Given that you wipe grease on your jeans and burp louder than I do (you think I haven't heard), I get that the idea of wanting to be better for someone else as much as yourself is revolting. But it goes both ways here, Davis. I want to be better because of you, too. I'm starting with exploring my poetic side. Lowry is teaching a poetry option for extra credit this semester, I'm late to join but he's letting me. So, immediately after shitty cafeteria lunch, I get to go dig deep. I think I got something already. Check it out:

Oh, chicken nugget, Mauled piece of meat,

I long to taste your nectar so sweet,

A love so great, so flavorfully profound,

A taste so cardboard-y, sing your sweet mushy sound,

I'll not give up on us, little nugget, I will not rest!

I'll indulge in temptation, which leads me to death,

Diabetes...

What do you think? Epic, right? I mean, I know I took creative license, adding the "diabetes" at the end, but... it fits so well I had to go with instinct.

XOXO

Kyler

Dear Kyler,

Epic? Not the word I'd use to describe a poem about your love affair with nuggets. It's like a tragic free verse, but I get why you want to take Lowry's poetry class and I think it's cool.

This will be our last letter! I feel as though I should seal it with hot wax and an iron press. Because I did it. I finally freaking did it. My impending homecoming is days away. I'm writing this because Jacob, Dad, and Claire are coming tonight to take my clothes and some of my other things home in advance. I don't know what else to say. I can't focus on anything. I keep replaying the idea repeatedly in my head of what it will feel like to kiss you again.

I don't want to talk about school. We can do it in person. Soon.

I can't wait to see you.

Love,

Lennon

KYLER

"I'LL WAIT FOR YOU AS LONG AS IT TAKES, I'LL NEVER LET YOU GO,
I'LL COUNT THE DAYS TILL YOU RETURN, I'LL NEVER LET YOU GO."
Fire to Dust, *Life-Defining Moments* EP, "Resistance"

ACCORDING TO JACOB, KNOWING INFORMANT and investigative reporter, Lennon from Maine with Serious Issues Who Sews and Is Broken and Beautiful and Badass returns home today. He'd informed me when he delivered her last letter. He'd been doing it on the sly. In between soccer balls, soda bottle rockets, and paper planes, Jacob is an infallible master of finding reasons to be outside. I couldn't sleep last night, and consequently I'm yawning every ten seconds while I gaze out the window straight into the early-evening rays of the California sun.

I've been here for the last forty-seven minutes...waiting...because the instant I see their car pull up, I'm making a break for it. For *her*.

Finally, Josh's Porsche eases up the long driveway and parks. The door swings wide and the first thing I see is her long, blond hair falling down her back, followed by one pale blue Converse and then the other. I watch for a moment, silent and spellbound by the sight of her—like I forgot somehow that she was so beautiful.

She doesn't turn around, and I'm struck with how similar this is to the first time I saw her. *Turn around, my beautiful girl. I want to see you.* Her hands swing out to the sides animatedly. Josh's face is stern. They're fighting. Lennon heads toward the house and turns back around to keep arguing with her father. When I spin on my feet, prepared to bolt, I'm stopped dead in my tracks. My father stands, arms crossed over his chest menacingly, blocking the doorway. Alone, that wouldn't bother me so much, but the expression on his face is one I've encountered only a few times in my life, and none of those times resulted in anything positive happening.

"Going someplace?"

I cast a glance over my shoulder. Lennon marches toward their front door, a duffel bag slung over her arm. I move to go to her a second time, but my dad readjusts his footing and stops me. Again. His teeth clamp down and his brows draw together in pinched irritation. "Don't even think about it," he warns.

"Shouldn't you be at work?" I ask. "Isn't somebody somewhere screwing up their life right now?"

He nods, then issues a cold smirk. "Probably, Kyler, but it won't be you. You won't be seeing that girl."

"Maybe not now, but what are you going to do, quit your job and stand guard over me twenty-four seven? You will not stop me from seeing her."

His face darkens.

"You can't stand here forever. And for every ounce of anger you have, I have triple the motivation. You won't keep me from her. Don't care what it takes." As I say it, I hope he believes every word.

The line I'm dancing is perilously close to being crossed, so I say nothing else.

"You're going to land your entitled ass in prison, Kyler. Restraining orders aren't something you want connected with your name. I can't allow it to happen, so if I have to quit my job and watch over you twenty-four seven, then so be it."

Quit his job? Yeah, right. Empty threats and hollow lies. I know this is true, because I've spent most of my life hearing them. I peer out the window again. The front door is closed at the Davis residence. Lennon was within feet of me and now she's gone, and, ironically, it begins to rain.

Lennon

FACT: THE TERM EVIL IS DEFINED AS PROFOUNDLY IMMORAL.
IF THAT'S TRUE, ANDREA IS LITERAL EVIL INCARNATE.

SWEAT PRICKLES AGAINST THE BACK of my neck when we get to the car. *I'm stronger than the thoughts.* My dad takes his seat behind the wheel and looks over to me, his eyes dancing across my hand. I don't move a muscle. And as we sit in the car and I tap *nothing*, instead of saying *Good job, Lennon,* or *Way to conquer your worst nightmare, Lennon,* my father hits me with a grenade.

If he'd done it any sooner, I wouldn't have been so eager to vacate the creature comforts of Willow Recovery Center. I am still forbidden from seeing Kyler. I'd bargained on a trip spent battling the thoughts about being in the car, but instead I find myself filled with so much rage, the only thoughts I'm fighting are the homicidal kind.

I mistakenly assumed I might be glad to see the Jenga house. It will never be home, but Kyler made it seem like it could be... almost... and now that's gone. I'm bitter. The instant the car is parked, I unbuckle, reach into the back seat for my duffel bag, and chuck it over my shoulder.

Dad steps out of the vehicle and makes a move to seize my bag from me, but I turn my body around so it's out of his grasp, sidestep him, and glare. "I don't want your help, thanks. God, it's bad enough you kept me from him for two months because you don't believe your stepdaughter is capable of something so evil, even though she is! Two months, Dad! Do you hate me or something?" My voice is escalating, but I don't care. "I did your stupid therapy. I'm better. I made it the whole way in the car without ritualizing. Isn't that what you wanted, a nice, normal kid? Well, you got one, but you're doing everything you can to make it so I'm not normal at all! Did you have locks installed while I was gone?" The tears burn in my eyes because everything is so unfair.

"Lennon, time for an attitude adjustment. He's violent. I'm your dad, not your friend. It's my job to protect you."

My body shakes with anger as I hold up a finger. "First of all, you're not protecting me. You're walking me straight into the place where the person I need protection from rests her vile head every night. Secondly, I wish he'd scared her more. He's not violent. He's been framed for doing something despicable to someone he cares about! He was mad! I'm not the one who needs an attitude adjustment!" I scream. "You do."

His stare is blank, expressionless, which only serves to make me more irate. He says nothing, so I pause and wait for any kind of reply, justification for his unjust decision, yet I still get nothing. Is he going to speak at all? His silent treatment continues, so I roll my eyes, spin on my heel, and charge toward the house, determined to make it to my room and never, ever emerge.

Jacob is sitting in the foyer holding his camera. There's a sign made from letter-sized paper taped together. In Jacob's rudimentary printing, it says, WELCOME HOME, LENNON.

Despite the argument with my dad, I smile when I see it. Jake, quick to catch moments of candor, takes a picture with his camera before letting it hang from the strap around his wrist. He throws his arms around my waist. "I'm so happy you're home! Mama went to get you a fruit bouquet. Whatever that is."

I ruffle his hair. "Me too, bud. Missed you."

It comes out with a croak. The type of vocal change that issues a clear signal of distress. Jacob's hands fall from my waist, and he looks up at me, head tilted. "Are you okay?"

I nod because if I try to speak, the tears will fall. I suck in a breath and gather my emotions enough to say, "Just tired is all."

He considers this but doesn't hold on to the information for long, because he asks, "Now that you're home, can we go to Kyler's? I want to make more airplanes."

Before I can answer and tell him we're both forbidden from seeing Kyler, Andrea comes sauntering into the kitchen, eyes fixed on her cell phone. Maybe I should return to the driveway and continue to yell at my dad, because surely it's better than being forced to look at her.

My stomach flip-flops and my ears ring, echoing the space around me. Andrea who sabotaged me, framed Kyler, and annihilated my entire existence is walking around like she doesn't have a care in the world. I narrow my eyes and wonder how on earth she can be related to someone like Claire.

Claire is good and kind. Andrea is not. As if she can hear my thoughts, she looks up from her phone. "Back from the nuthouse?" she asks, plucking an apple from the fruit bowl.

"Back *to* the nuthouse," I clarify. "Or maybe it's literal hell on earth. It could be that, too, because...well...you're fucking Satan."

Jacob's eyes go wide.

"That's a bit drastic," Andrea says. "Besides, you're far from perfect."

"Why don't you admit to doing it?" I ask her. "You destroyed everything, anyway, so you might as well have the guts to own it."

She turns the apple in her hand, lips slightly parted, her eyes glazed over as though she's seeing right through me. "I don't know what you're talking about."

"Of course you don't."

Dad closes the door behind us, locking me into a whole different kind of prison.

A flicker of relief dances across Jacob's face when my dad comes in, but as soon as I register the interruption, my gaze is back to Andrea. "I hope you get everything that's coming to you," I say to her. "Tenfold."

She laughs and bites into the apple. "Sure. Whatever you say."

Jacob tugs on my sleeve. "Can we play hide-and-seek? Please?"

My options are limited. I can play hide-and-seek with Jacob, continue to be disgusted by my father and Andrea, or I can go to my room and throw an epic pity party. I look at Jacob. "Twenty minutes, okay? I have to unpack and stuff."

Twenty minutes turns into an hour, most of which I spend finding Jacob versus the other way around. Claire returns with my fruit bouquet and a trivia book. She wraps me in a hug and I let her, because I hate my dad, I hate Andrea, and it feels like

Claire is the only person save for Jacob who is truly happy for my return. Correction: She's the only person whom I'm permitted to have contact with save for Jacob, who is happy about my return. Jacob leaves to have a sleepover with one of Claire's friend's kids, a boy named Lincoln. He assures me he'll be back, and when the door shuts behind them, I find no reason to stay outside the walls of my bedroom.

I grab my duffel bag from where it's been sitting in the foyer and head to my room.

I stop, momentarily wanting to turn the doorknob five times, but I don't. *Bad things might happen.* It's a thought. It's only a thought. The thought can't control me. I control the thought.

I swing open the door, and I gasp. Gone are the gray walls, gone is the gray bedding. Gone is everything. And everything in here is new or mine from home. There's a fabric headboard, romantic and in a shade of deep royal blue. It's old-fashioned-looking with diamond shapes spanning its width, and the bed is covered in blankets and pillows. Loads of white blankets in different sizes and textures. The walls are painted a clean white, and everything else in here is blue, green, or purple. There's a vase beside the bathroom door with peacock feathers.

I step into the room, feeling my lips pull upward into a smile. There's a large white dresser, and my heart skips for a moment before I open a drawer and see my clothing organized exactly as I'd had it. A sewing table is set up on the wall opposite my bed, and the contents of my trunk are unpacked into a cabinet with cubbies and labels. Bookcases on one side display my trivia books, stacked into clusters of five, and my mother's records, cardboard sleeves tucked inside plastic ones.

I run my fingers along them and notice they're in alphabetical order. A record player sits by itself on a shelf in the middle. I'm frozen into place, reeling from shock with genuine warmth in my heart, when there is a soft knock at the door.

I turn to see Claire standing there, her hands held together in front of her. She's in a pair of sweatpants and a matching hoodie, in muted gray. She smiles sweetly. "Your daddy said your favorite color was purple, but your friend Ashley told me it was blue, and Jacob insisted on adding green, so I told Trixie to use a little of each."

"It's beautiful," I say. "Thank you."

"Mind if I come in, sweetie?"

"No, of course not."

She enters the room and sits gingerly on the bed. "Listen, sugar, I know your daddy is being real stubborn right about now, but he thinks it's for your own good."

I wouldn't have invited her in if I knew she was going to defend my father. "It's not. Claire, Kyler didn't do it."

"He threatened Andrea, Lennon. And trust me"—she holds up a hand—"I can see how that might be easy to do if I were him, but he shouldn't have done it regardless of whether Andi is responsible for the incident."

I sit on the bed beside her. "Are you telling me you don't think I'm lying? That Andrea is the one who did it?"

"I'm telling you I'm not as willing as your daddy to rule out the possibility that she's not. Listen, I came in here to apologize for asking you about the interview. I wanted to wait until you were home so I could properly apologize, one on one. I didn't mean to make you uncomfortable. I thought it might be helpful for you."

I stop her before she goes any further. "Don't worry about it."

"I know I'm not your mama, Lennon," Claire says, "but I do love you. I care about what happens to you and I want you to know that I'll do my best to make sure you have the kind of life she would have wanted you to have. Nothing can bring her back." She reaches out and touches my knee." But I will make sure you know love any way I can."

My eyes burn immediately and as I nod, I feel the hot tears slipping down my cheeks. I swipe them away and mutter, "Thank you."

Claire reaches into her pocket and pulls out my cell phone. "Your daddy's opinion is loud, but I'm his wife, and sometimes my voice is louder than his opinion."

My hand shakes as I take it and throw my arms around her neck. "Thank you! Claire! Thank you."

She smiles. "You're welcome." She stands and points a finger with a stern look on her face and says something my mother would have. "Don't you be staying up all night looking at that thing, you hear me? Mind the time and get to bed at a decent hour."

I look down at my phone like it's a solid gold bar. "Okay. Thank you."

She nods and closes the door softly behind her.

Before I check a single app, I open my text message screen and compose one.

My dad thinks he can keep us apart. This means war.

KYLER

YOU CAN'T ESCAPE THE HYPOCRITICAL MIND.

Random Thoughts of a Random Mind

I MISSED THE ILLUMINATION OF the window on the far right of Josh's house for forty-two nights, so when the corner of my eye catches the familiar warm flicker, I pick up the remote and pause the movie I'm watching as I wait for the wonder of the Lennon Davis light show to commence. On. Off. Repeat. To my surprise and—I'll admit it—my disappointment, it doesn't. I knew parts of her would be *better*, but I hope they didn't erase the pieces of her brain that make her extraordinary. The gears and cogs that click and spin inside her mind, and make it turn in the opposite direction from most people, the same direction as mine.

I pad cautiously across the bedroom toward the window. I need to see her with my own two eyes, without my dad's presence threatening me. I try to convince myself that I'm not dreaming; she's home, she *is* next door, a mere ten yards away from my window. I want to confirm to myself in person that she's still Lennon. Beautiful. Badass. Lennon. Weeks have passed and I've been holding my breath the whole time, waiting for her to return.

I freeze halfway across the room when my cell phone vibrates in my hand.

My dad thinks he can keep us apart. This means war.

She has her phone back. I smile.

Well hello to you too Lennon. Welcome to this century. Text messaging is what all the young kids do.

You're funny. Sorry. Hi. I'm in this century but ready for a battle worthy of a bygone age.

A historic battle, huh? Did I ever tell you my lifelong dream of dying with valor, Davis?

This isn't funny!

No, I type. It's not. I'm sorry.

I hate him.

You don't hate him. You hate the circumstance not the person. I'm not Josh's biggest fan either but I think he believes he's doing the right thing.

I don't care what he believes.

If it makes you feel any better I tried to race outside and greet you when your car pulled up but my dad stopped me. Stood in front of me with his arms crossed, his neck vein popping like he's a member of the goddamned secret service. What a tool.

Why would that make me feel any better? It makes me feel worse. I hate this. 😞

Don't cry sunshine. Come to the window. I want to see you.

I wait for a few seconds before she appears. It's as if I'm seeing her for the first time. Her face is somber, her hair piled high on her head in what Macy has explained to me is called a topknot. She's wearing oversized gray sweatpants and a white sleeveless shirt. The kind I'd picture on a guy named Boris with a drinking problem.

Cute ensemble Davis, are you going for the convict/felon style? If so... nailed it.

Her gaze is on the phone screen as she bites her bottom lip, fighting a smile. Shut up. That sounds like something a convict/felon would say. Plus you're clearly jealous I can pull this style off far better than you.

Hate to break it to you Davis, but the only time I might be the better looking one is when we're both dead. Since it'll be closer to the natural version of me, and you'll be made up with blue eyeshadow and crimson lips courtesy of some underpaid makeup artist working in the morgue. As for today's fashion I'm practically a convicted felon anyway according to your dad. Violent and unpredictable.

My dad knows nothing. I miss you.

He assumes I did something terrible to you. Add to that the fact I punched a dent into the locker beside Andrea's head and I'm on the no-fly list.

What are we going to do?

Easy. I'm light years ahead of you. Are you ready for my wisdom?

If you have a solution let's hear it.

I don't want to type it because the answer is obvious and I'm not sure how she'll react to me pointing it out.

All you have to do is come to school tomorrow. We'll skip and I'll make you shine by doing speakable and respectful things to you in the parking lot of the country club.

She pauses before she types, I can't go back there.

Yes, I reply. You can.

Kyler... I can't... you don't understand. That was the most humiliating thing I've ever experienced in my life.

Wait. Is she serious?

I punch the Facetime button on my phone with my thumb. She answers. I don't even say hello. I open with "You're so many kinds of wrong on this, Lennon. I understand. I understand more clearly than anyone else."

Her eyes are extra small on the screen, yet they still bore into me like lasers. "You may understand what it's like to be different. I'm not saying you don't, because you are. But I can look at you and see right away what makes us different. When all the problems are a product of your mind, when it's not something logical or tangible... I guess what I'm trying to say is that we're different brands of different and there's a stigma with mine."

That's the stupidest reasoning I've ever listened to. "A stigma? Really? Is that some fancy word you learned at the world-renowned Willow Recovery Center?"

Her brows pinch together. "What?"

"A stigma. Pardon me, but fuck that. You think I don't know what it's like for people to assume something bad about me is true without ever so much as questioning it? Are you for real?" I suck in a breath. "I'm about to say something, Lennon, and it will piss you off something fierce. It's been my experience that when you call someone on their bullshit, they get defensive."

Her skin flushes pink. She's angry already. But I have to risk saying what I need to say because she won't get it otherwise, she won't understand. "I have to call you on it. Because in truth, it's a little fucking hypocritical that your letters were filled with meaningless garbage about having faith in yourself and fucking with fear when you won't even come to school."

I dare a glance at her. Her lips are pursed, her brows drawn down, her skin pinched pink with tinges of anger. "What do you expect? You're not the one everybody will talk about."

Those are fighting words. "Is that some kind of sick joke? Do you remember who you're talking to? I'm just saying it's pretty telling about your true thoughts on the situation. I haven't seen you in over a month. And you won't come to school, which is the only place you can be with me. It seems like a logical conclusion. It's within your power to return to school. You're just letting fear or pride control you, exactly like you said you wouldn't."

Lennon's glare could burn straight through the invisible screen armor on my phone. "Good night. Glad I got my phone back for this." With that, she hangs up.

Frustrated, I toss my phone on the desk and head for a shower. I won't be able to sleep now, guaranteed. I didn't mean to pick a fight with her, but I'd do anything. I'd swim across an ocean to be with her, so the fact that she won't return to school is surreal. A difficult problem with what should be a simple solution.

Lennon

I COUNTED THE DAYS AT Willow. Marked each one with a red X on the calendar. Clichéd, like something out of a movie, but it helped to have a visual reminder I'd see him soon. A countdown until I'd be able to throw my arms around him, text him thought-provoking questions, or spend time in his tree house.

Only one of those things happened, though, so instead I lie in bed, empty and hollow, just like when Mom died. That's what it feels like, as if he has died. Dramatic, yes, but also true. Sure, I can peek through the window and see him, and yeah, now at least I can text him, but I can't smell the laundry-clean scent of him, or touch his skin, or kiss his lips. And being deprived of those things is my definition of hell.

At home in Maine, my friend Ashley was obsessed with this kid named Benjamin Foster. She had the hots for him powerful enough to melt the atmosphere. I used to observe her in silent awe. How is it possible one person could be that important to another? But now, amid the chaos that my life has become, I understand.

I bury my head under the covers and try, without success, to fall asleep. Fighting with my dad, hating Andrea, fighting with Kyler. All exhausting and stressful. A constant pull between wanting to give up and wanting to fight harder for what I believe in, because I believe in us. My eyes are sandpaper and my throat is dry as bone. I head to the bathroom and grab a glass of cold water, checking my phone to see how much time I've spent willing sleep to come. A long text from Kyler is displayed on the screen, time-stamped 4:21 a.m.

I'm sorry I was an asshole. I'm frustrated and I took it out on you. I can't pretend to know what you're going through but I know what it's like to be talked about. They won't even give the courtesy of doing it behind your back. Thing is, fuck, Lennon, I miss you. I want to have you in my arms again Lennon and there is no obstacle that will stop me from trying so I'm having a hard time dealing with how you see it. But for what it's worth I accept it. You shouldn't do anything you don't want to do and I shouldn't try to make you. Assuming you still want to talk to me then I got us covered Davis. Plus Jacob is a diabolical mastermind. Surely between the three of us we can figure something out. I've waited almost two months but I promised you I'd wait a lifetime so what's a little while longer in the grand scheme of things?

Four thirty-seven a.m. is when I crawl back under the covers with a new understanding. The murkiness has cleared.

Life-defining moments are everything, and I'm going to have one tomorrow. A moment that's sure to inspire song lyrics from front men and forgiveness from boyfriends. I crawl back into the oversized bed, hoping I can wake up and be braver than I feel, and finally, I fall asleep.

It's a dictatorship around my house. My father has decided, in light of my recent mental breakdown and Kyler's display of affection toward Andrea, and my unwillingness to return to Bel Air Learning Academy, that I need to be under constant supervision until things are sorted. Until further notice, we are both working from home, where I can keep my pride and my father can keep me under his thumb.

Yet he still must work. His office is four doors down the hallway, but since this house is big enough to host a small country's worth of people, there's a decent distance between his space and mine. He'd told Claire about a conference call, at 1:00 p.m. sharp. It was with some record label from Atlanta. That call falling on the same day as my predetermined life-defining moment is a stroke of luck for me, bad luck for him.

I head to the kitchen but promptly spin in the opposite direction the second I see the back of my dad's head. I'm not that hungry. I'm also not a rebel in his eyes, so I need to be careful in case he can see through me like cellophane. Waiting until one is torture, but I'll do it, because I don't have a solid plan, just a wild idea. I head back to my room, without breakfast, and use dry shampoo and apply makeup but no lipstick, to prepare for what I'm going to do.

He'd better appreciate the extra effort. I curl my hair with a large-barrel iron so it hangs in perfect waves and select skinny jeans and a white cashmere scoop neck that slips off the shoulder.

During the time I take to do this, I stop to catch my breath outside on one of the front balconies where I observe Andrea getting into a Tesla with Liam. I watch as Claire ushers Jacob into her Mercedes and drives away, and I see my dad standing on the driveway in his robe waving good-bye.

With nothing left to do, I sit on my bed, look at my watch, and wait. I read some trivia books, watch a TV show, and try to enjoy the sanctuary of my new room. At 12:45 on the dot, there's a sharp rapping on my door.

My dad's voice is calm, even. "Lennon?"

"What?"

"You doing all right?"

I can't say I'm fine. He'll know something's up. If I do, I may as well put up a flashing neon sign telling him I'm about to go rogue.

"As well as can be expected," I yell at the door. "Watching a show."

"Do you need something for lunch?"

"Not hungry."

"Are you sure? I'm about to get on an important phone call. There's leftover pizza in the fridge."

"I'm fine." I add, "Thanks," even though I don't mean it.

"Sure," I hear him mutter under his breath. His footfalls echo down the hall.

My heart races in my chest, my gaze glued to my watch. The

seconds tick by, and I wait for precisely 120 of them before I tiptoe down the hallway and stairs to the front door. There's a small half table in the foyer that holds a tiny wicker basket used as a home for car keys. Dad leaves his in it every single day upon returning from work until the next morning or when he leaves again.

I snatch the Porsche keys and slip out the front door undetected, I hope.

OCD me wants to pause outside of the car and tap the roof five times, because if I get inside it who knows what could happen, but teenage girl Lennon, she's got one objective. Not to be a hypocrite. To show Kyler that I, too, can put my money where my mouth is, that I'm not full of grand ideas I can't bear to prove.

If I drive this car, Kyler could die, Claire or Jacob could die, even my dad, who is on my shit list, could die. And as much as I'm angry with him, I can't let that happen. I can't let him die.

People die in cars.

The twinge in my brain is small at first, but spreads fast and furious until OCD me is out full force. I could do it, five taps, just once. Maybe that would help. The pointer finger of my left hand twitches involuntarily, burning my fingertips.

It's a thought. It's only a thought. The thought can't control me. I control the thought.

I press the remote unlock on the key chain, thankful that the only noise it makes is a click before the headlights go on. There is no beep. I'm grateful because the last thing I need is to get busted before I even make it there.

The Porsche has been facing direct sunlight for the morning

and the inside is like a furnace. I don't have a driver's license, but before OCD controlled my life, I drove with my mom a time or two.

I slide the key into the ignition and crank the dials to their coldest setting while beads of sweat drip down my forehead. I have no idea if they're caused by nerves, or the actual sweltering heat of an LA day in June. I turn the key over in the ignition; my stomach squeezes my insides. I can do this.

I close my eyes and beg my memory to help me. Slowly let out the clutch and press the gas at the same time. The engine grinds and I cringe. I try a second time, only this time I'm successful and the car shifts into gear.

Maybe something bad will happen, because people die in cars. My mind tries to force an image but before it can, I stare at the road ahead. I only see the road, because the image of anything else, anything vile or repulsive, is a thought. It's only a thought. The thought can't control me. I control the thought.

Once down the driveway, I dare a glance at the house, in the unlikely event my dad heard my attempts at divesting the Porsche of its clutch, but the front door remains closed. I roll out of the driveway, shift into second gear, and I *drive*.

The class following lunch is already under way. The hallways of Bel Air Learning Academy are quiet, save for a student here or there. I walk toward Mr. Lowry's class with my head down.

I take seconds to find him. Slouched back in his desk, on first glance he looks like a bored teenager forced to endure modern education, but on closer inspection, Kyler is interested in whatever Lowry is speaking about. His brows knit together, and his jaw is tense as he traces the back of his pen along his bottom lip. His sand-colored hair hangs down enough to blanket his cheek, but it hasn't been set that way on purpose. He's wearing a Nirvana T-shirt. No beanies. No hoodies. Just Kyler.

Kyler, the boy I've waited six weeks, or forty-two days, to see. The boy I've spent the last 1,008 straight hours thinking about. And since I've waited 60,480 minutes to see him, my stomach twists itself into a knot before it wrings itself out. And because I'd dreamed about him for the last 3,628,799.996 seconds, my breath dies out when he's finally close enough to touch. I rap my knuckles on the door as a courtesy before I swing it wide open.

Lowry turns, and his eyebrows dart skyward in surprise as he pushes his glasses up the bridge of his nose. I'm as surprised as he is. Question is, which of us is the most caught off guard? Good chance it's me, because I *drove here* and I'm about to do the craziest thing I've ever done in my life. And trust me when I say I've done a lot of crazy, messed-up stuff.

Kyler is already out of his seat.

Mr. Lowry looks at me. "Well, hello, Miss Davis. I trust you have a superb reason for interrupting my class."

"I—I do."

He points a finger in Kyler's direction. "Sit down, Mr. Benton."

Kyler scowls and sits. The effort looks physically painful for him, but he obliges. Guess he figures he's in enough trouble.

The weight of everyone's eyes on me presses down so hard, my feet sink into the tile floor like quicksand. I take a deep breath. "I know we finished *Romeo and Juliet*, but I'd like to say something."

"This isn't even English," someone shouts out. "It's a poetry module!"

"Shut up," another yells, "let her speak!"

I look at Lowry. "Please. It's important. I know Kyler handed in our project, but I have a modern-day, documentary-style take on it I'd like to add."

The whole class is staring at Lowry. He gives a dismissive wave. "Go ahead, Miss Davis. Your project with Mr. Benton was both refreshing and original, so please, by all means, entertain us."

"Yeah, I can't promise it'll be that, but"—I pause—"when I was first partnered with Kyler for our project, we had many conversations about *Romeo and Juliet* and the debate about the balance of tragedy and love. I'd try to argue pro-love, which yeah, is stupid, but I liked to believe it could happen.

"And here's the thing, we could debate it for hours, because I have obsessive-compulsive disorder. And I overthink everything. All the time, every second, every minute, every hour of every day. I think about how clothing needs to be organized, how my books have to sit in groups of five, how I need exactly five notebooks, and if not five, then three or one. Never an even number, because something terrible could happen if things come in even numbers. I wake up thinking if I don't tap something five times, my dad will get crushed by a cement truck as he's crossing the street to get to work. And then I see him dead inside my head and no matter what I try to do to stop it, I watch it, over and over like a bad movie unless I tap the walls, the roof, the floor. So if you can imagine living that way, all the time, every second of every day, it would be easy to fall for the stupid idea of love being so powerful you'd die for it. That something so real could actually exist."

I have everyone's attention. The room is dead silent.

"But then I fell in love with Kyler, and he fell in love with OCD me. Suddenly, it was so obvious. True love, the kind that's real, should never make you wish to die for it. I know this because the only thing I want to do is live. But my dad, he's like Juliet's father, the Capulet head of the household, and he's trying to keep us apart, because he thinks Kyler would do something like post my medical records on his Facebook page for you all to get a good look at. My dad has no choice but to believe in Kyler's guilt to save face. He's married to Claire Davis, one and only heroine of *Cascade*, the soap every single one of your grandmothers or mothers watch on TV every day at noon, and Claire is the mother of Andrea, who is in fact the guilty party behind our sabotage but to this day insists on her innocence.

"But I don't care that she did it. I don't care anymore, because I never want to die for love. I want to live for it. I promised I'd never come back here, because I was humiliated. I was ashamed of how my brain works. I was ashamed of thinking about people dying all the time, about their brutal murders or horrific accidents all on me because I didn't tap five times. I was ashamed of being the person that I am."

I look at Kyler. "Until you taught me not to be. So that's why I'm here, I don't want us to be a tragedy," I tell him. "Not like Romeo and Juliet. I want us to live."

Silence blankets the entire room, the hum of the fluorescent lights the only thing bold enough to challenge the lull of twenty high school seniors.

Angela Markham is holding her phone up. Whether she's photographing or recording me doesn't matter. I don't care who in the world sees this, because I will defend it until I die. Kyler rises from his chair, but Mr. Lowry holds out his pointer finger as if he's magic and can render Kyler unable to continue forward.

Kyler looks at me, then at Mr. Lowry. He shrugs and proceeds ahead in wide strides. When he reaches me, his hand grabs my face, slides down my cheek, and underneath my ear. He smiles. "You're so fucking weird," he says. "I missed you, Davis."

I opt for one last push of OCD me into the atmosphere. I make it loud and clear to everyone I will never fit in, and that's okay. "I've waited three million, six hundred twenty-eight thousand, nine hundred thirty-nine point ninety-nine seconds to hear you say that. I missed you, too."

Kyler's mouth finds mine, there in front of Mr. Lowry, in front of the whole class, and I get lost in the taste of him, the silky touch of his lips. I close my eyes and inhale, searching for the scent of dryer sheets purporting to smell of ocean breeze.

Every single girl in the room issues a collective sigh of *Aww* until Mr. Lowry tears us apart with an ostentatious display of clapping. One of those slow and patronizing claps. "Well done, Ms. Davis. Am I to understand you're to have no contact with the boy you've just kissed in my classroom?"

I nod. "That understanding is correct, sir."

Kyler squeezes my hand. "Lowry," he says. "Cut me some slack, man-to-man. I haven't seen her in a long time."

"Let them go," Angela Markham says.

"C'mon, Lowry. Have a heart," a guy I've never seen before urges.

Mr. Lowry turns and looks at us, then at the class, then back at Kyler and me. "Should I turn my back for a moment, and find you both gone, there's not much I can do except have the school call and report your absences. That won't be until classes have been dismissed for the day."

Kyler squeezes my hand again, gives me a small smile, and winks. "Ready, Davis? Bonnie and Clyde style."

I've never been more ready for anything.

KYLER

I POWER WALK. I tow Lennon down the hallway so fast, I'm amazed we haven't set the place on fire with friction from the soles of our shoes. We attempt to avoid detection, but when we round the corner, there's Mae standing at her locker; I freeze. Lennon is immobilized, too. Macy's shutting the door, clicking the lock into place, when she spins and sees us.

She blinks. "Lennon, hi." She nods as though I'm an afterthought. "Going somewhere, dear brother?"

"What are you doing in the hall?" It's a valid question. First period after lunch is still ongoing, so technically, Macy should be in class.

She holds up a metal rectangular case and smirks. "Forgot my geometry set. What's your excuse?"

"We're on the run from authorities, parents, and academic institutions who try to fight fate." I hold up Lennon's hand in mine to show Macy. "They're failing."

"Glad you're back, Lennon," Macy says. She studies me. "Don't get busted."

"Cover for me if you have to," I tell her.

"Done," Macy says. "I'd better get to class. Dad's head will explode if you disappear and I get reported as skipping all in the same day."

I salute Mae and continue walking, steering us to the parking lot, where I spot Josh's Porsche. *There's no one in it.* My eyes go wide and as much as I try not to sound shocked, I do, because I am. "Did you drive yourself here?"

"I stand behind what I said when I was at Willow. I don't want to live like that anymore. I want to take risks and drive in cars and be myself without having to apologize for it. You were right." Her eyes are teary. "I can't let fear win. Not anymore."

Making out with this perfect girl should, in theory, be the furthest thing from my mind. We are, after all, *fugitives*. But I can't help it, so I stop walking to pull her close. "You keep kicking OCD's ass, Lennon. I'll be behind you every step of the way, because we aren't a tragedy, we're an epic love story. Maybe the greatest one ever told. And maybe we'll be happy for moments, days at a time, maybe even weeks or years. I don't care as long as it's filled with once-in-a-lifetime things with you."

I kiss her and feel her lips pull into a smile underneath mine. "We need to go," I say against her mouth.

"I know."

She veers ahead, toward Josh's car. My feet freeze for a moment, in horror I try to hide. To be honest, I'm not sure I want to trust my life to someone who was terrified to ride in a car a few weeks ago, even if it is Lennon the Badass. Thank God, she seems to have the same sense as she breezes by it and heads toward my blue beast.

"My heart is racing," she says, "probably shouldn't be behind the wheel."

"Solid logic," I tell her. "Don't worry about a thing, Davis. I'm a good driver."

She climbs into the passenger's seat with a lot less effort than I'd expected and buckles up. I start the car and put it into reverse before leaving the school, and our chances of being busted, behind.

I take us to the 101 North. "Hope you're really okay with driving, Lennon, 'cause we have a while."

El Matador State Beach in Malibu is the most beautiful beach in southern California. That's my humble opinion, but it's an opinion hard to argue with. The beach feels secluded from the world, nestled at the base of large, imposing cliffs that span the coastline. The sand is dotted with caves and coves perfect to escape from life, or in our case, parents. I love this spot because compared to Huntington or Laguna, it's got more character and it never fails to take my breath away. Kind of like the girl at my side.

Lennon leans back, crosses her arms over her chest while a smile tugs at her mouth. "I can't believe I did that," she says. "I drove."

There is unmistakable pride in her voice. We could be in a world of trouble right now and then some, but it doesn't matter because she drove, and because she loves me and she's with me.

I grin. "Can't lie, I didn't see it coming. I knew you had it in you, but I wasn't so sure you knew the same thing." I look at her. "I'm proud of you."

She rests her head against the window, her expression dreamy and content. "Yeah," she says, "I am, too."

An hour later, we park and navigate ourselves down the maze to the beach. Seagulls caw in the distance and the sound of rolling waves invades our ears. The scent of salt lingers in the air, enough for a mouthful. *This must be what life tastes like.*

Lennon reaches down and takes off her shoes, setting them atop a collection of seaweed gathered at the base of one of the rocks. A risky move considering all the things she could step on, but I get it; she wants to live life and take risks, and that includes stepping on a crab buried in the sand, so I do the same.

She heads straight for the ocean and dips her toes in the water, letting the tide come and caress her ankles. Her mouth opens, and her eyes widen with awe, drinking in the ocean in front of them. Meanwhile, I plant my feet there, too, and drink in so much of her that I'm scared I'm going to drown.

It was six weeks, but it felt like a lifetime. Endless days and sleepless nights filled with the echo of hollow thoughts have come to an end. I'll make sure of it because Josh may not know this, but every time he kicks me down, I will get back up and fight for her. I will prove she matters.

"This place is so beautiful," she whispers.

I step forward and wrap my arms around her waist. "Like you," I say in her ear. "Never go away again, Davis. Be weird if you need to be, be crazy if you need to be, just be. As long as it's with me."

She spins in my arms to face me and laces her fingers through my hair, pulling me so we're forehead to forehead. Her eyelids flutter closed. "I love you. I won't let him keep us apart, Kyler, I swear, I'll figure something out."

"Your old man will try to get a restraining order, or since his car was stolen, he'll probably try to pin me with accessory to grand theft auto, so he can send my ass to jail." I kiss her nose. "Doesn't matter, though. I'd go to jail for just a few hours with you, Lennon."

She shakes her head. "I won't let him. I promise I will never let him do that." Tears fall and slip down her cheeks. I grab her face in my hands and slide my thumbs across her cheeks to dry them. "Don't cry. We're here, next to each other in this amazing place. You fucking drove a car today. Let that sink in for a second, yeah? That's so badass. *You're* so badass. And, while we're here, in this moment, in this amazing place, I can kiss you, touch you, and hold you. That's nothing to cry about, is it?"

She smiles through her tears, bites her lip, and shakes her head. "No, it's not."

I pick her up, wrap her legs around my waist, and walk us over to one of the hidden coves. I lie on the sand, Lennon still affixed to me, and make her question whether Make-Out Junkie is the solid winner of the band name debate. I'd love to do more, and I think she would, too, but I hadn't counted on seeing her today, and I didn't come prepared.

I kiss her until my lips feel dry. I run my fingers along her skin, tracing small grains of sand across its surface. She lies down and rests her head on my chest, her fingertips tapping softly in time with my pulse, and we fall asleep that way.

Hours later, the sun descends slowly across the ocean, and we're awakened. My eyes open as the view of the sunset is shadowed by two men in uniforms. Police officers. I squeeze Lennon's arm. "Wake up," I whisper. "We're busted."

A tall, bald guy stands dutifully next to a short, pudgy one who should know frosted tips were out sometime around when Macy was born. Frosty looks at me, then Lennon, before tilting his head down toward the radio clipped to his shoulder. He pushes a button and in the midst of static says, "We found them."

Lennon gasps, but I bring my finger up and move a strand of hair that has settled over her eye. "Bonnie and Clyde style, Davis."

She smiles. "Are you suggesting a murderous rampage?"

"Not at all. I wanted to point out that we're wanted criminals now, hunted, just like Bonnie and Clyde."

"I thought we were Romeo and Juliet—"

The bald cop clears his throat. "Come out with your hands up where we can see them."

I link my hands behind my head and give Lennon the biggest smile I can manage. "Didn't know you were packing heat, Davis," I whisper. "Mighta changed my mind about bringing you here."

She giggles. "Shut up! They'll think you're serious."

"Relax," I tell her. "My dad's a lawyer."

Lennon

FACT: CALIFORNIA HAS ONE OF THE HIGHEST
RATES OF CAR THEFT IN THE UNITED STATES.

KYLER AND I ARE ESCORTED to the back of the police cruiser to wait while a tow truck comes to hook up his car. I assume something similar has happened to my father's car. Either that, or my dad himself has picked it up. The bald policeman, who I now know is Officer Hudson, pulls me aside and asks what happened, while his partner, Officer Lewis, talks to Kyler.

"You stole a car this morning," Hudson says flatly. "Tell me why you shouldn't be arrested."

"I can't tell you that. I can't even tell you I wouldn't do the same thing over again." My eyes drift to the side until my vision settles on Kyler, who is leaning against the hood of the police car with his hand behind his neck, as though he's been rubbing stress from it.

"You're in a lot of trouble with your father," he states. "You should apologize for stealing his car. He's obviously not pressing charges."

"I wouldn't care if he did," I say, even though that's untrue.

He shakes his head as though I'm a repeat offender, a career criminal he encounters often and not a teenage girl in love. It doesn't matter, though—I spent the afternoon with Kyler and I refuse to let anything, especially an encounter with a cop, ruin it.

Kyler sits in the back of the police cruiser when the officer opens the door and says, "Get in and watch your head." I do, and as we drive back to Bel Air, the tips of Kyler's fingers settle on mine and tap. Five times.

It took an hour to get here, but it takes almost two to get home. Traffic is congested the entire way up the interstate, but I don't mind. I close my eyes and feel Kyler's fingertips against my skin. Once we are driving and blocked in with the security bars between the front of the car and the back, the frequent dryer sheet smell is there full force, only now it's paired with the smell of the ocean. The real one.

When we enter Bel Air, I sigh and give Kyler's hand a squeeze.

"Don't be afraid," he says. "They can't stop us."

"No," I agree. "They can't."

The cruiser parks at the end of the drive, an equal distance between the Benton's house and mine. Officer Hudson opens my door while Officer Lewis extends the same courtesy to Kyler. They motion for us to get out of the vehicle, and as Lewis grips his forearm, Kyler turns and says, "It's not over, Lennon. Hold on to that."

I smile because I believe him.

Hudson raps on the front door with his knuckles, and it swings open to reveal my father. His eyes are bloodshot, his hair in disarray. The corner of his button-up shirt is untucked from his belt, and his tie is loosened around his neck. He scowls and doesn't even wait for Officer Hudson to leave before he lays into me. "What the hell were you thinking, Lennon?" He waves his hands. "You know what, don't answer that. You weren't thinking. What you did was stupid. It was dangerous."

Jacob's eyes peer around from the hallway corridor.

"You know what's stupid, Dad?" I shoot back. "Living your life in a bubble because of some ridiculous brain defect that tries to make you question your sanity. You know what else is stupid? Trying to keep two people from each other who need to be together."

"Give me a break," Dad says. "You don't *need* to be with anyone. What you need is a swift kick in the ass if you think this kind of behavior is acceptable. You stole my car, for Christ's sake. What you need is to deal with your obsessive-compulsive disorder in a way that is productive in helping you move forward with your life. What you need is to grieve the loss of your mother and to become a member of this family. What you don't need is the boy next door to make you feel whole."

I look at him as though he's sprouted a second head. "Maybe I'm not the only one who needs my head checked, Dad." My voice elevates, the pitch rising in irritation. "What you need, Dad, is to learn about OCD and stop trying to know me through Dr. Linderman. What you need is a little compassion. What you need, Dad," I practically spit, "is to open your damned eyes to the fact that Andrea is a vile, wretched bitch who could rival any of the villains on her mother's daytime soap opera. What you need is to understand that you can't stop me from seeing him,

I don't care what you do. I'll steal your car a thousand times if I have to. I'll go back to that stupid school, I'll be normal, I'll do whatever it takes."

"You will not be seeing Kyler Benton."

"Oh yes," I say, "I will."

Jacob steps forward from his hiding spot in the hallway. "Lennon, are you okay?"

"Go to your room, Jake," Dad orders.

Jacob shakes his head in defiance. "Don't make Lennon sad, Daddy. That's not fair."

"Jacob," my dad warns, "this is none of your business."

I glare at my father. "What you need is to understand that Kyler didn't expose my OCD on Facebook. I know you don't believe that, but it's true."

"You can't prove that," my father says.

Jacob's voice is hardly a whisper. "I can."

"Jacob," Dad says again. "Keep your nose out of it. Go and find your mother."

I look at Jacob. "It's okay, buddy."

He crosses his arms over his chest and gives my father his best threatening glare. "It's not okay. Kyler didn't do that. Andi did."

The tension hanging in the air bursts as both my father and I stop. I crouch down to look at Jacob. "What are you talking about, Jake?"

He brings his hand from its hiding spot behind his back to reveal his camera. "I have it on video."

Jacob's room is covered in paper airplanes. It's work not to step on them as we make our way to his small computer. He takes a power cord from the side and plugs it into the camera, and a window appears on the screen, populating all the pictures and videos he's taken. He double-clicks on one of them and we all fall silent.

Andrea is sitting on her bed in a silk robe with sponges between her toes while she coats them in a pale shade. Jacob's camera was clearly hidden, because the angle is skewed and makes it hard to see, but the audio is crystal clear. Andrea is speaking into the phone that sits perched on a pillow beside her.

"He thinks her idiot boyfriend did it," Andrea is saying. She smirks, even though the person on the other end of the phone can't see her. "Gullible. Even better, they're forbidden from seeing each other."

The voice on the other end of the line says, "How did you get into his Facebook?" I'm not sure whose voice it is, but that is not important.

"Pft, please," Andrea says in the video. "You know Liam's brilliant with that stuff, right? He's like a hacker. Facebook log-in is child's play."

"Wow," the voice says. "That's twisted, but well done."

"I know," Andrea admits. "Seriously, it was bad enough that all my parents see is her, I didn't need to have the fact that she's *sooo* in love thrown in my face."

My dad shifts uncomfortably, heads to the door of Jacob's room, and calls for Claire.

KYLER

A WISE MAN ONCE SAID,
WHY DON'T YOU ASK
YOUR DAUGHTER?

Random Thoughts of a Random Mind

MY DAD WASN'T HOME WHEN the cops delivered me. Good thing, too, because I think it'd be hard to see my notebook with a pair of black eyes. He's never actually hit me, but he's come close in belittling episodes where he likes to remind me what a disappointment I am. There's a first time for everything, and having a legit criminal as a son could prompt that side of him to explode. My mom sat me down at the table and told me I shouldn't be skipping school. More important, she told me, if Lennon was worth this much trouble, she'd help me any way she could. I told her she might start with keeping all this to herself—that is, my police escort and the tow bill to bring my car home.

I wonder how much trouble Lennon is in. She is now guilty of grand theft auto, a crime she committed to see me, so I'm sure in Josh's eyes it's my fault.

I alternate between working on her song, the one that's been haunting me for ages, and staring at my phone, waiting for her to text, until something catches my eye as it heads across the yard.

It's Josh.

I set my pencil on my notebook and stand. My dad still isn't home, and if Josh is going to scream at someone, I can't let it be my mother, so I make quick work of the stairs. I'm at the bottom and have the door open, just as Josh is raising his hand to knock. He looks shocked to see me. A little odd, considering he's the one standing on my front porch and not the other way around.

I don't say hello. I raise an eyebrow.

"Do you mind stepping outside for a moment?" he asks.

The raised eyebrow inches even farther up my face. "What?"

"I'd like to talk to you for a moment."

"You want to talk?"

"Yes."

I can't help it. I'm a skeptic. "Why outside?"

Josh clears his throat. "I've recently discovered that I owe you an apology."

"You're not here to kick my ass because your daughter stole your wheels and went against everything you specifically prohibited her from doing?"

Josh shakes his head. "I'm civilized, believe it or not."

I cross my arms over my chest and narrow my gaze. I'll believe it. I wave a hand at the door. "After you."

"Jacob presented me with some hard evidence that clears your name in the entire Facebook debacle, so I'll apologize, man-to-man. I was wrong. I chose not to believe my wife's child would do something that horrible to my own. The only other person who knew Lennon and her struggles, or would have access to that kind of information, is you. It was easy to blame you, and I was wrong to do so. I'm sorry."

"Don't worry about it," I say. "I get it. I want to protect Lennon, too. Shit happens, but so do everyday freaking miracles, and she can't go through life without experiencing both."

Josh smirks. I don't know if he thinks I'm trying to be a smart-ass. I'm not. "I see why my daughter likes you. You're very blunt."

"Or just honest. Can I ask you something"—I borrow his phrase—"man-to-man?"

"Certainly."

"You ever ask Lennon what it's like to be her? I mean, you can read all the books you want, you can Google the hell out of something, you can talk to the most expensive psychiatrist in the world, none of those will replace the words coming straight from her mouth to your ears. She's actually really good at explaining it, if you give her the chance." Josh looks at his shoes. I take it from his silence the answer is no, so I continue. "I'm not saying you shouldn't do what you've been doing. You're light-years ahead of my old man when it comes to giving a shit about your kid, so props for that, but what Lennon needs more than any doctor or any pill is some understanding." I shove my hands in my pockets and shift my weight around on my feet. "That's what I think, for what it's worth."

His expression softens. "A well-thought-out stance to have, Kyler."

"Thanks."

"I still can't condone your hostility toward Andrea."

"I still can't apologize for it, so maybe we can call it even?"

He considers this for a moment. "Yeah, I suppose we can do that. Lennon reminds me a lot of her mother, always so headstrong and tenacious in her pursuits. I know when I'll lose a fight before it begins, so with that in mind, I won't keep her from you anymore."

I bust out my best smile and it's not even on purpose. The weight of a heavy world that is filled with injustice eases off my shoulders.

"I won't hurt your daughters," I say. "Either one of them." I want to add more, because Andrea deserves a shitstorm of misery, but I won't be the one to deliver it. I'll let karma take that one. I offer him my hand. "I appreciate the apology."

"I appreciate the insight," Josh says. "You're a smart kid."

"I'm overcompensating for the hand I've been dealt in the looks department," I say drily.

Josh chuckles as he walks away.

Lennon

I PICK UP A BOOK and try to focus, but my eyes keep looping back and rereading the same paragraph until the words are nothing but blurred ink on the page. Claire had delivered Jacob to Mel's place, and I was banished to my room so she and Dad could talk to Andrea. I'm not sure what happened exactly, but there was a lot of yelling.

There's a soft rapping on my door. It could be Claire, or, if the Universe is unspeakably cruel, my dad. There's only one way to find out. "Come in."

My father peeks his head in. "Hi, bug."

Indisputable proof. The Universe is a monumental asshole.

I set the book down and flip on my side, facing out my window to see Kyler's room hidden by blinds. It's still better than looking at my dad's face. "I want to be alone right now."

"Lennon—"

"Please, Dad, just go."

"I can't."

Two words that are so simple, but effective in sparking my interest. I roll over again and look at him. "Why?"

"Because I owe you an apology, that's why."

Now I sit up, because it's the last thing I expected him to say. He points to the chair near the sewing table. "Mind if I sit down?"

I pull my knees to my chest and wrap my arms around them. "I guess not."

He walks in, shuts the door behind him, and, with a purposeful stride, crosses my room to sit down. "I've just been to see Kyler."

My heart skips at the mere sound of his name. "Trying to tame the wild beast?"

"Very funny."

"I'm not trying to be funny," I tell him. "It's a legitimate question."

"I went next door to apologize. I'm not above admitting when I was wrong."

Wow. Not what I expected.

My father continues. "He said something that resonated with me, bug."

My interest snowballs. "What did he say?"

"He suggested that I ask you about you."

"What about me?"

He pauses. "About what it's like to have OCD."

"Haven't you read about it?"

He nods. "I have. Not the same as hearing from someone who lives with it, which is something I should have realized before, so tell me, please."

"It sucks."

"My normal response would be something like 'I can imagine,' but I can't. I can't imagine. As your dad, that's pretty hard for me to admit."

"You don't want to imagine, trust me. It's horrible. You'd be an accomplice to the madness."

"I want to understand, Lennon. I really do."

"You don't."

"Please just talk to me."

And so, I do. I tell him *everything* about the burden I carry built of unsavory parts. I tell him I wish I wasn't this way, but I am because it's how I'm hardwired. When I'm finished, tears spring to my dad's eyes, so I use the opportunity to add, "Kyler may not be exactly the same, but he knows what it feels like to be on the outside looking in, he gets it. He gets me. So I can't understand why you are so determined to protect me from the only person who I can just be myself around."

"Because I'm a concerned father."

"I understand you're concerned, but when I'm around him I can relax, because he doesn't care if I'm tapping constantly, it doesn't faze him. My OCD doesn't matter to him. *I* matter to him. No one has ever made me feel that way, except you and Mom." Tears well in my eyes that now mirror my dad's. "And you tried to take that from me. To take *him* from me. And it hurt all over again. Worse than anything."

"I didn't realize why he meant so much to you, Lennon," my dad says. "I'm so sorry. I thought I was protecting you."

"I love him."

My father rises to his feet and comes to sit on the huge bed beside me. He pulls me toward him and wraps his arms around me. "I know you do, bug, and I love you."

I let myself stop hating my dad long enough to remember how much I love him, and it's all I need. I squeeze him back. "Please let me see him again."

Dad pulls away with a smile. "I came in here and told you I'm not above admitting when I was wrong. You can see him. After talking to him for a little while, he seems like a smart kid who cares very much for you. And that last part is something he and I have in common."

The tears that I'd been holding in fall and run down my cheeks. "I love you, Dad."

"I love you, too, Bug, more than you'll ever know."

Andrea has been reserved and complacent since Jacob's colossal bust. No outbrusts, no snide remarks. It's been peaceful. On Saturday morning, she and Claire walk through the front door, bags of groceries in hand. Today was her first appointment with an anger management therapist recommended by Levi. She doesn't look overly impressed, but she removes her hand from behind her back and reveals a chocolate bar and offers it to me. "My mom said you like this kind."

"Um, wow. Thanks," I say, touched.

She rolls her eyes. "Whatever. We were already at the store." Her voice is almost a whisper until she yells, "Jake! Mom got you a chocolate bar, but you can't eat it until after lunch."

I'm sure I'm gaping, but I try not to stare too long, because it'll flip her bitch switch, so wisely, I take it, thank her again, and head to the kitchen. My dad is pacing in the center of the room with his phone pressed to his ear, while Jacob is attempting to climb a footstool for access to breakfast cereal. Dad's voice is strained, his jaw clenched tight.

"What are you saying, Don? You assured me, guaranteed me, they'd be playing. I gave you an enormous check and didn't book a backup. What the hell do you expect me to do? The event is tonight, Don. Tonight." He glances at his wristwatch. "Precisely nine hours from now, my guests will arrive. That's not a lot of time to find a resolution, Don."

He continues repeating the guy's name, Don, over and over like he's making an effort to drive his point home.

I head to the counter where Jacob is and grab his cereal and a bowl. While he shakes the contents of the box, I retrieve almond milk from the fridge and splash it over the top. When I return the milk and shut the fridge door, my dad tosses his phone on the table and rakes his hands through his hair.

"Everything's fine," he says to nobody in particular. "Or it will be." He turns, strides down the hall, and bellows out for Claire.

Jacob, wearing his black cape, goes to the table with his cereal. "Daddy's mad," he informs me.

"I noticed."

"He said something about having a party for the music industry without music was hassle-nine. He screamed that part before you got here."

"'Asinine'? He screamed that it was asinine," I correct him.

He eats another spoonful of his cereal and crunches it thoughtfully before responding, "Yes."

Don was a band manager?

I touch Jacob's arm. "Put your bowl in the sink when you're done, okay? I need to do something."

"Okay."

I head to my room, pluck my phone from its charger, and text Kyler.

KYLER

"I'M BROKEN AND YOU'RE BEAUTIFUL, YOU'RE MY JULIET,
I MIGHT JUST BE YOUR ROMEO, THE ONE YOU CAN'T FORGET."

Fire to Dust, *Life-Defining Moments* EP, "Lennon's Song"

SIX MONTHS AGO, THE LAST thing I ever expected I'd be doing is sending a group text attempting to round up the members of my band for an emergency meeting, but six months ago, I also didn't expect that I'd meet someone like her. If Lennon can steal her dad's car, drive it to school, talk about us and her OCD in front of a full classroom of people, then I can do this. I have to because she's worth it—and oddly enough, she makes me believe that so am I.

Need you all at my house with your stuff. Stat. 911.

Emmett is the first to reply. What's up?

Last-minute gig.

The party next door is in full swing. Earlier in the evening I'd watched carloads of people arrive and the valet Josh hired parking their vehicles along their property until the space ran out. Then the valets switched to street parking, which pisses my dad off something awful every year.

Silas is the first to arrive. He points his finger next door. "Holy shit. We're playing a house party?"

I nod. Zero chance I'm telling any of them what Josh does for a living or whom exactly we're performing for. I'll tell them after, when it doesn't matter because I don't need anyone getting stage fright, so I say as casually as I can, "Helping my neighbor out. Last-minute cancellation."

"Cool," he replies, "I'm glad you decided to play live again. You may never want to do a demo, but if we can play gigs, at least that's a step up from garage band."

"Yeah," I say. "Big step."

Emmett and Austin show up about fifteen minutes later. "I was at the gym," Emmett complains. "And we would have been here sooner, but we had to park two blocks away. There's dudes sitting in town cars just waiting all over the street."

"I know. Listen, we don't have a lot of time." I pull the piece of paper from the back of my jeans and show it to them. It's the set list I wrote out after Lennon texted me.

Emmett squints. "Lennon's song? Aren't we still working on that?"

"Yeah. I'll do that acoustically. If that's okay," I add.

Austin grins. "You must really love that girl, bro. You're doing a live song by yourself. That's huge."

Before I can respond, Macy comes out of the house, jumping up and down and clasping her hands under her chin. "Lennon said I could come!"

"What? Since when do you talk to Lennon?"

"Since now," Macy says. "Get used to it. She's your girlfriend, isn't she?"

"Yeah," I say. "She is."

"I'm your sister. We're bonded now."

"You and Lennon?"

Macy just nods. "She also invited Mom!"

I don't have time for this, so I face the guys. "Ready?"

They nod.

The expression on Josh's face shows me he hadn't been expecting us. As we set up, I see him walk over to Lennon and talk to her with a smile firmly established on his face. I've seen those smiles often, though, and they tell me that the person wearing them is pretending not to be taken by surprise.

The guests are tipsy enough to be having a good time, but not rowdy. Yet.

I strap my guitar around my neck and connect to its pedalboard. Silas, Austin, and Emmett perform the quickest sound check I've ever heard, and I step up to the mic.

The buzz of the crowd lulls.

"Good evening, ladies and gentlemen." People stop milling about the pool and turn their attention to me. "I'm Kyler and this is my band, Fire to Dust. Josh, your host for the night, has graciously extended the invitation for us to play for all of you fine people."

Josh is looking at me with a hard stare. I can't tell if he's hopeful or trying to warn me that I'd better not screw this up.

"This is our second gig," I add.

Now he looks horrified.

"But we're going to do our best to entertain you for a little while."

A few of the women in the group cheer and it produces a ripple effect, so before it can die out, I sing. I sing the first song I ever wrote, then a ballad followed by three much more aggressive pieces. About midway through the third song, I notice people have stopped socializing all together. They turn, facing the makeshift stage, looking toward me. Some people's bodies move instinctively along with the music. I give Silas a glance and he grins. He's noticed, too.

After I do a few Nirvana covers, I know for sure people are entertained. Several of them look as though they could have been huge fans in their youth. Soon, we reach the bottom of the set list. "Lennon's Song." I swap my guitar for an acoustic, take a drink of water, and say into the microphone, "True story. I met a girl named Lennon." As soon as I mention her name, people turn around to look at her. They recognize who she is, they know her name because, after all, her father is the host of this party. "Lennon taught me that life is way too short to waste. That you only get a certain window of time to seize the things that matter. I wrote this song for her." To her I say, "Lennon, I fixed it. We aren't tragic anymore." I wink for her and explain to the partygoers, "Lennon's heard several versions of this song, because I kept screwing it up, but she hasn't heard this one."

Someone claps boisterously while several women in the group bring their hands to their necklaces or cover their hearts.

I strum the guitar. I didn't want to get overly complicated with the riffs because Lennon and me, we are plenty complicated, but I wouldn't have it any other way.

Once you were untouchable,
A girl meant for my dreams,
Until I made you mine somehow,
And then you set me free.

No faith in fate to speak of,
Forever just alone,
You walked in and changed me,
And showed my heart it's home.

The scars that burn inside my mind,
They fascinate you so,
You're my fateful fairy tale,
I'm never letting go.

I bit the poisoned apple,
And garnered just a taste,
The sweetest sin I've ever had,
In you I found my place.

The scars that burn inside my mind,
They fascinate you so,
You're my fateful fairy tale,
I'm never letting go.

I'm broken and you're beautiful,
You're my Juliet,
I might just be your Romeo,
The one you can't forget.

The scars that burn inside my mind,
They fascinate you so,
You're my fateful fairy tale,
I'm never letting go.

Where you go, I'll follow,
I'll drown inside your light,
Because you're my fateful fairy tale,
And I'm your star-crossed knight.

The scars that burn inside my mind,
They fascinate you so,
You're my fateful fairy tale,
I'm never letting go.

So stay with me, my sweetest sin,
Let me love you so,
Because you're my fateful fairy tale,
And my heart is yours to hold.

As the last chord fades and my gaze falls to Lennon. She's in a blue sundress, standing beside Macy, Jacob, and our parents at the bar. Her hands are clasped underneath her chin, and she has a huge smile on her face. Even more shocking, Josh is smiling, too.

Lennon brings me an ice-cold lemonade after our performance. For such a small group of people, they were so loud. We're standing poolside, and I'm hoping I don't look half as sweaty as I feel, when a guy with red-rimmed glasses and a pinstripe suit approaches. Lennon grins wildly. "Levi James Linderman!" she exclaims. "I didn't know you were coming."

Josh stands behind him while he holds up his wineglass. "Surprise. Your father invited me a while back. I guess I forgot to mention it." He looks at me. "Impressive performance," he says. "You're very talented."

"I'd have to agree," Josh says. "Perhaps I owe you another apology. Seems I've underestimated you."

Lennon beams.

"Thank you, Josh." I pause and look at the glasses wearer. "And?"

Lennon must notice. "Kyler, this is Dr. Linderman."

I extend my hand. "Nice to meet you, and thanks."

Dr. Linderman's grip is firm. "Ah, the elusive Kyler. It's truly a pleasure to finally meet you."

Before the conversation goes any further, another man approaches, dressed in a more expensive-looking suit. He reaches into his inside pocket and pulls out a business card. "Kyler?"

He says my name as a question, so I answer him with one. "Yes?"

"My name's Bradley Whittaker. I work for Springboard Records."

A fourth man approaches. "Trying to poach him already, Whittaker?" He, too, takes a business card out of his pocket. "I'm Michael Trevanni. I work for Electrified Records. If you aren't signed with anyone, let's talk."

Silas is looking at me. I'm looking at Lennon. One more life-defining moment coming up. As long as they're with her, nothing else matters.

I take the business cards as two more men approach. Josh steps in front of me. "Looks like you and your bandmates are going to need a manager. I'd like to help you guys find one, if you're interested."

I look at Silas, Emmett, and Austin. Macy's mouth is hanging open. My mom stands beside her, eyes glistening with tears. And when I look at her, I recognize something in her eyes. The spark behind them that believes in magic. It's the one I've been looking for since I was six.

"Yeah," I tell Josh. "I think we'd be interested."

Lennon

FACT: I'M SO IN LOVE WITH KYLER BENTON.

HE'S THE BEST THING THAT'S EVER HAPPENED TO ME.

THE TREE HOUSE IS MY favorite place in the whole world. It's Kyler's secret space, and for reasons I may never fully understand, he decided that I belong here with him. This is where I fell in love with him, and the place where I hope I never stop finding out all of the brilliant things that swirl inside his mind. We're sprawled out on his mattress, my head in the crook of his arm while he plays with my hair. I listen to his breathing, soft and even as the breeze outside carries a gentle song. I savor the quiet, especially the silence in my mind. Not so long ago, all my brain knew how to do was worry, but now, it takes frequent breaks from being anxious to appreciate all kinds of life-defining moments. Like this one, and every single moment to come after it.

"This is my favorite thing," I whisper.

His chest rises with a soft chuckle as his fingers comb through my curls. "Keeping your standards pretty low for Bel Air, Davis," he teases. "Spending time with me in my tree house. Cheap. Conveniently located and barrels of unparalleled fun."

I tap my fingers on his chest. "Shut up. As if this isn't the best thing."

He brushes a strand of hair from my face. "Yeah," he agrees, "it pretty much is the best thing. Maybe it's the best thing in the entire Milky Way and Andromeda galaxies combined."

I tip my head to look at him. "Definitely. Not maybe. Are you nervous about tomorrow?"

His tongue darts across his lips before he speaks. "No, I won't be nervous until like three seconds before. What about you?"

"Absolutely. I've been nervous for the last few weeks."

"Don't be," he says. "Be your weird-ass self. They'll love you. I promise. They'd be idiots not to."

"My weird-ass self?" I laugh. "I'm just hoping I can make it through without ritualizing."

"So what if you don't?"

My eyes widen at this idea. "Oh my God, what if I don't? That's going to be so embarrassing."

I sit up, but he smiles and pulls me back down. "Get back here. You have nothing to hide, nothing to be embarrassed for. If you have to ritualize, so what? All that means is a whole bunch of people who have OCD or know someone with OCD or love someone with OCD will feel like they have a voice. Ordinary people do ordinary things while people like you do extraordinary things."

Those few simple words make me feel so strong, it's like I'm made of steel.

"Don't be ashamed of anything, Lennon. Be who you are. You're amazing and you're doing people a service, even if you don't see it that way right now. Besides, there are definitely worse things than talking about a mental health problem that's misunderstood on television."

"What kind of worse things?" I ask him. "Like meeting with producers at the two major labels fighting over me?"

He turns his body and grins. "The struggle is real. Point is, tomorrow will be filled with big moments for both of us. You'll have publicly kicked OCD's ass and I'll know my fate: plant technician, petroleum transfer engineer, or musician. What will the future hold? Exciting to think about, isn't it?"

I giggle. "Plant technician? Petroleum transfer engineer? Don't you mean gardener and gas pump attendant?"

"Maybe."

"I love how your brain works," I tell him. "It's the strangest brain, but the coolest one."

"Strange Brains. Could be a band name, Davis," he whispers, and kisses my nose. "Think about it. Our slogan could be 'Mental Wealth.'"

"Strange Brains. Mental Wealth." I laugh. "That's the best one yet."

Lennon

Lennon from Maine

Lennon from Maine with Serious Issues

Lennon from Maine with Serious Issues
Who Sews

Lennon from Maine with Serious Issues
Who Sews and Is Broken

Lennon from Maine with Serious Issues
Who Sews and Is Broken and Beautiful

Lennon from Maine with Serious Issues
Who Sews and Is Broken and Beautiful
and Badass

. . . is mine

STRANGE
BRAINS
MENTAL WEALTH

ACKNOWLEDGMENTS

I NEVER CONSIDERED THAT the acknowledgments for a book would be harder to write than the book itself. If I were Kyler, I'd spend the next two pages arguing that there is no way to quantify a person's place in direct relation to how much they've impacted one's journey, thus earning their name a spot on this list. If I were Lennon, I'd spend the next two pages agonizing about the possibility of missing an acknowledgment, saying too much or too little. Am I being too personal or not personal enough? But I'm neither Kyler nor Lennon, so I'm going to give this my best shot.

I'm starting with Kieran Viola at Hyperion because quite honestly, GIRL POWER—*fist pump*! I'm decent with words except when they're meant to say thank you to the person who one day decided to make a dream I carried for a lifetime come true. *Thank you* feels like a truly insignificant speck of a sentiment, but thank you, nonetheless: Thank you for believing in this story, thank you for believing in me, but mostly thank you for loving Lennon and Kyler as much as I do. You've made this entire experience educational, uplifting, and unforgettable. I'm truly blessed to have you in my corner. And another round of "thank you" to Mary Mudd, Marci Senders, Amy Goppert, and everyone else on the Hyperion team—and to the talented Liz Casal and Torborg Davern for the book's beautiful cover and an interior design that illustrates Lennon and Kyler's story perfectly.

To my agent, John Silbersack. Thank you for having such faith in me from the beginning. I still remember running the idea for this book by you. I hung up the phone absolutely intoxicated by the possibility of the words that were about to flow. Each time I sent pages to see what you thought, you were so supportive and enthusiastic. I'm so grateful for your patience when I let anxiety best me and emailed you more than I should, and for your genuine appreciation for my firm beliefs in odd signs from the Universe. You take this all in stride and still offer me a warm smile and great conversation each time we meet. Your constant guidance, gems of considerable bookish wisdom, and support throughout my writing journey fill me with immense amounts of gratitude. Thank you.

My Wattpad4 (plus more) girls: Monica Sanz, Rebecca Sky, Erin Latimer, Fallon DeMornay, and Lindsey Summers. It doesn't matter if we've been together since the beginning, or we've picked you up along the way, the end result is the same. You girls are my sisters. We started sharing writing and now we share our lives. I can't imagine a single step of this journey without you fearless females by my side.

Monica and Fallon. Double shout-out: Thank you for reading

literally every single first-draft line of dialogue or narrative that I thought was good when I texted them to you (sometimes relentlessly). Thank you for never telling me to stop but for always telling me to keep writing instead. XOXO

To my little family: Jason, Dani, Trent, and Rylee. I love you guys more than the Milky Way and Andromeda galaxies combined. I'm mostly baffled but also grateful that you put up with me, not just when I was writing this but quite frankly, in general. I know I'm aggressive in most of my pursuits, which sometimes results in me locking myself away to write while I leave you to fend for yourselves. I can be a little hard to deal with sometimes, especially when I'm in the writing zone. Eternally grateful for your support and understanding. And to my children, please remember this: Don't let anyone tell you what your dreams should be. Only you get to decide that. This book is proof.

Thank you to Ursula Gutteridge for taking the time to speak with me and answer my questions about OCD from a medical perspective, and to the sensitivity readers who helped to guide me in the right direction.

To the staff and readers at Wattpad. This journey started with you. You've been here since the beginning. Thank you for giving me the courage to believe in a dream that once felt impossible. I couldn't have done it without you.

To anyone dealing with *any* kind of mental illness in yourself or in your families. You are bold. You are brave. You are badass. Talk about it. Please use your voices to shake up the world! Be informed and show support and understanding. No one should have to walk through life alone. Find strength in community and be good to every person you meet, because you don't know what their story is, you don't know about the scars they carry. Be kind.

Dear reader, if you're still here at this point in the acknowledgments, well done, you're in it for the long haul. Much respect. Thank you for giving my book some of your time. Thank you for making me want to keep chasing this incredible dream. Without you, there is nothing.

Here's where I get personal. I struggle, like many, with mental health, and sometimes I become a nervous, anxious, depressed wreck of a person. I have inexplicable panic attacks and worry to the point where I can physically make myself sick. A few short months after I typed the opening sentence to this book, my dad passed away. Having lost my mother years before, I was officially an orphan, and it doesn't matter how old you are, that's a hard pill to swallow.

It seems straightforward to thank the incredible people who helped me bring this book into the world in obvious ways: industry people, my family, writer supports. But *All Our Broken Pieces* would not have been without the following people as well. You helped me through a sadness I thought was never going to end and for that, I owe you more than an acknowledgment in some book.

Sam, my bff, my bestie, my ride or die. You should hold the number one spot on this list because you've literally been listening to me babble since the dawn of time when dinosaurs roamed the earth. Thanks for being there consistently for my entire adult life, and even well before then. You're the best friend a girl could hope to have. I love you.

Matt, I struggle to find the right words for you. Maybe I don't need them or maybe I used all the words up because I talked... a lot...*a lot*. Thank you for always being there to listen and not trying to "fix" things. Sometimes we all just need someone to hear us. When I quite dramatically informed you my fictional boy with a burnt face had no band name because positively nothing I could think of was right, you offered up Fire to Dust and it's still so perfect. I'm grateful for everything.

Simone, you're up there with Fallon, Monica, and Sam. Thank you for listening to me drone on about this book and my endless problems after buying me Starbucks. What an undeniable privilege for you! Just kidding. But how much I appreciate you (and the Starbucks) is no joke. Thank you. Also, so it's here and publicly stated: *irregardless* is not a word.

Lastly, Mom and Dad. Mom, I understand now why you didn't encourage me to be a writer—because you watched my father struggle and didn't want the same for me. That makes you a pretty kick-ass mother. Even better is that I proved you wrong (you would have loved that), and I think you're up there beaming with pride while Dad is beside you saying he told you so.

Dad, you're the one who gave this to me. A gift. A curse. A blessing. It depends on the day. Your faith in me never wavered. You made me believe I could do anything until I proved to myself that I can. I miss you both every single day, but I hope I've done you proud.